Galaxy of Phoenix

Book I:

Ontoo Neida Division Seventeen

ISBN:
978-0-9786845-1-8
0-9786845-1-6

LCCN:
2007934677

jadewinds™

Published by Jadewinds, Lakewood, Ohio

jadewindsTM is the publishing arm of Ascending Hall
www.AscendingHall.com

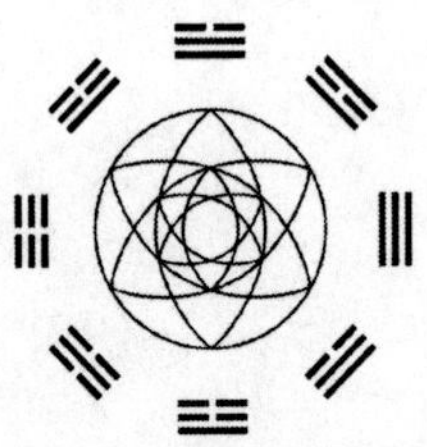

德豐觀

In sincere dedication to:
Mom, Dad, Jane's godfather, and Lulu's Mom

A Thank You to:
Grace1 and Tammy's Mom (Liang Hua), "Miss Margaret," "Miss Carol", and Dr. Albanese.

Of course:
None of this would not be possible without
Tao Huang
and his patience and faith in me.

Yin Tang
AUTHOR, ILLUSTRATOR, DESIGNER, CO-EDITOR

Tao Huang
EDITOR

TABLE OF CONTENTS

Intended for an audience age 18 and above.

Dear Reader:

As you are reaching the end of this book, please keep in mind it is not merely the conclusion of a piece of the story. This is an ongoing rhythm, much like life, and even though there are breaks in between, in the end, it all works together cohesively.

I initially wrote the entire series as one book. Later, it was decided that it was best to break it down and have them released individually. I hope you enjoy Book I: Ontoo Neida, the introductory book as much as you will enjoy the rest of the story.

你好，我的
名字叫天玫(瑰)
我出生时，是一位
普通的姑娘。

但是，宇宙
对我有另外的
打算。

这，就是咱们
的故事。

TERMINAL 4

CHAPTER ONE

A story has to be told. In the expanse of the Universe, there are many individuals who are worthy of receiving honor. It is only a few of these whose existence has brought a shining truth into the everlasting question of "why?" The souls in this story have been wrought with controversy, mystery, glory, and intrigue. Some regard them as heroes, while others believe them to be a plague brought upon them from a divine figure. Let me tell you the story, and you can decide for yourself.

Rose Tian came over to America at the age of three. There was just her and her older sister, Sarah. Her brother Joel had disappeared. She doesn't remember much about him. One day he was just gone, like their cat who had ran away.

Sarah was six at the time and she knew better. Rosi always listened to Sarah. Sarah told Rosi that Joel was gone and no one knew where to find him. She also explained that daddy was afraid to have his daughters disappear so that was why they went to America. Mom and dad never spoke to Rosi about Joel. Sarah always told her things though, even when she wasn't supposed to. Joel was supposed to be five years old when he disappeared. Rosi did the math, she was three then, so he would be two years older. He was one year younger than Sarah. Rosi was proud that she could do math on her own.

She didn't understand why everyone was so worried. Nothing bad ever happens in life. Joel was probably just at the park, even if it had been for months. Maybe he had found a cave or something and was living at the park. It sounded like fun, Rosi even wanted to join him. She would bring her little lantern and they could eat whatever sweet berries they could find. Sarah could come to visit them too, and bring toys with her.

One day, when Rosi was five years old, she came home to an empty house. That was strange. Sarah always got home a few minutes early. She was actually supposed to be at the bus stop to pick her up.

"Hello?" Rosi called upstairs. She waited, when there was no answer, she slowly started to crawl up the stairs. Despite the sunny day outside, Rosi was scared. She had never been at home all by herself before. What if the monsters in the towel closet got out? Cautiously, she leaned over the top stair. She peeped around the corner. The closet door was closed. She gave a little sigh of relief and crawled into the hallway. She stayed close to the wall. The closet was at the far end of the hall adjacent to the bathroom. Rosi's room was on the left two doors before it. As quietly as possible, she slipped into her room and locked it. Her parents didn't like it when she locked her doors. They were always afraid that something would happen. They had said in an example that if Rosi broke her leg and the door was locked, they wouldn't be able to help her. Rosi didn't care right then and there. She just didn't want the closet monsters to get her. She had seen them a total of four times when nobody else was around. They looked like people, but they wore funny cloths and were mean to her. They had pale unnaturally pink skin and spoke a funny language.

It was then that she remembered the note that was slid under the bathroom door a few days ago. Rosi was playing with her rubber ducky and didn't notice it at first. When she finally picked it up, she thought maybe Sarah had put it there. She had then taken the note to Sarah. There were too many big words on there that she didn't understand. Sarah looked at the note and didn't say anything. Rosi didn't think it was very important so she had forgotten about it. Where was Sarah now?

Then a thought struck her, what if Sarah had broken her leg in her room? That's not possible though, wouldn't she have heard when Rosi called out and answered? Bravely, Rosi put her book bag down and took a deep breath. There was only one way to find out.

She moved very slowly and quietly unlocked her door. She turned the knob very very slowly hoping that if there was someone on the other side, they wouldn't notice. When the knob wouldn't turn any further, she hesitated to gather her courage. Afraid to even breathe, she pulled the door open just a crack. She strained to see down the hallway. There was nothing there. The air was still and warm with the afternoon sunlight slanting in through the sunroof. She opened the door wide enough so she could slip through. Gently and as silently as possible, she let go of the doorknob. Again, she went down on her hands and knees and crawled towards Sarah's room. She never took her eyes off of the closet door's knob.

It seemed to have taken ages to reach Sarah's door. When she finally did, she hesitated again. Should she knock or call out? No! That would be a bad idea if the monsters were in the closet again. Without another moment's hesitation, Rosi reached out and grabbed Sarah's doorknob. With a hard turn, she threw her weight against it and fell in. She quickly got back to her feet and slammed the door shut.

Rosi twisted the lock in place. When Rosi turned around, she choked on the sigh she was letting out. What was this? Where was Sarah's bed? Where were her stuffed animals? The walls were still powder blue, but none of Sarah's things were there. Instead, there was a desk, her father's computer, and a filing cabinet. Sarah's plain brown bookshelf was filled with thick heavy hardbound books that looked like something her mom or dad would read. There were things from the den and her mom and dad's room, but nothing that belonged to Sarah. Did they move her downstairs? Why didn't anyone say anything at breakfast? Why didn't Sarah tell her? It was not like they were running late that morning. Rosi began to feel panic close about her throat. The closet monsters had something to do with it, didn't they? Rosi wanted to cry, and her breath was coming out in short gasps.

When Rosi's parents came home that evening, they found their little daughter shaking in the study upstairs. Her eyes stared blankly ahead and she kept muttering things they couldn't decipher, something about towels and a sister. When they had asked her what was wrong, she kept blurting out, "Where's Sarah!"

"Honey, you're an only child," they would reply. She was very pale and would not leave her mother's arms.

"It's the monsters wasn't it? They took her didn't they? Why don't you remember?" Rosi screamed. Her parents exchanged distressed looks. What on earth was Rosi talking about? Was it the stress from moving to a new country? Her mother was crying, what happened to their daughter? They had the police search the house and discover that it had not been broken into. The doctors looked at Rosi and declared that there were no signs of abuse. Who was this Sarah she kept talking about? Was she the culprit?

There was never anything in the news. Rosi's friends claimed to have never remembered Sarah. Even Sarah's friends started being mean to her like all the other big kids. Worst of all, mommy and daddy kept telling her that she's been an only child. Rosi couldn't help but blow up at her parents one night, "What do you mean no Sarah? Is it the same thing with Joel?" Her parents looked at each other, "How do you know about Joel? You were too young."

"Sarah told me," Rosi replied defiantly, "Sarah loves me enough to tell the truth but you don't."

Broken heartedly, her parents sent her to a children's mental institution for a little, while praying for hope that her "condition" would improve. Rosi hated it there and she resented her parents. No one there cared for what she had to say. They just wanted her to believe what they told her. It didn't matter that she was telling the truth about seeing the closet monsters or that she really did have a big sister. She was a kid and she was living in a grownup's world. Grownups made the rules and they had all the power.

Rosi grew tired. She finally accepted that Sarah was gone, and just wanted to go home. She didn't understand why everyone was so bent on telling her Sarah was her imaginary friend. It was as if they were playing a strange game of hide and go seek. She eventually learned to agree with what the elders said. Yet, she was extremely disappointed. Why wouldn't anyone listen to the truth? Sarah did exist. How come there was no trace of her? Sarah's things were gone, even people's memories of her.

"But how come I remember?" Rosi asked herself. No answers came. She didn't know what was going on, but she did know that her voice was too little to make a difference. She sat by helplessly and alone as the world around her turned without her control. Rosi's life was dark as she secretly mourned for her sister. She agreed to say that Sarah was just a dream, and learned that if she kept quiet, she could function in society.

That was also when she learned to disassociate with people who tried to tell her what she had to believe. She put her faith firmly into the idea that there is something bigger than the picture she was allowed to see. Maybe the grownups were really the kids, and they were being lied into believing something that was not real. In turn, they lie to kids because kids were still learning and they would listen most of the time. Except when sometimes something strange would happen. Like Sarah missing. There was no way Sarah was just a dream. Rosi couldn't explain it, and it caused her a lot of anxiety. Nevertheless, she lied and said Sarah was not real. That way, she could at least go home.

A year passed and Rosi had readjusted to life back at home with her mother and father. Rosi's mother had an old friend from college come visit her. Her name was Natasha and even though she was not Chinese, she could still speak the language. Natasha stayed for a weekend. She became close friends with Rosi's mother again after they did a lot of catching up.

Natasha took a particular interest in Rosi. She wasn't married but she loved children and would one day like to settle down and have some of her own. She was in her late twenties. Or at least she appeared to be. Somehow when Rosi looked into her eyes, she could fathom seeing the light from all the stars of the galaxy all at once. It was as if the woman had been to all of them and deep in her soul she had captured their essence. Rosi also saw that Natasha had a lot of pain like how she herself felt about Sarah. But there was something else too, something Rosi could not yet describe in her early years.

Summer rolled around. Rosi didn't have anything planned so she was absolutely thrilled when Natasha called and offered to take her to a summer camp in California. Her parents were doubtful at first and hard to convince. They could not help but remember Joel being missing, and the overprotective parental nature kicked in. In the end, Natasha was able to convince them that Rosi would be well supervised. Though still reluctant, Rosi's parents gave their consent.

It seemed to take forever to get ready. Mom helped Rosi pack and repack her things. She also made a checklist and made Rosi promise to go over it twice before the trip home. Finally, when Natasha rang the doorbell, it was time to go. Rosi's parents smiled and peppered her with kisses. She climbed into the taxi with Natasha and Mom and Dad stood back to wave goodbye. Rosi waved from the taxi's window. She was going to have a great adventure. She could feel it.

Rosi was quiet as she stared out the window. She was suddenly missing Sarah terribly. She wished that her sister could be there to share the adventure. Natasha would've offered to take both of them, Rosi was almost sure of it. Natasha liked children. She would have had fun riding the airplane with Sarah. They would have made a lot of new friends and there would be big kids who weren't mean to her like the ones back home. Rosi sighed shakily as tears threatened her eyes. No one even knew about Sarah. Not even her parents.

"You miss Sarah don't you?" Rosi swung her face around in shock. Natasha was giving her a compassionate look. Rosi opened her mouth to say something, anything. Nothing came to mind so nothing came out. Rosi felt like a fish staring blankly at Natasha. She looked away in embarrassment. She probably just heard Natasha wrong anyway.

"Its alright, I know about Sarah," Natasha continued in a soft voice. Rosi looked at her meekly. So she didn't hear wrong.

"How?" Rosi stuttered finally.

"I know a lot that most people don't," Natasha replied. All of a sudden, a knot released in Rosi and she buried her face against Natasha. She was bawling her eyes out.

"They thought I was crazy but I just missed her! Where did she go? Did the same people who took Joel take her away too," Rosi asked in between sobs. All the anguish poured out right then as if she were a baby again. Rosi was tired of trying to act like a "big girl" and she wasn't ashamed of herself one bit.

"Sh-sh, it'll be alright."

"Then how come mom and dad don't remember her?"

"Because they weren't allowed to." Rosi didn't quite understand Natasha's last statement, but it felt too good to have someone who knew about Sarah.

She had fallen asleep against Natasha and didn't wake up until the taxi stopped at the airport. It was hot and sticky outside, and Rosi's eyes were puffy. As the driver unloaded their baggage, Natasha wiped away her dried tears with a moist toilette. Afterwards, Natasha paid the driver and tipped him handsomely. He gave her a big smile and drove off. Rosi waited patiently, but Natasha made no move to go inside. They stood there like the other people who were waiting to get picked up. Rosi looked up at her questioningly. Natasha smiled warmly and a little apologetically, "We're not going to California."

A pang of fear shot through Rosi. She stared straight forward afraid to look anywhere else. Was Natasha a bad person? Was she taking her away like Joel and Sarah? Rosi started to panic. Was she shaking? Natasha must be taking her away. How else could she have known about Sarah? What if her parents were in on it too? They didn't know about Sarah, or did they just pretend not to know? She wanted to run, but she didn't know where to go. She didn't know what it was, but something was holding her back. Maybe it had to do with the way Natasha told her they weren't going to California. Natasha didn't squeeze her hand. It was loose around Rosi's. Natasha had trusted Rosi not to be afraid. So then why was she?

At that moment, a gray sedan pulled up in front of them. Natasha stepped down and opened the back door. She looked at Rosi patiently. The little girl swallowed. She looked from Natasha to the back seat. She could feel the cool air rushing out at her. There were leather seats too. Before she could let herself change her mind, Rosi climbed in out of the heat.

Rosi sat in the back by herself. Natasha had introduced the man driving as Marcuno. He didn't talk very much. He had acknowledged Rosi when she climbed in. Natasha threw everything into the trunk and climbed in up front. Rosi sat silently like a good little girl. No one said anything.

"Natasha? Where are we really going?" Rosi asked when she could not bite back her curiosity any longer. Natasha turned and smiled, "Don't worry, by the end of the summer, you'll be back safe and sound in your mother's arms." That made Rosi feel a little bit better. Maybe they were just going to a different summer camp and she was safe after all.

All of a sudden, the car accelerated so fast Rosi was thrown backward.

"Brace yourself," Marcuno called out a little too late. Rosi grabbed the seat's edge. They were moving too fast. This wasn't normal.

A control panel flipped from the dashboard and Marcuno pushed a few buttons. All around them, the shape of the car was changing. Rosi shut her eyes. The ride was very bumpy. When it went smooth, she bravely opened one eye. She peered meekly at the window and looked outside. All she saw was the Earth shrinking. She let out a gasp as the spacecraft eased off the burners. Rosi was speechless. Natasha and Marcuno were conversing, passing commands back and forth. The little girl in the back took no notice. She was absolutely dumbfounded.

Little Rosi stood with her back straight. Her large frightened eyes looked to Natasha for comfort, but the woman was standing as she was, with her back stiff. Natasha was staring straight at the wall, with her hands behind her back. Her face was wearing a blank and her eyes did not wander towards Rosi.

They were in parallel lines about six feet apart facing each other. Rosi wasn't sure what the arrangement was exactly. They were all marched in and asked to stand still. A man, his name was Matthew, walked back and forth between them. He was observing the line Rosi was in. He had a gentle, kindly face, but he wore a strict expression. Rosi was afraid to look around. She was aware that there was another girl at the end of the same line she was standing in. There was a boy to her left, his name was Dave, he looked like he was about eight years old. To her right, there were two boys and they were brothers. That was all she knew. Rosi was not sure, but she thought she heard someone call the other girl by the name June. She had white hair and looked about

11 or 12 years old. Later Rosi found out that she was only seven. In the line across from Rosi stood Natasha, a lady with blonde hair, a man with dark hair, and a boy about 13 or 14 years old.

The man they called old Matt was still pacing around in front of them. He stopped in front of the younger of the two brothers, "What is your name young man?"

"Wayne Easton, sir," he replied in a comfortable voice. The ease in his voice spread to her and calmed Rosi down a bit. If he wasn't scared, why should she be?

"Very good, who fetched you here?"

"My brother's friend, Richard, sir." The man nodded in approval and continued to pace. He walked by Rosi and she held her breath. He paused in front of Dave and looked him over. Then he turned to Rosi, "And what is your name young lady?"

"Wh- which name? sir."

"What do people call you?" He asked gently when he saw how frightened she way. After all, she was the youngest one there.

"My friends call me Rosi Tian. My mother and father call me Tian Mei." He smiled and spoke to her in Chinese. Rosi replied him in Chinese, she dared not to ignore a question from him. Surprise spread across her face. A small smile played around Natasha's face, but in a moment, it was gone.

The training began that very day. They started with the testing. They had to see what everyone was capable of. Rosi felt that she needed to see Natasha and find out what was going on. She couldn't get away though, not right now. They were being asked to jump rope and run up a hill.

They were at an institute called SHONDS. It was located in the Nurmana province on Mars. Mars was the military base for Earth, Venus, and itself. The institute was primarily underground, had many levels and was roughly four square miles. SHONDS stood for Solar Heave Ontoo Neida Division Seventeen. It would still be many years before little Rosi was to fully understands the meaning of Ontoo Neida: "forever captivated."

This was the only place for the people of division seventeen to feel at home. This was the only place where they can truly exist and didn't have to live in secret. This was where they will all rest one day, sooner or later.

That night, Natasha went to tuck Rosi in. She smiled warmly at the tired little girl. Rosi had forgotten how urgently she needed to find out what was going on. She accepted this to be her summer camp and as long as Natasha was there, Rosi trusted everything would be fine.

Natasha felt a little bit sorry for the girl, but no doubt she had great confidence in her. She had met a great many soldiers in her time and heard stories of when they were Rosi's age. She knew that this was for Rosi's own good too. Rosi was in danger, which was why her sister was dead. This was her one chance for safety and survival. Still, Rosi did surprise her. The girl showed a lot more potential than Natasha had originally estimated.

"Let me tell you a bedtime story," Natasha said. Rosi smiled and pulled the blanket up to her chin.

"Once upon a time, long ago in ancient China, there was a prince. He was not the heir to the throne because his mother was the fourth wife. But the emperor treated all his children fairly so the Prince was honest and good at heart. As he grew, he continuously helped his father keep council on who was a traitor and who was not. Thus he had many enemies. As a kind gesture, his father hired eight highly trained martial artists to be his bodyguards. The leader of these body guards was Dragon, the second in command was Phoenix, then Kirin." Rosi looked at her curiously. Were Old Matt, Cora, and Marcuno really from ancient China? Natasha continued, "The others were simply named One, Two, Three, Four, and Five. They were trained from birth to be the best.

Not long after the prince had recieved his bodyguards, a war broke out. The emperor's first two sons died in battle. This left the badly wounded third son to be the heir. His bodyguards did their job and saved him. But there were only five bodyguards left. When he became emperor, he ordered the remaining five to train new recruits from select children from the time they could walk. He also sent them to protect all of China. If a leader of the bodyguards were to die, the officer under him would be bumped up. For example, when his first Phoenix died, Kirin became second officer in command, but kept the name Kirin. Another a new Phoenix was chosen, he was to hold the position of third officer in command below Kirin. The tradition and the bodyguards have been passed down through time. They hide in the shadows, watching over the people of China.

One day, Earth needed guardians. There were eighteen groups

selected from Earth. Some were secretive organizations of top soldiers, some were gangs, even the dead emperor's bodyguards were chosen. They were tested and seven groups survived. Soon, five of them had to be destroyed because they were leaking illegal information about the aliens. They last two groups dueled instead of merging because the Chinese bodyguards were too stubborn to let foreigners join them. They were not yet able to see the greater cause of it all. In the end, the Chinese guardians came out the winner. Only the third officer was left in command. He was able to see the whole picture and agreed to have the foreigners join them and that was how division seventeen came to be."

"You call that a bedtime story?" Rosi asked incredulously. Natasha had to laugh.

"Lemme tell you a real one!" Rosi said, "Once upon a time, there were the moon fairies that only came out during a full moon, and they liked to scatter fairy dust on…" Natasha stayed until Rosi's mumbles could no longer be deciphered. The little girl was asleep. She smiled and kissed her forehead. She made sure that blankets would keep Rosi warm. Then Natasha left her to dream about her fairies.

Next day was the day where they were educated on the politics of division 17, and who their allies and enemies were. Old Matt explained to the new recruits why they were there on Mars. He told them that they were in a war. He was completely calm as he told them about the death of the old soldiers. It was due to an error in breaking the code a few weeks ago that division seventeen was sent into an ambush and lost many members. Thus, they needed the new recruits.

There were also a few "field trips" for the new members where they were to visit similar training centers nearby. They were informed later that day, they were to go into surgery, Rosi was a little nervous, but Natasha told her there was nothing to worry about.

Unfortunately, when Marcuno took them to tour Venus and meet allies, they were attacked. Rosi had fallen out of the jet craft. Luckily, it was as they were entering the landing zone. They kept her on life support as Marcuno phoned Old Matt to request permission for Rosi's alteration. Normally this would not have been allowed because it was not at the SHONDS institute. The division members were generally only given clearance to be operation on by approved doctors. However, this was a life or death situation.

At SHONDS, everyone was awakened just before the break of

dawn. This way, they could warm up before training started when the first rays of the sun touched Mars. Breakfast was quick and just after warm up. They were then injected with a serum that enhanced their mental learning and physical capabilities. June's mother, Cora, was Phoenix and she was in charge of the serum. Even though she was the second officer in command and held the official title of "Phoenix," everyone still called her Cora. Cora was her old code name and it stuck to her deeply. Her real name was Angie Stattler and she was married to a bureaucrat. That was a part of her life she left away from SHONDS and was to be kept secret.

Cora was a little superstitious. It was prophesized that the greatest warrior was to be found in division seventeen's next generation. It was no secret that Cora hoped her daughter to be that warrior. Even though Cora did not push her daughter, June was vigilant. She admired her mother very much and aspired to be just and fair like Cora.

Out of boredom one day, Rosi started to list off everyone's code names. Marcuno was the first stranger she had met. He was part Venusian. His great grandma was from Venus. Marcuno meant, "One who can be trusted." He was Kirin and Old Matt did trust him a lot. Cora was Phoenix, second in Command. June, her daughter, was Ciesa. Ciesa meant "piece." June was very proud to be a part of her mother and strived to please her. Rosi could understand that feeling, she was glad to be a piece of her parents too. However, some of it was forced, because after the Sarah incident, some of the security and faith she had in them left her.

Old Matt was Dragon, leading commander. He reminded Rosi of her own grandfather. He always had answers and never panicked. Richard was the last of the old soldiers besides Natasha. He was wounded back after their last mission. He was "Ornor" which meant "wind seeker." He never spoke much, but Rosi wasn't afraid of him. It wasn't an angry silence. It was determination.

Wayne was about a year and a half older than Rosi. He was Sandman because he liked to meditate. The more physical reason was his love of using variations of the sleeper hold. His brother Scott was Deklar, which meant "lightning" in Martian. Then there was the other guy, Dave. He decided to create his own name, Neroz. No one knew what it meant and he explained that it wasn't supposed to have a meaning, it was just mumbo jumbo. Natasha was Emerald. This was because of her Irish background. Rosi herself, was Dove, this was a nickname given to her by Natasha and one of the tech assistants at SHONDS due to her meek nature and unwillingness to fight on most occasions.

By the day after the alterations, everyone was able to leave the ICU. They slept back at their dorms and Ciesa was back to sharing a bunk with Rosi. Normally Ciesa had the top bunk because Rosi was a little uncertain about heights. For now, Rosi ignored her discomfort and courteously offered her weak friend the bottom bunk.

"Mother said that if we win this war, she'll take us to Liva to celebrate. She thinks you're a 'sweet little girl.' I'm glad she likes you, I haven't had a friend she approved of in quite a while." June chuckled weakly. Rosi joined in and was just plain happy that June wasn't in the ICU anymore. Ciesa sighed and continued, "I have not been to Liva to see my father in a while. He works for Yolukia. Do you know who Yolukia is? It's spelled E-U-L-O-O-K-E-Y-A, but Y-O-L-U-K-I-A in English."

"No."

"He's a politician who is running for the office of ruler of the local galaxies. I honestly do not know how many galaxies are in our group. I've barely left the solar system and they don't teach all that kinda stuff here."

"Barely! I've never left at all!" Rosi exclaimed in awe. She envied June. Ever since she learned of the other planets, she longed to leave and explore the galaxy. Maybe she would someday. When she was older and allowed to do more on her own. Maybe Natasha could take her. Natasha was becoming her best friend too. Rosi remembered her slight dislike towards the woman for dragging her into this, but now, it was all well compensated for.

"Well," June continued, "you will get to if we win the war. I pray we do. Do you pray? Do you believe in God? I do." That caught Rosi off guard, "I don't know, I never really thought about it, I used to, but now there are these planets with life on them that aren't in the bible . . . . . . let me think about it, I will get back to you. So tell me about Liva."

"My dad works at Liva. It's a long story. I'll start from the beginning. Did you know that the Milky Way galaxy has the highest crime and death rates? Did you know that of intelligent life, humans, throughout the rest of the galaxy, are considered third from the bottom on the intellectual scale? Well, anyway, Yolukia is trying to work at curiosity to win the election. He's really a cool guy. He's done a lot. He says that he will be able to take a human and make him governor of the Milky Way and the human would be able to clean it up. No one else in the galaxy cares about us so they are curious to see if it can happen. But Yolukia has faith in humans. He thinks we're not as bad as people say we are. That's why he hired my dad. My dad is half Chinese and half American. My mom is Russian and German but we live on Mars. Did you know that there are eight different genders existent in this one species of aliens? Did you know that we don't call aliens "aliens" we call them people because they are citizens of a place? Did you know that on Jupiter you can marry six people at once and there is such a thing as a temporary six-year marriage? A lot of things run by sixes over there. I used to like Jupiter, but they're being jerks right now, so we have to go kick their butts!" June started to giggle, and Rosi joined.

"That is, if we can! You know, we might die."

"Yeah, we might," she agreed. They were thoughtful for a moment.

"Hey June?" Rosi called mostly to see if she was asleep.

"Yeah?" She wasn't.

"What do you call an alien that's not a citizen of a place?" Rosi blurted out just to say something.

"I dunno, a bum?" They both tried to stifle their laughs so they would not get in trouble. After a few moments of breath holding, they calmed down. June was getting sleepy. Rosi stopped talking and closed her eyes. Soon, they were both in dreamland.

"What's the war over?" Scott asked.

"As a friend you can ask me that, but when taking orders, you cannot ask such questions," Mark said, "It is something over immigration rights to this new spot on Jupiter that was discovered to contain riches. Some people think that Jupiter is trying to hog it all. It was previously declared that such places belonged to the system, not the planet. I'm not quite sure of the details myself. These places are supposedly 'fountains of youth' or more accurately, it cures some pretty weird diseases. The esoterics believe it is an energy well from heaven, but I don't know what I believe, I am not allowed to as a soldier. These wells are only located on gaseous planets, none on the terrestrial ones. So those ancient Earth explorers, like Ponce De Leon, were really stupid searching for them on Earth. I mean, the people who go there were granted permission and the next thing you know, they're being kicked out. That, and some other 'countries' on Jupiter were having problems with Venus. So, naturally we sided with Venus. So, yeah, that's that. A little bit like World War One on

Earth crossed with the Cold War."

They flew in silence for a while and each were lost in their own thoughts. Then they rounded the sun. The windows were special glass, so Rosi could stare straight into the burning ball. The beautiful fire shown brightly, illuminating every part of the solar system at one point or another. The sun was the source of life. The sun stood for everything. The sun was what she wanted to be. She wanted to shine, she wanted to be admired, and strong. She wanted people to need her, to depend on her. She wanted to hold them up, to be that shining star!

The sun was also what was smiling at her the day Sarah disappeared. It was the only thing telling her to not lose hope. Now she couldn't tell if she had any hope left or not. Her world was completely changed.

"Okay people, look alive, we are approaching Venus," Richard called out. Rosi's breath caught in her lungs. It was a beautiful sight. Billions of stars twinkled at her and she felt lost in emptiness dotted with tiny pieces of glitter. They rounded the sun at a safe distance. The Earth was behind them somewhere. Slowly, a little green dot became more and more clear.

"Remember people, do not leave the vehicle until you are underground. Your body systems are not yet ready to handle these different planetary conditions. We will be only at the medical base here, the most notorious one, ranked fifth in the whole system, so if anything happens, its more than likely that we can save you. This place is called Wynds. Don't make fun of the name! They take their work very seriously." No one did, they were just as thrilled as Rosi to be in traveling through the expansive vacuum.

The planet was beautiful. Rosi stared in breathless awe. The yellow, white and green clouds swirled gently and invitingly. She just wanted to dance through them. It floated there in space, a graceful sphere, mysterious and elegant. She was fidgety, and could not wait to set foot and explore.

They flew to the side of the planet that was in night. They passed with ease as they descended through the thin atmosphere, which was the cause for Venus' extreme weather conditions that made living on the surface nearly impossible. They flew toward the Wynds landing area. Everything was cleverly disguised so that Venus' neighbors would not discover life there. Not that it would have been hard with all the clouds obstructing the view of the surface. As they approached, Mark picked up a radio and spoke into it in a language they had never heard before. A large part of the ground opened up. Mark reduced speed greatly.

They were about to enter the ground when the ship jolted. It flipped upside down, which is very dangerous with the effects of gravity. Mark skillfully got it steady again. He was yelling urgently into the radio, Rosi grasped her armrests like she did the backseat when she first rode with Mark. Her heart was about to beat out of her chest. What was going on? Before anyone know what to do, smaller areas of the ground opened up and other spacecrafts flew out. Suddenly the ship was hit again and everyone as jolted wildly. This time, a gash opened in the vehicle and Rosi fell out.

She forced her eyes open. Pain coursed throughout her. She couldn't breath, could not even writhe in pain. She saw the great doors closing above her and the Venus atmosphere was fading from sight, no longer beautiful due to the spacecrafts flying around, firing at each other. She heard yelling and people approaching her. Something odd seemed to be coursing through her veins and she felt very unnatural. Smelling blood, she slipped out of consciousness.

"Yes, hello? Is this Dragon? This is Kirin! We were hit! I repeat, we were hit! Recruit 117 is injured and is in desperate need of major medical attention." Mark yelled into the phone to Matthew.

"What?" he strained to hear. "No! Very serious! Brink of death!" he yelled into the phone, "She was exposed openly to Venus atmosphere, I need clearance for her operation!" He struggled to hear over the noise. He replied in a holler, "It can't wait! The Wynds army is fighting off the attacker! We can't risk a trip back! They need your permission to operate on her, which means she will have to be altered now! She can't wait or she will die!" He listened. A smile crossed his face, "Yes sir, Dragon! I will tell them to commence the surgery! Thank you sir!" Mark hung up and rushed back to the operating room where the surgeons were standing by. He nodded. They closed the doors and began to work.

Rosi was first aware of sound. It was breathing. It sounded close, as if it were next to her. She slipped in and out of sleep. Every time she tried to open her eyes, it felt like there were weights placed on them. She heard the breathing and realized it was her own. The breathing kept her connected to reality. She slipped into unconscious sleep again. There was nothing but black and emptiness. The second time she awoke, she was still breathing steadily. She thought she heard faint murmurs but was not sure. In a few seconds, she was back to black asleep again. Rest came over her body as it was slowly healing on its own. She was altered. An artificial substance was injected into her blood after her body was mostly patched up. This substance was made to assist humans in natural healing at an accelerated rate. She was given only a portion of the normal dosage. They did not want her to fall into shock. Every few hours, they gave her a check up, and a new injection.

After a handful of hours, Rosi was aware of sound again. She was awake. She could feel too. There was a blanket over her. It was comfortable, like the blanket she had at home. The one she would use to cover herself with when she curled up with a mug of cocoa in front of the fireplace. She attempted to open her eyes again. Slowly, like trying to drag deadweight, she finally managed to pry them open.

June looked up, she saw Rosi open her eyes. She jumped up with joy, "You guys!" she was barely able to whisper, "You guys! She's awake!" Everyone rushed into the room and crowded around her. Rosi was happy to see them there, waiting for her. It made her feel loved. She knew then, that her existence had become more significant that it had been before she had arrived at the SHONDS. These people knew her, and they would listen and support her because nothing she could ever say to them could be too crazy to be true. A doctor soon came in to give her a check up.

"Well, I see you're healing nicely! I will just give you the last of the injection and you will be fine!" he spoke with an accent she never heard before. She also noticed that he looked rather strange. He had a humanistic form, but not quite. She then realized she was on Venus, and this was the first alien, next to Mark, that she has ever seen! Even Mark was only part alien. She was quite excited, but was unable to express herself. She felt a prick on her arm, followed a few seconds later by another prick.

"Now, just close your eyes, relax, and rest up, you should be as good as new in an hour or two," the doctor said. She obeyed, and soon, she was asleep again enveloped in comforting trust.

Mark conversed with Matt, it was decided that Rosi was to receive a full alteration right there on Venus. That would include the translator in her mind that will allow her to understand various different languages, like a babel fish. An identification chip was to be placed into her arm too. Then a permanent version of the healing injection was to be given. It had the power to heal as much as a missing finger. It could easily allow her to heal bullet wounds, stab wounds, etc. But when it comes to missing appendages, they only heal into a stump. A new arm will have to be manufactured and reattached.

Rosi awoke feeling refreshed and energized. She pulled the blanket off of her. She looked around and panicked, no one was there. Did they leave without her? Just then Dave walked in to check on her and she sighed in relief.

"Hey! You're awake!"

"Yep!" she ran and gave him a hug. If her parents saw her, she would be in trouble for being that way with a boy, but she was on Venus, not at home. There had to be different rules!

"I'm all okay now! Where's everyone else?" she inquired.

"They're outside, are you sure you can walk on your own?"

"Yes!" Mark walked in and smiled at little Rosi, "Well, its sure nice to see you on your feet again!" Then in a serious tone he added, "We have to go over what happened and you have to know about the new you."

Rosi hid her confusion and followed him. First she was sent into a room where there were fresh clothes. She changed out of the hospital gown into a standard beige SHONDS uniform. She opened the door and Mark was waiting. She followed him down the corridor. She took notice of the nurses and doctors nodding respectfully to him. They treated him as if he were a nobleman. Rosi found it curious and made a mental note to ask him if it were because he was Kirin of division 17. She had a feeling the answer was "yes."

They were in a room with the same doctor that gave Rosi the last injection. He nodded to them respectfully and opened the door for them. Rosi followed Kirin in. He sat down at a circular metallic table, he told her to take a seat too. She complied. Once seated, she began to swing her feet, but then realized that she had to act like an adult now. The doctor seated himself and sighed. He began to explain the damage that was done to Rosi when she fell.

"Cool!" she said. Realizing she wasn't supposed to say anything, she shut her mouth. She couldn't help it, she was asleep for a long time and was as hyper as any child her age would be. The doctor smiled and continued. When he was finished explaining injuries, he went

on to explain what they had done to her body.

"We call it Alteration. It used to be genetic, it could only be done to a zygote, which is a newly formed baby, but now we have the technology to do it on any living being with a circulatory system. Each being has to have a specific formula for the different types of blood. We have thousands of different serums now. We also had to insert detection wires throughout your body. These will have to remain in you. Maybe years from now, technology will not require them. They are simply used to help you maintain homeostasis, or balance on the inside. You can also breathe any kind of atmosphere or in water. Your lungs are capable of separating oxygen from most substances. You can live for five hours without oxygen before you start to feel the symptoms of fainting. This is because your blood cells are now capable of storing oxygen on their own." The doctor was trying to find words to explain to a child.

"Also," he continued, "we have inserted a translator in your mind. This allows you to understand 550 living languages. You can also learn others at a highly accelerated speed if you pay attention to their dialogue, you know, the way they talk. The Alteration left you with prolonged stamina, which is endurance. It makes it easier for you to build up your muscles naturally and to stay in shape longer. So basically, you are a kind of superhuman. You can also go 56 hours without sleep, and then only 8 hours of sleep is required for your brain to rest itself. So, to end this, I would like to congratulate you for being reborn here on Venus!" He stuck out a hand and Rosi shook it. She was still trying to absorb all she just heard. She was now a superhuman? In what sense? She would have to speak with Natasha.

They all returned to the SHONDS institute as soon as possible. Natasha greeted her with a tight hug.

"Oh God! When I heard, I though I had lost you for a moment there!"

"I'm alright, I'm a superhuman now too!"

"So I've been told! Welcome to the club! You are the first qualified to fight!" Old Matt walked in, "Which brings us to topic. You were attacked, which meant Jupiter broke the stalemate, a diplomatic war has been set," he paused and in a grave voice added, "we are likely to get chosen. All of your training has been complete. The rest of you will be altered now, as soon as possible." Old Matt was obviously tired and something else seemed to nag at his mind. An hour later, the Martian doctors were flown in and everybody was operated on at the

SHONDS extensive medical lab where Rosi should have been altered as well.

The next day, the secretary of war of the Nurmana province, where SHONDS was located, was waiting for them. Division 17 was nominated to fight the diplomatic war. They will be informed tomorrow morning of any definite details. He left shortly. Rosi did not like him. He was a small and miserable man who probably didn't like children either. Later she was informed that he was the man who made Old Matt send division 17 in on the wrong side, causing the death of seven of the division's members.

"Natasha?"

"Yes?"

"What did happen to Sarah?" Natasha looked like she did not want to tell, but Rosi's eyes kept persisting. Something stirred inside of Natasha. Sometimes it felt almost as if Rosi had become her own daughter.

"She got a message that was sent to you, she went in your place, they killed her, we were late, we could not stop it. The people were from division 21, they no longer exist, such an act was a violation and they were terminated."

"Terminated?"

"Destroyed. Not just imprisoned and forced to reseign, but killed." Natasha felt that she could not and should not lie to someone who was entering the world where such things occurred. A chill ran through the six year old when she heard the words, but she kept herself steady. After all, she was the one who asked.

"But why?" in her mind came the piece of paper she got when she was five, she could only read her name and some more common words, but there were a lot of big words she didn't understand. So she asked Sarah what it meant. Sarah never told her, soon after that was when Sarah disappeared.

"First of all, they were not supposed to be on Earth, then, they killed somebody, an innocent child, and third . . ." Natasha paused, "They were trying to kill a future prophesized leader. It might have been Sarah, but I guess we will never know. No one knows if Sarah was supposed to die or not." Another chill ran through Rosi, she was supposed to be dead. But Sarah died in her place. She did not want to say anything.

She did not want anyone to blame her, to make her guilt deeper and harder to live with.

"Well, you'll be going home soon, I'm sure you will be alright, you've learned pretty quickly and in all honesty, I think you might very well be the strongest fighter." Rosi gave her a look of disbelief.

"Honest." Natasha's tone was definite.

"Thank you," Rosi smiled.

That night, she laid awake listening to Ciesa's light snoring. Tomorrow was the day of the diplomatic war. This was a way of settling disputes while minimizing casulties. Two elite fighting groups were set to compete. The conditions varied based upon what the politicians decree. Sometimes there were weapons, other times odd terrains, and rarely there were both.

Tomorrow they would all be placed into a maze and be given nothing more that a dagger with a Trex coating. Trex was a newly discovered chemical that had detrimental effects on altered beings.

This was the first time Rosi was to fight. Yet, she did not feel nervous at all, as if she had everything in control. The whole experience on Mars lacked a certain "real" quality to her. It was almost as if she was really at a summer camp. Nothing bad could happen. This was the same mentality she had when her brother, Joel, first went missing.

She let sleep take over and she slipped into the realm of dreams. There, she was at home again, sleeping in her own bed. Her teddy was tucked under the crutch of her arm and mom and dad were just down the hall. On the other side, was Sarah's old room.

Too soon, morning came. As she boarded the large craft that came to pick them up, she was overcome by extreme homesickness. She told herself that after this was done with, she would be able to go home. After this, maybe, just maybe, Sarah would be alive again and everything would be normal. Wasn't this just a test?

Rosi stood in line with the rest of division 17. She felt numb, as if she had left her body and it was running on automatic instincts. She was not nervous, everything just felt unreal. She looked over at June and then on the other side at Wayne. They were both stoic as the other soldiers were and Rosi became self-conscious. She should stop fidgeting and get serious or else she might get into trouble.

They landed the large craft and Rosi had no idea where in the world she was. For that matter, she had no idea where in the universe they were. The entire division followed Old Matt into a room and met with the opponents and faced the diplomats. Rosi kept a straight face and secretly tried to scan the faces of the aliens sitting on the screen who were scrutinizing her. Those were the men and women who were arguing over Jupiter and those were the men and women who needed her to fight. Rosi wondered why they didn't fight themselves. If she made a mess in her room back home, mom and dad always made her clean it up herself.

To the other side of the room stood a handful of people dressed in black with white trim. Rosi didn't look at them much. She vaguely noted that she was going to have to fight them later. A map showed on a large screen hanging on the wall. The two groups were to enter from the opposite sides of the large, sterile white room. Old Matt nodded and led the group out the way them had entered. The other group left the other way. Rosi obediently followed Ciesa who marched in front of her and they entered a large arena like room. Large halogen lamps hung from the ceiling giving everything an impersonal glow. To keep herself occupied until start was called, Rosi kept saying her codename over and over in her head, "Dove, Dove, Dove."

Start was finally called. They rushed forth into the maze, each going their own separate ways. Natasha called over her shoulder to Rosi, "Remember, don't underestimate them!"

Rosi tore through the maze, she braced herself as she went around each corner. There was no one. She was disappointed that she might not get to fight. Then again, that might not be a bad thing. They were all told in the beginning that there was a large room at the center of the maze. There would be more room there to fight instead of skinny corridors. If only she could find her way to the center room, she would be alright.

No sooner had she wished it, she heard brawling sounds and a right turn brought her to the center room. Ciesa was fighting with a male and Sandman was fighting someone else. Dove took a nimble step forward. Suddenly there was someone trying to restrain her from behind. Without thinking, she moved by instinct. She grasped the arm around her neck and tried to twist it away, but the person was much stronger and Dove could not grasp the arm tightly enough. Instead, she brought her leg up and kicked the person in the face. These people had two knees, one that bent forward and one that bent back. The person did not anticipate the kick Dove gave because she herself could not kick like that.

Dove faced her opponent. She did not know what to do. Her mind went blank. She bit her lip to fight the tiny burn of panic in her gut.

"Remember," she told herself, "fight to defend." The female lunged at Dove with the knife, she dodged it but the woman brought her arm around and cut Dove in the back. She cried out in pain. The woman was her height, a small creature, possibly a little bit older, but was very strong. Dove held her back in pain. The wound burned, it was deep. The trex coating on the knife kept her body from self-healing. Dove picked up her own dagger and the two continued to struggle. The opponent was very vicious and tried multiple times to stab Dove again. After being hurt once, Dove was extra careful and did not give the woman another chance. In a quick swoop, the woman kicked Dove's knee from under her, as she went down, Dove pretended to stab at the woman's gut, but she dodged the knife, lowering her face just enough. In one smooth motion, Dove slashed upward. She had hesitated for only a moment and that was enough to slow her. The woman recovered her balance and moved saving herself from a knife in the throat. She only received a small slash on her cheek.

She grasped Dove's wrist and tried to break her arm, but Dove did not allow it. With a quick twist, she restrained the woman. But stupidly, she had loosened her grip when the woman stopped struggling. Dove's inexperience gave her opponent a chance to get loose. Dove pushed her away and when the woman was off balance, Dove jumped and kicked the woman as she turned around. She read the anger on the woman's face as she wiped the blood off of her mouth. Dove stood, waiting, dagger in hand. Sandman had left the room, only Ciesa was in the room. The woman got up and came at Dove again with an aggravated cry escaping her lips.

Dove panicked and closed her eyes. Her favorite part of the training was when they learned to increase their other senses by eliminating eyesight. She heard the woman's breathing and focused on it. She heard the arm move the air and sensed the slight air current. Dove blocked and kicked the woman in the stomach. Ciesa almost backed into her. Dove gave her a hand by grabbing the man's arm and knocking him over by slashing what would be the Achilles tendon on a human. He cried out in pain but got up immediately putting most of his weight on one leg. This occurred at the same time Ciesa fell by the woman. For a period of time, they fought against the other's opponent.

When they were in close proximity to each other, they switched again. Dove made a mistake and opened her eyes again. The woman faked a punch to her face, as Dove dodged and blinked, she was left off guard for a split second. When she was aware of things again, the woman's arm had come down. Dove jumped back, but she received another deep wound across the stomach. She was loosing more blood. She could not help but drop her weapon. She clutched her stomach. Was this the end? Without realizing it, Rosi began to accept death and defeat. It was just much easier to give in. Besides, she didn't even believe in what she was fighting for. At least she would be with Sarah if she were dead too. She sank down on all fours, trying to force herself back to her feet and clear her head. The woman positioned herself to Dove's side and prepared to stab down.

Sandman had eliminated his opponent. There was exactly two minutes left. He went back to the center room to see if his help was needed. He arrived in time to see Dove fall to her knees. He had never seen that much blood in his life before and blanked out, not sure of what to do. His own opponent didn't even bleed that much, Sandman merely snapped his neck. Then, there was a scream. It was Ciesa who snapped him back to his senses. Ciesa had a dagger through her abdomen. The man who just killed her let go and watched her sink to the floor. Her blood flowed over him and left a pool on the ground that quickly grew. The woman raised her arms which brought Sandman's attention back to Dove. He saw that the woman was about to stab down. Before a second could split, he had thrown his own dagger and it struck the woman in the back. She sank as Ciesa did. At the same moment, the man turned around as Sandman sprinted up to Dove. Taking up her dagger, he turned to face the man. They stood staring at each other and Sandman was about to lunge when a loud buzzer sounded. Time was called. The man placed his hand on his chest and bowed, then walked away. Sandman checked Ciesa's pulse. She was dead. He heard a whimper and turned around. Dove pleaded with her eyes for him to do something. Not stopping to think, he picked her up and went back into the maze, hoping he would find a way out again.

Another loud buzzing sound made Sandman jump. Were they fighting again? Suddenly, the walls began to move and were sinking into the ground. The area was to become a single large room. He set her down and looked around for help. She held onto his sleeve as he tried to stand up. She was frightened. She thought she was going to die and she did not want to die alone.

The walls were gone now. The officials appeared. Sandman looked around again. He saw Scott standing by Old Matt. He let out a sigh of relief to know that his brother was fine. Suddenly, a scream was heard. Cora rushed to her daughter's dead body. She began to weep without control. The guards looked on. To them, this was nothing. The war was over. It was all collateral damage. Sandman was surprised at Cora's display of emotion. It was against everything they were trained to do. Yet deep down, he was glad to see her as a human despite her loss.

Division 17 was the winner. Rosi and Richard were rushed to the hospital. Richard died there. He and Ciesa were the only ones to die that day. His death did not count because he was still alive when time was called. The other team had three deaths and two wounded. Rosi did not know until later that the woman she was fighting with was the other team's leader.

Dragon was very angry. He knew that his team wasn't ready to fight. It was only on paper that they were all physically qualified because of their Alterations. That was how they were chosen, by random lottery between all of the nominated groups. This was all just diplomacy Rosi could not understand so she just laid quietly in the hospital bed waiting to heal. A few hours later, they all returned to SHONDS. Cora with a broken heart. She immediately requested to retire. She was only 38 years old while most soldiers stay on until fifty or even longer. Old Matt said he would think about it. He was 49 years old.

The war was ended with that battle. The treaty was left up to the diplomats and politicians. The fighting was done and over with. In three more days, Rosi was completely healed. She attended June and Richard's funeral. There was no fear, just sorrow in her heart. She thought back to the jokes she and June had cracked at Old Matt when they should have been asleep. June was a great best friend. She was really going to miss her. But, as Richard told her, "it's all inside."

A thoughtful calm had fallen over Rosi. She watched as they lowered the coffins, one by one. Richard sank below the land. His words were ringing in her ears. "You never forget, but there is nothing you can do." Rosi did not cry, she wanted to but could not. Richard told her that you can only go on taking orders. Like a robot. Emotions were not allowed to get in the way. She felt an aching in her heart as the coffins disappeared under the dirt. Looking around, she saw other tombstones. Those of earth were buried in an earthly fashion. This plot was for division 17. She looked at the past generations and knew that someday, this would be her resting place. She said her last silent good byes to June and Richard. The tears no longer held back in her heart. Inside, she wept, and understood her sadness. Outside, she was just a girl standing there. There was no mistaking, inside she had died a little bit too.

She expressed her condolences to Cora who was trying hard not to weep. Her former best friend's mother held her tightly and expressed how glad she was that at least Rosi was safe, for now. By the end of the week, Natasha took her home. Rosi understood that she was sworn to secrecy. It wouldn't be that hard, back home everything was a different world, a different life. She would just have to pretend that nothing happened. She had had plenty of practice because of Sarah's disappearance. Well, by now, Rosi had accepted that Sarah was dead.

A few weeks after Ciesa and Richard's funeral, Cora officially and formally announced her retirement. There was nothing to be done right then and again Old Matt said he would consider. All of the younger ones were sent back to Earth. After taking Rosi home, Natasha returned to Mars. The elders sat quietly in the meeting hall. Old Matt was the first to break the silence.

"I don't know about you, but I don't really have a home to go back to. This division has been my life." Natasha nodded solemnly, "I would like to have a child. Rosi is so wonderful. I wish I didn't have to do this to her." After hearing Natasha, tears started to slide down Cora's cheeks. Natasha caught herself, "I'm sorry Cora," she said sadly. They all felt old sitting there. They had seen and felt tragedy upon tragedy fall upon their heads. The apathy that they showed on the surface was starting to wear thin. It used to be a lack of discipline to cry or show any emotion when in an official meeting, but the old soldiers were just conversing their hearts. Nothing more, nothing less.

"Rosi was her best friend," Cora breathed. Marcuno sympathetically laid a hand on her shoulder and handed her his handkerchief, "Richard was my brother-in-law, I have to go home and tell my sister that I got her husband killed."

"But he died a hero," Natasha said somewhat sarcastically. They all felt the tinged tone and tasted the sourness in their hearts as well. The strength that lived in her soul for all these decades was finally beginning to burn out. They all knew that hero or not, Richard was still dead. Eventually, they were all going to die. They were not as invincible as they were once made to believe. What was their purpose besides obeying, serving, giving their soul and watching it die with the people they were closest to as they passed away?

A few months passed after the funeral of Ciesa and Richard. Everyone was called for a meeting at SHONDS. Natasha and Rosi were the first to arrive. Old Matt was sitting there with Marcuno. Rosi looked around curiously, where was Cora? Ritually, little Rosi walked up to Old Matt. He remained seated and gave her the smallest of his array of smiles. She knelt on her right knee and crossed her right fist to her left shoulder. Bowing her head, she paid recognition to her lead officer, "Dragon, Dove present."

"Take a seat," he replied. She listened. Natasha did the same thing and took a seat beside Rosi. One by one, everyone else arrived. They all went and paid acknowledgement to their leader and one by one he told them to take a seat.

Finally, when everyone was settled, Old Matt stood up. His usual kindly face was glum. He looked a lot older. The many years of strength through peril was fading fast. When he spoke, his voice carried the same authority, but a plague of exhaustion was taking hold, "I called this meeting for a very important reason. It seems that it is time for the new generation to find new recruits." When Rosi heard that she quickly looked around and caught Wayne and Scott's eyes. What did Old Matt mean? The brothers seemed to be asking the same question with their eyes.

"I received a message," he continued, "Cora's husband informed me that she has committed suicide." Rosi silently choked on her breathing. She looked around at all the faces and so did Dave. Cora was nowhere to be seen.

"I did receive her request to retire shortly after June's funeral a few months back. Her husband now told me her choice for replacement. I have the duty now to point out the new officer." He paused for a breath then continued slowly, "I am also announcing my own retirement. I have given this division my life, and now I wish to be left in peace." The new generation exchanged looks of surprise, but the older ones were quiet.

"This will leave Kirin as leading officer," Old Matt declared and gestured toward Marcuno. He continued, "Cora calls Dove to be her replacement." Rosi was bewildered. Cora wasn't dead. She couldn't take her place as Phoenix, what was going on?

"Approach me Phoenix," Old Matt said to Rosi. She wanted to shake her head and say no. However, it was instilled in her that she could not deny his command. Automatically, her legs carried her up to him. They moved her as if they were separate from the rest of her body and her mind. She lowered herself onto her knee again and bowed while still holding onto denial. Something inside of her was screaming in crazed fury. Old Matt placed his hand on her head, "Now, I declare her Phoenix in place of the old." When Old Matt lifted his hand, he pointed to a seat on his right that was left empty. Rosi obediently walked over slowly, letting all the information she had just heard sink in. She sat down as heavily as she felt. It hit her like a sack of bricks. People die, and Cora was dead.

"Since Natasha has also put in her retirement," Old Matt spoke again. Rosi darted a glance at Natasha. She felt her hopes slip, everyone was abandoning her and she was helpless. Old Matt continued, "I will not be able to choose her to take my place. I have chosen another that I believe to be a strong warrior. I choose Wayne." With that, the equally hesitant Wayne knelt before him and as he did to Rosi, Old Matt declared Wayne the new Dragon. Old Matt and Marcuno both rose out of their seats. Kirin sat down in Dragon's seat and Wayne sat in the chair Marcuno left. Old Matt was now standing.

"I have a question that I think you should all bear in mind every day you come here," he said in a booming voice. His strength seemed to have returned, but his tiredness was still apparent and ever present in his eyes.

"Can anyone answer me," he challenged, "what is the difference between a soldier, and a warrior?" No one moved. They could all sense that he was going to answer for them.

"A soldier follows orders. He can only do as he is told, he is bound by the law of a government. Like us." There was a dramatic pause and his voice softened, "but a warrior. A warrior is someone who acts with heart. The only laws he has are the ones of right and wrong he carries with him, and not just the words "right" and "wrong" but to truly understand that there must be a balance between all good and evil. I beg of you never to forget the origin of our division. Never forget the ancient bodyguards from Asia on Earth. They were warriors. Let that be an inspiration to you through hard times."

When everyone left SHONDS that day, they felt uneasy. Things were definitely changing. Never have so many of an older generation retired or died simultaneously in the course of a year. They felt that they lacked leadership and direction. What did the future have in store for division seventeen?

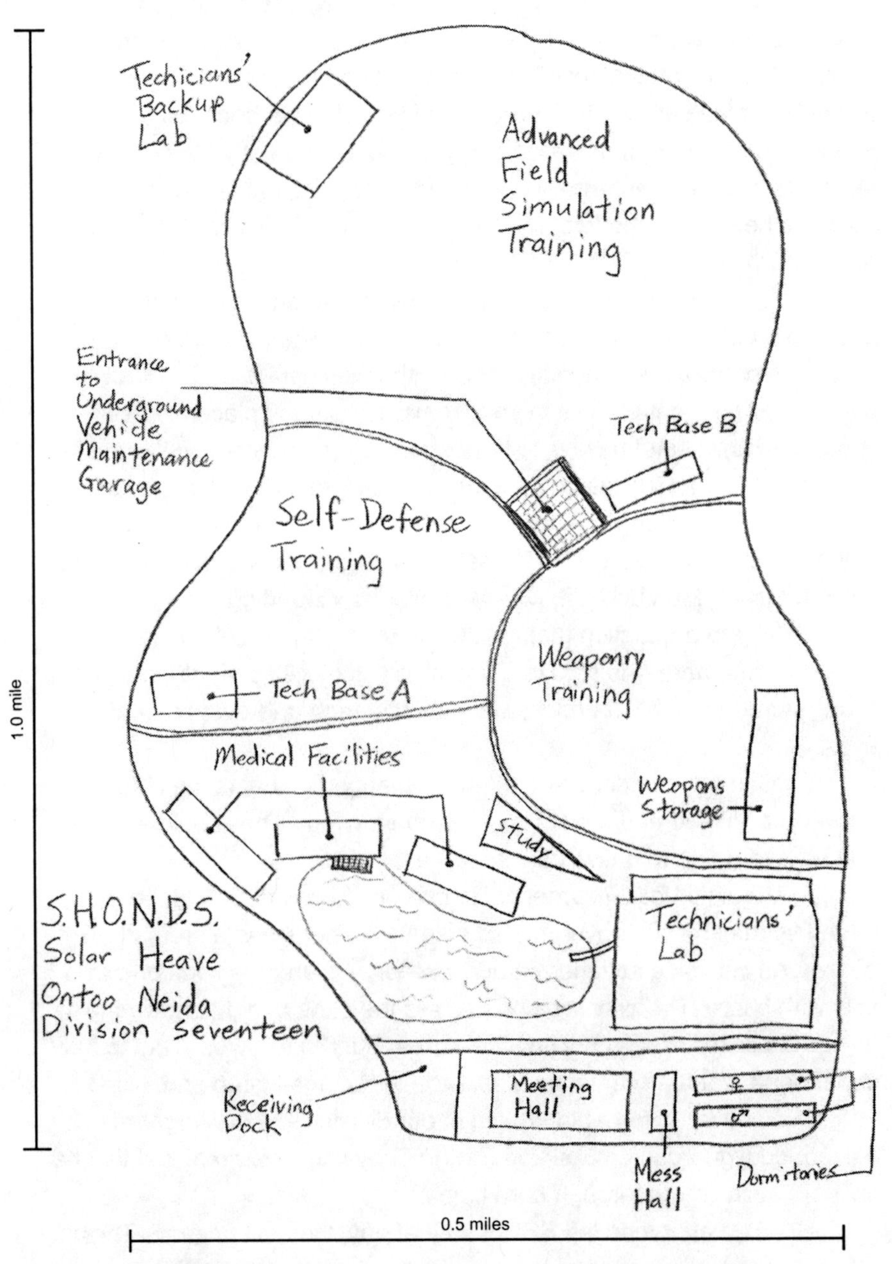

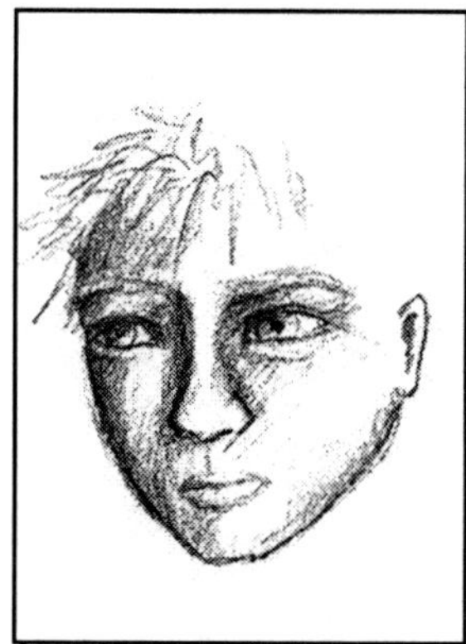

Age: 17
Wayne Trevor Easton
"Sandman"

Age: 20
Scott Frederick Easton
"Deklar"

Age: 14
Jessica Gretchen Easton
"Calm"

Age: 14
Darrel James Easton
"Zap!"

Age: Unlisted
Dave
"Neroz"

Age: Unlisted
Marcuno
"Kirin"

Age: 16
Lisa Joyce Sclaper (L.J.)
"Angel"

Age: 16
Rose Tian (Rosi)
"Phoenix"

Age: 16
Susan Linda Mateos (Su-Lin)
"Joy"

Age: 16
Erica Lucy Camus (Eureekuh)
"Sunshine"

Age: 16
Paula Eve Camus (Veea or V)
"Moongirl"

Age: 16
Araline Madeline Ashworth (Ara)
"Tinkerbell"

CHAPTER TWO

By the time Rosi turned eight years old, a relatively quiet two years passed with Marcuno as the leading officer in command. Without war, there was no unrest and no need to be on alert. Everything was peaceful and everyone was relaxed. The new recruits were only called to Mars for tests. Kirin had to make sure that everyone was still in good shape. He also demanded for everyone go on "field trips" again. This was to ascertain friendship amongst those who don't see each other that often.

There were three new members now. Jessie and Darrel were brother and sister to each other and cousins to Wayne and Scott. Dave brought a hometown friend, Joe. Rosi led a quiet life home on Earth. Her parents were overprotective because of Joel missing so Rosi never made too many friends. There was no one Rosi trusted enough to bring along, so she had no recruits.

They were all sitting in the meeting hall preparing to leave SHONDS when Kirin appeared with four doctors behind him. His mustache was twitching from agitation.

"They wanna clone somebody," Kirin spat out with total lack of formality. This shocked everyone because division leaders were supposed to act with poise. He was very angry, "I call this session informal, everyone is allowed to speak freely," he paused, "they are not cloning me though." The outburst made the doctors uncomfortable and they trailed a distance behind him.

The one who appeared to be the head doctor spoke up, "Well, now that I suppose you know why we all came here, let me explain a little. It is not our duty to question the ethics of cloning. We were merely assigned into this research field, much like yourselves when you are given orders. We were only granted access to ask military personnel for cloning permission. The council thinks that increasing the militia can't hurt. With that said, we are here to collect your personal consent for DNA samples."

Marcuno still refused to look at the doctors. Almost everyone said no due to personal ethical beliefs. Jessie and Darrel thought it was scary and refused. However, Rosi and Wayne, the two who were old enough not to be afraid but too young to understand what the big fuss was about, were very curious. They were the only two who gave their consent. Nevertheless, the doctors were overjoyed that there were any volunteers at all.

Not long after the clones joined the division, Marcuno retired and he selected Jessie for his replacement. He disappeared and no one has been able to contact him. Whether he was upset with the cloning, the clones or he was just tired of the way division seventeen was run, remained a mystery to the younger members.

"Oh my gosh!" Rosi exclaimed. It is exactly 5 hours before my birth time!

"Yeah, and we are lucky its night right now back home so our parents are asleep!" Wayne added. Marcuno sat silently against the wall with his arms folded across his chest.

"Phoenix," a doctor spoke to Rosi, "Your DNA was more successful, you have six surviving clones whereas Dragon only has two." Wayne rolled his eyes as if it were supposed to somehow be his fault.

"So, why are they still in the artificial uterus?" Phoenix asked.

"We are waiting for them to be born. See the wires attached to the fetus, as soon as it can breathe on its own and it's heart can beat on it's own, the light will turn green on the machine here and we can remove them. Thus, they will be born." As soon as the doctor was finished speaking, one of the lights turned green. He quickly approached the uterus and pulled a lever. The fluid drained and the door opened. The doctor removed a crying baby.

"But we're not done yet," he explained, "we need to place her into a growth chamber right away where she will be unconscious and will grow until she can grow no more, which is, your current age, age nine. That is all the memory the cells have." Rosi glanced at Wayne but he looked on in curiosity. This was strange to Rosi, but she was here to welcome her clones into the world. She supposed this is how a mother would feel, only maybe without all the pain. She didn't feel there was a need to correct the doctor on her age since she was going to be nine in a few hours anyway.

"The growth chamber may take a week to complete the growth process," the doctor informed them. They watched as the baby fell asleep. Two and a half hours passed by. Suddenly, another uterus light turned green and started to beep steadily. They went and removed the second newborn.

"Are you going to name them now?" Wayne asked. Rosi shook

her head.

"They're gonna be adopted right?"

"Why, yes," the doctor answered.

"Can't I let the adopting parents name them?"

"Well, yes, but it would be odd if they did not have a name before adoption."

"Oh well," Rosi said.

"Um, excuse me," Wayne intercepted, "but where are my clones?" He asked innocently as if looking for Christmas presents.

"Over here," another doctor called. Wayne and Rosi went into the adjoining room. There were several capsules lined against one wall. Only two at the end were filled. Wayne walked up to them. Inside each, was a human form that looked exactly like Wayne.

"Cool! Maybe we can all get along so I won't have to get my brother every time I need something."

"They are just about ready to come out."

"I've got a question here doc," Rosi piped up, "How come my clones are babies when they are born, but Dragon's aren't?"

"Easy, the methods we used are different. With Wayne's, they needed constant observation until they gain consciousness naturally. We attempted the natural division of the ball of cells that causes twins or even triplets to form. With yours, we simply injected the DNA into, what you might want to say 'separate babies.' "

"And it works?" Rosi whispered in questioning awe to herself.

"How come its not appreciated to clone people?" Rosi asked, "and how come you didn't mix up the samples, like clone me both ways and Wayne both ways?"

"Ah, I agree, that is the best way to conduct such a procedure if it were an experiment and they were testing results, but we have already proven the most effective way of cloning, we are just trying to perfect the procedure. Plus, there were budgetary reasons. As for what other's think, to many, cloning is a moral question, just like the death sentence on Mars a few years back. Only, I hope it doesn't cause rioting like the death sentence did," the doctor explained. He checked a few printouts, "Everything looks fine. They should gain consciousness within the next hour or two."

Rosi and Wayne walked back to the other room, Marcuno was chatting calmly with the doctor now. Another uterus turned green. Excitedly, Rosi approached to watch the doctor deliver her clone. But as the doctor reached in to pick up the baby, the light turned red again. Panic took hold of Rosi and she stepped back. Was it something she did? The doctor hurriedly placed the baby back in and reattached the wiring. He shut the uterus again and pushed a button, fluid swelled back into the uterus. They waited, but the light stayed red. The baby did not move. The doctor drained the fluid again and took out the baby, he went to the operating table nearby and began to perform CPR. Rosi watched in a semi-mortified state, "What's going on?" No one answered her. A few moments later, the doctor gave up. He picked up a white blanket and covered the baby. Even her face. Rosi imagined herself as the baby, trapped in darkness. A shiver ran down her spine. Even though she had watched Ciesa and Richard die, death was still a very scary thought. What did Ciesa feel when she died? What did her eyes look like before they closed? Was it like a candle going out? The baby never opened her eyes. What about Sarah?

"What happened?" Wayne asked. He did not want to believe what he thought he saw. The doctor sighed, "The baby just died. It happens every now and then. In this method, we run the risk of spontaneous abortion, or death, at every stage until they have finished in the growth chamber. But the other method we used for Wayne's clones only run the risk until they develop into the embryo stage. But as you can see, it does not produce very many of them successfully."

"What is the point of cloning?" Mark asked pessimistically, "they are only copies of real people." He had been in a bad mood the whole day. Watching a baby die did not help ease his tired bitterness. No one answered his question. He was not sure that he wanted an answer either.

With nothing to do but wait, Rosi glanced at her watch, knowing she would have to go home soon.

"Hey!" she said, "In half an hour I would have been born!"

"So, in a way, you are the third baby," Wayne joked.

"Maybe, unless the others are born right now."

"Yeah, that's true." They fell to silence again. Boredom overcame them both. They doodled pictures on paper for a while, but it soon got old. Rosi began to count the minutes to her birth time. A beeping sound made Rosi jump. It was another uterus. Rosi smiled at Wayne, "So I guess I'm number four right now."

"Yeah, unless that one dies too," he said absentmindedly. Realizing what he just said, he looked at her in deep guilt, "I'm sorry! I,

I-."

"It's okay, let's not talk about it," she said in a sad voice. Its true, this little baby could die too. Shame crossed Wayne's face. His eyes fell to the ground. The third baby was placed successfully into the growth chamber. The first three were born. Rosi's birth time passed. Fifteen minutes later, the fifth was born, and then not long after, the sixth. As soon as the door was shut on the sixth child, the doctor let out a cry of surprise. All three rushed over to see what was wrong. The other doctor came in from the other room too.

The babies were growing rapidly. In a period of ten seconds, they became toddlers. A few seconds more, they were about age five. They watched nervously because there was a chance some might have developmental problems, but all five grew in natural proportion. A few seconds later, the growth stopped. All of them had developed properly. The first child opened her eyes and blinked.

"Dragon, turn away," Mark said.

"Why?" he asked in natural confusion.

"She's naked!" Rosi cried in excited exaggeration. Wayne blushed but obliged. The doctor opened the chamber door and handed the girl a towel.

"Here, can you wrap this around yourself?" he spoke as if he were talking to someone who had a hard time understanding English. The girl held the towel in front of her naked body. She raised an eyebrow at the doctor.

"Can you understand me?" He then turned to the others, "I'm not sure of brain capacity, or intelligence level."

"Yes I understand you!" the girl snapped. She wrapped the towel around her, the doctor stepped aside and she walked out holding her head, "I've got a headache," she spoke fluently.

"Hi!" Rosi said. The girl looked at Rosi who was wearing a confused expression.

"You," she lifted a hand as if to touch Rosi's face, but then dropped it, "You're my original!" The two hugged and laughed at the miracle before them. The doctor was bewildered, he spoke to the girl, "You mean you know you're a clone?"

"Of course," the girl replied simply. They were interrupted by a coughing sound. The second child was coughing. Wayne turned around, but he saw Mark's face and turned back to face the wall. He decided to go see his clones. The doctor opened the chamber and let

the second child out, handing her a towel. Before he could speak with the clone, she cried out in joy, "Hey! Its you! Rosi!" she threw her arms around Rosi and the first child. Soon after, the third and fifth children were also out, and finally, the sixth. The sixth child was shy, but she greeted Rosi as warmly as the others did.

The doctor was bewildered, never in a thousand years did he expect the clones to possess the intelligence level they had, and even more so, to know who their original was, or the fact that they were even clones. He was about to call his partner from the adjoining room, but Wayne burst in.

"They're conscious! They're leaving the chambers!" Everyone rushed into the other room. The doors opened and Wayne's clones stepped out.

"Okay girls, back into the other room now, all of you!"

"Yes Mark," all six girls replied and went back. This surprised everyone even more that the clones even knew Mark's name.

The two boys were handed towels. They stretched and cracked their joints.

"Aw, I feel stiff!" one of them said. The other one kept a stony face. He looked at Wayne, "You're the reason why I'm here aren't you?" The negativity in his voice caught Wayne off guard. He lunged toward Wayne. The two began to fight and the clone had to be restrained.

"I know everything you know! I can do everything you can do!" he cried bitterly. Rosi and the girls peeked through the doorway to watch the commotion.

"Yes, that's true," Rosi's second clone agreed.

"What is?" Rosi asked.

"We know everything you know silly," her second clone smiled at her.

"Can I be a part of division 17?" the fifth clone asked.

"Yeah! Me too!" the sixth clone joined in, she was losing her shyness.

"Can we all join?" the first and eldest clone asked.

"Uhh," Rosi was caught speechless.

"Yes, you can," Mark replied them all as he approached. He dragged Wayne's delinquent clone by the ear, "That's what the cloning was for, more recruits."

"Let me go you fucking bastard!" he cried. The girls gaped at them as they walked through the room. When they were gone, the girls

looked at each other in surprise. Wayne and the other clone walked into the room followed by the doctors.

"It's cold," Wayne's clone said. The other doctor brought in clothes for them. The boys then left the girls and everybody changed.

"I wonder what will happen to the other clone of Wayne's," Rosi said.

"I hope they don't destroy him," the fifth clone said, "I don't know if that could be classified as dangerous or insane behavior."

"What do you mean?" Rosi asked.

"Well, usually they are forced to terminate any potentially dangerous result in any scientific procedure," the fifth clone replied grimly. No one else spoke. They finished getting dressed in silence.

"Are you gonna name us?" the sixth clone asked.

"I was gonna let you guys pick your names and I was gonna agree with them." They smiled, "you are so cool!" the first clone said to Rosi, "You are just like me!"

Lisa, the first clone, was adopted by a human family that lived on Mars. She became Lisa Joyce Sclaper. Susan, the second clone was adopted by an alien single mother that lived on Mercury. She became Susan Linda Mateos. Clones three and five were adopted together. Clone three was Paula Eve Camus, clone five was Erica Lucy Camus. They lived in Seattle, Washington. Clone six was Araline Madeline Ashworth and she lived on Mars with her widowed, half human mother.

Wayne's delinquent clone was given a chance to live. He was bitter for being brought into this world as nothing but a shadow. He did not value life, and he was not pleased with living. He was named Charles after a bully Wayne wasn't too fond of. And the other clone, who was the opposite, was William, named after an uncle. Charles was adopted by the same parents as Lisa, but she was repulsed by him and his attitude. When acceptance to division 17 was offered to Charles, everyone held their breaths, hoping he would not accept. He hesitated, but declined, saying, "What is the use? There's no goddamn point in me even being here. I refuse to be a puppet like the rest of you."

Paula Eve and Erica Lucy were well taken care of by the Camus'. Their father never told their mother where the girls were really from and she didn't mind the adorable Oriental twins. She dressed them alike all the time. Paula's favorite outfit was a cornflower blue overall set that their mother matched with a yellow daisy printed blouse. Erica (whom every called Lucy because it sounded more adorable) loved the pink Sunday dress with the white fringe. When it came to going out to dinner, they both bickered over which set they were going to wear. They both had wanted to dress the same because it made their mother smile, but they both had quite different tastes.

Eventually, by their twelfth birthday, they no longer cared to dress alike. Paula wore her purple baggy sweater almost everywhere with a pair of sweatpants and Erica wore tight fitting cloths with simple solid designs. It didn't bother their mother much. She had accepted that they were going through a phase and needed to find themselves separate from each other.

By their thirteenth birthday, Erica refused to be called Lucy. In fact, the kids at school found it fun to call her "Eurika" which she liked to spell "Eureekuh" for fun. Paula stole her first skateboard from the boy down the street (he actually left it at her house and never picked it up before moved away). After many sprains and scrapes, she finally managed to not fall off. She started to hang out more and more with the boys at the skate park. They didn't call her Paula because there was already a Paul amongst them. Instead, they called her Eve, Veea or just "V" for short. Due to her training with Division Seventeen, she learned relatively quickly and was soon keeping up with the boys and doing the same tricks.

One day, their mother saw Veea take a horrible fall during a beginners skate boarding competition. She could have sworn she saw the girl's arm snap under her. In a mad fury of panic she swooped the girl off to the hospital before she could make any excuses. To her surprise, the doctors said her arm was fine, she just had a few bruises. Veea's mom told the doctors she saw her daughter hit her head and was concerned there might be a concussion. She made them keep her there for the night. Just in case.

Veea was bored out of her mind while she waited impatiently for the minutes to tick by. She wanted to sneak out and board all night, but she was under surveillance. Every hour a nurse would come and check up on her. She wished desperately for some mission to call her to Mars or for some other excuse to save her from the boredom. That would give her a reason to think up a way to get out of the sterile box she was trapped in.

Veea had finally fallen asleep when she heard the windy noise.

She opened one eye and looked around. The room was dark and her curtain was drawn. Each room could fit three beds and each bed was separated from each other with standard hospital curtains. Veea picked up the flashlight Erica had brought her earlier that day. She flicked it on and a strong beam of light shot forth. It was a lot brighter than she remembered! She quickly turned it off. The windy sound stopped.

"Are you awake?" a voice spoke to her. Veea grew curious. Bravely, she answered, "Yes, who are you?"

"My name is not important, may I come in?" a smooth masculine voice answered. Veea had nothing to fear, she was perfectly healthy and having to take on an opponent did not even cross her mind.

"Sure," she replied. The curtain parted a little and a shadowy figure stepped in.

"Hello, I am Paula, but people call me Veea," she introduced herself boldly, "are you sick?" Veea couldn't tell, but it seemed as if the young man smiled, "no, it is my grandfather, he is going to pass away soon," he replied.

"Oh, I'm sorry to hear that," and she truly was.

"The doctors say he will be fine, but he says he is at peace and wants to leave the earth." Veea hesitated. She was thinking of all the life on the other planets. What if leaving the Earth was not really dying, but transferring yourself from one body to the next? It could be from a fleshy body into a celestial body.

"Are you hurt?" he asked Veea. She shook her head, "My mother thinks I might have a concussion so she made me stay here."

"Ah, her worry and care expresses her love for you," he replied gently.

"What was the noise I heard earlier?" Veea asked, "did that come from you?"

"Yes. I was singing," the young man replied. He remained standing.

"You can have a seat you know," Veea offered.

"Thank you, I thought you would never ask!" he sounded relieved. Veea realized he was being formal and polite and it was she who had overlooked the etiquette.

"What kind of song was it?" she asked.

"I am Native American, it was a song for the wolf. My grandfather says the wolf is the guardian for our tribe and he taught it to me when I was very young. I was singing it so that dark spirits do not plague his soul as he dies."

"You are Native American?" Veea asked, "what tribe are you?" There was a pause, then he spoke slowly, "You would not know of us like I do not fully understand the images in your head. It does not matter, you are from Asia and we share the same ancestors."

"All humans share the same ancestors!" she chuckled and he joined in with agreement.

"Yes, but did you know that humans are the result of animal DNA mixed with alien DNA?" he asked. Veea was quiet. It was a tense quiet. What was he saying? Was he aware of life outside of Earth as well? Was he there to hunt her for reason? Or was he there to help her? She turned up her senses to try to discover if he was a friend or an enemy.

"What do you mean?" she asked, leaving the question open for interpretation.

"I mean that there are old myths and legends in all sorts of ancient civilizations that deem they had received help from the gods. If we can't see angels or gods from the skies, why can't they be aliens from far away? I know that my grandfather can talk to animal spirits, so it makes perfect sense to me that we are derived from them as well."

"Quinn," Veea heard a weak voice calling. The young man got up quickly and went towards the voice. A soft raspy tone asked, "water, please?" Veea heard the young man walk away and go down the hall. It was quiet again. She sat still and could sense the old man. He was kind and gentle, she could feel it in her bones and he sent out a warm wave of welcome towards her. She nodded to herself. She marveled at him. She had been badly injured before and on the brink of death, but there was always a tight knot within her that just would not release. Her body could be ripped to shreds and blood and life would be pouring out, but there was always a safeguarded iota deep within her somewhere.

This old man was different. He was healthy on the outside, she could feel it, and the doctors think he was going to get better too. It was something on the inside that was different. There was a kind of peace as he sat back and counted the strands unraveling from the life within him. There was a kind of tenderness and patience mixed with gentle acceptance because he knew that the threads attaching him to this world were coming apart. Veea marveled at him. She had never felt that way before.

The young man walked back in and she could hear the old man sipping down the water. Finally, he was satisfied and breathed out a little refreshed sigh.

"Are you comfortable grandpa?" the young man asked. She could feel him nod in response. There was a moment of soft gray silence before the old man spoke again, "tell the young lady she will be fine."

"Okay grandpa." Veea heard him lift the curtain and he was standing by her bedside as he spoke the same words to her.

"But what does that mean?" she asked. She could feel him shrug, "who knows, I don't know, but if I were to ask him, he usually replies that you'll know when you are ready." With that, he returned to his grandfather's bedside and Veea fell asleep again.

She awoke with Erica shaking her arm. Opening her eyes slowly, she realized where she was. She gave a loud yawn as she stretched out the tiny aches in her body. The tiny tears dotted her eyes like condensation and she looked through them at Erica.

"Mom's getting your discharge papers in order," Erica said. Veea nodded, "How much homework did I miss?" she asked.

"No too much, you did miss a pop quiz though," Erica reported nonchalantly.

"Okay girls! The doc says you're fine, Paula, ready to go home?" their mom announced walking into the room with high spirits. Veea nodded eagerly and got up to change. When she pushed the curtains aside, she noticed she was alone. The young and old men from last night were gone. Veea followed Erica and their mom into the parking lot. As she was getting into the minivan, she happened to look up and catch sight of the young man walking out. Veea heard a bird call and saw the young man look up. He smiled. She followed his gaze and saw an eagle in the air. Somehow she knew that it was his grandfather.

Lisa Joyce Sclaper had a "funny uncle" and he called her L.J. Even though legally he was her adopted dad and they lived on Mars, he was very American in his ways. He liked the little idiosyncratic tendencies of speech so whenever he introduced himself with L.J., he would claim he was her "funny uncle," and called her a monkey. Her mother was the opposite. She was quiet and reserved and spent a lot of time alone. It was only her father, or "funny uncle" who could bring a twinkle to her eyes. L.J. knew her mother loved him dearly and if it were not for him, she would not know how to live. L.J. never knew exactly what her mother did for a living, but she knew her mother was the primary breadwinner of the family. L.J. and her father left her to do as she wished and was there when she needed them.

Though they lived on Mars, her father loved to travel to Earth. Her mother, not so much, so he would gladly take L.J. on his excursions. Together they would see Rome, tour Australia, venture to the Egyptian countryside outside of over populated Cairo, they would go thrashing through the safe parts of the South American jungles, and view what was left of the ancient structures in the fertile crescent. L.J. learned that her father had wanted to be a historian but spent too much of his time joking around as opposed to studying. He was brilliant however and met her mother at a think tank that was put together for a global defense mission. They needed the individuals on Mars so they gave clearance for their body alterations. Since then, they both grew accustomed to living on Mars and never left.

One day, L.J. and her father were touring Japan and he was in a heated half English, half Japanese conversation with the restaurant manager who kept pouring sake for him. They were talking about the roots of the Japanese people and L.J. had little interest. Like Veea, she believed that all people share the same roots. In the end, they were all human and it didn't matter where they came from, the final answer was: Earth. She had excused herself and was wandering around the little garden staring at the moonlight reflected on the backs of koi that swam diligently in the little stone lined pond. She heard some children talking energetically in a half quarrel, half fantastical tone.

"Grandma!" one of them ran up to an old woman and declared, "tell little sister that people can't change into animals!" L.J.'s ears perked up. This was interesting, something she had never heard of before. She had thought she knew it all. Even if it were just a story, it was one she had never heard.

"But Granny!" a little girl piped up, "you said that foxes, raccoons, and some cats can turn into people, so why can't people turn into animals?"

"Well little one, that talent has been lost because the connection to nature and the animals who understand it has been lost."

"See, I told you so!" the little boy cried, but the girl was persistent, "but that means they used to be able to!" she argued. L.J. had wanted to hear the old granny's response but her father was calling for her. He was unable to walk properly and needed her to hail a cab.

Back at the hotel, her father slept on his bed in a fitful sleep. L.J. pulled out her laptop and looked up information concerning human and animal shape shifting. Nothing made sense to her. In the stories, it seemed as if pure will could allow a person to change their shape. L.J. looked into the mirror and tried to force herself to turn into a cat. She really wanted it. She waited and waited, staring at herself for over ten minutes. Nothing happened. She was disappointed, but not surprised. She wasn't quite sure how to change back either. Would she have to will herself back too? The stories had no scientific basis and she let out a deep sigh. Either it really was a lost art, or just bedtime stories to lull children to sleep. She went to brush her teeth and crawled into her own bed to sleep wishing for a bedtime story of her own. Storytelling was a lost art too.

Mrs. Ashworth was the widow of Mr. John Ashworth. She was born on Mars and had never been to Earth before. She grew up in a very male dominant home and when her husband died, no one wanted to take her hand in marriage so she moved in with her brother and his wife. Mr. Mason and Mrs. Mason worked for the Preyal system's defensive team and told no one of their work. Mrs. Ashworth gladly kept house for them and took in little Araline Madeline when her brother and his wife brought her home.

Mrs. Ashworth did not ever ask the quiet little girl of her history. Instead, she talked to her like she would to the cats, telling her everything, pouring out her gentle heart full of sunshine and love. When the girl wanted to talk, she would. She would speak only to ask Mrs. Ashworth to teach her how to do the chores around the house. Mrs. Ashworth did so wholeheartedly. The little girl was so curious!

"Wipe gently at the soft surface, you don't want to scratch it," she would say about the Martian vases. Ara listened carefully. It was as if Mrs. Ashworth were putting her heart into the care of the objects and loved them as if they were a part of herself. She was a happy and simple woman. Ara liked her very much and was glad she was there to keep her company. The whole house was filled with the rotund woman's love and essence and it seeped through Ara like a dream potion.

Mrs. Ashworth adored the little girl who looked at her through the large black curious eyes. She just wanted to wrap her up in her large soft arms and tell her that no matter what had happened, everything would be fine. Mrs. Ashworth would not let anything bad happen to Ara while she was around, she would put her life on it. It worried her to no end when the girl would be called to go away on missions. Lydia

Ashworth had no idea what the missions entailed and in her mind, she saw exploding grenades and horrible weapons she could not name aimed at little Ara. Lydia Ashworth would then sigh and tell herself that she was getting carried away with her imagination. Ara was just a child, why would she be exposed to such things?

Ara stared soulfully at Mrs. Ashworth. The woman was teaching her how to properly pour tea. She suddenly felt very badly for her. The woman was not like her at all. Ara knew that she herself was strong and was able to hold up her own end in a fight besides division seventeen, but Mrs. Ashworth had listened to a man all her life. But isn't that what she was doing now? Kirin was Marcuno and he was a man. Ara had to follow his every command. The only difference between them was the amount of faith they had in themselves. Mrs. Ashworth gave her heart to objects and animals who would not, could not reject her. She was reliant on the good will of others to support her through her life. She would shy away from any negative comment made towards her and she was submissive.

Ara on the other hand was an individual and if the situation needed her to be, she was aggressive. She could survive alone in the world. She relied on the bond she had with the other division members and it did not hurt her when they would scold her. The only reason she was with Mrs. Ashworth was because she needed a cover life. She could leave if she wanted to, but she couldn't because of external rules. Mrs. Ashworth couldn't because she would be afraid to. She was locked up with fear from the inside out.

Ara admired the way the woman kept house and learned a lot from her. It was a sort of meditation when you slowly put yourself forth and let your thoughts drift as you lovingly care and appreciate all that you have instead of discarding it and wanting more. It made things in life hundreds of times more valuable if you came in contact with it every day and you learn every groove it holds. Did Mrs. Ashworth worry when Ara was away? Did she know Ara was training with dangerous weapons and fighting those much older and larger than she was? If she did, would she worry? Or perhaps she knew, and she kept calm and was under immense control of her emotions so she wouldn't get hurt. What would happen to Mrs. Ashworth if Ara were to die? Would the pain become unbearable? What would she do? Would she become so depressed she would just sit there all day and not clean and cook anymore? Ara felt as if she were the supporting beam for Mrs. Ashworth's emotional stability. She felt very attached to this woman, and vowed to take care in considering her emotions with every action.

William was sick and not well the first few months after his birth and spent a lot of time in the SHONDS medical facility. When he was finally discharged, he was already familiar with the in house doctors and technicians so he decided to stay there. He started an apprenticeship with Gary and was learning how to operate the machines. Gary was a little bit frightened of William at first because he didn't now how to accept clones. Over time, the boy's gentle manner won him over and he treated him equally like all the other men at SHONDS.

"That boy's got real talent!" he would say about William when others inquired of what it was like working with a clone. William never needed much and his curiosity could keep him going for miles studying whichever topic had grasped his mind at the moment. It wasn't long until everyone at SHONDS knew about him and grew fond of him.

Charles was a different story. The first two years after his birth were spent in a school for delinquents. There, he often got into fights because no one believed he was a clone. Eventually, when his staying there caused too much trouble among the other children, he was transferred to a juvenile parole home. The parents there were very strict with him and he learned to keep his mouth shut when not asked to speak. He still didn't care much for his life, but he cared even less to commit suicide. When his behavior finally improved, L.J.'s parents took him in as well. She didn't like the idea and she didn't like him. Yet, he kept to himself. He sat around and played videogames all day hardly saying a word to anyone. He didn't care for the excursions L.J. and their father went on so he never joined them. He knew his adopted sister didn't like him, but he didn't care. He would play pranks on her to jeer at her in secret. He would cover his tracks and leave no evidence so there was no way for L.J. to accuse him.

Whenever someone asked him to do something, a hot fire of resentment built up. It was as if he accused others of his unwanted existence and felt that they should just provide for him and leave him alone while they forced him to live, to feel pain and to feel anger. He would always retort rudely and refuse to do anything. It is only when his mother looses her temper towards him that he gets up to do as she asks of him. His mouth would be set in a firm and silent line that dictated in a singularity how much he hated everything. Still, it was less of an effort to comply than it would be to fight and resist. What did he give a care for in this world anyway?

Occassionally, Charles would still run errands for division seventeen. Although he would never admit it and denies from the root of his heart, he feels a sort of connection with his original. He could never hurt Wayne, nor William. They were too much like a piece of him. It was as if William took all the good things and Charles was left with the bad. Still, he approached it all with a kind of apathy. He did things just to do them. He didn't try to derive a higher meaning out of it. Like an automaton, he strived on to live and waited patiently for the day when his life would be taken from him as inconsiderately as it had been given.

Unlike the girls, the boys hardly spent any time together. William was busy training with Gary and Charles was busy doing nothing more than sulking. The girls would plan little outings together and they were quite a sight to see. It was usually L.J. who planned the trips and sometimes her father would tag along to chaperone. Most times they went to see places L.J. and her father had passed over during their trip. They went to Russia and everyone exclaimed how great of luck it was that their parents had six adorable identical girls. When they went to France, they were all stared at in wonder. Even though people would ask from time to time if they were truly sisters, they made no comment concerning the six of them together. In Africa, they had been mistaken for being six goddesses and in Antarctica, the scientists were fascinated by them and asked them questions concerning their birth. They all looked at each other and answered incredulously, "we were newborns, we have no recollection and our parents never told us."

"And your mother carried you full term?" they kept pushing.

"We don't know," always came the same answer.

The traveling around helped to meld all six girls together and they became like true sisters in a short period of time. They learned each others' movements and speech patterns and were more than capable of filling in for each other mid-sentence. It was as if each one of them had five others as extensions of themselves and this helped them greatly when timing and movement demanded highly organized precision. As the years were to wear on and on and the girls grew closer and closer to each other, they were inseparable and virtually indestructible.

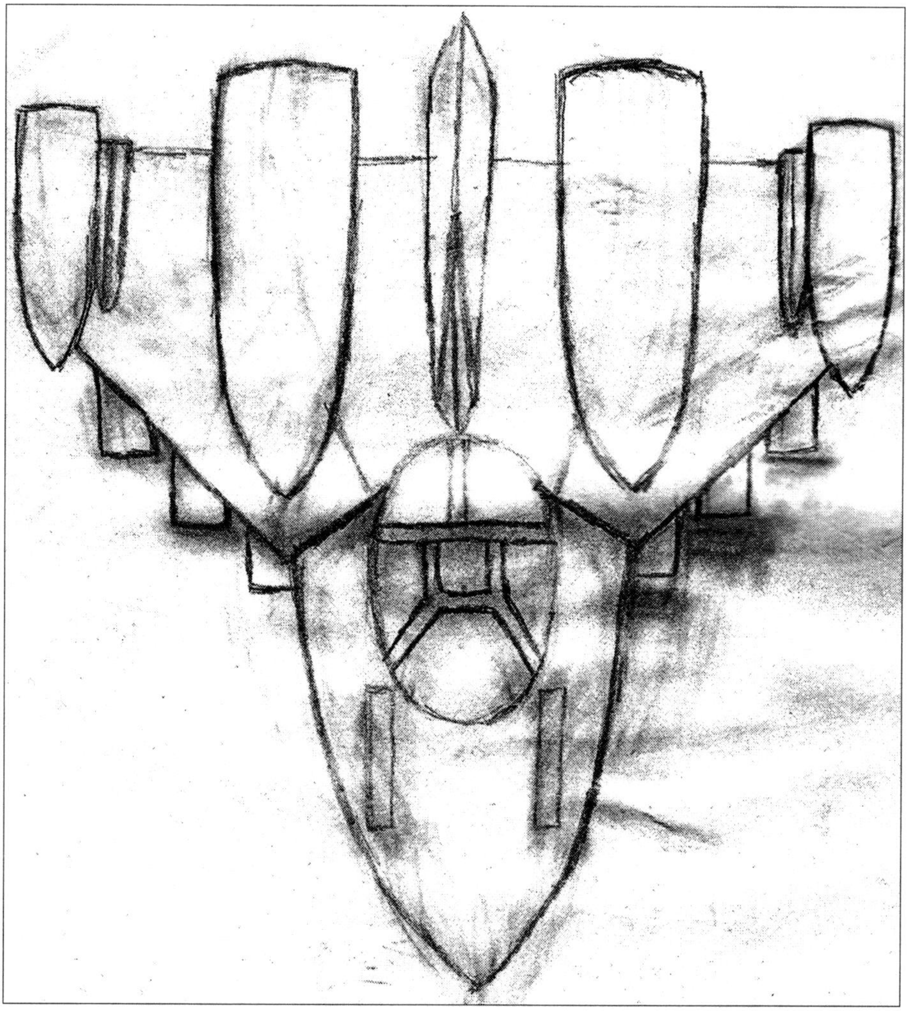

Original Napkin Sketch of the QBC-435 Tink and the CP 4-9

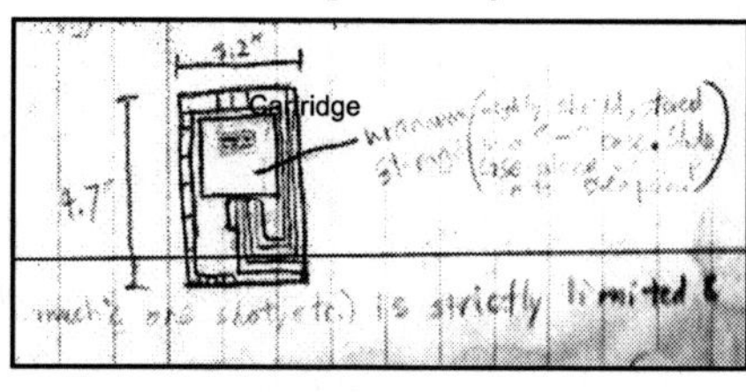

Cartridge stores 165 short blasts or 12 hours straight nuclear stream

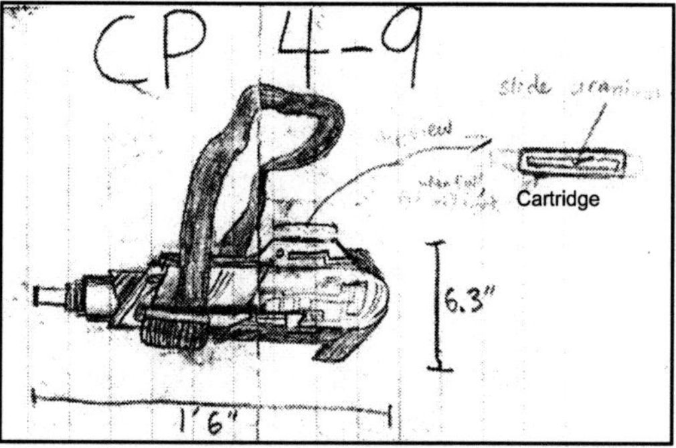

CHAPTER THREE

Rosi, who was now accustomed to the name Phoenix and left behind the name Dove, walked into the SHONDS meeting hall. The walls were stainless steel with large windows cut into them. The blinds were closed to keep out what little light there was. Living on Earth most of the time, Rosi was used to more sunlight than what Mars was able to receive. So seeing the blinds closed all the time always raised a single pointless question in her mind: Shouldn't more sunlight be better?

Absentmindedly, she walked over to the blinds and opened them. She smiled at the rusty landscape. The color was beautiful. It was such a warm feeling when the sun kissed it just right. It made her smile and momentarily forget that she was a killer. The slopes danced with shadows that seemed to hold secrets and stories from ages before her existence. It was almost as if it were a puppy teasing her soul to go and play with it in spirit.

Her lovely thoughts were interrupted by a knock on cold steel.

"Come in," she called out flatly and shut the blinds in one singular cold snap. Turning around, she faced the door. The glint of the overhead lights made the long table at the center of the room seem cold and impersonal. Phoenix closed off her emotions and walked the length of the room to the door. Hector, one of the technicians at SHONDS came in, "This is Mavius, the man who contacted us earlier."

"Thank you, Hector," Phoenix said. She stood solidly on two feet with her arms behind her. She turned to the man named Mavius, "Shall we have a seat?"

"Of course," he smiled warmly. Rosi didn't like him. He was a typical politician. He had the power to sway the councils into commanding her missions. His presence here could only mean trouble.

The two seated themselves at one end of the long meeting table that had been at SHONDS since Rosi first arrived.

"My, you are awfully young," Mavius spoke.

"I am thirteen years old, according to Martian law, I was considered an adult four years ago."

"Of course, but you are not a Martian, you are a human." Phoenix ignored the insinuated instigation, "What are you here for?"

"Ah, right to the point, I like that." Mavius took his time pulling out some papers from his tote. He arranged them on top of the table this way and that until he found his liking. Phoenix stared neutrally at his hands. His hands were soft, even for a Jupiterian. He was born into wealth, no doubt, and probably quite clever. She would have to be on her guard.

"I am to understand," Mavius began. He folded his hands on top of his papers and leaned forward to look Phoenix directly in the face, "that your division was meant for the protection of earth. I also am to understand that a lot has changed these last few years. An unusual number of, what you refer to as 'old soldiers' have retired simultaneously. Simultaneously, you understand that word right?" Phoenix ignored his tone and nodded once, curtly. If it were not for his rank, she would have ignored the remark completely.

"I am offering to reinstate a new division in charge of your duty and offering you and your current followers to come work for me. What do you think?" He stopped abruptly. Phoenix looked at him incredulously, "What do you mean exactly?"

"I am offering to buy your loyalties."

"Why are you asking me, why don't you speak to the military council?"

"I did, they left the final decision to you." Phoenix was shocked. Was the council allowed to do that? She would have thought they would have laughed in his face and turned him down. Was the council saying that they were willing to sell military loyalty? Since when was that legal?

"No," she replied flatly.

"Surely," Mavius began.

"Because I don't like you and I don't have to, please leave," Phoenix cut him off. He stood up and looked as if he were to speak again. Phoenix walked by him to the door and opened it. She turned to look at him. He got the idea. He gathered up his papers and shoved them back into his tote. He was suddenly serious as he walked up to Phoenix. He towered over her, trying to intimidate her. She was not threatened. She had taken down many who were much larger than he was. It wasn't that she didn't know she was acting brashly, she did. She knew that she should keep cool especially when dealing with a man of his standing, but she just didn't trust him.

"Mark my words," he said coldly, "this is just the beginning." Then he gave her a deviant smile. There was something else that he knew and would never share with her.

As Phoenix shut the door behind him, she couldn't fight the

shiver that went down her spine. She felt as if there was a trap being set around her that she couldn't see.

They were far away from the blue sky and gentle winds of Earth. Rosi and Wayne were standing before Yolukia. She was fourteen and he had just turned sixteen. Yolukia had won the seat as ruler of the local galaxies two years ago. He was making plans for the future and one of the things was to have a successor. He wanted someone to train in his politics. Rosi hated most of the politicians she had met, but there was a gentle sternness in Yolukia that she felt she could trust.

He felt that he was too old to be a father and a ruler so he called forth two of his favorite subjects at the accurate mating age. They were two humans, Rejianiticana and Dygheild. Those were their public names. Their secret names were Rosi and Wayne. He told them that he wanted a son. Rosi was distressed. The first thoughts to pop into her mind were that of her mother. What would she say!

Wayne on the other hand was confused at first. He was raised in a religious family and was still adjusting to fact that the Bible was incomplete. He liked Rosi, but he didn't want to have the responsibility of being a father, not to mention Rosi would be brought into his family's life forever. She was also his boss and he had no doubt things would be quite difficult. There were just too many taboos for Earth!

"I understand your traditions," Yolukia said, "I have arranged for a wedding to be held right now." Rosi and Wayne looked at each other in panic. They had both lied to their parents and said they were going to a sleep over at a friend's house of the same gender. Wayne was at Bob's house. Rosi was at Jasmine's. This was definitely not what they expected Yolukia to call them for. According to her parents, Rosi was too young to even date. How was she supposed to explain to them a husband that lived in Colorado?

"Your honor," Rosi spoke and got down on one knee, "I understand that we are of the perfect breeding age, but our society has changed and I am afraid that a marriage would cause a lot of difficulty." Rosi had known Yolukia to be gentle, but for the first time she experienced him putting his foot down to her. Under normal conditions, Rosi wouldn't even have spoken up, but she was more afraid of her mother than the ruler of the local galaxy groups.

"My word is final. I will marry you two and you will be escorted to the wedding chamber where you will spend the night." He motioned for them to be led into the dressing rooms not allowing either one of them to object anymore. Rosi donned a simple white dress with a triangular train. A veil was pulled over her face and she was handed a bouquet of drofas, her favorite white flower with the scent of heaven. At least Yolukia took her favorite flower into consideration. Wayne put on a nobleman's vest. The style was from the planet they were on, Juyvine. It was deep blue with matching trousers and a burgundy edge at the sleeves and cuffs.

The two of them nervously crossed the large hall to stand in front of Yolukia. Rosi was so nervous she thought she was going to faint. Her parents were going to kill her if they found out. There was no way to hide it, she would swell as she got further along in her pregnancy. She wished that she had the option die instead of going through with everything.

To Wayne none of this seemed real. It was like a play and he wasn't too sure if it was a good idea to participate, but if he didn't, Yolukia might have his head. He wanted neither a wife nor a family of his own. He wanted to be at home biking or swimming and playing in his band like most sixteen year olds. He couldn't fight the feeling that his own personal life was now over.

It wasn't until he had to turn and face Rosi when the realization soaked in. He looked into her scared pale face as he took her cold shivering hands. Suddenly he understood exactly what she felt and he became frightened too. They had no control over their lives. It was lost the moment they were selected for division seventeen. Whoever said "ignorance is bliss" must have been in a very similar situation of despondency. If only they had been left as civilians, they would have been able to lead the life they believed they could. His heart suddenly went out to her. Her fear and desperation were the same as his.

They had both hesitated at the "I dos" but they said them out of fear for their lives. Rosi didn't think Yolukia would really execute them, but she didn't want to risk it. Rosi liked Wayne as a friend, but she wasn't so sure she wanted to marry him, or for that matter, anyone in general. Wayne didn't feel that he was ready for a responsibility so big as providing for two living beings and wanted to run as much as Rosi did, but Yolukia's commanding force kept them there. They leaned forward and gave each other a shy peck on the other's lips. Rosi looked away with blushing cheeks. That was her first kiss.

The peck reminded Wayne of his first kiss. He was in preschool and there was a girl with beautiful angel blonde hair. His friend Mickey dared him to kiss her and he did. She ran to the teacher crying and he was sent to time out. This time, Rosi wanted to run as much as he did, but they couldn't. Their timeout would be death and he wasn't done living yet. Even though he lived to take lives, Wayne knew that there was something more he was still missing and he refused to die before he found out what it was. Besides, Rosi was good looking and he admired her. She was smart too, so there was no rational doubt in his mind that she would agree to a divorce after the child was turned over to Yolukia.

Rosi's thoughts dwelled on being disowned by her family. She feared the look of disgruntlement from her mother and losing contact with her. Most of all, she feared her father. Her wouldn't strike her with child, but he would never let her in sight of the family's eyes ever again. Her mother just gave birth to a little sister named Mia. Rosi wanted to be there as her baby sister grew up. Rosi was just a child herself. She didn't want to be having a baby of her own.

The two of them were escorted by Yolukia's guards to their wedding chamber. They stood there solemnly as they heard the door being latched on the outside. Wayne turned to Rosi, "Well Phoenix, you tell me what to do, and what we are going to tell our parents." Rosi felt annoyed, "Stop it," she said shakily. Her mouth was dry, "I didn't know this was a part of the job description."

"Don't yell at me," Wayne said. Instantly Rosi felt sorry for snapping at him, it wasn't his fault after all. He walked to the far end of the bed and took off only his shoes.

"I'm tired," he said, "so I'm sleeping regardless. This bed is big enough so we could share it. Maybe if we just pretend, Yolukia will leave us alone for a while thinking that we actually…you know." Rosi swallowed, "You have a point." She looked at the bed. It was the only piece of furniture in the room besides a chamber pot and she was getting tired. She walked over and took off her shoes. She pulled back the covers and folded the long dress in front of her. Delicately she slid under the covers and pulled them up to her shoulder. She slept as close to the edge as she could and kept her back to Wayne. She was still nervous being in the same bed with him, but the sheets were very comfortable and she was just so tired. She blinked sleepily but was still too nervous to relax.

"Do you think we will actually get out of this?" Wayne asked. Rosi opened her eyes, "I don't know," she said sadly and confessed,

"I'm very scared." She didn't think they could get out of it, but she could still hope. Wayne gave a little tired chuckle, "When I was little, I never expected this to happen." Rosi smiled, "Ah yes, childhood, we obtain a false illusion of everything." She realized that she sounded a bit pretentious but was too uncomfortable with the external situation to care.

"I hardly know you," Wayne continued, "My parents warned me against marrying someone I hardly knew, but I guess they never counted on it being a life or death situation." Rosi giggled a little bit. She rolled onto her back but still stayed near the edge.

"Well Wayne Easton, since we have never really hung out before like normal kids our age, tell me a little about yourself and I will tell you a little bit about myself."

"Well, you know Scott. I'm the middle child. We have a little brother named Albert at home too. Scott was named after our father's ancestry, we're from Scotland. I am named after my mother's brother and Albert is named after my father's only other sibling who died in Vietnam. You?"

"It gets complicated," Rosi said staring at the dark ceiling. She was thinking about Sarah. She knew that Wayne could be trusted. He was as deep into this whole mess as she was, but she wasn't sure where to begin. She sighed then started, "My parents just had a little girl named Mia. They want me to tell her that I am the oldest."

"Are you saying that you're not?" Wayne asked. Rosi puckered her lower lip in concentration, "I had an older sister Sarah, she was three years older than me, and a big brother Joel who was two years older." She had paused. Wayne was lying on his elbows now. Rosi knew that his curiosity wasn't going to let her get away with just that and leaving him in the dark was just plain cruel.

"Joel disappeared when I was three. I don't really remember, but Sarah told me about him. And when I was five, Sarah disappeared, but no one remembers at all. There was never anything in the news and her things in her room disappeared. My parents really don't know about her because they sent me to a children's mental hospital for talking about her. But somehow Natasha knew about Sarah."

"So they don't know anything about Joel or Sarah? Wait, you mean, our Natasha?"

"Yes, Emerald. They do remember Joel, we think he was kidnapped, that's why we moved to America, but Sarah..." They were both quiet for a while. Wayne wasn't sure what to say. He didn't want to say the wrong thing. Finally, he spoke to break the silence, "I'm sorry for your misfortune."

"It's okay," Rosi said weakly. She needed a hug, but it would feel wrong if Wayne gave her one in bed like this. Even though that was what they were there for, she wasn't quite ready for it.

"Is it better now that you have new sisters?" Wayne asked referring to the clones. Rosi smiled, "Yes in a way, but it never replaces the ones we lose. It's like bits and pieces of a puzzle because I have mom and dad, and then them. Sometimes when I'm extremely sad I can feel them. I wouldn't say it's the telepathy but I've been getting these feelings even before the procedures. How about you?" Wayne thought for a moment, "Just once. I got really angry at Scott over something stupid and I could hear Charles in my mind telling me to completely trash his room and burn it."

"Hmm," Rosi said leaning up on her side to face Wayne, "I've never felt them in anger before."

"I think its because Charles is so pissy all the time," Wayne said. They both shared a laugh at that.

"Oh, something I remember, up in front of Yolukia, when he told me to kiss the bride I remember my first kiss back in preschool, my friend dared me to kiss this girl, I did and she ran screaming," Wayne shared. Rosi cracked up laughing, "You made her cry?" she choked. Wayne nodded. The two of them laughed even harder. Soon they were gasping for breath. Perhaps it was the laughter that broke the tension, but it felt good for them to feel a bond. It was almost like sharing a bunk with Ciesa back at SHONDS a few years ago.

"Did you get in trouble?" Rosi asked with tears in her eyes from laughing too hard.

"Yeah I got a time out and the teacher called my mom." This led to another burst of laughter. It lasted for a couple of minutes. It eased the situation and reminded them that they were still just kids. Somehow, the laughter made them better friends.

"You know," Rosi said after she finally caught her breath, "I wish you were a girl, then you'd be allowed to sleep over." Wayne wasn't sure how to take that, "Wait, are you saying I'm gay?"

"No! I'm saying you're cool."

"Oh, well, thanks, I mean, I don't have a sister so I don't really know much about girls. So how am I doing?" he asked jokingly.

"As your wife, I'll give you an A."

"Oh my God," Wayne said hiding his face in the sheets. He mumbled, "Wife, wow, I almost forgot about this whole thing."

"Yeah I know," Rosi agreed, "I take it you're a virgin too." Wayne nodded.

"What kind of girls are you into?" Rosi asked.

"Hmm," Wayne said pulling his face out of the sheets, "Is this a trick? Are you trying to trap me into having an affair so you can file for a divorce?" he joked.

"Why of course," Rosi joked back.

"I like girls who are pretty but don't try to look like everyone else. Someone smart and likes the same things I do. How about you, what kind of boys do you like?" He asked. Rosi was thoughtful for a moment, "Someone easy to get along with and that can actually understand girls. Someone who actually cares about how and why things in the world works and gives a crap. Oh yeah and I have this thing with blue eyes," Rosi blushed, "I saw this picture once in a magazine and this guy had these beautiful blue eyes."

"That's it for looks?" Wayne asked.

"I believe that you can read a lot from someone's face," Rosi was curled up on a pillow facing Wayne, "If they aren't a good person at heart, they like to grimace or frown a lot and you can tell by the lines on their faces. And if they like to smile, they are usually a good person. I'm not really sure. You don't have to be drop dead handsome to have a kind face is what I'm trying to say. That and it also justifies what my mom always said about not making weird faces or my face'll get stuck like that!"

"What about me?" Wayne asked, "do I have a kind face?"

"I can't see in the dark silly!" Rosi replied, "Do you have blue eyes though?"

"Yeah, haven't you noticed?" Rosi blushed, "No, I'm such a horrible wife, I don't even know my own husband's eye color!" she exclaimed pulling a pillow over her head in embarrassment, "Although if I were at SHONDS I would be able to pull out your file and check!" Wayne chuckled with her then added, "Yeah, talk about favoritism with your boss!" This led them both into a fit of laughter that didn't die down until a few moments later. Finally, Wayne spoke sleepily, "I'm getting kind of tired so I'm gonna get some shut eye. I'll see you in the morning."

"Okay." Rosi could almost feel Wayne close his eyes. She had a pleasant feeling inside of her as she listened to his breathing grow soft and even. What she felt was a major crush on her husband. She slowly leaned forward and gently kissed his lips. He smiled and kissed her back. They fell asleep embraced in each other's arms.

The mission was a simple one, they were to escort Yolukia around the Inner planets of the Solar system. It was low profile so only division seventeen was there. This was only Rosi's second mission and she was an excited seven year old. Unfortunately, it did not go smoothly. The ship was attacked and forced to land on Mercury. Rosi was trapped in a collapsed cave with the new ruler of the local galaxy groups. She was given orders to lie low and remain dead over the radio while the rest of the division fought off attackers until the backup arrived.

Rosi pulled the large rubber band out of her hair that kept it in a ponytail. She started to play cat's cradle. Yolukia was fascinated with her. He noticed the power of innocence in such a small child and asked her to teach him how to make shapes out of the elastic string. He asked her about her family, her planet, and most of all, her species. In the two Earth hours they were trapped together, Yolukia learned all that he needed to know. When they were finally rescued, Yolukia looked to little Dove and spoke mystically, "I shall be, how do you humans say it? 'See you around.'"

It wasn't long after that he awarded the division for bravery. It was just a small honorary token that didn't mean much. Every division usually receives one when they persevere in an unforeseen circumstance. Yolukia used this excuse to secretly accept Rosi as his goddaughter. She was asked not to tell the public, and she complied. All his other plans were kept hidden. Rosi was thoroughly confused, so she went to confess to Natasha. Natasha was quiet and had no answers for Rosi concerning the Ruler's actions. She merely told her to keep her chin up.

It was 1 o'clock AM and a fourteen year old Rosi could here her father snoring. Carefully and quietly, she opened her window. She looked around praying her neighbors were not awake to catch her. She had the darkness in her favor as she leaped from her second floor window. With her training, she was able to land softly on the earth.

"Woof," came a muffled bark. It was her dog. Being chained outside, he awoke when he heard the window open. He knew it was Rosi and just wanted to know where she was going.

"Shh," Rosi said going up to Cyrus and scratching behind his ears, "I'll be back boy." She took off running at top speed with soft steps. She slipped through backyards with perfect stealth until she reached the nature preserve park. Hidden in the trees, she pulled the control chip for her jet craft out of her pajama pocket. Pushing a few commands, she pulled her jet craft out of the storage dimension. The dimension was created artificially for space conservation and convenience especially for military personnel. Rosi hopped in quickly and silently. She activated the invisibility shield and took off with no one ever knowing she was there.

There were knocks at Natasha's door. She had moved to Jupiter after the war many years ago when she had lost a lot of her friends. Things have been tranquil in her life. She settled down and had been married for two years now. She was pregnant and patiently awaiting the newest member of her family.

"Hello?" Natasha called out in a warm voice. Her hand was on the doorknob.

"Hi, Its me, Rejianiticana," Rosi replied, never using her real name. They all had civilian identities away from Earth. It was optional but available for the convenience of keeping their true identity a secret. Natasha was not her real name either, it was Selena. She shared this with Rosi after she had retired, but Rosi still called her Natasha.

"Come in," Natasha greeted her warmly, "what a pleasant surprise!" she exclaimed. She gave Rosi a warm hug and swept her into her home as if she belonged there.

"Can I get you anything to drink?" Natasha asked.

"No thank you," Rosi said. She wore a concerned expression on her face. Natasha sat her down on the luxurious low back couch and shuffled into the kitchen. She brought Rosi a glass of water anyway and set it on the end table.

"What's wrong dear?" she asked while easing herself onto the couch beside Rosi. The younger human looked around, "Is anyone home?"

"Nope, its just you and I and we can talk about anything," she took Rosi's chin in her hand, "Anything," she repeated. With her eyes, she gave Rosi permission to speak of division 17. With a sigh, Rosi confessed the newest occasions in her life.

"I'm married," she said nervously. She stared at her hands and played with her nails. Natasha patiently awaited for Rosi to explain herself. The girl was still trying to gather the right words and calm her fluttering stomach. A few moments later, she continued, "It was an order from," she lowered her voice, "Yolukia." Natasha did not stir. With no surprise, she waited a few moments, then asked, "Who's the lucky young man?" Rosi was silent. Natasha was patient, giving Rosi her space. She took a sip of water and unintentionally made Rosi felt as if she was wasting time.

So she blurted out, "It's Wayne." Natasha sputtered out a laugh and elegantly spat her water back into the glass. Rosi's cheeks felt as if they were on fire. Natasha managed to control her hysterical laughter into a small chuckle. Never in a million years would she have thought Yolukia to be that silly. They were both children. She understood that the Ruler treasured Rosi for reasons she didn't understand but wasn't going to question. However, she would have expected him to demand a spouse from some other nobleman or at the least someone not so close to home. He had the power to select anyone, why did he pick Wayne?

"It wasn't our idea at all!" Rosi defended herself. Natasha had composed herself again, "What's wrong with being married dear?" she asked soothingly, "I am."

"But Natasha, I am just fourteen years old and I don't know what to do is right. It feels like I have no control over anything," Rosi cried. Natasha smiled, "come here." She took Rosi by the hand and led her to the huge floor to ceiling windows in her apartment. It faced the great city she lived in and had a beautiful view. Natasha placed a chair in front of the window and sat Rosi down. She pulled a comb out of her pocket and loosened Rosi's hair. She began brushing the hair and humming a tune. This was very relaxing for the both of them. Rosi sat silently. She enjoyed the moment of tranquility and felt it wrap its arms around her. Natasha was like her second mother, she could understand issues Rosi could never speak of to her real mother. Rosi cherished Natasha's existence and the position she held in her life.

After a few moments of golden silence and comfort, Natasha spoke up in a warm soft voice, "I don't know why you two were forced to be married, but I know that there is some reason. It doesn't matter if you understand it now or many years later, you will see it eventually. Not everyone gets the freedom to choose." The comb scraped gently over Rosi's scalp. Natasha kept up a steady rhythm and when she spoke, she followed that rhythm, almost as if she were reciting a poem, "You and I, we are fortunate ones. We were given permission to see more than our world is allowed to see. We were chosen for a higher purpose. Of course, some would say it is a curse, to have to follow commands and live a certain lifestyle. However," Natasha place her hands on Rosi's shoulders and whispered in her ear, "That world out there," she gestured out the window towards the view they had been admiring with the comb, "that world is yours. The many different cultural societies, the many different beautiful ways of living that you would never have dreamed of on Earth, that is yours. You are allowed to love it and become a part of it, and that is something not everyone is privileged to have." Rosi's eyes filled with understanding as Natasha returned to combing.

"Besides, you don't think you know what to do because you think too much, yet not enough. You are always worrying, but if you analyze yourself, you will find that the correct actions have been conditioned deep inside of you, and even though consciously, you are confused, a part of your mind is always in control," Natasha finished. Rosi smiled. She looked out at the Jupiter city, Ghinsota. The lovely buildings were hiding and reappearing behind the clouds of deep reds and golden oranges. It was like living in a sunset. She loved the way Natasha broke things down for her. Whatever happens, she would not be left without a home or a family. What she really feared was losing her Earth family's trust. It was a weakness she had to hide. It was one that might betray her in the future if she were not careful.

"Right and wrong are just words, the truth is, outside of Earth, my family on earth, there is nothing wrong with what is happening," Rosi said calmly. Natasha smiled.

It didn't matter that she was forced to marry Wayne. Her parents never had to find out. She had become their guardian, selecting the information they were to know and protecting the Earth. In return, she had the freedom, and burden, of awareness.

The solar system was asked to join a defensive mission by neighboring systems. They wanted to increase their number of secret operatives. Thus, the solar system was asked to send at least 40 of their highest trained professionals. Twelve of those were division 17. Without any briefing, they were put on a ship and told that their orders will be given once they arrived.

Two systems over in the Tweila system, division seventeen finally arrived. All the members including young fourteen year old leader was not quite sure what to expect. Still, every one of them kept a professional attitude. They all had on a stoic face, and a silent composure. They were seated in a dark room on a long bench. Their commanding officer stood in front of them. She would have preferred to pace about, but was afraid that would appear inappropriate. The other eleven members sat stiffly on the bench with their hands on their knees and a blank expression. All their assigned standardized equipment from Preyal, their home solar system, was neatly packed inside their travel packs that lay in straight order underneath the bench they were seated on. Moments later, a person in uniform entered the room. The only person he acknowledged was Phoenix. He handed her a stack of folders and quickly left the room.

Phoenix opened the top folder. There were maps and a list of times. She studied them quickly. Her scientifically enhanced mind absorbed the information at an accelerated rate. In the last folder was a flat piece of metal with a tiny hole in the middle. She recognized it as a hologram projector. She dropped in on the floor and gave it a good hard stomp to activate it. She had never used one before but her training in SHONDS was not in vain.

A cartoon popped up. In an overly enthusiastic voice it started to give them their orders. It was a voice that you would use for a child with lyrical ups and downs in the pronunciation. No doubt this was to disguise the sincerity of the mission in case it fell into the wrong hands. All twelve members watched indifferently. But their minds were absorbing every detail in the message. Whatever else they were to know from the folders, was up to Phoenix.

"Self-destruct in 5, 4, 3, 2, 1." It was like a typical action movie, which stirred a slight amusement from Phoenix's otherwise dead emotions. There was a tiny "poof" and the piece of metal was gone. Phoenix walked over to the bench and grabbed her pack. With an effortless swing she slung it onto her back.

"Let's move."

They formed a line. Phoenix walked in front followed by Dragon then Kirin. Behind them followed Phoenix's clones: Angel, Moongirl, Sunshine, Tinkerbell, and Joy. Behind them, was the rest of the division: Zap, Neroz, Skull, and Deklar. They would have tingled with excitement due to the fact that this was their first mission away from home. However, they were all trained properly. This meant they did not feel until after the mission. Each one of them could have been labeled as a cold-blooded killer. They were as dangerous as any predator on Earth and ten times more deadly.

Phoenix led them to an elevator. In her mind she was going over the maps in the first folder. She learned to section off a portion of her conscious and use it like a computer. She stored information in a way that made it easy to retrieve. The maps told her where to take her division and the hologram projector had given the rest of the instructions. The elevator took them down to a basement level. She walked forward and passed two corridors. At the third, she turned left. A few meters down they made a right and faced a massive set of double doors. Phoenix pushed them open and continued forth. They passed by small sleek fighter jets adapted for space travel. Those were not theirs. The next section however, contained three larger, meaner looking fighter crafts. On the side of each one was a number written in Latin, a language that expanded beyond Earth.

"Dragon, take Moongirl, Neroz and Joy into Craft two," Phoenix said calmly and sternly. She turned to Jessie, "Kirin, take Angel, Zap and Sunshine. I myself will be followed by Deklar, Tinkerbell and Skull." Phoenix paired everyone with those who had the least amount of emotional attachment between them.

"I will take first fleet followed by Dragon then Kirin, do not act without my command." Phoenix climbed into the first fighter craft and everyone followed to their assigned places.

The fighter crafts were similar to those in the Solar System. Phoenix tested the digital communicator, "Dragon, Kirin, come in."

"Roger."

"Roger."

"Does everyone know how to fly one of these?"

"We'll figure it out," Kirin replied in her usually cool manner. Inside, Phoenix smiled. This was going well so far. They all powered up their ships and taxied them to the launch pad. Phoenix did not question the mission. She was trained never to do so. She simply followed orders. If she were allowed to think twice beyond tactics and assault, she would realize that they were violating a treaty. The three divisions from Preyal were brought in for defensive measures. But their mission was clearly stated as a top secret information retrieval mission. To any rational being, that would have registered as offensive measures. It was like tossing a match near open barrels of gasoline.

The three fighter ships were leaving Tweila boundaries. They activated the invisibility shields and continued to fly under silent on their way to Fa Relarious, the capital city of the system Pillur. The city was its own small planet. Phoenix went over the map again in her mind. The orbit of the planet should bring it to the outer edges of the system. Even though they have their own private militia, it would take a while for them to arrive.

"Kirin, stay behind, Dragon, follow into orbit but stay at a distance," the leader commanded. Phoenix slowed down the ship as she prepared to enter the atmosphere. This was a gaseous planet. She hoped the orbit would not throw her off. She recalled the first time she set foot on Jupiter. She could not stand upright and kept falling over. Her guide had to hold her up.

Jupiter had to build its cities on artificial islands that floated around the core of the planet in different layers connected by bridges. Needless to say, the first settlers were quite advanced. Jupiter now has 29 layers that orbit on their own. Each island is anywhere from hundreds to thousands of miles apart and held together horizontally by beams. The travel done between these are done in jet crafts that follow special beams that act as bridges.

They set down smoothly. The superior vehicle landed undetected within three miles of their target. The four got out and started towards the location. They sprinted with ease over the metallic ground. To Phoenix's relief there was no motion sickness whatsoever. Within a few moments they had reached the 12-foot fence surrounding the perimeter. There were no trees around for them to push off of and flip over the fence so they had to do it the hard way. Deklar and Skull braced their arms together. Phoenix took a running start and then leaped off of their arms as they tossed her up. In one summersault she made it over the electrified fence. As she passed over it in the air, she could sense the current with her delicate skin follicles. It would kill anyone, altered being or not, in an instant. Next was Ara, after her Deklar sent Skull over the fence. Then he returned to wait patiently back at the fighter craft.

The three moved silently and in the shadows. They barely touched the ground as they ran quickly towards the main building. The people on Fa Relarious were not anticipating any "visitors" so there was minimal security. They safely made it to the target building. Phoenix looked around. She put a finger to her lips to indicate quiet. The alarms were triggered by sound. She pointed up. They were going to break in through the roof.

They left their shoes hidden in the dark shadows behind the building. Then, silently and swiftly they scaled the wall using the tiny spaces between the large bricks. Their fingerprints were not on file anywhere and if they were, Tweila had them erased before this mission. The cutoff gloves were meant to help with grip but in this event they merely got in the way. Still, they made not so much as a grunt as they effortlessly made it to the top.

Once there, Phoenix analyzed the ventilation system. The gigantic fans were controlled from within and it would make too much noise to enter that way. At the far corner of the building, they noticed a tiny moon roof. Phoenix verified with her mental map that it led inside. Peering in, she did not sense any cameras. She calculated measurements in her head. Only she and Tinkerbell would be able to fit. Skull would have to stay behind. The window would not allow for an easy abort in case something went wrong, but it was the only quiet way in. Without further questions Phoenix took a tiny flask out of a pocket and poured solvent all around the moon roof. Within seconds it pulled free. She made motions for Skull to stay and for Tinkerbell to follow. As quietly as possible they two fourteen year olds dropped into the room. It was a janitorial closet.

Phoenix went the door and put her ear to it. She listened for the tiniest vibration. If she focused, she could even hear the pulse of a sleeping guard and nothing else. Cautiously they opened the door a crack and checked for cameras. There were two, one at each end of the hallway. Phoenix attached the silencer to her gun. Holding her breath, she took out the cameras. They waited counting to ten. No sirens, not shouts, no one knew they were there. Automatically they moved into the hallway. About half way down they found the room they were looking for. Phoenix did not let pride get to her head just yet. The fact they slipped by undetected did made her heart swell. Her teenage ego seemed to shout, “oh yeah!” She quickly tucked it back under control and kept her senses alert.

They entered the room. It was a laboratory. Towards the back there was another door that led to an office. It was THE office. They moved to the door so stealthily the air barely moved around them. Tinkerbell took a pin out of her hair and picked the lock. The door opened effortlessly. There on the back wall was a huge safe. Phoenix knew inside that safe was the computer and inside that computer was the file they wanted.

Phoenix took a magnet generator out of her pocket. She placed it against the digital lock and pulled numbers from the memory. She proceeded to type the numbers into the screen next to the safe. They waited for the safe to open.

"Denied," a voice said, "please enter correct code or alarm will sound." A ten second countdown started. Without wasting a second, Phoenix tried to pull another code from the lock. She typed in the new code.

"Access granted." There was a soft beep and the door opened. No time to sigh relief, Ara stood at the entrance of the safe as Phoenix approached the computer.

"Welcome," the computer spoke. Phoenix placed the 300 TB storage unit into the tiny hard drive. With slight amusement, she thought of how technology here was the same as on Earth and all throughout her home system.

She scanned the contents of the computer and quickly located the file she was searching for. After selecting it, she recalled the password she was given. She typed it in and the file spread before her eyes. She pushed the download button and patiently waited. The download initialized. She continued to stare at the screen. The file was all in code and she understood nothing of it. It was nothing more than a texture to her, running about the screen. A few moments later, the download was finishing.

Out of nowhere, the voice spoke up again, "Warning, illegal download. Warning, illegal download." The hard drive sparked and caught fire as an alarm went off. Phoenix grabbed it and tried to retrieve the disk, but it was too late, it was a huge melted lump. A metal gate started to come down from the entrance of the safe but Ara caught it just in time. Her girlish frame relinquished amazing strength as she held the heavy crushing gate about the ground.

"Phoenix hurry," she said in a calm voice. The two went under the fence and let it slam down behind them. They were headed out the way they came. In the hallway five uniformed men were running towards them.

"There's a corridor to the right that leads to those fans on the roof, I don't think we need to keep it quiet anymore," Phoenix commanded Tinkerbell. They faced two of the guards who were about to tackle them. They easily rendered them to the floor in a series of smooth actions. They bound them with plastic rope the guards' belts were made out of. Without a moment to waste, they turned the corner. Phoenix could hear more people joining the remaining three guards.

"Remove the fans I will hold them off," Phoenix called. Without a word, Tinkerbell wrenched the door off of its hinges and ran into the steam room. Phoenix kicked the face of two guards as they came around the corner. The third dodged her and tried to restrain her arm. He was not strong enough. Phoenix shook him off and tossed him into more approaching guards. She followed quickly with a swooping kick that knocked all of them backwards. She had the advantage of a corridor where she only faced a few opponents at once. She dropped to her knee and disarmed two guards. She swung around up and leaped into the air landing them each a kick in the face. She arched back and landed on her hands. Doing an effortless back walkover, she took off after Tinkerbell. As she was about to jump up onto the roof she was tackled from behind and fell forward. Before she landed, she had reached back behind her and grabbed the guard by the collar. With her free hand she caught her fall and with her back legs she flipped over the guard and landed her feet on his stomach. He doubled over in immense pain. She heard a ping near her head as a bullet bounced off metal. They were shooting at her. Closing her eyes she focused on the sound of breathing and cocking of the gun. With a fraction of a second she heard another fire. By then she had already drew her own gun and fired in the same direction. Her shot was dead accurate. It met the other bullet head on and pieces of tiny hot shrapnel flew everywhere.

There were four guards in the doorway, two kneeling in front. They were lined up to fire. Before they could begin to pull pressure on the trigger, Phoenix had let fly with her gun and they were all dead on the floor. As she put her gun away, she was jerked upward. Skull had grabbed her by the collar and pulled her out of there. No time for regrets, not now. There never should be any regrets for them. But it was when Phoenix was alone late at night, she dreamed about what families those guards would have had.

"Jump," Phoenix called. The three launched themselves from the building. They pulled out their daggers and dug it into the side of the building as they fell down the eight stories. This slowed their decent until they finally jumped to the ground. They jumped into their boots and headed back the way they came. More bullets were shot at them. They listened carefully and dodged left and right avoiding any wounds.

"Deklar, where's our ride?" Phoenix radioed through the tiny chip built into her glove.

"Right here," he replied. In front of them the fighter ship landed sending a rush of air out to greet them. The door opened and the three jumped in. Before Deklar could take off, jet crafts appeared and started to fire at them.

"Dragon," Phoenix called calmly, "we are under ambush, be prepared to defend." Deklar maneuvered around the shooting jet crafts and took off away from the planet. Phoenix manned the lasers and shot down more jet crafts. This was more for her nightmares later. But for now, there was no time now to think, just to act according to how she was trained.

Soon they made it past orbit. With Dragon and Kirin's help they were able to fight off the first fleet of attackers. Before the second fleet could be launched, division seventeen was already on their way back to Tweila.

Back at the base in Tweila, Phoenix was being given the fifth degree, "How could you possible fail the mission?" the general demanded, "You were promised to be the best from your system! Is this all Preyal has to offer! Some stinking humans?" Phoenix kept silent. She felt nothing. To her, scolding was merely a formality. Success was never rewarded, failure always punished.

"I have the file sir, just not the storage unit you gave to me." The general just looked at her in disbelief. He smirked, "well then where is it?"

"In my mind, I have it all memorized," Phoenix replied. The general sighed. He kept silent while thinking over what to do, "Alright, I'll let you off easy this time because you are nothing more than a dumb human, but I want that file as soon as possible. We will escort you to a facility and you are not to leave until every last character is recorded, is that understood?"

"Yes, sir."

Phoenix was escorted to a computer lab. She sat there for a painstaking fifteen hours recording everything from memory. Her division had been sent home, but Dragon stayed. Deklar, his brother Scott, was going to tell their parents he was sleeping over a friend's house. Rosi was going to have hell to pay when she returned home.

"Finished," Phoenix stood up. The file was now in the hands of the Tweila Galaxy.

"Are you sure that is everything?" The general asked.

"Yes."

"You are excused until further notice, you will be escorted back to Earth," the general then diverted all his attention to the computer. Phoenix silently left the room. Dragon was holding her pack. She was surprised to see him.

"Thank you," she said slinging the pack onto her back. A man appeared out of the computer lab, "I am to escort you back to Earth," he informed them.

"Lead the way," Phoenix replied. Wearily they followed him into the ship that brought them back to the Preyal system.

They were silent the entire seven hours back to Earth. Phoenix and Dragon sat side by side not speaking to each other. Even their thoughts were quiet. They were one hundred percent soldiers, only doing as they were told. But now, they were also husband and wife binding them closer together in a state of being where they did not need to speak.

Rosi was grounded. She was forced to miss her first homecoming. Her parents even had the police there when they had found her room empty. She was in unspeakable trouble. Yet, she could secretly care less. She would just have to be smarter about things next time. She sat on her bed. Her parents were starting to sound a lot like the general. They were telling her how much they sacrifice for her and how much worry she had put them in. Rosi sat there with her head bowed like someone who was doing penance. She just let her parents yell at her. This was yet another formality. The only thing different was their justification for yelling. The general was in charge of something she could not question. Her parents still remembered Joel disappearing and just loved her. Love, what a funny word, was all this yelling a true expression of love? Rosi would have to remind herself never to fall in love.

"And further more," her mother yelled, "your sister is moving into your room!" Rosi snapped her head up, "No! I like my privacy!"

"We can't trust you! Besides, Mia is too old to share a room with Tommy anymore!"

"But Tommy's three and he'll be scared!"

"Then would you rather have Tommy move in?" her mother demanded. Rosi knew she had lost this war. Her seven year old sister moved into her room by the end of the week.

"Hey Rosi," Mia whispered from the other side of the room.

"What?" Rosi demanded. She was exhausted after two make up exams and wanted to sleep.

"Where did you go that one night?" Mia asked innocently. Rosi sighed, "none of your business."

"Why can't you tell me?"

"Because you might be spying for mom and dad," Rosi pulled the covers over her head.

"That's not funny," Mia said.

"Go to sleep, I'm tired," Rosi commanded.

"But I had a dream that night you didn't come home."

"Mmm," Rosi moaned. She had half a mind to go sleep downstairs. If she did, she would never hear the end of it from her parents.

"I had a dream you were dancing in the stars with this girl that looked like me, but her name was Sarah," Mia paused, "You guys didn't see me because I was standing on Earth, but I wanted to come dance too. I was yelling but you didn't hear me," Mia finished. Rosi was silent. Mia was thoughtful as if she was trying to relive the dream, "It was a beautiful dream." Tears threatened Rosi's eyes. She quickly brushed them away. She did not cry, and Sarah was gone anyways.

"Go to sleep Mia," Rosi demanded gently. Her little sister finally rolled over and in a few moments was breathing deeply. Across the room, Rosi lost all sleep. She should really be nicer to Mia. If Rosi disappeared, Mia would be just like herself when she lost Sarah. She couldn't do that to her. Rosi wished deeply that Sarah was still around. Then someone would be able to stay with Mia when Rosi went away. Of course, then Rosi would probably be dead or would have never heard of division seventeen.

"Nothings perfect," Rosi whispered to herself. The night faded into dawn. Rosi went to her window and looked at the last of the fading stars, "I still miss you, Sarah."

More domestic trouble. Yolukia called Rosi and Wayne to Juyvine again. He was extremely persistent. This struck a tinge of fear inside of the two young newlyweds.

"Why haven't you conceived yet?" Yolukia asked Rosi gently,

"Have you not performed the mating ritual?" Rosi blushed a deep crimson, "No, your honor." The two young humans desperately wished to be somewhere else at the moment. This was far worse than any humiliation they could think of at that age.

"Is there something wrong with your fertility?" he asked both of them intently.

"No, your honor," they replied in unison.

"Not that we know of," Rosi added.

"I did not ask you to feel an attraction to one another, I asked you to conceive," Yolukia said in a strict voice, "You do not understand how desperately I need a successor! This should be a great honor for the both of you to be chosen."

"I understand," Rosi replied.

"You must spend the night here again," Yolukia spoke in stern tone, "drink this." Two bowls of dark red fluid was brought into the room. Rosi cursed to herself, her parents were going to murder her when they find her missing again.

The next morning before they were allowed to leave, one of Yolukia's servants gave Rosi a test. She was pregnant.

"Oh my God," she clutched her stomach. She suddenly felt very sick. Her parents were never going to let her live. Her first impulse was to bawl her eyes out. This was everything against her upbringing. What was she going to do? She could handle breaking her way out of a prison and killing massive amounts of people. But this was something else altogether.

"This is so wrong," Wayne said to her under his breath trying to comfort her.

"Screw you!" she pushed out in a breathy whisper, "I'm the one carrying the evidence in my womb!" she was hyperventilating, "I am so dead!" A tiny tear found a corner of her eye. Wayne did not know what else to say. They were alone in the room at the moment as the servant went to bring Yolukia the news. Rosi needed to sit down. She collapsed onto the floor. Leaning her head back, she let out a long nervous breath. Wayne felt guilty and sympathetic.

"Do you hate me now?" he blurted out, "I'll understand if you do, but this might cause problems for, you know, our job." Rosi snapped her head to look at him. She had not thought about that yet. Wayne sat down beside her and studied his hands. Rosi watched as he followed the lines in his palms and studied his fingerprints. What did it matter?

In four more years Rosi no longer had to put her parents through the torment of worrying about her. Even if she had to spend the rest of the four years in perpetual lockdown, it was all worth it. She leaned her head against Wayne's shoulder. He looked at her in surprise. Rosi felt warmth spreading from his body to hers. Perhaps it was a good thing they had no recollection of the night before.

"Do you love me?" she asked, forgetting how she questioned love a few nights ago. He hesitated, "I think I have to. We have to be together until death do us part." Rosi smiled. It was definitely not a romantic comment at all, but he was still hers, and she didn't feel as alone. Wayne didn't tell Rosi the truth that he had already felt himself fall for her. Perhaps it was the fact that she had a higher command or that they would never be able to have a normal life. Either way, he had always denied any potential feelings he had for her. Or maybe it was just that, something he shouldn't have. People always want what they can't have. Now, everything was to the wind. It was in that moment when he finally accepted the fact that they were both in division seventeen for life. This meant having a normal life was never going to happen.

Rosi raced down the hallway of her high school. She was extremely late and her school was probably going to call her parents. She approached her classroom and was about to yank open the door when, through the window, she caught sight of herself in her own seat. Shock came over her. She quickly moved away from the window to avoid being seen. A few moments later, the bell rang. Rosi pulled out a pair of sunglasses and put them on. When the girl who looked like Rosi walked by, Rosi grabbed her.

"There you are!" the girl whispered.

"Ara!" Rosi exclaimed, "Oh my God, what are you doing here?"

"Covering your ass! I had dinner with your family last night," Ara explained. Rosi looked at Ara with adoration, "I LOVE you so much, you will never know."

"And they never suspected a thing!" Ara said proudly, "hurry, lets go change in the bathroom then you can get back to your life." Rosi hugged her sister tightly. She was a lifesaver. Rosi was still a little bit hurt that her parents didn't suspect anything. Or maybe Ara just knew Rosi too well. For the moment, the baby in her womb was forgotten.

The next morning, Rosi was feeling extremely sick.

"Mom!" Rosi called. Her stomach was upset, "what did you put in dinner last night?" even though she hadn't eaten a bite of it.

"We had leftovers dear, the same thing you had the night before" her mom called back from the bathroom where her sister was brushing her teeth.

"Can I stay home from school?" Rosi pleaded. Her mother walked into her room and leaned on the doorframe. She gave the pale girl a look of disbelief. Rosi just sat in bed and stared back blankly.

"This is your karma for sneaking out and worrying us half to death!" Rosi's mom said. She walked in and felt Rosi's temperature, "Well, you're not burning up, but you do look very sick."

"Please mom? I feel like I'm about to puke everywhere."

"My, isn't that orthodox," her mother said sarcastically, "Well, you were acting funny last night, I suppose you could stay home today, but tomorrow not 'buts' you are going to school, is that understood young lady?" her mom said tapping Rosi on the nose. She smiled, "Yes mom." Rosi pulled the blankets way over her head and snuggled in deep. So her parents were able to see the difference between her and Ara after all. A few moments later, she was sound asleep.

"Rosi," someone whispered. Rosi was still thick with sleep. Someone shook her. She moaned and pulled the covers tighter around her. There were some giggles, then, someone yanked all the covers off. Her mind still fuzzy, Rosi opened her eyes.

"Surprise!"

"Oh God!" Rosi shrieked. Wayne, his brother Scott, L.J. and Ara were all in the room holding a cake to her face.

"What are you doing here?" she was pleasantly surprised, but worry soon overcame her, "my mom doesn't work!"

"Oh yeah she left you a note," Ara handed Rosi a slip of paper. Rosi read it out loud, "Errands til three pm, soup on the stove, Mom." Rosi let out a sigh of relief.

"We came for the baby shower," Scott said.

"How did you know?" Rosi asked exasperated.

"My brother is the father," Scott chuckled smacking Wayne on the back, "way to go buddy! Score!" Wayne turned crimson.

"You told!" Rosi demanded, "I didn't tell anyone!"

"We know," L.J. said, "you should have told us too! Instead I had to hear it from cheese head over here," L.J. indicated Scott.

"I don't think it should be a secret amongst the family in the division," Wayne asserted. Rosi was embarrassed, "I don't know what to say you guys, thank you!" At that moment, Rosi felt a bond between herself and her duty. What once felt like an obligation, now started to feel like family.

Even after the rest of Rosi's visitors had left, Wayne perched on the roof of her house to watch for a few moments more. It was his baby too, he would never be too far. He knew that Rosi was still doubtful about their attachment, but what was fact was fact. He was her husband and like his own father he would not fail his duty. She was a very sweet girl, he wished he knew more about her. It wasn't fair they lived states apart. At least they were on the same planet. For now, he had to return to his parents and keep up the façade for the other ones he loved.

It was the weekend on Rosi's Earth. New Years was coming up and Rosi was busy. Nonetheless, duty doesn't wait. Phoenix and the leaders of the other two Preyal divisions were called into conference. Incidentally, Rosi was sleeping over Tina's house. Tina did not know, and Rosi prayed that her parents trusted Tina enough that they wouldn't call.

On a planet in the Tweila System, Phoenix was being briefed on their next mission. The Pillur System was upset with the Tweila, Preyal and Iroliem Systems. Divisions seventeen, twelve and nine were to work together on a sabotage mission. Like previous missions, the leaders were instructed, and then they were to pass down commands. As the leaders of the divisions were preparing to leave an explosion flattened the facility. This was no doubt a reconnaissance due to the information that was stolen from Fa Relarious some months ago.

Everything was fuzzy. Phoenix felt a bleeding in her gut but she could not move. Life was seeping out of her. She tried to move her hands and drag herself out of the fire, but she had no strength. The last thoughts she remembered were those of her baby. Would it be alright?

There was consciousness, but no sight, no sound. Everything around Phoenix was dark. Her eyes could not see. She began to fret and her skin began to feel pain. Suddenly, a wave of rest swept over her and she was back to sleep.

The Neptunian doctors had given her another injection to keep her unconscious while her body slowly worked on repairs. She was suspended inside a horizontal tube. There were many wires attached to her body monitoring her healing progress. She had been cut badly by shrapnel and suffered many burns. Her eyes were gone. The fire had cooked them to a crisp. She could not hear because she was suspended in a solution of Tenopuiharexia. It was more commonly known as Tenorex, the reverse of Trex and was used in healing. A day later, Phoenix body was fully repaired. All, except one thing.

Her eyes opened slowly. Everything was yellow. A few seconds later she was able to piece together her thoughts. She knew she was in Tenorex. This was a first for her. She had read about it before but it was such a rare chemical only the best medical bases had them. She slowly stuck out her hand and knocked on the glass. A doctor walked over and released the fluid from the chamber.

"How are we feeling?" he asked. Phoenix opened her mouth to speak but gagged on the yellow liquid. She choked and coughed it up as the doctor patted her on the back. When she finally cleared herself of the disgusting fluid, she replied in a croak, "Alright I guess." She rubbed her eyes.

"Good," the doctor placed a stethoscope to her back and asked her to breathe. He checked her pupils and declared that she was ready to be discharged. He handed her a paper gown and was prepared to leave the room.

"Doctor," Phoenix called out shakily. He stopped, sensing her next question in sad fear, "Where is my baby?" The words stood out stark and cold as her voice quivered with high strung tears. He didn't have the heart to look at her, "I'm sorry, but the little boy didn't make it." He then proceeded out of the room, leaving her all alone.

Phoenix didn't move. Somewhere, deep down, she had already known that she miscarried, but she still needed to hear it. She needed someone to confirm the devastation. What were the odds that her child would survive anyway? She began feeling very strong emotions. She took a deep breath to calm herself down. Then another, and another. She put self into motion and got dressed. Another deep breath escaped her chest. She was a good soldier, and she was not allowed to feel. Just a couple more breaths and this feeling would go away.

A knock came at the door.

"Come in," Phoenix called out. There was more strength in her voice than she felt. Dragon peered in. She was so relieved to see a familiar face she almost lost herself.

"Hi," he said softly. She couldn't smile back. If she didn't keep emotions out of herself, she would fall apart. That was something no one was allowed to see.

"How are you feeling?" he asked walking up to her. His voice was hollow and told her he already knew.

"Very shitty," she replied. Her voice was still hoarse. There was an awkward silence between them. He didn't know if she knew about her baby. She didn't know what she was supposed to say. Finally, Dragon broke the ice, "So, did you hear about the baby?" Phoenix nodded, "Its such a shame." She couldn't look him in the eyes. She could not believe she replied so coldly. It was his child too.

"Phoenix," Dragon spoke to her in a stern voice, "don't hide to me how you feel, your eyes don't lie very well." His straightforward remark made her uncomfortable.

"Well then that just means I'm not a very good soldier!" she screamed and pushed him away and left the room barely able to contain herself. Dragon let out a deep sad breath. He was not upset with her. He had never been as near death as she had been twice in her life already. He was just trying to make things the best that he could. Maybe Phoenix was right. The message she was sending was that they were not a family. The marriage was still just strictly business, and they were to be nothing more than friends. Rosi seemed to have shut herself off, forfeiting the concept of needing anyone. It was as if she had lost so much in a life before division seventeen, she chose only to be alone.

The day after Rosi was discharged from healing in Tenorex, Yolukia called Rosi and Wayne to Juyvine again. He was saddened to hear of Rosi's misfortune. Rosi herself was running in soldier mode for most of her days. She was afraid to feel anything at all. Yolukia gave his sympathies but also stressed the importance of wanting an offspring between the two. Rosi and Wayne obediently drank more of the dark red fluid and by next morning the two had conceived another child.

They were to conduct a Pearl Harbor excursion. Or at least that was how Phoenix described it to her division. She had shoved her baby out of her mind for the time being. They had a job to do, and that was what was most important. In two days they were to meet with the other two divisions. The division nine leader was going to be the head commander and everyone was expected to pull their own weight. A week later, they would swing into action.

Child Two (inside the womb)

I do not understand very many things in life. Mine has not yet begun. I am about six months before birth. Every minute of my life I have the comforting sound of my mother's heart to lull me back and forth. I can tell that she is a strong woman. She is always so active. My world is nothing more than a warm cubicle and sleep. I do not know this consciously, but something assures me that I would be greatly loved once I enter the world on the other side of this piece of skin.

One day, something strange happens. From the darkness of the womb in which I reside, I see a light. The light is so very far away. I am able to think as well. Not clearly because my mind is not yet fully developed. I put my hand out to touch the light. A much larger hand takes a hold of mine. I look over. Even though I have never seen the woman before, I can feel deep in my soul that she is my mother. She smiles at me and her mouth speaks to me. No sound comes out, but my heart can hear her words, "Let's go home," she says. I notice other people around me. We are all flying towards the light. I look back at my mother. She is smiling at me and there was never anything more beautiful in my life. Suddenly, she is being pulled backwards. Her face wilts into a saddened expression.

"I have to go," she mouths to me, "My work isn't finished." I beg her the only way I could, my eyes were full of protest. I did not want to be alone. She gets pulled further back as more people pass us by towards the light. My hands are small and my grip is weak. My mother removes my hand from hers. She kisses it gently then lets me go. I continue to float towards the light as my mother is being engulfed by darkness. The last thing I saw of her, were her eyes. They were so deep, so beautiful. She would have been my own personal guardian angel if I would have ever made it into the world of the living.

The dream was fading. What was it about? Phoenix struggled to hold onto it as her mind was becoming more and more clear. It was something so beautiful she was sure she would never find it again in this world as long as she lived. A single tear emerged from under her closed eyelids. It paused to gather courage. Then it slid down her cheek to find refuge in her hair.

Dragon, Zap and Ara sat silently beside Phoenix. Her body

signs were stabilized. She had lost all signs of life when they rushed her from the wreckage. They were sure that they had lost her for good. Her body was cold and lifeless as the doctors worked on her. It wasn't until eight hours later they told them she was going to be alright. Wayne did not want to ask about his child, but Ara did.

"I'm sorry," was all this doctor could say.

Yolukia did not call the two to Juyvine this time. He merely contacted Phoenix, "I am very sorry to hear about this tragedy. I have decided that this is a sign. Even though I wish for a successor from you two individuals, I will no longer rush things. Whenever you are ready, I will accept a male child." Phoenix acknowledged the ruler and they ended the transmission. She looked at Wayne. There was something unexplainable she was feeling inside. It felt worse than her own tastes of death. His eyes were gentle and sympathetic. She realized how selfish she had been. They were his babies too and he loved them. She was responsible for their deaths. Suddenly, a gate opened and all the emotions her self-discipline held back, escaped. She burst into tears and cried in the arms of someone she had once refused to accept. Losing Sarah and having her parents think she was crazy had scarred Rosi into abandoning trust and attachment. Dragon had just won her back.

Natasha received another visit from Rosi. This time, the girl looked very different. She wore an expression not fitting for someone her age. Natasha bustled Rosi into her own home. While she went to fetch Rosi some water, the young girl sat down beside the crib of Natasha's baby. She studied the tiny fingers and the soft round features. Rosi had no recollection of her death. She wondered what her babies would have looked like.

When Natasha returned, she found the girl in tears. The next few hours Rosi told Natasha of what had transpired within the last few months. All her heartaches and stories of death poured out of her. When the baby started crying, Rosi sobbed even harder.

"Its just not fair," Rosi vented, "I know what I have to do and I know we were trained not to feel, but sometimes I just can't do it."

Natasha picked up her baby and cradled him. The crying stopped.

"Would you like to hold Sally?" Natasha asked. Rosi shook her head. Natasha spoke more sternly, "that was an order soldier, don't forget I still rank before you." Obediently, Rosi took the tiny person in her arms. Something deep inside of her connected. Every tiny movement felt like it was a part of her own. There were moments when Rosi would prop something against her hip for balance and something deep in her subconscious screamed that a baby should be there. It was almost as if every second of her day, her soul was preparing for a baby. A baby she would never have. Holding little Sally helped to fill in that hole. Even if it was just a little bit.

"Thank you, Natasha," Rosi was truly grateful. Even though this woman had brought her into division seventeen to help keep her safe, Rosi has faced nothing but death and destruction. But Natasha being there to console her made all the difference in the world.

Dikara
"Governess of the Galaxy"

CHAPTER FOUR

Rosi (age 6)

"War is vicious, war is bloodthirsty. Can any of you kill and be able to live with it? If you are weak, then get out! We only accept the strongest here!" Natasha was lecturing. More like yelling. This frightened Rosi. She had never seen Natasha like this before. It was as if she were a whole different person.

"Can you wear a mask over your emotions and do what needs to be done?" Each word that came out of Natasha's mouth made Rosi shrink. Did Rosi have to kill these people here? What if she got herself killed? She might end up like Sarah!

"Now I ask you, what does it mean to die? Is it the end?" Natasha shook her head, "death is only the beginning, dying is a part of life. Before you came into this world, you were dead. When you sleep, you are a small step away from death. Do not fear it, stare it in the eyes and kill it before it takes you. You must know how to judge, how to separate good from evil, you must never enjoy killing, but do as you must. You are the hope, the protectors. You, all of you here are potential guardians of Earth. But, when push comes to shove, don't hesitate to kill. It is the ultimate defense. Soon, all will make sense. Now I want all you to keep what I just said in mind and we will continue to the self-defense training field. We will continue to learn all forms of martial arts, including alien forms. You were learn multiple ways to strike, the block, to fall, and to do all three at the same time."

Everyone learned fast. The injections that enhanced learning in the younger individuals were working. Scott was ten, Wayne was eight, June was seven, turning eight in autumn, and Dave was already eight, turning nine. Rosi's seventh birthday was coming up. She had forgotten because she was so absorbed with learning the history of the planets and the causes of war and all the mathematical and technical skills along with the defense and penetration of defense. But Natasha remembered Rosi's summer birthday. She spoke to Old Matt about making some arrangements.

"Surprise! Happy Birthday Rosi!" Rosi had followed Natasha into the kitchen. They burst into song as they presented her with a cake. Rosi smiled and hugged everyone. Although they learned of war, these people were still human and they still knew how to love.

Later on, she called home, her parents wished her a happy birthday and asked how camp was.

"Its great! A lot of fun! I met a lot of new people, like Wayne, from Colorado."

"That's nice, we'll see you in about another month?"

"Yep! Don't worry!"

"Okay, take care and listen to Natasha alright?"

"Sure mom! Love ya!"

"Love ya too!"

"Bye!"

"Bye!"

"Natasha?" Rosi sought her out.

"Yes?" the woman replied. Rosi took a deep breath. This was not an easy question.

"When the others died, you know, when you were given faulty instructions, how did you feel when they were gone? What do you do when your friends die and you were not around to help them live?" Rosi made sure her voice was gentle and held no malice. None of the division members spoke of the previously deceased soldiers. Rosi had to know. She had to know what might happen to her when she died.

"I," Natasha began. Then her face stiffened and a tired aggressiveness took over, "Cold, cold and angry. Helpless. I don't like talking about it, whats past is past and only lives in our hearts." Rosi saw the strength leave the woman's face. She had never seen that before. Natasha always kept a cool, placid expression no matter what. She never faltered before, but the years were breaking down that wall they were all trained to keep up. Rosi tried to make herself satisfied with the answer, but could not, so she turned to Richard.

"Hey, Richard?"

"Hey little Rosi, how can I be of any service to you?" he greeted with his usual warmth. His face didn't move much to show emotion, but his voice gave it all away.

"I talked to Natasha, but I wanted to know more. I mean, what happens if we die? You guys never talk about the other division members who've died. What did you feel to find your friends gone?" Again, something in Richard changed. With him, it was surprise and anger. The surprise was that Rosi came to him to ask that question. But Rosi knew the anger was not directed toward her.

"How did I feel?" he shook his head, his eyes were focused on something in the distance, "I was angry at the universe and how it works. I was angry with all the violence and how it was taking people away from us. I hated with a passion that I could not relish upon my enemies. No, you never forget those you've fought with side by side. Let me tell you something," his eyes switched back to Rosi, "When you are in division 17, a bond forms, you can't help it, its magical, yet, you know its there. And when one leaves, the others mourn, but they hold it all inside." He sighed and looked away with melancholy showing in his eyes, "We never talk about it because nothing is supposed to affect our work. But every now and then, when someone asks, you really can't stop yourself from telling. It's just that there is no point, they're all gone now. All you can do is keep going, keep fighting, like a robot. A soldier is a robot. You take orders and you follow. Stuff happens, what are you going to do? You can either let it get you down, or shrug it off and move on. Sometimes moving on isn't as easy as it sounds." A sadness came over him. It was a sadness that slowly grew in him throughout the years of his membership in division 17. He had shared the joys and sorrows. He was one of the "old soldiers."

Wayne (age 16)

Meditation, it was so deep and tranquil. Breathing deep, he was barefoot in the snow with nothing more than light pants and a t-shirt on. Eyes closed he moved through the slow tai-chi motions. Every fiber was insensitive to the cold. There was pleasant warmth that spread throughout his body. The pitch black of the small hours hid him in his parents' backyard. He felt his spirit lifted and playing in tune with the entire universe from the furthest stars to the air around him at the moment. There was beauty in mere existence.

The snow crunched softly as he pivoted his feet. They were blue and cold but Wayne took no notice. He was going to be a father. As upset as his parents would be if they knew, he was ecstatic. They would never have to know. He finally formed an attachment to division seventeen that was beyond necessity. As a result, he was living two lives. Even though honesty was something he had to sacrifice at certain times he felt that it was for a good cause. After all, he was able to justify it. He was protecting his family and all humans on Earth.

Switching to a different stance, Wayne breathed out deeply,

pushing from deep within his gut. He didn't remember much of his younger years in division seventeen. He was in for as long as he could remember. Many times he had wondered, which life was the lie? He kicked and landed in a new stance. He had never had emotional attachments through the division. They trained him to act without feeling. Was it wrong to feel protective over Rosi and his child? In a way it was how he was supposed to feel protective towards Earth. Was this different? Rosi was his commanding officer. His family had always told him that the only real men were gentlemen. Shouldn't he be in charge? Then again, his parents didn't know everything. As much as he loved them, he understood that he and his brother were the only two in the immediate family blessed to know more about the universe.

It was Christmas day. All the Eastons were gathered in Wayne's house. After many cheek pinches and, "Oh my! Look how they have grown" the aunts and uncles finally settled down to dinner and conversation. The potluck dinner covered the entire twelve-seat table. There was hardly any room for the plates and glasses.

Aunt Lee was telling a story about her lap dog Tickles. The little rascal still chases the mailman who was many times his size. Uncle Jeffrey brought in a new line of hair products for his store for everyone. He was happy because it was selling well. The holiday cheer was spreading well throughout the family and the evening was bright. Wayne could not stop thinking about his baby. He just wanted to shout it out to everyone and sing from the highest peak to the world. He wanted to share his great news with the people he loved the most in the world, but his damned secret had to stay just that, a secret.

"So how is your girlfriend, Scott?" Aunt Jenn asked.

"Oh she's doing well, she's with her family tonight, we spent all day yesterday together," Scott replied.

"What about you Wayne?" Uncle Steve teased, "Isn't it about time you find yourself a little sweetheart?" Wayne turned a deep beet red. Uncle Steve was looking at him devilishly, "there is someone isn't there?"

"Well, not really, we don't, I dunno," Wayne said. He didn't know what he could possibly say! He didn't want to keep Rosi a complete secret but how on Earth would he tell them about her without saying too much?

"Wayne's got a secret admirer," Scott rescued him, "we're still trying to figure out who it is." This aroused a raucous cheer through the family followed by laughter.

"So Uncle Steve, why are you teasing Wayne? When are you going to get married?" Scott asked diverting attention from Wayne. Another laugh tore around the table. The wine had given everyone a warm glow and soon Wayne's secret admirer was forgotten. He gave Scott a thankful glance.

Later that night as the adults sat around in the living room the children went outdoors for a snowball fight. Scott and Wayne were huddled behind a rock.

"So what was all that blushing about?" Scott asked Wayne in a half serious tone, "she is your commanding officer, do you really have feelings for her?"

"What's wrong with that?" Wayne asked defensively. Scott put his hands up, "Hey, nothing at all, just be careful and don't get burned. I mean, this is a lot bigger than me dating Trina, this isn't just the girl down the street. You and Rosi, man, that's something big right there. I mean, pairing the two of you up, the Ruler is either screwy or he's got something up his sleeve."

"I'm not following," Wayne said.

"You are both in the same job, she's a higher official than you. You're second in command, that's a cause for drama right there. I don't know why he has so much interest in the two of you, all I'm saying is maybe he wants to disassemble the division or something like that."

"Scott, we're all just kids in the end. We are short sighted and we don't care, we'll recover."

"Right, I know that, but our system might not. Catch my drift?" Wayne was silent, "I never thought about it that way." Wayne thought for a moment, "He rules all the local galaxies, why should he care about Preyal? We're nothing more than just a system." The two of them were quiet. Scott peered over the rock. He launched a snowball, "Gotcha!" He hit Mary Ann in the back.

"Hey!" the twelve year old cousin shouted, "Jessie! Help!" Jessie was thirteen, and also Kirin in division seventeen. She came running with a huge grin on her face.

"I need a snowball!" Jessie shouted to Mary Ann. Mary Ann throws one to her as Jessie runs by. Jessie jumps up and grabs a branch, swinging over the rock, she nails Scott in the face. Wayne doubles over laughing as Scott starts to chase Jessie around the yard.

Scott finally catches Jessie. She was laughing hysterically as Scott picks her up over his shoulders and throws her into a deep pile of snow. He then commences to sit on her, "I'm gonna fart!" he teases.

"Ew! Get off!" Jessie laughs, "that's so gross! Stop picking on me!" By this time, all the cousins around the yard are rolling around in the snow laughing. Wayne wished deep down that Rosi was there to join in the fun with them. She was his wife and that meant she was family. He wanted her to be in every aspect of his life. Sadly, some things were just not possible. Still, there was also the possibility that she didn't feel anything for him at all. No matter what words can be said, true emotions can be different.

A week later Wayne made a decision to see Rosi. Late at night he flew to Rosi's house. He peered through the window to see a sleeping girl about six years old. That must be Mia, Rosi's little sister. Rosi's bed was empty. Wayne proceeded to SHONDS and woke up the live in technician.

The live in technician was an old man named Gary. He was on call at all hours. His primary job was to provide information to the division members. He was always notified of where the division members were and what their status was. Wayne asked Gary to find Phoenix for him. He couldn't help but almost feel as if he were stalking her, but something just didn't feel right and he was worried about her.

"Don't you know?" Gary replied, "she's on Neptune. She was in an explosion." Wayne's mouth went dry. He forced himself to swallow hard, "explosion?"

"Yeah she was at a meeting in Tweila, I can give you the address to the hospital if you want it."

"Yes please." All the recent holiday cheer that built up inside of Wayne was gone in an instant. He was back in the cold world where Christmas was frivolous and unnecessary.

He took the directions Gary printed out and thanked him. Hopping back into his jet craft, Wayne flew away praying that Rosi and his baby were safe. He couldn't do this, this was too much. He wanted her to be in his life, but she could never be. He wanted to walk away, but he just couldn't anymore.

Wayne had changed into his division uniform just in case. He wasn't sure what to expect and having Division Seventeen as an alibi couldn't hurt. He called and requested permission to enter the top secret hospital as Dragon. He was granted, after parking quickly, he entered the hospital.

"Sir, how may we help you," he was asked by a man in uniform.

"I am looking for Phoenix of division seventeen," Dragon spoke smoothly.

"I'm sorry sir, you need special clearance to view her."

"I'm her second officer in command," Dragon held out his left arm where an identification chip was installed. The man in uniform held a small machine over his arm. A few seconds later, words appeared on the screen confirming Dragon's identity.

"Right this way," the man took Dragon to the room where Phoenix was being kept. There were two doctors keeping watch for any changes in her medical condition.

"Hello," one doctor greeted, "May I ask who you are?"

"Dragon, division seventeen," Wayne replied briskly. He caught sight of a lump of flesh inside a Tenorex tube. His stomach threatened to churn. An icy hand gripped him and his heart felt like it could explode from worry.

"Its great that you are here, we were going to contact you in a few hours to discuss her injuries," the doctor spoke in a gentle tone. Wayne swallowed, "go ahead, I'm here now."

"First I would like to say how lucky this young lady is. There were two other casualties at the scene. There was a terrible explosion of which the cause is still not yet determined. Shrapnel ripped away most of her face and cut off her foot right as you can see," the doctor gestured to the tube. Wayne did not recognize the black and brown burned lump at all.

"We retrieved the foot and Dr. Hinderson is attaching it as we speak." The other doctor did not look up when Wayne had come in. Behind a glass wall, he had on a helmet that was connected to a magnifier inside the tube. He sat at a massive control panel that controlled the smallest instruments ever invented. He was manually attaching the bone and major blood vessels in Phoenix's foot.

"She suffered major muscle and organ tears," the first doctor continued, "through the shoulder and lungs. The most tragic was her reproductive organ. She was under top secret to carry a larva, or as you humans call them, a baby. That was lost." Wayne tuned out the doctor. The rest of the words went inside one ear and right out the other. His face and posture remained stoic. He went numb. All the joy and excitement from the previous days came crashing down. It was like waking up the day after binging extensively on drugs and the plague of going cold turkey hits you. Wayne could even feel his heart bleeding and wanted to double over. His self-control was astounding. He did not falter for a second. He couldn't. A part of the secret was that no one was to know who the father was. It just wasn't fair. He wasn't free to love, and he wasn't free to mourn. His life was nothing more than a parade of self restraint.

In his minds eye he was holding her broken body and weeping. It wasn't fair. Not to him, not to her, this life was too cruel. It was like living in an emotional prison where truth in itself was a heaven they were never allowed to touch.

Months Later (Phoenix conceived with second child)

"Scott?"

"What's up little bro?" Scott replied.

"How do you know when you love someone?" Wayne asked. Scott guffawed, "Lemme guess, Rosi?"

"Yes, I mean, I know the feeling of being in love where you're all dizzy, but dad always told us that wasn't real love. What is real love?" Wayne inquired. Scott was thoughtful, "I guess its how you feel with mom and dad. I mean, you're not 'in love' with them but you know that you can rely on them and they will support you and they will be there as you grow."

"Is that it?" Wayne asked. Scott gave him a look of pity, "I feel so sorry for you little bro, being tied down and all, you should be out discovering what love is, not already married."

"I'm pretty sure I love her," Wayne said.

"Or maybe its because you lost the first baby, and you feel sorry for her because you gave her that baby and this time with the second baby you want to feel more involved or something like that," Scott said. Wayne furrowed his brow, "You lost me."

"Never mind," Scott turned back to his homework. Wayne sat with his pencil above his own homework, but his mind was elsewhere.

The next day they were assembled for another mission. They were to meet at SHONDS and they were taken to yet another facility in Tweila. Dragon pulled Phoenix aside, "I don't want you to go on this mission, is there anything I can do?"

"Dragon," Phoenix had a flat expression and spoke with a professional tone, "I have a job to do just as you do. Don't ask me to change, I'm the leading officer and I have a duty. Know your place, you are never to speak of this on a mission, ever again."

"But you have my child," Dragon continued.

"The child is neither mine nor yours, it belongs to Yolukia. Desist or I will demerit you." Phoenix ended the conversation and walked away. Dragon understood that her dry personality was her professional side, but he could not help but feel anger towards her. She brought up a good point though. One that he didn't let himself think too much about. He would never be in the child's life. Why did he care so much for it then?

Fa Relarious was not the only target planet. On the very commercial planet of Jonix Newim there were top secret underground information storage facilities. There were also farmers there who were really disguised guards stationed to protect it. It was their duty to pretend like there was nothing there but crops. This was where division seventeen, nine, and twelve were sent in. They obeyed and destroy all the military weapons underground. In the process, they had damaged whole fields of crops and caused civilian casualties.

Once again, Phoenix, as her duty called, sent her division back as she continued to hold off oncoming attackers. She was positioned at one of the gates and Dragon and Kirin were positioned at another. Dragon knew that Phoenix sent him to fight with Kirin because of the conversation earlier. Under normal circumstances, he would have preferred to stay by his little cousin, Jessie. However, he knew that Phoenix was with his baby and if anything went wrong he would rather be by her side.

Dragon and Kirin blocked off their gate and sealed it shut. They entered their jet crafts and proceeded to follow the first group. Phoenix would rendezvous with them later.

They were ten minutes in their flight back and everyone had checked in except for Phoenix.

"I'm going back," Dragon radioed brashly and without further comment he whipped his jet craft in a 180 and headed back in the direction they came.

"Me too," Tinkerbell radioed.

"Halt!" It was Kirin, "Before we all go crazy like Dragon lets find a little structure. Tinkerbell, you volunteered, go with Skull and Moongirl to retrieve Phoenix and aid Dragon, the rest of you stay on course." Good old Kirin, she always had her head on straight.

They were too late. Phoenix's body was torn from limb to limb as the ultimate form of insult. She was deceased. The tiny baby was stuck on a stake along side Phoenix's head. What occurred next was an even bloodier mess. The four division members followed Dragon's command. They killed nearly a quarter of the civilians on the planet and retrieved the body parts. The sight was apocalyptic in measure as fire consumed most of the populated areas.

At top speeds, the division took off to Neptune. They must hurry before too many of the cells in Phoenix's body die and she is lost for good.

As they flew away, the bombs set by the three division leaders went off and all the equipment hidden under the surface was destroyed. At least the mission was accomplished. If Phoenix were to live, she would not be reprimanded this time. If she had failed, death would have been a granted wish.

"Doctor, what about the baby?" Dragon asked.

"Well, the mother," the doctor began, but Dragon coolly interrupted once more, "You told be about Phoenix, what about the larva?" The doctor sighed, "It was in its first human trimester, there was nothing we could do."

"Thank you," Dragon replied flatly and walked back into the viewing room. Behind a glass window, he watched as the doctors reconstructed Phoenix's body once again. He was able to find a tiny bit of conciliation in the fact that she was going to be alright. His disappointment and pain of loosing a second child were threatening him to cry, to let it all out. Yet, he stood there like a robot. Not even a furrow was found on his brow.

Dr. Spalling sighed deeply as he operated on Phoenix. He remembered little Rosi when she was ten and on her first trip on Neptune. He was established as her pediatrician. He also treated her cloned sisters. She had grown so much and it was such a shame her life was headed towards disaster. His own son was turning ten soon. He felt blessed that he would lead a safer life than Rosi.

Division seventeen was under suspension. They had disobeyed commands. They were supposed to have set the bombs and leave, but Dragon going back jeopardized the situation. Division seventeen's position was replaced by division eighteen. Even though it was an insult, this allowed Phoenix to stay at home and recuperate.

"You should have been careful Rosi," her mother scolded, "now you're sick in bed and you can't do anything." Rosi closed her eyes. Her body was in excellent running condition and stable, but she was still very weak. Her pride was also hurt. Here she was supposed to be the leader but she had gotten over powered and her division was expelled from the mission. It was her pregnancy that made her mind woozy and her body slow. Still, she didn't allow herself any excuses. She just wanted to get better. Knowing Yolukia, he'll call her soon and ask for another baby. Pulling her knees up to her chest and wrapping her covers over her head, Rosi tried to pretend that she was dead. She wanted to forget her duty and get away from her parents nagging her to be perfect.

Her mother yanked the blanket off of the bed exposing Rosi shivering in her pajamas. It was rude of Rosi to turn away from her mother while she was being verbally reprimanded. She was too tired to care and her mother took her attitude as an insult. She began to hit Rosi out of frustration. Her mother and father fought while she was away and now her mother was taking it out on her. Rosi automatically huddled into a ball as a civilian would do. She felt physically naked in her thin cotton clothing, but the truest self she kept locked up behind a door deep within her. She didn't want to exist anymore. These negative thoughts plagued her mind as she slipped into a fitful sleep. Her mother felt scared and guilty, thinking Rosi had fainted. She shook her awake again.

"What mom! I'm fine! Just really tired, please, just leave me alone!" This frightened her mother, and she quickly and quietly walked out of the room in a confused daze.

Months had passed and Rosi was past her post partum depression. Life was going as well as it could. Everyone in the system was still unhappy with division seventeen but that was quickly fading from sight. Yolukia had taken note of the two dead babies and decided that it was a sign meaning Rosi was not yet meant to conceive. He pardoned her saying he would excuse her for a few more years.

Phoenix called a meeting to SHONDS. She was feeling a lot like Old Matt, old. As she waited, she reminisced about the days when Natasha would fetch her and they would go to SHONDS together. Wayne, Scott, Darrel and Jessie arrived together. Not long after, Joe showed up. Then the cloned sisters showed up, followed by Dave who came right after his final exams.

"I have some interesting news," Phoenix spoke up after everyone knelt before her and paid recognition, "We are getting an alteration upgrade. Neptune has a prototype discovery they want to test on humans and because of our suspension, they think this is a great way for us to get involved again."

"So we're guinea pigs," Deklar piped up. Phoenix nodded, "Yes, Scott I know." With a tired look, the division members signed the release forms. This next operation might kill them, or it might make them more superhuman. Either way, with their sins on their shoulders, they were very far from God as it were.

The alterations were incredible. There were many unexpected results. One of which, was telepathy. This led to a lot of problems at first. There were a lot of fights and eventually, Joe was asked to leave the division. He was the first ever to be asked to leave. He had anger issues. Like all the other members, he could keep his façade as cold as ice, but he did it by imagining violence. After many of the division members had received mental threats from him in images of their body disemboweled, he was asked to leave. This was a brash decision, but since all the members were quite young, it could not be helped. Instead of working with Joe and the problem at hand, they merely cut him loose.

Like all things, the division members eventually learned to control their thoughts. They learned to package the telepathy and hide it in a deeper part of their mind apart from their conscious. It didn't take them much longer after that to learn to use it only when they wanted to.

Rosi was dying to know what Wayne was feeling, but she was afraid to know so she pushed him from her mind and focused on her work. Wayne felt the same way, and he had tried asking only to find nothing on the other side. Rosi justified herself by making her believe that they would be nothing to each other until the day Yolukia wanted another child from them. She didn't dare think anything else.

Rosi was pushing past all the popular girls in the hall. She didn't care.

"Excuse me, pardon me," the bell was about to ring and she was going to be late for class. She made it through the door just as the bell was ringing.

"Just in time Miss Tian," her teacher teased, "Its about time you learned by your senior year."

Giving a quick smile, Rosi went to sit down in her chair only to fall over. The earth had shook violently. There were surprised shrieks throughout the school. Everyone was thrown around and the atmosphere was tense. They all waited with their nerves on edge, getting ready to react in an instant and flee from threat. Nothing happened. There were multiply, "what the hell was that?" flying through the air. No one answered.

Rosi was straining her ears. Could she hear something in the distance? Was that a humming? She knew that it was below the frequency of normal human hearing so she couldn't ask if anyone else had heard it.

The principal walked from classroom to classroom telling everyone to evacuate the building. There was madness as screams let up and people ran over each other to leave the building. Rosi lagged behind, mostly to avoid the stampede, but also to try to figure out that noise. Suddenly, without warning she flew through the ceiling and was flying upwards through the air. She was smacked against something hard and she almost lost conscious. Just as she was about to gain her bearings, a body slammed into hers and there was a mutual "oof!"

She was stuck to a giant magnet. Travis, a junior from her school was stuck too.

"Help!" he screamed, but it was too late. They were flying upward at an alarming rate. It didn't take Phoenix long to figure it out. It was an invisible spaceship. The humming was the large magnet that had sucked her through the ceiling. It detects a certain type of metal. The kind of metal that just happened to be the kind the detection wires in her body were made out of, and somehow, Travis' belt. He had found the belt buckle at a pawn shop and they told him it was made from metal that came from a meteor.

The pilots of the giant magnet were probably looking for the other division members as well. Rosi put her arm behind Travis to prevent his back from breaking. They were going incredibly fast.

Before she could make up her mind on what to do, there was a large blast and they were suddenly free falling. Division eighteen had blasted the ship. Rosi and Travis fell through the air and both landed with a thud.

Rosi moaned. Her face was planted about a foot into the soft dirt. She couldn't lift her head. Her neck must be broken. Her right arm was definitely broken. Her right fingers shouldn't be able to touch her elbow. Rosi focused hard. A few cracks later, her body was realigned properly. She grit her teeth and tried to push herself up. Bad idea. She let out a muffled cry and dirt got into her mouth. She laid still and waited patiently for a few minutes. When the throbbing pain subsided, she tried again. Even though she was achy, she was able to sit up. She raised an unsteady hand to her face and tried to rub the dirt out of her eyes. She missed and swiped her nose, which was still broken. She uttered a tiny yelp of pain. When the nerves in her arm finished healing a moment or two later, she was able to clear the dirt successfully from her swollen face.

She opened her eyes to see a mangled Travis looking at her helplessly. A few of his fingers twitched hopelessly and his eyes were wild with fear. Something seized Rosi. This isn't right, this wasn't supposed to happen, not to Earth. The people who she killed were soldiers. They were trained to accept death as a part of life. Rosi struggled to keep her torrents of panic under control. Through a broken jaw jutting out of a fractured skull, he undulated out a painful, "why?"

The shock of hearing his voice made Rosi lose control of her telepathy. She read his distressed thoughts. Because they both shared a moment close to death, she could see herself through his eyes. She was cold and inhuman sitting there, watching him slowly die. He wanted to know why she couldn't feel anything. Or at least appear to feel nothing.

"No!" Rosi screamed inside of her head. Was she really a monster? Without thinking further, she pulled out her communicator.

"I need transport to Mars medical base immediately."

"Phoenix, we can't save him if we can't alter him," the doctor spoke. Rosi was in torment. What was right? Only division members and those who had gone through clearance were allowed to receive alterations, not civilians. It would take months to gain clearance. She was supposed to let him die and become a casualty. Yet, wouldn't that be the same as inviting others to attack earth? Rosi's head was still a little foggy, some of her body functions were still trying to stabilize. To her, Travis represented Earth. Earth was her home and her sanctuary, she wasn't going to give it up.

"Then alter him, we need someone to replace Skull." Her decision was brash, as was cutting Joe loose.

Travis became Wolf. He was very scared of the world he was brought into at first. He had countless questions and Phoenix answered all of them. She kept seeing him as herself when she first arrived at SHONDS. She trained him personally and looked after him. He lived at SHONDS, making it his home. He hated his family. He called his mother a whore and didn't care about his stepfather. That's why he chose to let them think he was dead.

Rosi couldn't do that to her family, making them think that she was dead. She went back and the media swarmed around her asking about the alien abduction. She feigned amnesia of the event and after being hospitalized for a few weeks, she went back to school just in time for graduation. Her parents didn't say much to her. They were encompassed in a fearful sort of quietness when confronted with something they didn't understand.

Dragon didn't openly object to the inclusion of Travis. Kirin did. Dragon's little cousin Jessie argued the confidentiality of the division with Phoenix. Phoenix stuck with her excuse that they needed a replacement for Skull. Phoenix didn't want to hear many more objections. She seated Wolf at the meeting table and then commenced to bring up political issues. They had a video conference with Division Eighteen who were on Venus. Their division was notified to be on alert when individuals on Venus went missing. They followed the ship to Earth just in time to save Phoenix from abduction. It was obvious that the ship was after altered beings due to the fact they had the giant magnet. However, since there were no survivors to question, it was difficult to say why.

Both divisions agreed to be on high alert. Phoenix had a funny feeling in her gut. She couldn't help but remember an annoying man from a few years back. A man named Mavius. Perhaps she should look into what he wanted. After the meeting, she went to see Gary.

"Gary, I have a top secret request."

"Yes ma'am," he complied right away and went to work looking up any information he could on Mavius.

Wayne wasn't hurt. He tried telling himself he wasn't hurt. Rosi had to have reasons for bringing Travis into the division. He wasn't going to ask. Did he really love her anyway? He wasn't even sure what love was. That night, he didn't eat dinner and crawled into bed early. He shared an apartment with Scott and they attended the same University.

Wayne couldn't sleep. Somehow, he felt very far from reality. What was real? Was the division real? Was his marriage to Rosi real? What about school? His life on Earth? He snuggled deep under his sheets. This Egyptian cotton was the only thing real right now and it felt great. Nothing else he could give a damn about. He choked on that lie as he tried to swallow it.

Rosi knocked on Natasha's door.

"Hello?" an unfamiliar voice called from the other side.

"Its me, Rejianiticana," she replied using her Jupiter civilian name. The door opened and an unfamiliar but friendly woman answered, "Can help you?" She was a pure Jupiterian.

"I'm looking for Natasha?" Rejianiticana replied.

"I sorry, no Natasha."

"Selena?"

"No, no Selena, you have wrong address?" she asked Rejianiticana in a silvery voice.

"I'm sorry, I must have. Sorry to bother you," Rejianiticana walked away. That was strange. She checked the address again. It was right, that was where Natasha had been living. What was going on? She wouldn't move without telling Rosi, would she?

"Ara, Natasha's gone," Rosi told her youngest cloned sister on Mars.

"Did you ask the technicians at SHONDS?" Ara asked.

"You know we are technically not allowed to keep track of them anymore," Rosi was depressed. Ara nodded in accordance, "I don't know what to say."

"Oh Ara, I'm so confused, I need someone to talk to, that's all," Rosi spewed forth. She was frustrated.

"I'm here," Ara said comfortingly.

"I tried calling Wayne the other day to see how he was."

"He didn't answer?"

"No, he did," Rosi hesitated, "He wasn't cold, just, distant." She didn't know how to continue.

"You love him?" Ara asked gently. Rosi looked her in the eyes, the eyes that were exactly like hers, "What is love? What do we know beyond what ours parents gave us? How do we deal with sexual tension and separate it from lust?" Ara paused, "Do you think you love him?" Rosi sat quietly. Thoughts were playing around in her mind. She had question after question about how she felt, but she had no answers.

"I think, I think I didn't know it before because I was hiding the truth from myself. But, I think I do."

Ara shoved a spoonful of ice cream into Rosi's mouth, "Silly, he's probably jealous of Travis." Rosi was surprised, "Travis?" she muffled through ice cream. Ara giggled.

"Yeah, I mean, he's a new member you picked. He's a guy, and he lived by you. If you ask me and I were Wayne, I would be thinking that you didn't take the marriage seriously and you were dating Travis."

"But I haven't dated anyone yet in my life, you know that!" Rosi defended.

"But does Wayne know that?" Rosi lapsed into quiet thought.

Rosi was called to Juyvine again. This time, she stood alone in Yolukia's presence.

"Your honor, you have sent for me?" she said with a polite bow to the ruler of the local galaxy groups.

"Ah yes, Phoenix, so glad you can come," Yolukia said standing up. In her mind, Phoenix was thinking about the conversation she had with Ara last night. Was Yolukia telling her she no longer had to give him a child with Dragon? Did he think she was dating Travis too? How often did Yolukia looked into her life anyway?

The ruler stood up, "Walk with me, dearest little one." He had a habit of calling her that sometimes. Phoenix obeyed and they walked through the enormous halls of the castle-like building. The internal buttresses were lighted up with millions of tiny bulbs that twinkled happily, making Phoenix feel as if she was underwater on Earth.

"You probably don't recall this, but when I was campaigning, I promised to show the galaxies the power of a human."

"I actually do, your honor, an old friend of mine, Ciesa, her real name was June, she told me."

"Ah yes, Stattler's daughter."

"You knew her?"

"I knew her father, he worked on my campaign. Such a pity that she died." Rosi was silent. So was Yolukia. They kept walking, letting the lights dance around them.

"Dearest little one, Phoenix, I have a proposition for you."

"Uh oh," she joked, "Does this mean I have to marry again?"

"I'll get to that later," as soon as Yolukia said that, Rosi felt a pang go through her and she regretted that she had even brought that up."

"I am going to make you Governess," he said while stopping to turn and look at her. His eyes studied her every reaction.

"I'm afraid I don't understand," Phoenix said with genuine confusion.

"When I first met you, I know that you were the one for the job. You were still young then, and you still are young now. Eighteen is a very green age. However, there is no one else I would rather give this position to than you," he paused. "You are going to be Governess of the Milky Way, you will be governess of Quandonta."

Phoenix felt her lungs stop working but forced herself to breathe mechanically, "I can't! I always pictured someone much older and with more experience and I'm sure the rest of the galaxy groups feel the same way!"

"Now now," he put a comforting hand on her shoulder, "You just fear failure, not the responsibility, since, you are a military member, I have no doubt you can shoulder this weight. I will ease you into this. I am assigning officials to you, all you need to do is remain pure and answer the decisions they place before you with objectivity. In time, the council will reduce in size and everything will be left up to you, but that is still a ways off."

"Your honor!" Phoenix was exasperated. What else was this man going to demand out of her? She wanted to curse the day she met him, but deep down, she knew it was because he feared too. He feared those he couldn't trust, so having her around was like having a priceless jewel.

Yolukia had let her get comfortable with being the Governess and settling into a new life. Like he promised, she had hundreds of advisors and she only needed to answer what they placed before her.

Things were changing on Earth too. Rosi moved away from her parents and went to college. This was a load off of her shoulders. As long as she called every now and then to assure them she was alright, they would leave her alone. She no longer had to tend to the emotions of her family, which made time for her to tend to the Galaxy.

Paula Eve and Erica Lucy were living with the Camus' in

Washington. Their father was a retired CIA agent and didn't explain to their mother where the girls really came from. She thought they were abandoned twins from one of her husband's crazy missions so she gladly accepted them into her home. She was a little curious though when the girls never got sick and every hospital checkup was perfectly normal. There was no mistaking that she was thrilled to have two perfectly healthy girls. Yet, at the same time, shouldn't third world country children be malnourished?

The two cloned girls were as different as could be. This was easily explainable. Their mother dressed them a like all the time when they were younger. Gradually, they started to find distaste in what the other liked. Erica was the prom queen, Paula, who was referred to as just "V," was a skateboard champion. They fought quite a bit at home and frustrated their poor mother. Even their laidback father scolded them from time to time. However, when they were on missions, Phoenix knew to pair them together because their thoughts were so in sync.

Paula had to find a job because her mother was pressuring her. Erica had already graduated with an associate's degree and was temporary working as a secretary. She was going to study to be a paralegal. Paula didn't see a point in getting a job. This life was merely a mask for her real existence anyway. She was cloned for a purpose and that was to serve in division seventeen. Her father and mother were assigned to provide for her, so why should she bother?

"V, you are just like Charles," Erica would say about her pessimistic attitude, "We've got one life, it doesn't matter how or why we were born, if we have this opportunity, why don't you take it?"

"Shut up, honky," Paula would snap as she grabbed her board and headed out to the skate park. She would also duck as a hairbrush flew at her head.

Charles was the one that despised everything. Paula wasn't really like that, was she? She would always be disturbed after Erica would say that to her. When they were growing up, Charles was the poster child for being a bad kid. William, Dragon's other clone, turned out okay. He went to work as a technician at SHONDS, and was still invited to their private parties and gatherings. Charles had wanted nothing to do with them. Phoenix even had Lisa Joyce live with him to keep an eye on him. He couldn't be trusted. Paula hoped she wasn't like him.

Paula and Erica showed up at SHONDS together when Phoenix summoned them. They immediately went to sit at opposite sides of the room. It was apparent that they just got into a fight. After the routine briefing to catch them up with recent events, Phoenix turned to Paula.

"V, I've got a mission for you. You'll be the first to take this kind of mission." All eyes trained to Phoenix in hidden surprise. They were all waiting to hear more.

"You are to go undercover and be a personal bodyguard for a protected witness. We have a paranormal expert from Earth also paired up with you. That was just a part of the negotiation, there was nothing I can do."

"Yes, ma'am," Paula accepted.

Paula was never told why the man was in the witness protection program, but it was not her place to ask. Her partner was Jim Overman, a typical American. At least, that was how Paula labeled him. Though he didn't speak much, she could tell by his air that he was very self righteous.

"There will be bounty hunters after him," Agent Overman said to Paula as if she didn't know already. She sat quietly.

"What's your real name," he asked her suspiciously.

"Moongirl," she replied using her codename, the one she knew that he already knew.

"No its not, don't get sassy with me, what's your name, how do I know you can be trusted?" he pushed. Paula ignored him.

"So that's the way it is then," he turned away and focused back on the road. Jim Overman was probably not his real name either, so why did it matter?

They were riding silently in an SUV. Agent Overman was driving, the witness was in the back seat. They only had to watch him for two weeks until the Martian government finished setting up his new life. Paula told her parents she got a job in a different state teaching skateboarding. Even though they thought she could get a better job than that, they still counted their blessings and were glad that she was doing something.

The three of them were to stay at a cabin deep in the woods owned by the United States government. It was highly secluded and had no phone or internet. Besides Agent Overman's satellite phone, which was to be off most of the time, there was no way to contact them and no way to track them.

They finally pulled up to the cabin and they all trucked out of the vehicle. Paula studied the witness. He was short, five foot two. He had sandy hair and wore huge rimmed glasses. He had a meek face and his hazel eyes darted around nervously searching for danger. He had short, blunt fingers that were calloused at the tips. No doubt from constantly being on a computer. If it were her guess, he was probably a hacker of some sort. Either his boss turned him in or he stumbled across something he wasn't supposed to find and the Martian government traded his safety for the information.

"You gonna cook for us?" Agent Overman asked Paula.

"Incredulous," she said flatly. She never cooked at home, didn't even know where to start. If he was going to continue with his chauvinistic attitude, they were going to have problems.

Agent Overman turned out to be an excellent cook. Paula figured he was secretly showing off. He probably grew up without one of his parents, his mother, most likely. That compensated for the lack of understanding of women and the cooking skill to fill in for his culinary ignorant father as he was growing up.

"Delicious," she complimented hoping to extend a truce. He waved his hand matter-of-factly, "Not my best." But she could tell he was secretly pleased with himself. The truce was accepted as subtly as it was offered.

"Get in the car and stay there," Paula said to the witness. There were three people in the perimeter. She could sense them. It was towards the end of the second week and it had been mostly quiet. It was after dinner and they had heard unusual rustling outside. The witness, whose name was also Jim, obeyed. Paula and Agent Overman circled the car with alert senses.

"Moongirl," he whispered to her. She walked silently to stand beside him.

"I've got two in my sights, I'm going to take them out."

"Wait," she said, "we don't know if they're hostile."

"What the hell do you mean not hostile, they have to be here for the witness," he said in a loud agitated whisper. He was not one for keeping a cool head.

"Or to warn him, lets be sure first, but stay on alert," she said calmly. He just snickered at her. Moongirl couldn't sense a threat with her telepathy, but she could be wrong. Maybe Agent Overman was right, they should just take them out anyway.

A shot rang out and a squeal was heard.

"Holy shit it was right by me!" Agent Overman screamed. Moongirl ran to the other side of the SUV. Agent Overman kept firing at the squirming body of a little girl from Romirry, a race of aliens from Saturn.

"Stop!" Moongirl screamed at him. He didn't listen. To him, she was just another paranormal anomaly. Moongirl tackled him and easily wrestled the gun out of his hand. She held him down with her knees in his armpits and repeatedly laid fist after fist into his teeth. Three punches down, she finally struggled to compose herself. Pushing him out of her mind, she ran to the little girl. The witness, Jim was already holding her, crying.

"She was my niece!" he screamed. The other two aliens showed themselves and stood by with large frightened eyes. No doubt they were just teenagers who went along with the Romirry girl who wanted to see her uncle. When Agent Overman groaned and sat up, they took off running in fear of acquiring the same fate.

"Are you human?" Agent Overman asked the witness aggressively.

"Of course he is," Moongirl answered flatly, "He must have been married into the alien race, or adopted."

"Its just a damn alien, it ain't human," Agent Overman tried to justify himself. A dark wave of anger swooped over Paula like a hot wind. She stood up quickly and turned to him. She studied him thoroughly. He really did feel okay with it, to him, the little girl was as expendable as the chicken cooked for dinner. In his book, only humans were allowed to live. Only beings like himself knew the epitome of life. With swift steps she approached him.

"Oh don't you look at me like that," he threatened her, "You know what I did was right, our job was to protect him at all costs." His words had no effect on her. Paula grabbed him by his collar and slammed him against a tree. Technically, he was right, as soldiers, they were to eliminate all possibilities of threats to complete their mission. But she was almost sure the little Romirry girl was an exception. She was there to see her uncle. They could have just told her to go home and warn her about how dangerous it was coming out this far.

"You think you are so fucking great, you think us humans know exactly why we are alive? Well let me tell you something you pompous piece of shit," she shook him hard. "That little girl was from the Romirry race, a race of people known for their peaceable behavior. They don't judge before they know and even when they do know, they still ask. They are not like you and I, dirty filthy humans who can't even admit that we are broken. They go out and try to save all that is desecrated. You and I, will never be like her, so don't you ever dare say that we deserve to live more than them."

Suddenly, Paula felt drained. She let go of Agent Overman and walked up to Jim, the witness. She laid a gentle hand of mourning on his shoulder. Suddenly, something started to beep. It was coming from inside the dead little girl.

"We have to go," Moongirl said to the witness.

"I'm not leaving her body!" the witness cried.

"You have to, there is a bomb inside of her," Moongirl shouted. She grabbed the witness by the collar and with a cold heart, wrenched the dead girl's body from him. He cried out in strong objection but Moongirl shoved him into the back of the SUV. Agent Overman headed towards the driver's seat but Moongirl got in first. There was no time to object, he climbed into the passenger side. Moongirl hit the quick scan button and the SUV scanned itself for any foreign objects or threats. It was clear. Moongirl pulled out the key from around her neck and started a hidden ignition underneath the steering wheel. The entire vehicle changed into a jet craft. They flew away just in time as the little girl's body consume the cabin and the forests surrounding it in flames.

Moongirl was receiving a debriefing back at SHONDS from Phoenix. She told her commanding officer about the little girl. Phoenix told her the culprit had been captured. Someone had given the little girl some candy with explosives hidden in it and directions to find her uncle. The girl was innocent and there was nothing Paula could have done to save her anyway. How Agent Overman didn't set her off when he shot her was pure luck in itself.

"No, not luck, she still died," Moongirl said. Her tone was calm and emotionless, but deep down she was sad. Phoenix hugged her sister. They shared a moment of silence.

Back in Seattle, Paula went to find Erica who had rented a room in a house her friend bought.

"Hey sis," Paula said walking up to her, "You're not as pigheaded as I thought." She was comparing her to Agent Overman. Paula threw her arms around Erica and let out a deep sigh on her shoulder.

"Veea, whats wrong?" Erica asked. Paula didn't answer. She didn't have to. Erica was able to absorb her sadness. Erica returned the hug.

"It'll be fine sis," Veea let out in a sigh. Erica stroked Veea's short hair as she started to cry.

Yolukia introduced Phoenix to Trinala, the royal dresser. Only he introduced Phoenix as Dikara. Dikara was the name of his deceased granddaughter. Phoenix didn't dare ask questions in front of Trinala for fear of leaking out something secret. Yolukia had to have his reasons.

Trinala was excited as she showed Dikara to many different silks and materials. Many of them were so breathtakingly beautiful Dikara had a hard time believing she was to be clothed in them. There was the shimmering black and gold cloth that hung elegantly and swooped gracefully around her shoulders. There was the soft green material that felt like she was petting a baby kitten. Then there was the three-tone dark gray material that could appear a deep wine red or a goldenrod yellow depending on the angle you viewed it from. Little Rosi was so ecstatic she could hardly contain her joy. She threw her arms around Yolukia and gave him a deep grateful hug.

Trinala first slipped Dikara into a graceful white robe. It was more like a baggy dress. She adjusted the neck to fit, then the waist. The dress was down to Dikara's ankles and swished when she walked. The sleeves covered her hands. When Dikara went to roll them up, Trinala stopped her, "No, you cannot do that! You are the Governess, no one may see your hands!"

"They are not to judge you by your physical form, rather, how you rule," Yolukia explained. "They are not to know what species you are either, but I will be telling them you are human, because of the promise I made to put a human in power, so that doesn't matter."

"And also, you are a noble woman, they cannot see your hands," Trinala added.

"Ah, but that is so old fashioned, no one cares for that anymore," Yolukia joked.

Next, Trinala picked a deep blue cape and slipped it around Dikara's shoulders.

"You must always wear a cape to further hide your form," she

explained, "and that is not all." Trinala picked up a smaller piece of cloth that matched the deep blue and fitted it around Dikara's face as a veil. Looking into the mirror, Rosi was thrilled to see an elaborate design over her nose. Trinala attached trinkets and jewelry into her hair that hung forward onto her forehead as a headdress. Trinala then picked up the final piece of the garb. She placed a large scarf-like headdress over Dikara's hair, leaving only her eyes to show. Trinala then picked up a makeup pen and did the traditional markings of planet Liva onto Dikara's face.

"You will be stationed to rule on Liva," Yolukia explained, "That is where your home will be as Dikara."

Later that day, Yolukia let out a broadcast that was shown on the news station of every progressive planet across the local galaxy groups. He introduced Dikara, as his adopted human daughter. He made it clear that this was a part of the promise he made to clean up the Milky Way galaxy. He called the Milky Way galaxy Quandonta, which was its universal name. Dikara was now in power, and she had the full blessing of one of the most powerful figures within billions of light years around.

CHAPTER FIVE

A star shaped box. Inside was as photo. It was of Trisha and Alex. Su-Lin, as her sisters called her, smiled. She was in Trisha's room. Trisha was her best friend. Around the golden star shaped box was a hairbrush, and a heart shaped necklace. No doubt, the necklace was from Alex. Su-Lin had not seen Trisha in a very long time. They had grown up together. Five long years had passed since she had been home to Mercury. Her foster mother was dead and Su-Lin was back for the funeral. Her mother was old to begin with and behaved more like a grandmother. Still, Su-Lin loved her very much.

Su-Lin looked around. Right now, she was afraid to say anything for fear her emotions would let fly. Trisha had the same lavender curtains and the soft smell of lilac was still emanating from the little jar Su-Lin had given her some years ago. It was a pretty jar. It was dark violet with intricate silver vines curling around it. It was about the size of a baseball but definitely heavier. Su-Lin had bought it for her when she was stationed at Turnika Jos. She remembered that as her first major assignment. She had been extremely homesick. When she came back, she found her mother ill. Su-Lin was only able to stay with her for about a year until she was called away on another assignment. Her mother had passed away quietly. Su-Lin made it just in time to say goodbye. She had said nothing about the baby in her womb. She knew what was going to happen to it. No need to bring up the dead.

Trisha walked up behind Su-Lin. Her footsteps were soft and the carpet muffled any sound they made. But Su-Lin could feel the sorrow in Trisha's movement. The girl was shorter than Su-Lin and a year younger, but they still moved the same way. She stood next to her right now, as if they were one. She was the only friend of Su-Lin's that was at the funeral. Everyone else there were her mother's friends. Her sisters could not make it. It was a miracle Phoenix let her go at all. Su-Lin understood the circumstances and knew that she should forgive them. She knew, but still, it was her beloved mother that died. She could not help but bear a little bit of resentment that none of them cared to even say anything at all. Her division hardly knew her mother, so she tried to convince herself it shouldn't be a big deal. It was still hard for her to swallow the bitter feeling though, no matter how much she tried to reason. Perhaps it was the bitterness that division 17 stole her life and the only friends she has are those associated with violence or those who don't know her real life. Irony has it, this peaceful life was merely a cover, it was never meant to be real or lasting. She felt so alone.

"That's Alex," Trisha spoke up about the picture, "I met him about a year after you left, he is a great person." Su-Lin smiled, "He has a very kind face, I know that he's taken good care of you for me." They managed a few chuckles but were quiet soon afterwards. Su-Lin could sense something nagging at Trisha.

"I don't know what it is that you do," Trisha started, "I won't ask though. But I have a feeling that this may be the last time I see you, either for ever, or at least a long time." Su-Lin was quiet. Trisha turned to face her, "I know there is something you don't want anyone to know." There was a silence. Su-Lin didn't know if her close friend could tell she was with child or if it was the sorrowful expression on her face. Did Trisha mean that she was asking to hear what she didn't want others to know? Or was she simply stating that she knew and it was alright if Su-Lin didn't say anything.

"What is it Su? You don't have to tell me, but I'm still that same girl you grew up with. I might be able to help." So she didn't know. Su-Lin was quiet for a moment. She was starting to feel very lethargic, and it was difficult for her to gather her thoughts. She let her mind drift around for a second before opening her mouth to say anything. She thought about Rosi, then the first time she met mother. She named her Susan because she always like that name. Mother then gave her own name Linda for Su's middle name. She was Susan Linda Mateos. She grew up believing she was someone and that she had a choice in life. She was wrong. Sure, there were "choices" but circumstances only allow you to take a certain path. There were invisible chains everywhere dictating people's actions. Her thoughts finally drifted back to Trisha.

"I have a baby I can't keep," Su-Lin blurted out. If Trisha was surprised, she didn't show it. She waited patiently to see if Su-Lin had anything more to say. When she didn't speak, Trisha asked, "Do I know who's?" Su-Lin shook her head, "I was on Yeyla." Trisha gave her a blank look, "Where?"

"It's a planet, I'd rather not say where, but very far away. In the Trials Galaxy."

"Su! You were as far away as the Trials Galaxy? My God! That's! Why that's very far away! You might be the only one on Mercury to have been there!" Su-Lin wouldn't have been surprised if that were true. She regretted her words, she had said too much. She kept quiet.

Her jaw clenched to fight away tears. Tears were a weakness.

Trisha hugged her, "Su, what are you going to do." Su-Lin didn't say anything. Trisha gazed into her eyes and in a moment was able to read her expression.

"Oh no, are you sure?" She asked. Su-Lin nodded. Trisha sadly ended what protest she would have before it left her lips.

"I don't have a choice, I can't tell you anymore," Su-Lin said. What could she say? That her child would be used for leverage against her and the whole of division seventeen and that risk could pretty much be considered treason. Besides, Rosi had had two miscarriages. Wasn't the same likely to happen to her too? Rosi was forced into marrying Wayne by Yolukia. He wanted a successor and he chose their DNA. Their first two sons were unborn and lost in action. Rosi almost died both times. For now, they were to wait until the new technology on Neptune was developed. Rosi would just have to carry for one month, then the fetus could be transferred to an artificial uterus. None of them were ever supposed to get married or have children unless they already did before entering the division. That was the policy of the division. Only Yolukia had the privilege to override that.

"I can't be like Rosi," Su-Lin accidentally said out loud, "I'm not special enough." Her mind was fuzzy from the grief and undoubtedly her hormones were making her confused as well.

"Who's Rosi?" Trisha asked gently. Surprised, Su-Lin looked over, "Did I say that out loud?" Trisha looked confused but nodded. Su-Lin gazed at her best friend. She had soft blonde hair to her shoulders. Her eyes were a sweet chocolate brown. This was Trisha. This was the Trisha that might die if she, Su-Lin "the plague," did not get out of her life soon. Su-Lin tried to give her a smile but failed, "please don't dwell on it. I should go and never come back."

"So I was right?" Trisha whispered with tears in her eyes, "I'm never going to see you again?" Su-Lin was fighting her own facial waterfalls. She nodded, "Maybe, just pray for me please." Trisha was sobbing now, "I'll walk you out." Su-Lin nodded, her throat would not let her say anything more. Trisha led her way out. Su-Lin turned and looked once more at the room where she used to have sleepovers and parties. Trisha owned the house now, but she kept this room because she cherished the rare kind of friendship they had. It was the kind they knew that would last forever and was never forgotten. Taking a shaky breath, Su-Lin closed the door and walked away from her past and back to the life she had to live. A single tear broke free from its prison and slid down her cheek in a short-lived freedom to die under her chin.

Su-Lin sat in the waiting room thinking about her goodbye with Trisha. She was on Neptune and this was the last stop before going back to live at SHONDS on Mars. Since her mother died, she had decided to move out. She was thinking about all the cookies they had baked and the secrets they shared. There were also all the dances and all the crushes they shared. Trisha was more of a sister to her than any of the others. Su-Lin was glad she left when she did. Any longer, nothing good could have come from it. Trisha could have been put in danger.

She would never forget the last time she saw Trisha. It was not a happy image like all the others. Trisha had tear stains on her face while she said goodbye. Her eyes were puffy and Su-Lin could hear both of their hearts breaking. A very large part of her died and was buried with her mother. Now at this hospital, it was time to tie up the last loose end. They had just called her name.

Su-Lin sat on a platform. It was very cold. The nurse wheeled the screen in front of her abdomen. She attached some wires below Su-Lin's navel. She flipped a switch and an image came on. It was a very clear image. Su-Lin could not look away. It was an image that showed heat signatures. She saw her baby. It was moving as if it were already free in the world. It squirmed as if it were kicking away stifling blankets. The nurse went to turn off the switch but Su-Lin called out for her to stop. She just watched and started to smile at the tiny piece of joy.

All of a sudden she realized why she was there. She felt lost and too scared to say yes or no. She just stared at the heat signatures. It struck her as amazing that she was never there, she was never in a womb before. Not one of a human at least. This little creature captured her heart and she melted.

"I can't do this," she said despairingly to the nurse, "I'm going home I can't do this." The nurse just smiled, "I understand." She unhooked Su-Lin and handed her back her cloths. Shakily, Su-Lin got dressed. A thought teased her, maybe they showed the mothers their babies to make them change their mind. Maybe this was a trick. Either way, Su-Lin was glad it worked. Once again she apologized to the nurse for wasting her time, then left in a hurry. She jumped into her jet craft and drove away from the hospital to an exit point. She waited patiently for her cue to take off. It was rush hour and she expected to be there for a while. It would be ironic, she thought to herself, if Neptune were to fall under attack and she would lose her baby anyway. However, she knew that it was highly unlikely. It was true the terrorist rates had risen though. It happened when Dikara came into rule. There were many rebellions and gatherings of people who called themselves freedom fighters who didn't like the idea of the Governess lording over them. They express their grievances anyway they can throughout the entire galaxy by attacking government owned buildings. Neptune was secure though. It was a neutral progressive planet with plenty of protection because they did not care one way or another about the Governess. There was no reason for anarchists to act on Neptune.

Su-Lin got the sensation that her baby was curling up against her. Like a puppy would on a cold winter day. Like a baby who only knew its mother and she was it's God. This led to a rush of emotion and a longing for the good old days where she could at least pretend that she led a normal life.

Exit points were like a combination of freeways and take off strips where crafts lined up to take off and leave a planet. It was invented decades ago when jet craft collision rates increased. It was Su-Lin's turn to take off, the attendant signaled her and she got into position. They raised the panels behind her jet craft and the attendant gave the go signal. She fired up her engines and was gone in a few seconds. As Su-Lin flew back to Mars she made up her mind not to tell anyone about her child. She was going to have to disappear for a few months when she started to show. That was a crime that could lead to her being exorcized. She didn't care anymore. They didn't go to her mother's funeral, even if she never asked them too, it was an unspoken expected courtesy. Without Trisha, her baby was her only family now.

Su-Lin arrived on Mars earlier than expected. Phoenix greeted her with a smile and a hug, "Sorry I couldn't go," she whispered into Su-Lin's ear. Su-Lin left her face emotionless and Rosi did not press. They went into the technician's floor. Gary was training a new girl, Angela. She used to work security on Neptune, the medical base for the solar system. Su-Lin didn't mention that she was just there. "What a coincidence," she thought silently to herself.

"I have some bad news," Phoenix said right off the bat. Su-Lin sighed, "Lay it on me." Phoenix nodded. She admired Su-Lin's resolve to do what needs to be done.

"Yeyla is having some more problems in the Providence of War sector of the Trials Galaxy and they want someone back there again." Su-Lin could not believe her ears, she stared at Rosi, "Why are we even in a different galaxy anyway?" she asked incredulously. Rosi gave a crooked smile, "Because they are avid traders with Turnika Jos."

"Ah, the planet of commerce," Su-Lin commented. Rosi nodded in agreement with, "And statistics say its one of the most important planets to the Milky Way. The Providence of War wants a large share of Turnika Jos, you know that means, easy access in case of an invasion. We cannot comply with the Providence of War and they are threatening to cut off trade and completely take over the planet Yeyla. We need someone there who can handle herself just in case something happens and you're already familiar. The governess' councilmen were set on sending you too," Phoenix paused, "but if you don't want to go, I can see about a different arrangement." Su-Lin shook her head, "Nope! You are leading officer, your word is law." Su-Lin figured she owed it to at least follow this last request. Meanwhile, she could have her baby there.

Su-Lin was back to being Kinadr. Kinadr was one of her many identities, like Rosi, she tried her best to keep her civilian life a secret.

Kinadr had a baby now. She did not contact Groyu, the father. He was human, which was probably why Su-Lin thought she loved him. She met him last time she was stationed on Yeyla. It was a familiar face so far away from home. She was lonely and she wanted to be happy. This time, she felt different. She had a different resolve. She was going to stay out of social events and keep to herself until Phoenix called her back. She wasn't a young woman out to be loved anymore. She was a mother who left everything else behind and only had her child to be the center of her universe.

It was nighttime in the dark apartment. It was a rundown place with thin walls. Su-Lin remembered when she used to think it was exciting to be living in such a rundown place. Now, she had no choice. She supposed she could've asked Phoenix for a better place, but she didn't want to explain herself and she might leak out information about her baby. It was her precious secret, something no one else could have. She stood in front of the bathroom mirror. She pressed gently into her abdomen. She wasn't bulging yet, but she did gain weight. She wetted a towel and gave herself a towel bath. The bathtub was dirty and she never even thought of using it. She used to soak at the public mud pools and bath in the healing herbs. She would like to do so again tomorrow, but first she had to find something to trade for entry. She decided to take up embroidery again, something her mother had taught her. She stayed up all night tediously picking out delicate designs.

The cheap flame lamp was getting overheated. Su-Lin turned it off and plugged a smaller one into the gas outlet. It worked the same way as an electric outlet on Earth. Since there was such a large supply of natural gas on Yevla, that was what most things ran on. She switched

on the gas flow and lit the lamp. She stayed up all thirty four hours of nighttime and made several lovely images. She almost didn't want to part with them. She wanted her baby to see them, she wanted to share with it her own joy.

Su-Lin let herself disappear into the relaxing mud. Just her face was visible. These places were much like the public baths of Rome. Yeyla was a semi gaseous planet. There were semi-solid gasses in the Trials Galaxy all mixed in with rocks like fruit in yogurt. They floated around like heavy gelatin with chunks of vegetative rocks stuck in them. Sometimes the rocks were as big as moons. Upon these mountainous chunks was where most of the population made their homes. Most of the populations were humanoids. There were some creatures that thrived upon certain emissions from the collision of gasses. They lived away from the humanoids and were sometimes hunted for food. Most of the humanoid population were able to raise their own food.

Yeyla was the largest planet of a very small system named Yeylacore. Their sun of course, was just called the Core. The other four planets were quite insignificant and were nothing more than trading ports. Most of the activity, was on Yeyla.

Su-Lin meditated to her breathing. It sounded very loud. Blood was drumming in her ears too. She wondered if her baby could hear it yet. If not, it should probably feel her blood. Su-Lin never knew the comfort of a human heartbeat. The only pulsing she knew was that of the artificial uterus pumping nutrients in her body as she was cloned. She only knew what Rosi experienced, but it was not first hand, just pieces of memories. Su-Lin was sure that it was a wonderful experience and she regretted missing out on it.

"Hello there." Su-Lin opened her eyes slowly. Someone had tapped into her meditation. She was a little agitated, but not angry. She looked around, poking her head a little out of the mud. A younger girl was sliding in next to her. Su-Lin smiled politely. The girl giggled excitedly as the cool mud slid over her slightly orange and pink skin. Her eyes were a dark red and they sparkled like rubies when she spoke to Su-Lin, "Hello, my name is Tanyui, what's yours?"

"Kinadr," Su-Lin answered neutrally. She let herself slip back into the comforting mud.

Su-Lin was a little scared, but she was upset too. She knew she was doing something wrong. She had the responsibility to make sure everything in the Providence of War was quiet and orderly, but she fled. Her baby was to be born in two months and she had a confrontation with Groyu, the baby's father. He was very demanding and wanted answers from Su-Lin. He was still the careless, self centered individual Su-Lin had first met. He threatened to have the court take the baby away from her. So she screamed that she would leave and take the baby some place he could never find. He replied that he had connections all over Yeylacore and throughout the entire system, it would only be a matter of time before she was found. The reason for the argument was because the baby was a boy. On Yeyla, the fathers were in charge of raising the male. Su-Lin did not trust him. She did not see him through the rose colored glasses she once did. She saw him for what he really was, an irresponsible human who felt he could bend things to his will. Typical, no wonder humans were so depreciated. Su had stormed away knowing that he would not be able to find her where she was going.

Su-Lin did not want to go to the Milky Way galaxy, but with the exception of Yeyla core in the Trials Galaxy, she didn't have clearance to go anywhere else. She would have been red flagged immediately. Still, the Milky Way was a big galaxy and she could still find ways to avoid the governess. With determination, she sought out a tiny backwater solar system and made a life for herself.

Archimedes was a system at the edge of the galaxy. It was one of those underdeveloped places that was assigned a random name by the governess so it could hold a spot on a map. Su-Lin found a nice planet, Ceve, and settled down on it. It reminded her of a third world country on earth. The only visitors were tourists or missionaries. Su-Lin negotiated to stay in a small village. When she showed them how much she knew about technology they were unimpressed and skeptical about letting her stay. Since she could not do most physical chores in her condition, she showed them her embroidery. They were absolutely fascinated and she was accepted as a tailor and teacher to the local women who wanted to learn her needle work.

Years flew by and Su-Lin's son was three years old. He was born gauntly and remained that way no matter how much she fed him and fussed over him. She stressed over what she should do. She wanted to take him to a doctor she trusted in the Solar System, but she did not want to risk it. There had been an attack on Turnika Jos from the Providence of War. It was nothing major and repairs were almost complete, but she knew that it was her responsibility to prevent any unpleasant encounters. No doubt division 17 was required to set a bounty on her head. Phoenix probably sent a search party out for her right now. She would want answers for the attack on Turnika Jos.

Her son was now in bed half of the time. She wasn't sure if he was dying or he was just allergic to something on the planet Ceve. She had gone to a neighboring system to birth him and gave him a basic black market alteration so he could survive on Ceve. He should have no problems, so why was he sick?

Su-Lin heard a happy commotion outside of her cabin. She went to the door and saw the happy blue skinned boys running towards the slowly approaching tour bus. They carried with them little trinkets they had made in hopes to sell or trade with the newcomers. She smiled at them. She wished desperately her little Julian could run with them. As she stared at the oncoming tour bus, she decided that if Julian did not turn for the better in five Cevan days, she will have to risk facing Phoenix and return to the Solar System. After all, he was all she had left after her mother passed away. She refused to let herself come in contact with Trisha. The girl was much safer without her.

Su-Lin stood outside her door as did the rest of the village. There was a main road at the center of the village and there were little shops that lined both sides. The residential cabins were scattered carelessly about from this road forming a lopsided circle. Su-Lin's cabin was at the far end of the main road. The tour bus stopped at the little inn that sat at the beginning. Roughly twenty tourists stepped off. Half of them went into the little inn, the other half started to wander down the main road bargaining with shop keepers. Su-Lin went back inside to be with Julian. He was asleep. She leaned over and kissed the skinny little boy's forehead.

A knock came at Su-Lin's door. She tucked the blanket around her son's shoulders and curiously went to see who it was.

"Hello?" she said coming up to the open front door. The villagers all trusted each other and shared everything anyways, so almost everyone left their doors open when it was light outside. A figure stood in the doorway. Su-Lin recognized him from somewhere, but it couldn't be! She paused, "I'm sorry, can I help you?" she asked crossing the front room towards the door. A surprised look came over the man's face, "I know you don't I!" he exclaimed happily. Su-Lin looked at him blankly.

She knew his face, it was one of the first faces she had ever seen in her life when she stepped out of the growth chamber, but she could not put a name to it. What as his name?

"Rosi! It's me!" the man said in an excited yet calm voice. Su-Lin smiled, "I'm not Rosi, but she is my sister." She did not give up her own name just yet, what if he was sent to trap her. She only hoped that he thought she was one of the other clones. They had clearance to be around the galaxy and were not guilty of running away from duty.

"I'm sorry," he apologized, "Its me, Marcuno. I know I met you before but I can't remember which one the five you are." Marcuno, that was his name.

"Anyway," he continued, "I was surprised to see the jet craft at the outskirts of the village. So I asked one of the shopkeepers about it. He said it belonged to the tailor, and now that I see you, I'm not surprised! What mission are you on or can you not tell me?"

"I'm sorry," Su-Lin replied, "I remember your face and name, you were there when I stepped out of the growth chamber, but who are you?" The man chuckled then returned his face to the serious expression he wore most of the time, "I used to be Kirin from the old generation of Division Seventeen." Suddenly, it all flowed back to her, "Oh, I remember," she said apologetically.

"Its alright," he replied. Su-Lin didn't know if she could trust him or not. It was unlike Rosi to ask someone like Marcuno to find her, wasn't he the one that went missing? Him and Natasha both went missing, Old Matt had contacted them about it because even he couldn't find them himself.

Marcuno had stayed for tea and they mostly talked about the past. To her relief, Marcuno did not ask why Su-Lin was there. He did however, mention to her that he was searching for a place to call home and start a family. Su-Lin did not know if he was implying anything. Why didn't he call Venus home? That was where he was from. Soon it grew late and Marcuno went to the inn. Su-Lin gave a sigh of relief, she didn't know what she would do if he had tried to arrest her. She was not going to let him know about Julian. After she cleared away the teacups, she went into her son's bed room to check on him. She turned the flame down on her little hand held lamp and placed it on the nightstand. His breathing was raspy and he had kicked the blankets off of him. When she sat down next to him she began to worry. His body was drenched with sweat but he was cold. Quickly, she pulled the blankets back over

him. His face was hot but the rest of his body was freezing.

"Julian," she shook him gently, "wake up honey." No response.

"Julian?" she shook him harder. He should have been awakened by that.

"Honey please wake up!" she almost yelled. No response, the boy stayed unconscious. Su-Lin panicked and all of her precautions went out the door. She rolled her son up in blankets and took off running towards her jet craft. She knew that every time she turned it on she was traceable, but she didn't care, no punishment could be greater than losing her son. She gently strapped her son into the passenger side. Giving his hot little face a kiss, she buckled herself in as well and started the engine. It turned on with a roar that no doubt woke the entire village. It took her two minutes to drive to the foot of the mountain that was about 60 miles away. She aligned herself against the foot of a steep drop using it as a launching pad. Soon she was flying through space at maniac speed. She was headed to Neptune, the medical base of the Solar System and still holding the position of one of the most renowned.

Asteroids and space dust were a hazard to space travel so the Milky Way Galaxy finally received a grant to clear certain areas for fast travel. These areas started at Liva, which it used as the center and radiated out. Needless to say, it was dangerous for Su-Lin to travel through the outskirts of the galaxy through all the random dust and asteroids but she was in a hurry and traffic would have been an issue on the cleared paths. When she finally arrived at Neptune, she had been in many chases with patrolmen after her and she lost them all in her desperate fury. She was going to have hell to pay, but for now she was only worried about her son.

Su-Lin crashed through the doors of the Gyrhart Hospital, "Dr. Spalling?" she called out. Angry nurses appeared from doorways.

"Ma'am, please, you need to be quiet," they urged.

"Fuck you!" she screamed hysterically in the nurse's face, "Dr. Spalling please!" she continued to run. She clutched Julian to her chest. She didn't stop to check but was almost sure he had stopped breathing. With a mother's psychotic rampage, she tore around corners pushing past security guards.

"Young lady I am right here, please quiet down," she heard someone yell strictly. To her relief she turned around and saw her old doctor.

"Dr. Spalling please," she continued with a lowered volume, "Its my son, I need your help."

"Rosi," Dr. Spalling said in surprise.

"No its me, Susan!" Su-Lin said in an agitated voice. All six of them had gone to Dr. Spalling as their pediatrician, it was annoying how everyone always remembers Rosi. The clones were human too, their births were just different.

"Susan?" Dr. Spalling was surprised, "you have a son?" Before Su-Lin could say anything else Dr. Spalling took Julian in his arms and called out to a nurse, "prepare the ICU right now, this boy needs to be there." Su-Lin didn't know whether to be relieved that her son was in good hands or devastated that he needed to be in intensive care. Of course, what did she expect?

"Follow me," he said to Su-Lin over his shoulder. Obediently she followed. She stood at a distance watching helplessly as doctors and nurses attached wires and stuck needles into her son as if he were a pincushion. She held her breath, afraid that breathing would make her fall apart. All around her, the air hung a heavy green with dread.

"Oh Julian, I'm sorry that I didn't bring you here sooner," Su-Lin said so only she could hear. Finally, Dr. Spalling turned to face the mother of the young patient. He took her aside and spoke to her gently, "Susan, why didn't you tell me or any of your doctors when you were pregnant?" Su-Lin looked at him with tears in her eyes, "Its complicated." The doctor nodded with understanding. He knew their lifestyle.

"The reason is this," he started sympathetically, "You are a clone. That is why I thought you were Rosi when you said you had a son. She had been asked to conceive. You though, you theoretically are physically unable to carry a child because you are not an original. I am very surprised that he is even here with us today. You should have miscarried." A shock went through her body. Su-Lin felt like she was struck by lightning, she could guess the doctors next words, "so what your saying," she asked in an exasperated whisper, "is that my Julian will definitely die?" Grimly, Dr. Spalling nodded. It didn't seem real at first. Su-Lin was ready to give her life for her son's future. Now she had just found out that he wasn't even supposed to have been born. When the truth had slowly seeped through her, the doctor had already helped her into a chair. A single sob broke through. She swallowed it down hard. She didn't want to cry. Another sob fought through. Well why the hell not? Her son was dying. The finality of him dying finally hit her like an avalanche. She was suddenly crying uncontrollably as the last emotional restraints crumbled like a broken bridge. She sat there, alone, in the giant hospital with it's blaring white walls echoing her cries.

Su-Lin stood at her mother's tombstone. There was a single red glass rose that lay there peacefully. Organic roses could not survive on Mercury. Su-Lin knew it had to be Rosi. The message was clear almost as if Rosi was in her head right then and there. It must have been the "twin thing." Rosi was worried about her and wanted her to come home. Her mother's grave was the only place she knew to find Su-Lin. If she could feel at the moment, Su would have been touched, but her son had died. That was it for her, the end, the final wall that hit. If she could commit suicide, she would have. But she had no access to Trex, and whatever else she would do, her body was just automatically repair itself. She was condemned to walk the galaxy as a living deceased.

Thinking back to her last moments with Julian, she broke into tears again. Su-Lin had sat carefully next to him so she wouldn't crush the wires. She held him in her arms. She had finished crying then and was determined not to let her son see her tears. She was afraid that it would stress him. He had gained consciousness for a little while. He placed his little head on her bosom.

"Mommy, I love you," he whispered with a crackling voice. Those few small words were enough to send Su-Lin's insides into turmoil. Julian slipped peacefully back to sleep. That was where he died painlessly. Su-Lin was left all alone in the world.

"Well mother," Su-Lin spoke to the tombstone with a heavy sigh, "I had a son, but he died." She stopped for a moment, then added softly, "everyone around me dies," another pause. A thoughtful expression crossed her face. She already knew what she wanted to say. She just wanted to feel the air around her confirming the decision she had made, "I want him to lie next to you. Could you watch over him for me?" Su-Lin tried to smile but failed. She was beginning to feel the fingers of anxiety and insanity close upon her. Fighting them off, she turned and walked away. Perhaps she could go see Trisha again. No, that would be a bad idea. All she could bring her was danger. Maybe she could go somewhere and relax for a little bit, but who was she kidding? She would only drive herself crazy if left alone. So there was only one thing left to do. She knew it was not psychologically healthy, but she didn't care anymore.

The life of joy and happiness had ended. The memories of her mother and son were those of bitterness. So she took these memories and crammed them into a little box deep within her soul. She pushed it way back into a corner where no one else could find it. She was just as good as dead inside. She had no reason to live for herself. She became what she was originally cloned to be, an empty shell whose only use was to serve.

No one in her division would ever know all that had transpired. No one will ever know about her son, he was by far too precious to share with the people who would never appreciate him. She would have to come up with an excuse for the attack on Turnika Jos, but that was all trivial. No punishment could be worse than what she had just suffered. With that, she returned to Phoenix. To follow orders like a zombie.

A very meek child, Angela's parents were concerned for her. They were both doctors and lived on Venus. Angela was always quiet and didn't speak much. She was slow to reply and her parents were concerned that she might have learning disabilities.

Angela knew better. She didn't speak unless it was necessary for her to say anything. She saw the world differently. There was a highly recessive gene in the Venus species. Both of Angela's parents were unaware that they carried the gene. It just had never occurred to them.

Angela was able to compute answers in her mind at a highly accelerated rate. As a child, she was able to understand why she should not wiggle around in a highchair. She could fall. Angela was always looking for connections in her mind. She didn't see any need to ask questions. Banter was used between people to communicate understanding. Angela knew that if she used insight to study her surroundings long enough, any answer would come to her.

One day, her parents sat her down and had a talk with her.

"Angela, honey, we are worried about you," her father said. She did not ask why. In her mind, Angela located the problem. Her parents were concerned that she did not have much of a social life.

"You don't have any friends," her mother spoke. Angela never saw the need for friends. Her parents loved her, and they meant the world to her. However, she saw that it would comfort her parents greatly to know that Angela was socializing.

"Okay mommy and daddy, if you would like me to acquire social interaction for your comfort, I would be very happy to do that," Angela resolved the problem before her parents could even speak it. They looked at each other. This was the longest chain of words they had heard come from their daughter's mouth in a very long time.

"Angela, what did you say?" her father asked. Angela looked up from her doll. Her big green eyes were captivating her father, "daddy, I read your books. I have the Hernandez syndrome." Her parents were dumbfounded. They had spent all their time on new research with their patients that they completely oversaw their own daughter's unique medical condition.

From that day forth, Angela's parents never bothered her about being quiet. In turn, they often asked her complicated questions. When Angela was eighteen, she was recruited in a think tank on Jupiter. After a few terms there, she was hired at a medical base on Neptune. It wasn't long after she was moved to Mars to work for division seventeen as an accelerated technician and information collector. It was there that she meet Veea who showed her that there are more things than those that meet the eye.

Angela Wallisky had been working for division seventeen for quite some time now. She didn't really care much for violence, people died anyway so why rush it. She did however care for her parents and their safety and she personally felt that the Divisions Council was doing an excellent job. A part of her job was to monitor Earth and bring to Phoenix's attention anything she thought was relevant. One day, she called Phoenix to SHONDS. She had noticed a strange pattern on Earth she thought the leading guardian should know about.

"There have been reports of missing peoples from Earth," Angela informed her superior. Its been unexplained by the officials there, I don't think it would hurt to look into it.

"Roger," Phoenix replied. The next routine meeting was the week after. She assigned Araline Madeline Ashworth or "Tinkerbell" to the project. They created a fake alias for her in Canada and she was set to work.

Ara's first task was to find out why the humans were missing. They could have been abducted by poachers who harvested human organs for tea, or they could have been kidnapped for slavery. The latter wouldn't make any sense since it cost a handful to alter humans. Still, there were planets with oxygen in their atmosphere as well, that would explain it. But usually those planets had different gravity and most unaltered humans would die under those unfamiliar conditions. Her only hope now was to lie attentively and wait for the next human to go missing.

Months had passed. Ara was able to ascertain that the majority of the people missing were from South Africa. There was one individual who was missing from France, two from Asia, and five from Canada. Besides that, there were nine missing from Africa. Wouldn't it be ironic if it were indeed for slave trade? Anyway, it was up to her to prevent further abductions and return those who were missing to their home. That was, if they were still alive.

She studied the profiles of the abducted individuals trying to decipher a pattern. They were all in excellent health, and were athletes of some sort having high performance endurance. None of them had contact with the top secret government departments aware of life on other planets. So then why were they missing?

Marcuno had watched Su-Lin take off from the planet Ceve. She was holding a bundle in her hands as she ran to her jet craft. He could sense something was wrong. Nevertheless, the girls were much older now and no doubt could handle themselves. He hoped that running into her wouldn't jeopardize his situation. It was true he was looking for a place to call home. He was actually looking for a place to squat and develop his own alliance. The ruler of the local galaxy groups had placed a governess in Quandonta. Marcuno didn't like the idea. He wanted to have an army of his own just in case things were to turn for the worse. He had avoided a paper trail and as far as everyone knows, he was as good as dead.

All across Quandonta, there were similar alliances formed. Armies that were lying patiently, waiting for the governess Dikara to make a mistake. Marcuno had been asked to join one of these massive armies but he declined. He didn't agree with a lot of their beliefs. They were more aggressive than he was. They were going to sabotage Liva and overthrow her rule. Marcuno thought that was folly. The governess had the support of Yolukia, which meant much larger armies. Any attack on Liva would be like a bug flying into a windshield. It would be better to wait for her to make a mistake, then by following procedure, remove her from office. The army of followers was a safety defense measure. Quandonta was able to function just fine without a ruler with the singular power to make decisions in her own hands, so why was she there now?

Something just didn't smell right. Marcuno had even thought about asking the loyalty of division seventeen but they served the system, and the system served the galaxy. He didn't want to put them in an uncomfortable situation.

There was no method or system to the way Macuno recruited people. He would travel from backwater planet to backwater planet hearing what people had to say. If he thought they would be an asset to his alliance, he was ask them to leave behind all their traces and join him. If they declined, he would play it off as a joke and disappear from their life forever. No one was able to track him. The years in division seventeen left him with incredible stealth techniques both physical and political.

Perhaps he should speak with little Rosi. He should ask her to denounce service to the system and join him. No, that would be too much pressure for her, he wouldn't want to burden her with that decision. Running division seventeen itself was a big enough chore. She wasn't mature enough to think for herself yet.

Mavius sat silently in his living room. He was not a bad man, at least, he didn't think so. Sometimes people who existed for the wrong reasons needed to be removed, that was all. He thought back to the first day he had met Her. She still hasn't given him her name yet. She was a serious young lady with long black hair and cold black eyes. She was just a child and he spoke to her lightheartedly. However, when she opened her mouth, all that spewed forth was venom backed by intelligent thought. He had no idea how she became so embittered, but she had very strong beliefs.

She had asked him what his view was on the Solar system and he told her that it was running smoothly and there was a fine but delicate balance. Somehow, she was able to convince him that the beings living there would never be able to progress without coordination, they need to share similar goals. He wasn't sure how she did it, but she swayed his mind. He was a very stubborn man, but she brought out point after point supported by factual documentation. He had an odd feeling that she was staring into his soul and manipulating him from the inside of his very mind. But that's not possible, was it?

He shook himself to rid of the prickly feeling on his shoulders. He didn't trust her, but she was right. She had won his loyalty and he enlisted to help her. She would not accept his help at first. Not until he promised to follow her every command without question. He hesitated there, but only for a moment. He swore a blood oath on his life that he would listen to her or die. She smiled coldly as if harboring an even darker secret. She gave him his first order. Upon hearing her request, he felt a tinge of regret. She wanted him to assassinate her clones. She said that were cloned without her consent and were set to destroy her. She gave Mavius their names and told him that he could find them serving division seventeen on Mars.

CHAPTER SIX

After a few years of independent growing, Rosi and the other sisters once again started to spend more time together. They could not help but notice how withdrawn Su-Lin had become. She was much quieter now. She had always spoken softly, but occasionally a shy joke would surface here or there. Now, her face just seemed to be frozen. They respected her space, maybe all she needed was time.

The girls were twenty years old and things were pretty much quiet. The disturbances with Tweila were worked out and the thousands of deaths were ignored and written of as history. Yeylacore was having some internal problems and the Providence of War was no longer looking for problems with Turnika Jos. At least, not for the time being. Though Division Seventeen had been promoted to serve the governess of the galaxy, they were merely one out of hundreds of other operations.

L.J. (Lisa Joyce) moved away from her family and Charles to live on Earth in America. She turned gothic. Her raven black hair had three distinct white-blonde highlights and her lower lip was pierced on the right side. She wore red eye shadow with heavy black eyeliner. Her clothes were always black and flowing. Sometimes, there would be a splash of purple or red. The girls joked that she was filling in for Charles' attitude.

Paula stilled used the name "V" and added snowboarding, skyboarding, and surfing to her list of activities. She got along a lot better with Erica after the witness protection incident with Jim and Jim. Erica on the other hand started to express her physical femininity. She wore revealing clothes and walked in alluring sways.

Ara was still the sweetheart. She laughed and looked through you with sugary innocence of her inner child whenever they were not acting on behalf of division seventeen. She moved to Jupiter because she wanted to be near large populations. She wanted to study the economic flow of an advanced civilization. She still called Mrs. Ashworth quite often to let her know that she was safe. She even brought Mrs. Ashworth to visit Jupiter a few times. The aging woman was not very comfortable traveling to such a populated place and generally chose to stay home. She accepted the fact that little Ara was moving on and could not stay by her forever.

Rosi was still nagged by her family. She loved them dearly, but feared for them. Now, instead of calling home to ease her parents' nerves, she called to ease her own nerves, just to make sure they were alive and well. There was no knowing who knew who the governess was and what they might do. There were too many secrets and too many hidden dangers.

Scott, who had always been a top student and charismatic bookworm started to secretly crush on L.J. who secretly had a crush on his good friend Billy from school. Neither said anything and Billy was the one to usually do all the talking when the three hung out together. When L.J. started spending time with her sisters, Scott started dating Bethany from his Calculus class. Bethany was also into heavy metal like L.J. and kept up a Mohawk. If you were to ask Scott, he would deny that L.J. was the reason he was dating Bethany.

Darrel spent a lot of time with V and Ara, but usually not simultaneously. He enjoyed the same sports as V, but Ara's fascination with Economics coincided with his own. He was nothing like his sister Jessie who read books in her free time. It didn't matter what books she got her hands on, she loved the flow of words and language. Jessie also sang. It was unusual and inspiringly beautiful to hear the vocal notes emanate from her thin and delicate lips. Her eyes were long and ovular and they remained impassive like stone most of the time. Darrel and Scott were usually the only ones to make her laugh. This stoic and seemingly apathetic girl transformed every time the flow of music would lift her soul to express itself through words. That was where all her shy, secret passion would hide.

Travis was fascinated with Angela Wallisky, the new technician for SHONDS. He would try creative ways to ask her out on dates and she would find equally creative ways to refuse him. She always used logic to trick him and he loved how smart she was. He wanted to grasp her and kiss the insolent words from her mouth with tenderness. She would never let him. She saw him as a pathetic ignorant brute. She was a new breed of woman, a fascinating creature of esoteric mental quality and he wanted to grasp it, share it, make it his own. She was unique, he wanted the uniqueness.

Dave spent a lot of time with his father. He was getting old and had a lot of lifetime knowledge to share. Dave did not chase after the opposite gender like most people his age. He sat and absorbed humans through the medium known as culture. Modern idiosyncrasies evolved every few years. What was history is only changeable by perceptive, but the facts stayed the same. He looked up to his father very much.

Dave was also a stoic figure like many of the others in the division. He didn't like to show his feelings and in many ways he was a hardcore soldier. Marcuno's father worked with his father so the two knew each other as children. He still got lost in the past sometimes. Marcuno, who was older, would take him on excursions when their fathers were in a meeting. They never stayed in the company day care, they snuck out and explored underground Mars. They would shoot rubber bands at rocks that they pretended to be dangerous enemies, and collected "specimens" for research and dissection. They had been good friends until Marcuno went to Business school on the other side of Mars. It was just a few years later that Dave himself went to military school. He had just graduated when Marcuno asked him to join division seventeen. He could not refuse. He withdrew from his original path and followed his hometown friend. He then found out that Marcuno had been in the division since he was thirteen. This explained Marcuno's lust for adventure which had rubbed off on Dave. Why Marcuno did not choose him to be Kirin, left a sore spot on his soul. Yet, he trusted the judgment, and left it alone.

Dave had always had eyes for Erica. He had never said anything though because he knew that she was still immature. He found something attractive about the constant energy she had and the interest in bending people's will with her gifted ability to flaunt her figure. What most engaged his interest was the fact that she seemed so removed from the rest of the division. He wasn't saying that she wasn't sincere with her work, but she didn't seem to belong in division seventeen. She belonged in a civilian life, but she was still able to turn on a dime and do what needs to be done.

He lacked respect for Rosi. He had to admit that he was jealous of her being selected as an officer. She seemed so uncertain when it came to taking necessary action. He would have made a better leader. It seemed to him that most of the time she would just bungle her way into something and jerk around until she got free. The girl never seemed to make up her mind one hundred percent. This drove him nuts.

Rosi still thought about Natasha. Why did she just leave like that? Did someone get to her? She disappeared much like Sarah, people who she thought loved her enough to share secrets with abandoned her without a trace. There was nothing Rosi could do. She would say a prayer for Natasha whenever she got a chance.

Rosi was still going to college. A young man named Evan was constantly vying for her attention and for her to be his girlfriend. Her family liked him very much, but Rosi thought of him as immature. He was a typical person for his age, acting infallible and as if he had his entire life mapped out, answers in his pocket, and control on his keychain like his discount cards. It almost made Rosi sick. She just wanted to scream at him sometimes, "You don't know, you never know what will happen to you, fool." She kept her mouth shut. She even acted like him, stupid, infallible, as if she had all the answers. She went to the rock concerts he and his friends went to. She went drinking with her college girlfriends and even though she physically couldn't get drunk, she still faked it. It annoyed her to a great extent whenever Evan tried to take advantage of her falsely presented lack of sobriety. She always pushed him away and many times bit her tongues as the words, "I'm married, you fucking pig!" would surface in her mouth. Those words weren't fair to Wayne. Their marriage was for a higher purpose, not to be used as a scapegoat.

"Rosi sweet pea!" a voice traveled to her window. She cringed. Taking a deep breath, she prepared herself for the following annoyance. The only reason she put up with Evan was for a suitable cover. Rationally, an average girl her age would be attracted to a prospective young man like him. She should see it as a blessing.

"Good afternoon, Evan!" she called down the window in a Juliette-like voice.

"How are you this bonny afternoon, Love?"

"I am not your love," she replied sweetly in a singsong voice that took away the harsh bite she really meant with those words. She almost hated him, but she recognized it wasn't him that she hated directly, it was having to put up with his ridiculousness.

"Ah, always the good girl, but I bet you won't be once we're married!" he called back up, "your family loves me!" He saw her as a good Asian girl being chaste according to her family's wishes. Rosi laughed loud and harshly at his comment but still revealed nothing. She wanted to chuck a brick at his pompous airy head. She didn't. Instead, she called back, "I'll be right down." She grabbed her jean jacket and picked up her keys. Taking another deep breath, she left her roommate a note and went down to pay penance for something ridiculous. Perhaps God was punishing her for stealing the peanut butter cookies out of the cookie jar when she was little. Or maybe, He was killing her soul slowly for all the people she had killed outside of Earth.

Wayne was in a similar situation with Cindy and Belle. They were twins who attended his university and they both had a thing for him. They would send him little notes and inappropriate images of themselves together in the shower. At first Wayne lusted and kept the pictures as anyone his age would. Then one day, when he was looking at them, he saw Rosi's face. He suddenly felt guilty that he had no respect for the twins. Rosi he respected and he knew that she respected him as well. Maybe she didn't love him and maybe she did have a crush on Travis, but she saw him as a person. These twins only wanted him for physical pleasure.

Wayne deleted all the pictures. It was spring break and his mind was tired from pretending to struggle at the workload. He dialed Rosi's number on his phone. There was no answer and he didn't feel like leaving a message. Wayne took a deep breath and stretched. Looking out his window, he saw people walking around. Some were in a hurry and walked with headphones on. Others biked with backpacks on their back. A group of jocks walked by with some cheerleaders. The ones at this school weren't as bad as some colleges he had looked at. These jocks and cheerleaders actually had brains and did well in their classes. A few couples walked together hand in hand. Cindy and Belle walked by with a boy from their chemistry class. The boy looked like Wayne and he sensed they had hoped he would be looking out his window and become be jealous. He wasn't. They would have been disappointed.

Wayne looked to the sky. It was a soft blue. If he were to travel straight up into the sky, through the atmosphere, it would turn to black. A brilliant, beautiful velvety black studded with diamond-like stars. That was his secret, that his life was literally written in the stars. He stared at the colors some more. They were truly beautiful, like the colors of Rosi. He missed her incredibly. He picked up his phone to call her again but hesitated. A road trip would be better, it would be just what he needed to unwind.

Getting up, he packed a few things, a toothbrush and his secret communicator that was disguised as a small but heavy solid black rectangular paperweight. Getting into his car, he humored himself with the realization that he was traveling in a normal way to see her. He could reach her in moments if he used his jet craft. Yet, slow was better, he needed time to think. Would she be happy to see him? Should he call? He liked the idea of a surprise much better. He was thinking of her lovingly, as her husband and destined life partner, not as her subordinate and accomplice to her orders.

"Well Evan, what are you here for today?" Rosi asked with a sweet but fake smile.

"Your love," Evan leaned in to kiss her. Rosi turned away. He had been getting more and more pushy about physical activity and she could not stand it any longer.

"Oh come on Rosi! You know its undeniable that we are going to be together! It's destined! Why are you being so prude!"

"Because Evan, I don't love you," Rosi spat back unable to hide all her blackness in her words. Her hands in her jacket pockets clenched. She looked at him calmly and coolly.

"You don't mean that do you?" Evan said, he looked hurt. Rosi was tired of him, "I do mean it. I like you and your company," she lied, "but I am not attracted to you." She was stern and he sulked silently.

"We could go see a movie," she said with false pleasantry. He nodded his consent. They walked slowly to the theatre without speaking to each other. Evan behaved like a little boy who was scolded for breaking the window with his baseball. Rosi wanted to reach over and slap his cheek good and hard for his idiocy. She clenched her fists tighter in her pockets, not allowing him to hold her hand this time. This was becoming intolerable, her patience was about to be worn out.

The movie was mediocre at best. Rosi was agitated by Evan's constant mentally nagging. She could hear his loud thoughts telepathically. He would go from scolding her to wooing her in his mind. He would imagine scenes of ridiculous romance where she was nothing more than an objectified "perfect wife." He would be her hero saving her in times of desperate need. Usually it involved another man that he could better. His thoughts would drift to her cool words and he would get upset with her again. She wanted to turn and scream at him, "SHUT UP AND GROW THE FUCK UP" but held her tongue. He didn't know she could hear him. When he started to fantasize about ravishing her body, she excused herself to use the restroom. She spent more time than she needed to in there. When she returned, he made fun of her "making a poopy." She ignored the comment and asked what she had missed of the movie. At least during his recap, she didn't have to put up with his silent thoughts.

After the movie they decided to get a smoothie. Rosi was praying for the night to end soon and was wondering if the sacrifice for her hidden identity was worth this headache. They walked along the lit street as a few other college students walked around with their friends. The walkway was stone and made a lovely clacking sound as different shoes walked by. Rosi wore tennis shoes and was pretty much quiet. A sorority girl walked by, strutting in obnoxious stilettos, but the sound the stone made in response allowed Rosi to forgive her. Rosi was lost in the moment of beauty that existed in this exquisite little street. She didn't hear what Evan was saying.

"Hmm? Could you say that again please?" she asked politely looking at him. His eyes looked like a little animal that was cornered. He moved quickly and reached out to grab Rosi's wrist. She watched it as if it were slow motion. He was sluggish to her. He swung her around and pushed her against a wall. For Rosi, he moved slow enough that she could have easily stopped him, but she didn't want to give any signs of her combat know how. She turned her face away as he leaned in to try to kiss her, but his lips never got anywhere near her. She sensed an interruption even before the anticipated gross kiss never occurred. Rosi turned back to look.

Wayne was standing between Evan and herself. She was surprisingly overjoyed seeing him there. Even though his back was to her and she could not see his face, she could tell he was glaring at Evan.

"Who the hell are you?" Evan demanded shoving Wayne's shoulder. Wayne didn't budge. Rosi wished he would have faked a little in reaction to a perfectly normal push like that, but she didn't grudge. She was too relieved. He was saving her from herself and her over indulgence in putting up with others unnecessarily.

"I'm her-," he started in response.

"Boyfriend," Rosi finished for him. Wayne didn't speak. He behaved as he was accustomed to, as if she were his commanding officer. She had the final say. Rosi was relieved he didn't try to say anything afterwards. Wayne stood tensely, eyes glaring at Evan.

"What? Rosi! You never said anything!" Evan was exasperated and kept babbling, "and dude, why did you overreact?"

"Oh come of it Evan, like you wouldn't have done the same. I never said anything because you never asked," Rosi replied calmly standing beside Wayne. She was acting very military like as well. Her body harmonized with Wayne's and she grew tense as well.

"Vile woman, you played me!" Evan shrieked, they were drawing a crowd.

"Fight! Fight! Fight! Fight!" people started to chant. Rosi placed a hand on Wayne's arm. He understood that he was not allowed to strike. His personal emotions were locked deep down. Seeing this boy with her made his blood curdle and he was hurt. This did not mean he couldn't obey her like an officer would.

Before Evan moved, they both knew he was going to strike. The two of them gracefully stepped apart and Evan over lunged stumbling towards the ground. He caught himself with one arm and prevented himself from planting his face into the stone. Rosi walked away with her back to the two of them and merged into the crowd. Simultaneously, Wayne walked the other way with his back to Evan. The three didn't face each other. Rosi and Wayne were one, they could sense each others' movements. Wayne knew he could not walk out of the circle of people who had gathered around. If he would try to, they guys would throw him back in until either he or the guy trying to kiss Rosi were defeated. To force his way out would mean taking down more than half of the guys in the crowd. That kind of attention was not allowed. With Rosi observing, he wouldn't get away with it. His only option was to keep dodging until Evan finally tired himself out and forfeited.

The crowd cheered as Evan strutted up to the stranger. Even before he struck, Wayne read the idea in Evan's head. Evan was the type of guy who needed to stubbornly set his mind to do something and give himself a rage inspired pep talk to do it. Evan lunged at Wayne's shoulders. Wayne easily dropped down and swept Evan's legs from under him. He caught Evan by the collar before his head hit the ground. He sensed Rosi's glare without looking up. The emotions he locked from his conscious stirred but they were under control. The rules she set for him in this fight as his commanding officer was that he was only allowed to dodge. No touching, let the stupid boy wear himself out. Wayne complied out of familiarity. He let go of Evan's collar as the young man caught his own fall with his arm. Wayne took two steps back. His body was still. Rosi wished he would have faked fighting like a normal person, but that would chip into his composure. His composure was what was keeping his emotions under control. It was also why he was obeying her and not beating Evan to a bloody pulp.

Wayne was very upset underneath. His anger grew. His eyes filled with hate. He did not move. Evan walked up to him and grabbed him by the shoulders. When he couldn't throw Wayne to the ground, he started to slam his knee into Wayne's stomach. Wayne barely budged. He stared back at Evan full of hate. He focused it all in his stomach, which hit Evan back as his knee met Wayne's abs.

The crowd moaned and groaned and cheered for this new stranger who barely cringed at Evan's attacks. Evan was a fairly average sized young man who would have put up a decent fight with anyone else.

"Stranger! Stranger! Stranger!" they cheered for Wayne. Wayne wanted to slam Evan mentally, but even he was afraid of that part of himself. Mental attacks were very dangerous.

Rosi couldn't tolerate it anymore. She couldn't bare to see the sight of Evan bashing mercilessly on Wayne, even if it was nothing more than a feather brush to him. It didn't feel right, it hurt her heart. Wayne was taking the disrespect because of her, for her. She knew from that moment on, that his love for her was pure, and that even though she made a secret unconscious oath never to love, she felt something for him. His love was genuine, why was she abusing it by making him restrain his self-dignity and tolerate this imbecile's stupidity as she had?

Rosi marched forward and grabbed Evan's shoulder, throwing him back, she stood between him and Wayne, "that's enough Evan," she commanded him coolly. Her eyes bore into his soul, she knew she made an impact.

Evan looked away in fear but his rage was still present as an expression of his sexual anxiety. His sexual anxiety was a result of social pressures and personal anxiety. It was not Rosi's burden to relieve him of it. That he just couldn't see.

"Why did you lie to me! Not telling me you had a boyfriend is the same as lying!" he screamed unable to look into her eyes.

"Whore! Whore! Whore! Whore!" the crowed chanted. Rosi was about to stare down the crowd when sirens sounded. The crowd immediately began to disperse. Rosi mentally made Evan look up, looking into his eyes, she spoke titanium words, "Our decrepit friendship is over." She turned and took Wayne by the hand, leading him away. As soon as they were out of Evan's sight, Wayne jerked his hand away. Rosi felt slighted, but she knew that she deserved it on many degrees.

"Why didn't you call me before you came?" Rosi asked calmly. Wayne replied telepathically, "I tried, you didn't answer." There were tears in his heart. Rosi was silent. She had her phone off, she knew that the question was pointless.

"Does Travis know about that jackass back there?" Wayne asked Rosi as if she were a comrade. The militia mentality was melting away.

"No, why?" she asked. Wayne was silent. "You didn't really think Travis and I had anything did you?" she implored. He was still silent. They walked towards the campus, it was still a good ten minutes away. Plenty of time to cool off.

"Wayne!" she exclaimed stopping to look at him. His expression was worn. He looked so disappointed. Rosi wanted to reach forward and kiss his cheek but her restraint prevented her from feeling anything. He had stopped too. He glanced in her eyes, afraid that his emotions would betray him, he looked away dejectedly with a stubborn sigh.

"Do you have a place to stay tonight?" Rosi got down to business to prevent emotions from expressing themselves. Wayne shook his head, "I'll find something."

"Unless you are too upset, you can stay with Carly and myself."

"Would you be okay with that?" what he really was asking was, "how many guys do you invite to stay with?" That was the question Rosi answered, "You would be the first." She looked at him, he looked up sensing her eyes. In her heart she felt a tenderness, a connection with him in that moment. She felt the warmth of her pregnancies. When she carried his babies, she felt a strange kind of love she had never felt before. She now attributed this emotion to him.

"Lover," she spoke with her mind in a gentle whisper. He blushed and turned to watch the sidewalk. All the negatively charged emotions from a few moments ago melted away. They walked side by side in peace. Everything was calm between them, everything had been forgiven.

"When I saved Travis and had him altered it was because he was innocent of the mess he was drawn into. I was weakened by guilt of all the other's I've killed. I saw him as I saw Earth," Rosi finally communicated to Wayne in a low voice. In her mind, she sent him the image of Travis' mangled body and the dying "Why?" that had escaped his lips. Wayne caught onto her desperation. He grabbed Rosi and passionately held her against his chest. She was surprised at this sudden expression of emotion, but did not reject him. She was a little bit uncomfortable, but it was more from her own affection towards him than his towards her.

Back at the apartment, Carly was there with her boyfriend.

"Wow Rosi! Who's the stud?" Carly asked in a slight drunken

stupor.

"This is Wayne, my childhood sweetheart" she spoke gently. The words were more for Wayne than Carly.

"Well, my dude and I are spending the night at his place and I'm taking off early tomorrow to go home for spring break. I'm skipping my last class."

"Lucky, I got an exam in Macro on Friday night," Rosi conversed.

"Ooh, that sucks!" Carly cooed.

"Nice to meet you man, I'm Nick," Carly's boyfriend introduced himself to Wayne. Wayne shook his hand politely, "how are you doing, Nick?"

Rosi and Wayne retreated into Rosi's room to give the other two their privacy in the living room. It was suddenly very awkward for the two of them.

"So, I take it your spring break is a week after ours," Wayne said to break to the uncomfortable silence. The moment was a little reminiscent of their first night on Juyvine when Yolukia first married them.

"Yeah, I'm assuming you're on spring break now?" she asked. He nodded. It was awkwardly quiet again. Rosi could sense something rising out of Wayne. He wanted to ask something. His exterior was quite unchanged, his mind as well, but there were words.

"Did you love our children?" he asked finally.

"Of course!" Rosi breathed out. He believed her. Her self-discipline and control were undeniably extraordinary, as were his, but he always knew what he was thinking. She was a different matter.

"Why would you think I didn't?" there were tears in her voice. He looked at her guiltily, "I never doubted you, I just wanted to hear it, I'm sorry if I made you break down a wall."

The two ended up in each others' arms. They sat on the floor leaning against Rosi's bed. They played within each others' minds, sending sweet thoughts and images back and forth. When they heard Carly and Nick leave, Wayne bravely reached down and kissed Rosi on the lips. Rosi's cell phone rang. She had turned in on after Wayne had stated he tried to call her. It was her parents. Rosi gently pulled out of the kiss, "Yes, Mama?"

"Evan just called! What did you do to the poor boy?" her mother demanded.

"Nothing Mom, I've told I didn't really like him that much, he just pushed too far," Rosi rolled her eyes at Wayne. She wanted to shout at her mom, "he's always trying to have sex with me! Do you like him now?" but that would have been disrespectful and crossing a line.

"Who is this other boy he's talking about?" her mother pressed into her life.

"Oh you mean my fiancé?" Rosi responded. Wayne's ears perked.

"What?" came the sound over the phone.

"I was going to wait until I came home for spring break to tell you," Rosi lied.

"Are you going to bring him with you?" her mother asked.

"N-," Rosi began, Wayne nodded, Rosi immediately shopped short and corrected herself, "Yeees Momma, he's a nice boy, you will like him."

"What does he do?" she asked. Rosi rubbed her throbbing forehead into Wayne's chest, "he goes to college in Colorado mom." She could feel him giggling on the inside. It tickled her too.

"Oh, college," Rosi could hear her mother's thoughts and so could Wayne. Her mother was silently wondering about Wayne's grades compared with Evan's and how he might be able to provide for her daughter in the future. Rosi looked at Wayne with embarrassment. She mouthed to him, "sorry."

"Hey! Colorado! How did you meet him?" she asked.

"Mom, I told you about him twelve years ago, when I went to that summer camp in California with Natasha."

"You kept in touch all this time?"

"Yes mom."

"Wow! So he knows you pretty well then?" her mother implored. Rosi placed her hand on Wayne's knee and thought to him, "yeah, he knows me."

"Momma, I have to go, I have an exam on Friday," which was the most sincere thing she said in the entire conversation to her mother.

"Okay, be a good girl, bye-bye."

"Bye mom." Her mother forgot about Evan by the end of the conversation. After she hung up, Rosi shared a loud laugh with Wayne.

"Oh my gosh! You're going to meet my parents!" it suddenly hit Rosi. It hit Wayne as well, "Oh shit!"

"Do we tell them we're already married?" she asked.

"I don't know, should we?" he was at an equal loss.

Yolukia sat at the head of the table. The committee was discussing the newly appointed governess and her dangers.

"Her life is constantly under threat!"

"What would it mean if she is dethroned? Would they try to dethrone you next?

"You are too deeply linked to her, you must be careful and wary of her and what happens to her."

"We must clone her and keep the clones safe, that way if anything does happen to her, we can reinstate a clone. This way, the image would keep you and this state of ruling safe!" All the members had different ideas. Yolukia hated the idea of losing Dikara. He hated the idea of secretly having to clone her, but they were right. Their plan was that they would secretly clone her, and hide the clones in the newly discovered dimensions where time and space were different.

"We have to have more than one clone!" someone exclaimed.

"Two, that is it, not more," Yolukia boomed his final decree. The meeting was adjourned.

It was V's turn to train Angela. Angela was going to be a field tech, which meant she would be cleared to travel with the division on certain missions. She had to have the basic physical training to qualify. Being mostly a scholar, this was hard for her, even with the aid of physical enhancers. V had worked with many younger boarders and skydivers in the past and was able to break down certain movements for Angela. She could explain things to her and Angela was very grateful. V liked Angela because she was not like Erica. Though V's bond grew better with Erica, she still disagreed with her ways. Erica was caught up with her looks and getting boys to do her bidding. Even though it was all just a show for cover, V thought it was sickening.

Angela on the other hand was extremely intelligent. She was like V in that she didn't say things unless they need to be said. There was a sort of profound truth in silence and they both shared that. Their friendship grew. V would go to Angela with questions, Angela would seek her help in understanding sports or other physical movements concerning coordination. It was a perfect contract between them. They began spending enormous amounts of their free time together. Erica and V's parents were much older than the average parents. They passed away in their 70's and Angela attended both funerals. V wouldn't admit it out loud, but without Angela there, she wouldn't have felt complete.

Even when V shaved her head, it was Angela who did it for her. When she dyed her spikes green, it was Angela again, experimenting a new hair dye formula she had invented just for V. Even Erica liked Angela. Angela understood that Erica's behavior was just an act to be an airhead. She had seen Erica in action and knew that she was just as smart as the rest of the division. Angela even understood the satire in Erica's choice of a façade, it was to tease V. Angela could never tell V this, V would refuse to see it. Still, they loved each other dearly.

Tanyui (Yeylacore)

Tanyui never forgot seeing the governess' face at the mud bath a few years ago. What was she doing there? Was it a test? Tanyui's father was the King of Yeylacore. She was his bastard child. No one cared for her. But not too long ago, the governess of the Milky Way galaxy kidnapped the royal family. Dikara didn't want Tanyui because she was illegitimate, but they took her mother away even though her mother was just a mistress.

Her father refused to agree to the governess's terms so she killed his first family, then his second. Soon, it would be her mother's turn. Tanyui could not let that happen. She killed her father and being his only kin on Yeyla, she assumed the throne. She obeyed the governess and launched new attacks on Turnika Jos and began a slow invasion to take command of Yeylacore. Still, the governess wanted more before her mother was to be returned. Out of fear for her mother's safety, Tanyui did everything she was asked.

Yeylacore was located in The Providence of War. The Providence of War was named after a philosophy. Survival of the fittest was a theory in more places than just Earth. Almost everywhere in the local group 47 people believed that in the end, scratch the politics, it's the violence that answered all the questions. Tanyui was brought up on this belief and her mother in the hands of the Governess of the Milky Way Galaxy proved this to her.

Tanyui had tried to contact the Trials Galaxy leaders for help, but they kept turning her down. Yeylacore was on the outer edge of their galaxy and they had more important things to do. Tanyui had no choice but to ask her father's council for advice. The council was not happy with her as the ruler. They knew that she was acting out of fear for her mother's life and she could not be trusted to make wise decisions. It was foolish of them to speak up against her. She had them executed and she hand picked new advisors. Amongst them was Groyu. His uncle was one of the few councilmen that Tanyui kept alive and that put Groyu in her favor. He had forgotten about Kinadr, or rather, Su-Lin, and his baby by this time. He was more focused on obtaining power for himself.

Tanyui didn't really care to keep Yeylacore in the same state her father had. Her main objective was to bring home her relatives that were still left alive. She completely tossed out her father's politics and made her own. This included not trading with Turnika Jos. Her new policy caused many uprisings and riots. She was in no mood to have the people cry out against her so she made harsh decisions turning herself into a tyrant. Not once did she hesitate to lift her iron fist. She had no care for the people. Her weakness was her mother, and the governess had her. In turn, the Governess really ruled Yeylacore.

When the Governess told her to attack Turnika Jos, she fulfilled the terms immediately. This returned one of her father's mistresses and one of her children. Tanyui knew that it was just a token and the Governess of the Milky Way was leading her on, but her mother was the only one she had in the world. It would be a long while before she would see her mother's face again. Tanyui and Yeylacore had become a pawn in Wrie's game to take over Dikara's life.

Mavius

"So you believe in totalitarianism?" a young Mavius asked the woman with dark hair. He was a young politician from Jupiter. She smiled at him. Even though it was a friendly smile, he could feel no warmth coming from her. He did not sense a soul behind those deep black eyes. He was afraid of her, but she was brilliant. Damn it he down right admired her. She knew a lot concerning the way the Solar System was run. It was strange how he had never heard of her before, such a glorious mind must have had written books or have papers published somewhere. Like himself, the woman believed that in such a wretched state of society, the best thing to do was to control everyone under one single commanding force. Letting things slide around the way the council did was never going to accomplish anything. There needed to be one voice that commanded all. They needed a dictator who could straighten out all the chaos.

However, after the woman made him swear his loyalty, she

explained what she wanted. That was when he hesitated. She needed to use him, push him up the ladder of leadership. She also needed him to kill six people. The six of them were her clones. She claimed that they would stand in the way of their goals. Mavius hesitated. It was true that he would never leave the solar system because he loved his home. However, he never expected to commit murder. Yet somehow, as he stared into those bottomless black eyes, he lost his own reasoning and believed that everything the dark haired woman told him as truth set in stone.

It was not difficult to find Wrie's clones. The one named Rosi was the leader of a military division. The other five were also in that division. Wrie commanded him to get rid of Rosi first. The rest would be easy. Mindlessly, he called upon his most trusted servant, Stregatori. He had become Wrie's puppet. Soon, Jupiter didn't matter, his life didn't matter, his mind was in the clutch of her hand.

It was Mavius who acted on behalf of Wrie with Yeylacore. It was Stregatori who kidnapped the royal family. Wrie showed her face to Tanyui through a video conference. She knew she had the true governess' face and she knew that a simple girl like Tanyui didn't know any better but to believe her. Wrie did keep her mother and she used her leverage well.

To get to the dimension of the Governess, Wrie sacrificed everything in her "home" dimension. She had always had a calling to somewhere beyond that which she could reach. People at her "home" treated her cruelly and she only learned to hate. Once she discovered that she was truly from another dimension, and that she was a replacement clone for a ruler, she became greedy. She salivated at the idea of ruling a galaxy. The power could all be hers, all she needed to do was destroy the existing governess.

Since her home dimension operated on a different time line that fluctuated apart from her original dimension, she was able to see certain events before they would occur. She learned the secrets of the governess, who she really was, and what she would be. She learned of the other five clones and knew had to get rid of them too. The other clone made of the Governess was in a different dimension and that portal was lost when an extreme time slippage occurred. Wrie would be the only alternative.

Wrie watched Dikara's progress and identified her weakness. She knew all of Dikara's allies, enemies and things that made her tick.

She picked a moment in time that was best to start her plot, and, with the sacrifice of her "home" dimension, transported herself back to the dimension that had cloned her.

"Tell me, Mavius, how many systems do we have allied against her royal highness?" Wrie spoke coldly. Mavius was more or less in a trance now. His wishes were originally for bettering his system, but now Wrie had forced him to travel beyond what he cared for. It was as if he couldn't stop. He was her mask, his actions were somehow dictated by her.

"We have four dominant planets in three separate systems secretly allied together. Three minor systems gave their loyalty, Yeylacore is obeying out of leverage, but I don't think they would be willing to crash their explosive planet into Liva just yet, or blow it up for that matter. We are going to have to replace the girl ruling there. I myself am working up the council ladder. Stregatori is mixing in with the local rebels." Mavius was silent after his brief report. There was a long, cold steel moment, then Wrie replied with a cruel curl in her voice, "Good." Then she got up and walked away.

A part of Mavius had millions of questions for himself and her as well. The dominant part that felt as if Wrie were controlling her, was silencing him. One question did break through though, "Where did she come from?" Following by another, "Who is she?" Suddenly, it felt like a dark hand coming out of no where, and the stream of questions stopped. His eyes turned stony. He got up and walked out of the room behind Wrie like her dog.

CHAPTER SEVEN

Zyolious Sarces

The Haiokasheeba was the name of the dark force that lived at the southern pole of the Solzan moon, Quar. Legend has it that it was a lost element of nature that had once destroyed the people of Solzan. It was banished to the moon by the gods. Sometimes when the moon is on its most tilted rotation, you could see it. It is a small dark hurricane slowly spinning in torment allowing terrible tales to be told of its destructive forces. Some say it is the lost spirit of a female searching for her lover who sacrificed himself for her and he was buried beneath the land they set foot on. He would be the Almarion, and she destroyed most of the planet surface, trying to break free, to free him, to love him.

The planet Solzan had limited traveling abilities. Only the most advanced countries were able to send and receive ships once in a while. Yet, it treasured it's separation from the rest of the galaxy. It allowed them to be free from the corruption and kept them close to the natural essence of their planet.

Sarces was a little girl who grew up in the tribe of Zyolious. She listened intently as the elders told her about the Almarion and Haiokasheeba, and how she had to be a good little girl or else Haiokasheeba will send out a demon in the middle the night and steal her soul. She listened to how the village would be frightened and sad to find little lifeless Sarces. Living in a matriarchal society, Sarces feared the wrath of an angry woman as any child would. Even if the woman were a dark spirit entity on the moon.

Her eyes were always wide as her elders' voices rose with the wind rushing through the blue leaved Kicadble trees. Those were the trees that were believed to be the guardians of life and planted to protect the citizens from the Almarion. The roots were said to suck the essence of the Almarion and keep him subdued. The curled blue leaves made a great dish that was only eaten during the bi-annual celebrations. The seeds were baked and eaten before bed as a personal protective device against the dark force on the moon. Haiokasheeba would never harm the Almarion.

It was upon the Kicadble trees that Sarces trained. Targets were set up all around and she practiced with darts every single day until she could hit them blindfolded. At age eleven, she started training with her triple edged pell swords. They were short and slender but razor sharp. She was trained to handle them as if there were her appendages. When Sarces was twenty years old, her family encouraged her to enter into the Ability Contest. The Ability Contest was held every three years in her country of Flazerth. At first Sarces was shy and humble saying that she was not good enough. However, when the whole village began persuading her, she finally gave in. Zyolious had not had anyone from their tribe enter the Ability Contest for about a decade. Sarces was their pride and joy.

The contest was long and grueling, but she had won. Never in her dreams had she thought she was that skilled. Her victory came as a surprise to everyone in Flazerth, especially herself. When she returned to Zyolious, there was a feast awaiting her. She celebrated and danced with everyone under the deep purple sky around a light blue flame that shined with a white light.

That night, when she returned home, her mother and father approached her with pride.

"We love you so much daughter," her father said.

"We wanted you to seek a husband and bring him home and take our name of Zyolious," her mother started. For on Solzan, women were superior. Her mother continued, "but now we know that you were meant for so much more."

"Mother what are you saying?" Sarces asked.

"We want you to leave Solzan," her mother said with tears in her eyes, "We want you to travel to the neighboring planet Callyna and find yourself, what you were really meant to do." Sarces father nodded and smiled proudly at her, "We love you sweetheart, don't worry about making us proud, we always will be. We just want you to find a better life than this humble little village." Sarces walked into their outstretched arms. She knew that her parents meant her well, but she didn't want to leave. Yet, no matter how gently they told her or whatever sweet kind words they used, she knew that it was a command and she had to go make another life for herself. She must obey her mother, or else she might set a curse upon her village. Mothers were meant to be obeyed.

The next day, the whole village was there to see Sarces off. She smiled with a warm feeling in her heart. She loved her home and her heart would always be here. She knew that she would die there when everything was done. She turned and boarded the space bus then found a seat. She waved to her village disappearing in the distance. She didn't feel desperate or lonely. She felt full of the love her village had given to her and knew that no matter where she went or what she did, that will always keep her strong.

The ride was long. As she idly watched the landscape, her grandmother's voice seeped into her mind. It was the very first story she had heard about the Almarion and Haiokasheeba. This version in particular did not inspire fear in her. It was the other stories that did. The stories about what happened to Haiokasheeba after she had lost the Almarion.

Once upon a time, before life forms ruled Solzan and the planet was still molten and hot, there were spirits. They dwelled in their own dimension, much like an after-life, or in this case, a before-life. They were just a soup mix of souls. When these spirits died, their bodies turned to dust and came into our present dimension and spread upon the earth. This dimension is what we know today as the world of the living and their ashes are the seed of our existence. Billions of years later, they had evolved into Life. Even as the prehistoric creatures roamed, the spirits were still alive and coexisting peacefully.

A possible explanation was that these spirits arouse from the heat or the "heart" of the new planet. They maintained animal and humanlike forms and had complex emotions. It is said that these spirits set the precedent for patterns in peoples' behavior. There were no rulers or policy enforcers, the spirits did not quarrel much. They were ruled by compassion. There were the sprites of the air, the earth, and the oceans. Those of the ocean chose to keep to themselves living an elusive life of beauty and wonderment. They approached every problem with rationality and viewed the land sprites as coarse and mundane and thought little of them.

The land sprites were crafty and inventive. Their behavior was a lot like the humanoids and they created little systems of management, but nothing too extreme to the extent of an empire. They merely made a lot of agreements and treaties and functioned in group activities. As for their appearance, they had various different physical forms and moved in different ways.

The sky sprites lived in the name of freedom and harmony. Every now and then, the land sprites would become jealous of the sky sprites because they maintained harmony so much better than they could.

The earth sprites based their life around order because without order, there would be chaos and that meant destruction. They were not evil, they just wished to learn, and obtain what they lacked. Their ultimate wish was for Harmony and in their minds, the only way to obtain that was to study air sprites. Thus, they began attempts to capture air sprites.

There were five main body forms for the sky creatures. There was the large bird species with the enormous tail that possessed a hauntingly beautiful voice. Today we know them as pyre sirens. The serpent with the head of a lion and the heart of gold we call Mosuns. There was a smaller dove-like bird, which blessed the land with fertility in the spirits' dimension. Much like the pomegranate today, this small bird was a good sign. There were also the large tentacled beings that slept most of their lives. They were extremely docile creatures and held the appearance of a flat-shelled turtle. They also had a turtle shaped head, but nine tentacles (one of which was a tail). These creatures allowed the other four species to build their cities upon their backs. The last of the five sprites was a very agile deer. It was believed that they were once land sprites who grew so light by shaking worry and duty off of their shoulders, that they bound up to live in the sky, in harmony.

The land sprites would have worshipped the air sprites if they did not look down upon them for their lack of organization in their lifestyles. As life on the planet began to grow, the earth sprites walked amongst the land creatures, unseen. They shared the same earth, never touching each other. As the dead sprite's essence transferred dimensions they turned into the creatures that live with us today. They roamed free, forgetting where they had come from.

Haiokasheeba was her name and she was one of the large songbirds, a pyre siren. Almarion was a lion-headed serpent. Spirits could not reproduce. Of the thousands upon thousands of sprites born from the molten earth, none of them were unable to reproduce. Their numbers were dwindling. They were all dying. Even though each of their lives lasted for hundreds of thousands to billions of years, the only creature able to reincarnate, was the large songbird. This creature was the pyre siren. This glorious songbird sang its beautiful song shortly before its death. (Much like the bamboo blooming right before it dies.) The songbird would fly about the ocean and sing with the ocean siren sprites (mermaids). The bodies of the ocean sprites turn to foam after their death and were mourned by the songbirds. The songbird would then die in a burst of flames high in a hidden nest of a mountain. But these sprites have been dwindling too. For the earth sprites have been stealing the eggs and although in an innocent enough attempt to find the answer to spiritual freedom and harmony, they would accidentally kill the songbirds. Their remains would turn into ashes, which scattered to the four winds. This created new life in the world of tangible flesh.

It is now the age when humanoid forms are starting to flourish in the dimension of flesh. This would be the same dimension that had forgotten their spiritual essence and roots. The sky creatures have been forced to build their nests upon mountaintops. The turtle-squid sprites had all died out. The smaller bird sprites have died out as well, thus leaving behind barren grounds for the earth sprites. Life was extremely difficult for everyone left in the spirit dimension. The earth sprites now began to believe that the secret to eternal life lie in the songbirds and their eggs became very precious. The earth sprites became engulfed in their own selfishness.

The deer sprites have become messengers for the few songbirds and serpents left alive. They were extremely faithful and thankful to the air sprites for accepting them into their lives. They did not want to be associated with the earth sprites. The few serpents and song birds left flew inland away from the water in order to escape the land sprites.

Haiokasheeba (high-OH-kuh-SHEE-buh) and Almarion were in love. Very few sky sprites experienced love because love was not freedom. But their love was Harmony. Something most living things cannot understand anymore. After spending billions upon billions of years together, they became each other's halves. Haiokasheeba was the only songbird to have a guardian while she sat in her egg waiting to be reborn. They would have been a legend, if the flesh dimension would have acknowledge their spiritual roots. But only a few humanoids living today can understand what transpired then.

The only battles fought between the sky sprites and the Earth sprites were when Almarion went out to seek back Haiokasheeba's egg. He guarded her carefully whenever she was weak. Unfortuneately, he could not live forever. When he finally passed away, his ashes spread upon the thriving Earth in the dimension of flesh.

Haiokasheeba was devastated. She sang every day and every night over the ocean. She never ceased, even when the sirens avoided her. She vowed to never stop singing her sad song until she was reunited with her Almarion. She had lost a piece of herself, and it hurt her terribly. Gradually, her songs filled with anguish. She had no answers. She swore to herself that she would not rest until she was whole again. With that oath, she ripped out the fire gem from within her. (the gem or "gland" which caused the large songbird to burst into flame when they were old). She tossed the gem into the ocean and flew to a village filled with land sprites. She flew into unnatural fire, birthed by the sprites of earth. And then she flew towards the ocean. As she burned, her ashes fell into the ocean. Until nothing of her was left. And that was how she entered the world of flesh. This was so she could begin her search for her Almarion. Even at night, when the sun is setting and the wind is still, you can hear the haunting hollow voice of the Haiokasheeba coming from Quar.

It is a shame that no one remembers Haiokasheeba and Almarion. They no longer exist, only in lore that is used to entertain child folk. There is no proof of what is real and what is not. They are forever lost. Will they ever be reunited? They were left with no closure and nothing but eternal pain. It had become too painful for Haiokasheeba to live in her dying world without Almarion. Everything about the two of them that had lasted for billions of years became no more and will never be acknowledged nor worshipped. But what was carried on through their ashes into this world, was the search for the other half. Whether or not soul mates exist, beings or any creature with higher thought long for their spiritual fulfillment. This was the only thing left of Haiokasheeba and Almarion. It fills each one of us, and we call it “searching for destiny.” It scattered far and wide throughout the stars and some have found their home within the souls of others far away.

The space bus stopped. Sarces got up and gathered her things. As she boarded the larger space craft that would bring her to a new life, the story about the Pyre Siren and the Mosun stuck with her deep in her heart. She was out to find her destiny.

Ara had two good friends, Shelly and Rachael. After Travis finally gave up on Angela, he started to go with Shelly. Shelly was a sweet Martian girl with grandparents from Earth. She had never been to Earth and Rachael was there once when she was very young. Travis decided it would be a treat to take them. He went through the necessary procedures and got them clearance to travel with him. They did not know he was a member of division seventeen, but they did know he had more freedoms than an average civilian. They understood and respected his privacy.

Before the girls left, they had to get fitted with artificial skin to appear more human-like. They only knew a few words in a scatter assortment of Earth languages, so Travis promised he would do most of the talking.

As they were walking along a boardwalk, some teenagers were walking towards them. The girls were nervous because they had not been that close to humans on Earth before. Travis calmly whispered to them that everything was fine. The group of four guys and one girl walked by. One of the boys was muttering something.

"Damn Spic," was all Travis caught. His grandparents on one side were Puerto Rican, they were the ones who had raised him lovingly. His own parents were spat out rejects of American society but his grandparents understood things like reverence and respect.

"Excuse me?" Travis turned to face the speaker, his blood was hot. The poorly postured boy turned and looked at him through a crooked eye. Travis read insecurity in the young man's mind and understood the puffery to merely be a show for his friends. It did not warrant the unnecessary insult.

"You heard me," he said full of insolence. Travis took a step forward, but Shelly placed a hand on his arm. He turned and looked at her. Suddenly, he realized how foolish he was. Here he was, about to pound a boy who had no reasoning power of his own. Travis himself had transcended beyond flesh and the human race to a higher power of emotional experience capable of extending beyond stereotypes. The boy, was simply not worth his time. Travis smiled at Shelly. Without another look, the three turned and left while the group shouted more obscenities at their back. They didn't matter anymore.

"Why were those humans like that?" Rachael asked.

"We're not all like that, some of us are plagued by our own minds. Shall we visit another place?" Travis asked pleasantly. Shelly smiled.

"Give me back my folder Zapariah!" Ara shouted to Darrel. It was wrong of her to a modified form of his code name, Zap! (exclamation point included) but no one else was around. He was helping her with a research project. She was interning at an auditing firm on Jupiter. He had enrolled in a school nearby so he could taste the society. It wasn't because of Ara that he went to Jupiter, he loved the planet as well, he was just glad there was a familiar face there, that was all. Darrel loved the night life there. There were many extraordinary social games the youth would play. They were often filled with stupidity, much like the youth on earth, but to a more extreme extent.

Ara and Darrel were very straight forward and honest with their feelings. They cared greatly about each other as mutual members of the same division, but they were simply not attracted to each others' personality. Thus, they held a strong but platonic friendship.

Though Darrel was excellent at socializing on Earth, Jupiter was a different story. He had a difficult time connecting with the people there and was awkward at many times, unlike Ara. Ara had a sugary patience with everything and everyone and if it weren't for her, he would have been socially bankrupt. He loved it though. Back on Earth, he was popular, on Jupiter, he held the opposite social status.

The groups Ara associated with would have outings together to Saturn whenever it would orbit near Jupiter. This didn't happen that often and it was quite a treat. Swimming in the rings of Saturn was an ethereal experience. The gentle dust particles slipped by on your skin in a silky manner. The larger chunks of frozen ice sent energy shooting through your body when you sat on them to rest. There was a magical energy charge in the Saturn rings that soothed anyone's soul and put their hearts to rest. Darrel loved these outings and would often float alone in the rings, staring straight up and out at the expansive sky. That sky, was where his home, Earth was located. The rest of the sky was his as well, his to protect.

Ara gazed softly towards Darrel. She admired him. He gave up his prominent social life to live in more or less seclusion on a socially active planet like Jupiter. Not everyone could give up what they had that easily. He was something special indeed. She was glad he was there to fight beside her and Phoenix. She had the utmost respect for him, he never let anyone down.

She recalled when they were younger and there was the last sweet treat Marcuno had brought them. Ara had unknowingly ate the last one and there was none left for Jessie who arrived later. Jessie looked sad as Darrel teased her and Ara thought he was cruel. She had felt bad enough she ate the last treat unknowingly, but Darrel had to rub it into

Jessie's face. Just as Ara was about to say something, Darrel retrieved two of the treats from his pocket. He had been saving them for his little sister. Ara smiled. People like that were rare. People like them, were rare. She was glad they were bonded together by a singular mission.

Since things were peaceful, Su-Lin was granted permission to travel the galaxy. Phoenix saw something was still eating at her sister and her heart went out to her. She gave her a pass signed by the governess that gave her free access to travel about the galaxy as long as Su-Lin kept her communicator with her and could make it back to Mars within two Earth days. This was something that Phoenix probably should not have done, but the power went a little to her head, and her heart was ruling. Either way, as long as no one knew their real connection, there was nothing anyone could say. As far as they would know, Su-Lin was on a mission for the governess.

Phoenix also granted Su-Lin permission to use one of the systems fastest jet crafts which allowed Su-Lin to travel further and still hold the guarantee of returning within four Earth days if the occasion of an emergency would arise.

Su-Lin was thankful though she was extremely depressed and unable to feel much joy (despite that her code name was Joy). She finally cried in Rosi's arms. She gladly took the leave and wandered aimlessly around the galaxy searching for something, yet nothing at all. About a year after Sarces left, Su-Lin found herself landing in Flazerth on Solzan. A few months later, she found her way to the tribe of Zyolious. Immediately, she sensed something was different about this place. She had a sort of connection with the peace and discipline they offered. They trained in martial arts but didn't let forceful anger dominant their practice. She met the elders, who were able to see right through her.

"You have suffered devastating loss young one," an old wise woman said to her, "but you were selfish as well." Su-Lin was taken aback and little insulted. In her mind, she wrote off the woman as a fool, but somewhere deep inside, she was afraid that she was right. The old woman planted a seed of thought into Su-Lin's brain. Was she selfish in holding onto her pain? Was she selfish in expecting to be worth more? Was she selfish in hating the others for not caring about her mother, especially since they had their own families? Was she selfish in leaving Trisha? Was she selfish in wanting to keep her son? The thoughts were getting too loud for her. Tears were in her eyes and she felt like she was going to break. She turned and walked to the edge of the village toward the woods.

"You are free to stay with me when you feel ready to return," the old wise woman called gently after Su-Lin. She didn't turn around. That night, she slept in a tree like she did whenever on a rare occasion she would visit Earth. She was visited by a dream:

A ball of fire that danced around and occasionally sprouted wings to move itself around, was flying through water. The ball of fire was herself yet not herself. It was everyone. It felt safe with the water around itself, as if it were itself. The water would extinguish the fire, only if it let it. Otherwise, the two enemies in nature coexisted harmoniously.

Su-Lin awoke in the middle of the night and walked back to the village. The old woman sat in front of her cabin before a fire. She was waiting for Su-Lin. She smiled a pure smile that turned her eyes up and made them disappear.

"The fire is yourself, the water is yourself. The fire and water are Almarion and Haiokasheeba before desire set in. Only with nothing but pure love and emptiness in our hearts, can we give ourselves room to be full of happiness, Joy." Su-Lin's breath caught in her throat. How did the old woman know her name?

"No surprise young warrior, my destiny was to aid you. My whole life I have learned much and gain much wisdom. Before I pass on, I must give you all of my wisdom through teaching. Will you accept me as your master and learn with me?" the old wise woman asked. Su-Lin swallowed, she was dumbfounded. She felt herself nodding. The old woman smiled, "good, get some rest tonight, we will start tomorrow."

The old woman was surprisingly nimble. She started by teaching Su-Lin the secrets of the Zyolious martial arts. No one objected because the old woman was greatly respected in the village. They all trusted that she knew what she was doing. Even though they knew Su-Lin was leaving, they accepted her into their hearts and their homes. Su-Lin had never felt so much love in her life. Except, maybe with her mother and Trisha. With Julian, the love was tinged with pain.

"We learn to stop running from ourselves before we can face any other opponent," the old woman spoke to Su-Lin. She was not sure what those words meant, but it didn't matter, she will one day.

A married couple approached Su-Lin one day, "You are a gift from the wind. We sent our daughter away and the wind blew you here. We can feel your fate is later intertwined with hers. Please give her our love, when you learn to love." Su-Lin was insulted. She knew how to love. Didn't she? Yet, the tone in the couple's voice was warm and loving, Su-Lin could not be angry with them. Instead, she felt humbled.

The second year she was there, the sword smith woman teamed up with the rest of the elders. The three women and two men joined in a circle around Su-Lin and the sword smith. They channeled into Su-Lin and helped the sword smith devise a weapon especially for her. It was the same initiation Sarces had gone through years before. After the procedure, the sword smith woman took Su-Lin to her cabin. Amongst the many lumps of unshaped metal in her work area, there was a large bookshelf. It was an organized mess. The sword smith took a book down and looked up the formulas the elders had channeled to her. The woman gasped and she looked up at Su-Lin both questioningly and struck with awe.

"You, you're connected with a pyre siren!" she exclaimed, "not just any, but one with Haiokasheeba in her soul!" Su-Lin had heard the stories of Haiokasheeba and the Almarion, but she had no idea what the sword smith was talking about, so she kept quiet. The woman looked into the book again and looked back up at Su-Lin. Something that was a cross between fear and wonderment shown on her face.

"The Almarion too," was all she said. Su-Lin looked back at her imploringly for a few moments. She tapped gently into her mind, but the woman spoke again, "you may very well be the connection from us, leading to the reunion of the two entities who long for each other. Their longing causes war and destruction and desecrates the purest of love." Su-Lin looked to the sword smith blankly.

"I may only fashion weapons, but I know the myths!" she exclaimed tossing the heavy book onto her messy table. She dug around for something, "I have it here somewhere." A few papers shifted and a stack of cards with leaves pasted on them fell to the floor. The sword smith pulled out a half rolled up scroll, "Here! The pyre siren and the mosun!" she showed Su-Lin the painting of two airy entities. A chord of recognition struck inside of Su-Lin. She was looking at a foreign depiction of a phoenix and a dragon. Something stirred inside of her as she began to feel. She began to feel a cosmic connection as truth was dawned upon her. Maybe there was a God, and maybe He was what connected all things together with His divinity.

"You must give this to Her!" the sword smith whispered loudly to Su-Lin. She shoved a tiny bottle into her hands. There was black smoke inside, but the essence was stronger. It looked to be the material that circled about the black pole on Quar.

"And this to Him!" she exclaimed excitedly. She thrust an equally sized bottle of white smoky essence into Su-Lin's other hand. The smoke seemed to glow softly.

"But you must take care when smuggling this, it is highly forbidden! Imagine! The very essence of Haiokasheeba and the Almarion, captured! When they receive it, have them mix the essence with water, they must drink it!" Su-Lin stared at the two tiny bottles cradled by her two palms. They entranced her.

"You are the true Kirin, but you will not live long enough to carry out the full role of messenger," the old wise woman said coming up to Su-Lin. Su-Lin's eyes looked at the old woman full of empathy. Something deep inside of her surged, as if coming alive for the very first time. She was finally tasting destiny.

"When Haiokasheeba was searching for the Almarion, she was searching for her love. When we search for love, are we not but searching for our own destiny? Without loving through ourselves, we cannot love at all. We cannot connect with our destiny, we cannot respect others, and we cannot become whole. What is destiny but finding the harmony within ourselves?" the wise old woman smiled profoundly into Su-Lin's eyes. Then turning to the sword smith, she spoke, "now, what weapon are we pairing this girl up with?"

Su-Lin mastered her moon swords. There was a pair, and the sword smith mixed the essence of the Almarion in one, and the essence of Haiokasheeba within the other. They were made of a titanium and cezonite alloy and shaped equally in two curved triangles. There were two points at the tip, one longer than the other. Beneath the handle was another point used for backward stabbing. One represented the waning moon, the other the waxing moon.

It was the end of the second year when Phoenix called Su-Lin back to Mars. Something was changing, and Phoenix wanted everyone close by. It was about time too. The wise old woman said she had taught Su-Lin everything she could by then. In a private sacred ceremony, the old woman took both of Su-Lin's hands in her own. She spontaneously combusted and left her essence inside of the young girl. When she returned to say goodbye to the village, they sensed the spirit of the old woman inside of her, and they all bowed to her in respect.

The unpleasant man, Mavius, was head of Preyal system council now. Phoenix had followed the election through the news, and when he won, she called everyone to Mars. She told them about her meeting with him nine years ago when he offered to buy the loyalty of division seventeen. This made everyone uneasy. They stuck close and stayed at SHONDS whenever they could. They could not help but feel Mavius was out to get them. Even Dave's father, who served on the council for Mavius felt distaste towards this new leader. He appeared empty when speaking to the council, devoid of his own thoughts.

It was also around this time that Phoenix had her first brush with the rebels against the governess. There was an attack on Liva and division seventeen chanced to be there. They had captured the leader Stregatori and held him for questioning. He said nothing and was near dead when more rebels rescued him. The governess told them to not pursue to rebels, they appeared to be nothing more than disgruntled citizens who had change forced upon them that they did not negotiate for. The governess Dikara actually shared their point of view. After all it was Yolukia who instated her with the position and not her choice to be there.

It was Angela who had voluntarily stayed up many nights in a row hacking away at multiple communication devices who discovered that Stregatori was working for Mavius. They could not share this information with anyone since it was discovered illegally and no one would believe them anyway. They appeared to be two disconnected cases. Mavius was bound to Preyal while Stregatori was a free lance rebel who squatted on backwater planets. Their positions appeared to be completely opposed. Nonetheless, this was valuable information for division seventeen to keep in their pocket.

Zyolious Sarces stayed for three years on Callyna studying more martial law. When the riots between the anti-governess and governess supporters got out of hand, she decided it was time to leave. She found herself broke down on Ceve in the Archimedes system and surrounded by anti-governess rebels. She left as soon as she could. She didn't care one way or the other about having a governess, she was learning to make peace, not war. One more trip brought her to Salineptra, the first artificially created planet in the galaxy. There, she was surrounded by intellects and scientists. That she could tolerate. She spent her days meditating and practicing her martial arts.

It was around this time that Dave's father passed away. He died of natural causes and left peacefully. He knew that he had done all that he could. Dave stayed by his father's bed every free moment he had. His father told him to warn Phoenix of Mavius. He told Dave that he knew Mavius was plotting against the governess, but there was just no damn proof anyone could get.

Dave accepted the information bravely. He had closure when his father passed away. He found a new devotion towards Phoenix and division seventeen. He would follow his leader now because his father respected her. For reasons he didn't understand, his father supported Phoenix and he would too, wholeheartedly. He felt as if he were the division's guardian. He would see things through until the end. If not for anything else, then for his father.

CHAPTER EIGHT

Blank pages on a diary, being filled up. Another secret identity, another life. Another point of view. Stories all the time, what was real, who knows anymore? People lose the way to their own heart sometimes.

"My name is Hannah. I am not gorgeous. I am not ugly." I don't know how, but I managed to screw things up. I don't do it on purpose, I guess I'm just too stupid to see the things going on around me. I don't think I'm self absorbed. But if I'm not, then what else could I have been?

It started a few years ago. Three to be precise. I was asked to go into hiding by a friend who knew that there were those out to harm me. I ran away to this place and changed my name to Hannah. I picked up life and kept low. It was the first time I had ever been in an urban scene like this. I had grown up in a moderately well off suburbanite family. I had never experienced first hand gangs and murderers and killers without self-control. It had everything to do with the ego and self and not purpose. I am not saying that I support purposeful killing or anything like that. I plead the fifth on whether or not there is blood on my hands. Since I've been here, I pretty much stay away from society and keep to myself. Living like this way was difficult. I had moved four times in the past three years.

I have a husband you know. I love him very much. At least as much as I humanly can. I mean, I would give my soul for him. My life is expendable. This however, could not prevent us from being excommunicated. For three years. I carry him in my heart. I don't know what he is up to and though I wonder sometimes, I know deep down that I can trust him. I am afraid for his safety and I know he is afraid for mine. For now, there is nothing I can do but sit tight and be away from him. Until it is safe again.

Toddie's is a bar a few blocks from where I live. I've been there a few times now and then. Trying to make some new pals. Or not. It was just something to do. I've noticed the regulars but no one has spoken to me yet. I guess its because I zone out at the TV. I figured if anyone wanted to strike up a conversation with me, they would.

There were two kinds of women in this city. The hardworking bitter women. And the bitches. The bitches outnumbered the hardworking women. The waitress at Toddie's is a hardworking single mother. The first time she served me, she didn't smile. Maybe she couldn't smile, it looked to have been a long day for her. Her face was emotionless. I've often heard the owner Toddie ask about her daughter.

"Hows your little gal?" he would ask. I tipped Kalle handsomely the first night. Since then she was able to offer me a tired grin whenever I would come in. I knew they probably talk about me when I wasn't around. I would be curious about me too. A young woman all alone.

There was Toddie behind the bar and occasionally Peggy would work too. Peggy was a bitch. I wouldn't blame her though, she was very pretty. Her motto was to be safe and not sorry. There were six regulars that were almost always at the bar. There was Billy and Jason who worked together in construction. Tom and his hardworking girlfriend Eliza were there every Tuesday and Friday. Then there were the Bevon brothers. They were twins but one of them had a slightly longer face. This intrigued me because I remembered what a wise old friend of mine had once said.

"Twins are always as one. It is just a pity that most of them can no longer tap into their connection." Some people believed this to be a scientific fact. Some just laughed. I had always believed it though. I'm not sure if the Bevon brothers possessed the connection or not.

One night, someone had accused Kalle of short changing him. I was watching and I know that she didn't. The Bevon brothers stuck up for Kalle. The drunk man pushed her and she fell into my table. I helped her up and asked if she was alright.

"Hey man, Kalle's our girl, she wouldn't short change you, let me buy you a drink," one of the brothers offered.

"Who the hell are you?" the man fumed. He punched him and before long, his friends were in the brawl. Of course his brother had to stand up for him. I don't know how I got dragged into it, but the fight was coming in my direction. As I tried to get away, some other drunk guy grabbed me in an offensive place. Of course I had to punch him in a place like this. Then one thing led to the next.

The brothers and I came out on top. Needless to say, we were all kicked out, but not before I left a shoe mark on the face of the man who started the fight. Outside, the first brother stuck out his hand towards me.

"Hi, I'm Ben. This here is my brother Ken." I smiled politely trying to stifle a laugh at their rhyming names.

"I know I know, our parents weren't very creative," he added in a lighthearted voice.

"I saw the way you kicked ass in there," Ken spoke up, "I'm very impressed. Ken was usually the quieter one.

"I like Kalle and I know about her daughter," I said in a soft voice, "Its late though and I've got to work tomorrow."

"Late? Come on, its only midnight. We know a bar a few blocks down owned by Toddie's friend, you sure you don't wanna grab a drink?"

"I'm sure," I said with a smile and turned to go.

"Please, we're just trying to get to know you," Ken added.

"Yeah," Ben added, "you've been at Toddie's quite a few times and we've never said hi, now that we got kicked out together and we all like Kalle, I say we should at least go get a bite to eat."

"Thanks for the offer, but I really can't," I turned them down gently.

"Will we ever see you again?" Ben asked.

"Yeah I'll be at Toddie's tomorrow," I called over my shoulder.

"Promise?"

"Promise!" With that I picked up my pace and left them behind.

It was about five in the morning when there was a knock at my door. Naturally, I wasn't asleep. I didn't really have a job. However, I do have roughly four million dollars at my disposal due to my banishment. I have to spend it sparingly because I do not know how long this will go on for. Plus, it isn't really my money.

Upon opening the door, I recognized four of the men from the drunken brawl at Toddie's. It wasn't long until my anger took over. More people died that night. They were trying to burn me in my apartment, they deserved it. I don't get a sick pleasure out of killing people, but sometimes I just get very angry. I was disappointed in myself. My anger had been raging out of my control more and more often. I am usually coolheaded, but being excommunicated for three years had done something to me. I don't know what it is, it is almost as if I were losing my mind. I wasn't here long and now I should probably move again.

All the residents escaped and were physically fine, but the building was gone. Along with it, burned their cherished memories and livelihood. Now, there will be more homeless people and the city never really do too much for them. I always tell myself, "Look what you did?" but the other part of me is numb and I just plain didn't give a crap.

Before I hit the road, I decided to keep my promise to the Bevon brothers in order to avoid suspicion. Fires and death happened all the time in the city. Even though I doubt anyone would really investigate further into the situation, I wanted to make sure I was kept in the clear.

I took a deep breath as I walked into Toddie's. I should've left, but I missed interacting with people. I just wanted to have a few drinks and laugh. The music was lively and my mood was a little better. Ben saw me first and waved, "Hey, how's the tough little fighter tonight?" I smiled a friendly smile and coolly walked up to Ken, "Is he always this loud?" I joked. They must've had a bet going onto see who I'd warm up to first. Ken turned and laughed mockingly at his brother as Ben sighed and ordered the next round of drinks.

They introduced me to Bill and Jason. Only Eliza was there. She was a bitch to most people, but she managed a smile for me.

"Its okay, Eliza's just an extreme feminist, if you hadn't whooped those guys' asses yesterday, she probably wouldn't even look at ya!" Bill said. The chat was friendly. They mostly talked about work. The brothers worked at a tractor factory. Not much later Eliza had to go. Toddie came over and said goodbye. He then joined in on our conversation and brought up the fire last night.

"Yeah I lived there," I said honestly. They all gave me a concerned look.

"My God, so you got anywhere to go?" Ken asked.

"I was just gonna get a hotel and then go to my mom's."

"But what about your job?" Ben asked. I had slipped but I caught myself, "Oh well, I hated it anyway. I'll find another" The two traded looks and Ken spoke up, "You're welcome to stay with us for a while if you don't mind." I gave a hesitant look.

"Shit, you could stay with any of us," Jason said.

"I mean its up to you," Ben ignored Jason.

"I really shouldn't."

"Alright," Ben agreed, "but if you ever are on the street, you could stay with us. I mean its not much, but there's at least a roof," he chuckled. No one hinted at me being the cause of the fire, nor the deaths. I relaxed.

"Come on guys, lets see what you're made of," I said buying everyone a round of drinks. After that, Toddie offered us a round on the house.

"So how come you never came over to say hi?" Bill teased. He was borderline flirting and I hid my discomfort.

"I dunno, I was in a new place and kinda shy I guess."

"That and she can't trust us hoodlums!" Ben joked before taking a shot. None of them questioned how I was able to leave a new job so quickly since I told them I was leaving for sure. I was slipping up more and more these days, but thank goodness the alcohol slowed everyone's awareness.

The hearty laughter felt great. It was something I had lost touch with the last couple of years. I had finished college at twenty two, and then things got messy and I was ordered to go into hiding. I tell people I'm thirty five but I am really only twenty five. That's what my fake driver's license says too, that I'm thirty five. Ben had asked me how old I was and we spent the last fifteen minutes comparing mug shots on our licenses. He was thirty two.

Soon, Bill and Jason had to leave. Not long after, it was closing time. Toddie let the three of us stay to keep him company. He gave Kalle a doll to take home. He said that his own daughter had outgrown it long ago. Kalle thanked him and left in a hurry to get back to her little girl.

"What's her daughter's name by the way?" I asked. I was acting pretty sloshed. Toddie answered, "Bridget," then let out a loud burp. He tried to continue over our laughter, "she's a sweet little thing, I've met her a few times. Such a pity she has to grow up here though." After a short silence, Toddie continued, "You know Hannah, I never thought you to be such a spirited young lady. No offense, but I thought you were one of those uptight bitches like Peggy," here he started to crack up, "uptight bitches that were tired from a day of being fucked and then have your pimp take all your money." Everyone exploded in laughter.

I laughed heartedly. It felt great to laugh. We laughed for a full minute before stopping. By then we were all exhausted and pretty drunk. Toddie told us that we had to go because he had to get home to his "old hag." Though they loved their women, men still feared them and covered their fear with insults.

The brothers lived in a studio. I think they offered me a bed but I passed out on the couch after a quick shower. I slept unable to be awakened.

I awoke lying on my stomach. The sunshine shown through the bare window and made a trapezoid on the ground. A gray musty smell tickled my nostrils mixed in with the smell of grime. I couldn't remember where I was. I heard mumbling and my head hurt. I sat up. Big mistake!

A sharp pain shot through my temple. I was pretty disoriented, it wasn't the alcohol, it was falling asleep for the first time in five days. I had slept awkwardly and my neck was pinched.

"Good morning sunshine, need some aspirin?" I turned and saw Ben holding a bottle towards me. I started to remember last night.

"Yeah, thanks," I got up and took the bottle. The two looked away from me, their faces red.

"What?" I asked. They didn't say anything. I looked down. The blanket slipped off when I stood up. It took me a while to realize that I wasn't alone and in my confusion last night, I had slept naked.

"Oh sorry," I wrapped the blanket around me and went into the bathroom. I put on yesterday's cloths making a mental note that I needed a toothbrush. I tried my best to brush my teeth with my finger. It didn't work when I was thirteen, I didn't know why I expected it to work now.

The coffee smelled good. The boys tried to make bacon and eggs but it came out a solid lump. I didn't care because it was thoroughly cooked and tasted fine.

"This is good," I said taking a bite, "Thanks."

"Hey that's ok," Ben joked, "we owed ya for the peep show earlier." I blushed. I put my fork down and looked at both of them.

"Listen up guys. I don't want to inconvenience you. I value your brotherhood and I trust that neither one of you would be stupid enough to give that up for a plain old girl like me. And sorry about the nude thing, I didn't remember where I was last night."

"That's fine, we've all seem naked chicks before," Ken said with a straight face. I didn't know if he was trying to be sarcastic or helpful. I dropped the topic.

I knew that I had to get going. But why did I have to be responsible? I was banished wasn't I? I wasn't supposed to be me, so why am I so concerned about responsibility? All I had to do was lay low. Besides, I was really tired of moving too. I kept telling myself that I had to go, but next week just kept being pushed along until it was next month, then it was another month later. I have been here for two months. It didn't bother the boys though and I wasn't itching to move again. That was until I saw Stregatori. He did not see me. I was out walking one morning and he was sitting in a car at a red light.

Stregatori meant Mavius was around. Mavius was the reason the counselor had banished me for my own safety. I was not allowed to act against Mavius for political reasons. So theoretically, he could kill me and no one could do anything. I hated it when the law failed to protect. No doubt Stregatori, Mavius' right hand man, was out looking for me. How he tracked me here, I'm not sure. But I had to leave soon before everyone I knew was in danger. I made plans to be gone by the next evening. However, when I had gotten back that night, the brothers were drinking again. They had gotten kicked out of Toddie's again for defending Kalle.

"Hey Hannah! We got a shot here with your name on it!" Ben called. I put a smile on that looked more genuine than I felt. I downed the shot. It couldn't hurt to spend one last night with my friends. It was a relaxed evening. Even Toddie showed up for a little while to drink with the boys. He wanted to show there was no hard feelings for kicking them out, it was just his job. I looked around at the laughing men and the feeling of being alienated and distant hit me like a supernova. Why couldn't I shake the feeling that it was too late?

I hated myself. Why couldn't I even cry? Was it because things like this have been happening since I was six years old? Things like Ciesa? Was I really as cold as I felt? I was walking to the store for some eggs and bacon. That seemed to be the guys' primary food. I walked by Bridget's day care. Kalle's daughter. I had never met the girl. But outside, there were police. Even though I was across the street, I saw the deep red letters on the white brick wall. "Phoenix." I shuddered.

"Another murder, such a shame, a little girl," I heard someone in the background say. Looking at the letters, unable to tear myself away, I knew everything Stregatori wanted me to know. He had gotten to Bridget. He knew me, my life here. How? I thought I did well to keep low. It didn't matter! Why was I being so goddamn selfish? The little girl was dead. I stood and stared at the bloody word. Me, I was Phoenix. I was written with innocent blood. I could feel it in my soul. Even from across the street on the other side of traffic. I knew I should have left two months ago. I brought this upon Kalle. Speaking of which, she was tearing through the crowd. She was crying. I could hear her in my mind and feel her in my heart. My heightened sense did not let me miss out on her emotions and for a moment it was almost as if I was in her body. I felt her pain and it stamped guilty all over my soul. No one around me paid any attention to me. They didn't know that I was responsible for that little girl's death. But I did. I knew and I hated myself. I wish I could make it all go away. I wish that I could turn back time and somehow prevent this from ever happening.

I heard a gunshot. Kalle was dead. She had taken a gun from an officer and shot herself. She couldn't go on anymore. Her life was too hard and just not worth it to her anymore.

I know that feeling. Believe it or not, this monster can feel. I know what it feels like not wanting to live anymore. I know that feeling. I do. I deserve it. But not Kalle, not Bridget. It was all my fault. All my fault. Everywhere I go, pain follows. Pain and destruction. I realized it was just like Ciesa dying, then Cora dying. They were dead. Dead. I wanted to laugh hysterically. It seemed as if the last tiny bit of sanity was slowly seeping out of my ears. I don't know why. I felt the same way I did when Ciesa died. Has my world shrank that much? How did I become trapped within my own head?

Ken was suddenly by my side. This reminded me of an incident last night. Ben had passed out early and Ken and I were attempting to pick up the mess we left. Out of nowhere, Ken fell into me and pushed me against the wall kissing me. The last time something like this happened, my husband stepped in. I pushed him off. I was alone.

"That's not fair!" he yelled. Ben snoozed on in deep sleep.

"Kennedy, stop."

"No! You walk around naked and you expect me to not want to fuck you! Its all your goddamn fault you fucking tease!" With that he knocked beer bottles onto the floor in a swooping motion. I watched in a trance as glass tinkled beautifully and loudly in miniature explosions sending shrapnel everywhere. Ken didn't turn to notice, he merely threw himself onto his bed. I picked up the broom and swept up the broken glass. When I was done, both of the guys were snoring. I brushed the incident off because I knew I was leaving soon. I felt no affection towards Ken and my husband was who my heart belonged to no matter what. Only he knew me and my secrets.

"Hey stranger," Ken said, diverting my attention to the present where we stood across from Bridget's daycare. I gave him a smile feeling a little uncomfortable. He probably didn't remember last night after all the alcohol.

"Hey," My voice was cracked.

"So whats going on across the street?" he asked. I didn't answer. He turned to me and saw my face, "what's wrong?" I turned and looked straight into his face, "Bridget," I choked and couldn't say anymore. For some goddamn reason tears decided to show in my eyes. I covered my face with my hands as the look of horror crossed Ken's face. I choked back a sob. Goddamn these fucking tears! I realized then that I loved Bridget. I had compassion for her hard working mother who loved her little angel. I realized that I felt like Bridget's guardian too. We had all watched over Kalle so she could take care of her little baby. We were all family in a way, all of us at Toddie's. Now Kalle was dead too. All my fault. So why am I still here? I started to wipe my tears away.

"Where's Kalle?" Ken asked gruffly. That did it. I started crying again. Why? Wasn't I strong enough to hold back my tears? I desperately needed my husband, anybody, Ara? Just a shoulder to cry on. As if he read my mind, Ken pulled me against him. I wanted to pull away. It just wasn't right to be against him, but inside I was hurting too much and I needed someone. Just long enough for me to get a hold of myself.

"Where's Kalle?" Ken asked again. I opened my mouth but couldn't speak. I always felt like a fish when this happened.

"Hannah?" He took my shoulders and gazed at me steadily as I wiped my tears away. The same way Natasha did so many times, and the same way Dragon did.

"Dead." That was all I could say. Ken waited patiently and I took a deep breath. Was I really this fortunate to have run into such a decent being in this city of hell? I continued, "she just shot herself."

"Oh God," he said with color draining from his face. I felt more tears coming. I bit my lip to stop them. Ken looked carefully at me, "we better get you home."

The walk home was short. I sat down at the table and Ken handed me a beer. I would've preferred tea, but I didn't really care. I was grateful not to be alone. I might just sob uncontrollably. I took a swig and noticed tears in Ken's eyes too.

"So its over huh? Just like that, their lives."

"Yeah," I squeaked.

"Why?" I knew that it was a general question, but all the guilt flowed back to me. I took another sip of the beer. It was never my favorite drink. The boys drank too much. I was drinking too much too. The answer to Ken's questions was: Me. I was the reason that they were dead.

"When is your brother gonna be back?"

"Soon."

"I need to talk to you guys, maybe Toddie too." Ken leaned over and looked at me with a look I didn't care to identify, "If you're in any kind of trouble," he said softly, "We can help you." I smiled politely but it could not cover the worry on my face. I got up and went to the window. My mind was in the clouds. I was thinking about home, about Mars and Jupiter.

Once, a sensei had told me that life and death came as karma, nothing we do should we blame on ourselves. He told me everyone I killed with my own hands were to die at my hands. It was all planned by a higher force. Still, it was hard for me to accept Bridget dying at such a young age. She was only four. I was six when I was recruited. Such young ages. I felt a tinge of resentment. I was angry that I was chosen and could not lead a normal life. Even when Natasha chose me, why didn't Old Matt and the committee reject me when I was up for review? I didn't care if I would have shared the same fate as Bridget, living was just terrible with the burden of a broken heart. I was so engrossed with my thoughts that I did not notice Ken's arms around me until Ben cam in.

"Hey guys," he said looking at us hesitantly. That's when I realized Ken still held an interest in me. Oh fuck how could I have been so damned naïve? I'm a fucking adulteress! This was an even bigger mess. I thought I saw jealousy or perhaps anger on Ben's face. How was I going to explain myself? I was stupid, but would anyone believe that? I thought I was finished with this bullshit in my younger years.

I sat them both down to talk. I got them both beers and they lit cigarettes. Ben looked a little pissed, Ken looked innocent. I took a deep breath and started.

"Guys, this is going to be complicated. I don't know if you know yet Ben, but Bridget and Kalle are dead, in a way, I am responsible." Ben looked a little surprised, "go on." He did not see the police and did not know about the blood. To him, what I had just said were just words. The loss had not hit him yet. I took another breath.

"I don't know if you remember when I said I stayed here because I expected that the two of you valued your brotherhood over me." Neither of them moved, they were still listening and sucking on their smoky tobacco sticks. "I'm also married," I slipped in at the end. Ben glanced nonchalantly my way.

"Sure, that's why you and Ken were holding each other."

"Oh come on now, you're just pissed because I made a move!"

Ken exploded.

"You knew that I liked her!" Ben shouted back. I covered my face and tuned out the shouting. I could not believe this was happening. They sounded like a bunch of little boys and they had the gall to fight in front of me like this. Why can't male and female coexist androgynously?

"Stop!" I shouted, I was getting pissed.

"You stay outta this!" Ben shouted. I was amused that he was ordering me to stay out of a dispute that was over me.

"Don't talk to her like that!" Ken shouted back. I was getting very angry. I was going to talk to about Kalle and Bridget, but they were fighting over me like a piece of meat. It was intolerable, but I sat still trying to keep myself neutral. I wasn't even this pissed when I had to put up with Evan a few years ago. They completely missed the point that I was married and didn't have interest in either one of them. Soon, a punch was thrown. That was my last straw. I got up and grabbed both of them by their collars. They struggled out of my grip and shoved me out of the way. I stumbled back a few steps in agitation. A bottle found it's way beneath my foot and I fell. Pissed off, I got back on my feet. They cat was out of the bag. I had no reason to hide any of my secrets, Stregatori knew where I was. I built up my adrenaline and used my real strength. I grabbed both of them by the collar and separated them, lifting them a little of the ground. That got their attention.

"Stop," I pleaded to both, "I'm just not worth it." I put them down and they straightened their cloths.

"We'll see about that." Ben took off as if he didn't realized I had just lifted him up as easily as a sack of potatoes. Ken walked into the kitchen. I locked myself in the bathroom and gathered what little things I had. I washed my face with cold water and looked at my reflection. What could have possibly made me worth fighting over? It didn't flatter me, it distressed me. Chaos followed me. I have an ordinary face. I am athletic, but there are many women who have figures similar to mine. It didn't matter, I still felt horrible. There is nothing worse than breaking siblings apart. Especially those who were bound by the same birth.

When I came out of the bathroom, Ken was sitting at the table again. When I told him that I was leaving, he got up and handed me my jacket. I didn't say a word. I noticed the pain in his eyes. I had to leave. I was causing too much agony. They thought that they were in love, but they didn't even know what love meant. They were fighting for possession.

I picked up the book bag containing all my things and slung it onto my back. Maybe I should introduce him to one of my sisters. I quickly rejected that idea. It was so stupid I didn't even know why I thought of it. I just missed them myself, that was all.

As I was opening the door, Ken reached over and gave me a hug. It was strange, how much he felt like my husband. The feeling quickly passed, but not before he stole a kiss from me. It was a deep kiss and I did not let it continue for longer than a second. Still, as I walked down the hall I was shaken with guilt. I felt like I was betraying the man I was bound to forever, till death due us part. It upset me so much that I could not breath properly. I did not look back as I quickly darted down the stairs.

I was lucky I had not run into Stregatori. The day I saw him on the street, he was oblivious of me. I am not sure why Mavius wants me dead. All I know is somehow, I am a threat to his tactics. The counselor had banished me to the planet of my real birth because it was a silent planet. Earth's ignorance protected me.

I do not know what happened. Or why I am here. I am still a little vague on the details due to my banishment. L.J. was locked up with me and Toddie. Why Toddie, I might never know. We were all arrested for some reason by the system's patrol officers under the counselor's commands.

"What the hell am I doing here?" Toddie fumed.

"Apparently the governess has a death sentence for division seventeen and a reward for whoever can do it." L.J. replied.

"Which is impossible," I added.

"Well why the hell not, and what the fuck did any of this shit have to do with me?" Toddie yelled. It was clear that he was exasperated.

"Because I am the governess. You could just be a mistake," I explained out of sympathy. I regretted the words immediately. I am not good with secrets. Toddie let out a sigh and slouched to the floor. The poor man. He didn't understand any of this. Whatever was going to happen, he didn't deserve a share of it. I myself was a little numb right now. First Bridget and Kalle, now Toddie might die. Could I never stop it? I was feeling attachment again. Perhaps I was getting old and craving family, who knows. Why couldn't I feel the way I once did, like death was just a part of life? Like I killed because I had to. Why was I feeling? A soldier doesn't feel. She or he merely acts on orders.

L.J. explained that we were in an underground prison in Oklahoma somewhere. She also updated me on Dragon. He was sent on a mission by the counselor and was granted immunity from Mavius. Still, I was very uncomfortable with him on a mission alone.

"He's not alone," L.J. added, "Scott is with him." She had said it solemnly. I didn't say anything. What could I say? Both of our husbands were on this mission. What can I do?

"I'm sorry," I finally stuttered. She didn't say anything. I realized it might have been better if I didn't say anything at all. Toddie was silent too, lost in his own thoughts.

It wasn't long until V came to join us. Angela Wallisky was with her.

"She's a lawyer on Mars now, she's going to be helping us out a lot," Veea explained of Angela. This had happened during my exile. I accepted the information with gratitude. I was just too happy to see these familiar faces once again.

It was only a few moments later when we were informed of the counselors arrival. We were brought into a questioning room, just me, L.J., V, and Angela. Toddie had to wait outside in the sitting room. The counselor sighed.

"I have some bad new Phoenix," he said to me, "apparently one of your friends was talking to someone who worked for Stregatori. He did it innocently at first. However, when Mavius made him an offer, he couldn't refuse. Do you know Benjamin Joseph Bevon?" Oh shit. I closed my eyes for a moment. I could not believe it was Ben. Or could I? I knew they were too good to be true. I opened my eyes and looked straight at the counselor, "How did he know who I was?"

"He didn't, Benjamin's friend thought you matched the description, he told Stregatori who then went to spy on you. Afterwards, Stregatori found Benjamin." I took a deep breath, "How deep are we in?" Now it was the counselor who sighed. He continued with a sympathetic look, "Mavius grows stronger in politics. I am afraid that there is not much I can do anymore. He has made you a public enemy on Uranus and amongst the Hayessans. I am afraid I cannot do much to protect you." He paused and I was deep in my own thoughts.

"Tell us about the governess," L.J. asked.

"I don't know, but I think right now you should be worrying about Dragon," he said sympathetically. Bewildered, L.J. and I stared at him.

"Why?" she demanded in a tense whisper.

"He's been missing for a few days now. Our trackers went off line and we couldn't find a reason."

"And my husband?" L.J. demanded.

"The same. As you know, they were together."

We left the room in a dark mood. First things first, what to do about Toddie. And Ken. I was still disturbed from that kiss. I didn't have a chance to tell my sisters yet. Now wasn't the time. After some discussion which brought up the topic of Kalle and Bridget, we decided that Toddie should stay at the prison. The people at the institute in Oklahoma would look after him. Before we set out to find Ken, we said goodbye to the counselor as he left. He was a good man. I just hope he doesn't get pulled deeper into this mess and get killed.

"You never said you were a triplet," was the first thing Ken said to us when we approached him. V looked at me questioningly. I ignored the look. She was merely questioning the company had I had been keeping.

"You have to come with us," Angela demanded firmly.

"Why?"

"To keep you safe," L.J. interjected. I didn't say anything. I had a frog in my throat. I was no longer comfortable around Ken. He though he loved me, and he shouldn't. I could never love him back. But it was my fault wasn't it? I was too ignorant to see it, I just led him on. I was overly confident in myself and thought that I had everything under control. The exile and living with oblivious people must have clouded my mind.

Ken was finally persuaded and he was brought to the same cell as Toddie. They were happy to see each other, but not too thrilled to be in the cell. We made sure that there were proper furnishings to make living as comfortable as possible. After all, they were there to be protected, no to be imprisoned. I still haven't found the right time to tell him about Ben yet. I just kept putting it off, like I kept putting off moving away from them. I knew it was wrong, but I needed time to find courage. Battlefield courage I have. I can kill the enemy, I simply slip myself into an apathetic mode. That's what soldiers were trained to do. But people I know and have had in my life make things difficult. Like now. It's hard when you know someone. It's funny, after all I had been through, there's still a lot I have yet to learn.

V and Angela started to hunt for Ben. We had to find out what the damage was before it was too late. L.J. and I were to track our husbands and find out what was going on.

The four of us lived in a little house in Texas not too far from the institute in Oklahoma. It wasn't much, but our large basement was packed full of equipment and weapons. Everything was standardized. I pray that this would all go by smoothly without any violence since I was still not allowed to leave Earth. If anything were to happen, civilians would undoubtedly be dragged in.

Three days passed since the counselor left and I finally worked up the courage to see Ken. I was nervous being unsure of his reaction. I didn't want to be cruel and speak to him as a stranger, but if I did not keep my voice clear of emotion, I doubt I could've done it. I chewed my lip as I walked through hall to their cell room. I knocked twice and entered. Toddie smiled and greeted my happily, "Hey young lady! Never thought you'd be responsible for me getting this here royal treatment. Still haven't thanked you yet." It was true, their cell had been made very comfortable. They were fed three square meals a day and had access to a recreational facility.

"Its alright," I replied, "I should be sorry, I come bearing bad news." The two sat in their easy chairs. I myself chose a straight backed chair.

"Kennedy Stephen Bevon," I started in my official voice, "your brother Benjamin Joseph Bevon has joined with a very powerful politician who is set out to find my demise." I swallowed. The two just look at me, confused.

"Keep in mind that you do not have to believe a word I say. However, I know he has someone impersonating an extremely powerful figure in law. Why he wants me destroyed escapes my knowledge. I am just here to tell you what I know," I paused. No one even twitched a finger.

"Thank you for your cooperation, have a nice day." I got up to leave.

"Wait what is this?" Ken asked standing up. I slowed my walk towards the door. I didn't turn around, I couldn't face them.

"Stop!" Ken cried, "please." My steps stopped. I shouldn't have to be here listening to this fool. Ken sounded in pain, "I mean, you're coming in here and telling me that my brother is out to kill you. Not just that, but you're talking to us like you don't even know us. What kind of shit is this? It's like we didn't even know you! We don't fucking know you!" His was very angry but I could feel a twinge of pain in his voice. What a fucking mess.

"I'm sorry," I said flatly.

"And you won't even look at us when you're talking to us! You're afraid! I don't care if there are people trying to kill you and you think you're all high and mighty. You're just fucking scared, you can't even face us," he cried, "not even me." I didn't say anything. I didn't move. I could sense Toddie's discomfort.

"I really thought we had something," Ken continued, he was a lot calmer now, "and you're telling me that you are already married and my brother is some psycho. I can't believe you, he had a thing for you too." I turned to face him. He was a little taken aback by my eyes, I could tell by the way he looked unsure of himself.

"There never was an 'us,' thus, we never had anything. I apologize for my own ignorance towards your feelings, but this ridiculous courtship has to end. I have to leave now."

"Why?" His voice was very soft. I don't know what it was, but blew away all the anger I had a moment ago. The poor man was just stupid. He could never comprehend what I was nor could he understand why I killed. At that moment, he alienated me. It was just Dragon, division seventeen, and myself versus the world. No, versus the galaxy.

"I'm not that pretty," I blurted out. I bit my lip to prevent anything else stupid from spilling forth. That was not what I meant to convey at all.

"No, but you are a hell of a person. To all of us at Toddie's, you are just the most fucking gorgeous thing. Just you, something about you. You grab a hold of people and you don't let them go, even Eliza. She admires you. It's a power. You think we're the only ones who see it? What about Bill and Jason?" his voice turned emotionless, "I guess you just don't know what kind of witch you can be, casting spells left and right." I was floored. I reached a new emotional low. The compliment was more of an insult, a parent inflicting emotional abuse to a child who was very bad.

"Isn't that right Toddie?" Ken asked. Toddie let out a heavy sigh, "Leave me outta this," he sounded tired. I swallowed, "I have to leave now."

"Fine then leave." I walked out of the room. "Where the hells that husband you love so much, not fucking here," he muttered pessimistically under his breath as I shut the door. I rubbed my eyes and walked quickly down the corridor. I should have slapped Ken to defend Dragon, but this whole mess was my fault. A few steps more and the feeling disappeared. I once again felt a connection with my division, no matter how dispersed we were at the moment. I stopped dead in my tracks, turned and went back to the room. I had all intentions to slap Ken but I couldn't. Everything he felt was partially my fault as well. I picked him up by the collar and stood him in front of me. I gave him a look a teacher often gave a naughty child, "I am not afraid of having feelings, I have them and I have been broken more times and in more ways than you can possibly fathom. And you, don't you dare ever to speak about my husband like that ever again. He is a man you will never be. And me, I am something that will only hurt you more and if you were wise, you should have learned your lesson on women long ago." I turned and left. I could feel the cuts I have made on Ken's heart. I am not a very nice person. Why do I even bother pretending to be? That whole scene back there was totally unnecessary and quite immature. I just needed to find a release and end what should not have ever been started. Ken would be alright. Ben was the real problem.

I went to Bridget and Kalle's funeral alone. I explained to Ken and Toddie that it was not safe for them to go. Ken ignored me. Toddie was not too happy, but he asked me to say a prayer in his absence.

There were not that many people at the funeral. There were some of the regulars at Toddie's. Kalle's mother was there. She was sobbing. I forced myself to stay throuh the entire funeral process. My self loathing was unbearable at times. Bridget's father was there too. He was no where near Kalle's mother. Bridget was obviously not in Kalle's plans. But what does it matter? They were both dead now. I didn't let myself think too much or else my emotions would have overflowed.

Not long after, I was on my way home. Kalle's mother and best friend stood by her and Bridget's graves. I gazed sadly at them. There was nothing I could do. I started my car and left.

On the way home I forced my thoughts away from the funeral. I let my mind wander over facts. After some cross calculations with Earth's calender and Livan days, I realized that the governess was due for a meeting in two weeks. It was urgent that I speak with the counselor again to see what else he could tell me. What am I going to do when I arrive on Liva and there is someone on the throne? How are they going to believe that I am the real governess?

The house was empty when I got there.

"Hello?" We were out in the middle of nowhere so they had to have taken the cars to go anywhere. I checked. All three were still there. That was strange. I checked the basement. No one. It was starting to get a flash back of when I was five years old. I came home and Sarah was missing. I went back into the kitchen. On the floor I found the note V had left me. I sighed with relief. "Angela and I took a cruiser to Mars. -V." I relaxed. I read the note again. Where's L.J. then? That was the last conscious thought I had.

I awoke hours later jammed in a tiny space. My mind was woozy and I could not figure out for the life of me where I was. I opened my mouth to ask no one in particular about what was going on, but all that came out was a groan. I closed my eyes to avoid my blurry vision. I was fighting to stay conscious. Somehow through the mind fog I realized how strange this was. There were hardly any accessible drugs that could do this to me. It had to be someone from Mavius. I would have panicked about now, but I was too drugged. Just before I slipped into darkness again, the craft jolted violently. I squeezed my eyes tightly shut and swallowed hard to avoid vomiting. I hit my head and fell back into darkness.

When I opened my eyes again, my mind was much clearer and I saw L.J. holding a cotton swab over my arm. No doubt she just injected me with the antidote.

"What was that?" I asked groggily.

"Antidote to diluted trexia, it was attacking your healing systems," a familiar voice answered above me. I looked up and saw that my husband was holding me up.

"Wayne!" I exclaimed and weakly wrapped my arms around him. All the pain and guilt was swept away with a rush of happiness. It had been too long.

"I missed you so much," I whispered with tears in my voice.

"Me too," he replied softly, "you scared me for a moment there kiddo."

"I saw your buddy Ben," L.J. spoke up getting straight to business, "I followed him. I didn't want to bother you at the funeral and V was gone. I figured since we're not under mission I acted alone and silent. I found these two on Venus in a coma with the same trexia dilution in their veins," L.J. indicated Wayne and Scott, "Now we know that Mavius has access to inhibitor drugs." Her eyes turned steely to reflect the gravity of the situation, "It's gotten more dangerous, sis."

"That's not all," Deklar added, "Ben's been altered. Its not advanced like ours, but he can live on other planets. He has slightly increased speed and physical strength too." Scott officially saluted me as I got to me feet, "I have already contacted Moongirl and Angela on Mars. They left a message at the institute and wanted us to know that they were taking Kennedy to Mars for a body alteration too. They were hoping that his enhanced telepathy would help us locate Benjamin, who has been labeled a threat."

"Jesus, is there anything else?" I asked tiredly, " I can't believe how little I've been informed." L.J. and Dragon exchanged looks. I rubbed my temples, "shit, what is it?"

"We have the false governess in the basement right now," Dragon replied. I perked up. This was interesting.

"Who is it?" I asked. Deklar answered, "A clone, of you." I immediately knew that I had fucked up far beyond what I had imagined. Ben, it had to be Ben. He got them a tissue sample of me.

"How the hell did Mavius know she was the governess anyway?" Dragon exclaimed.

"Damned if I know," his brother answered.

"He hasn't released anything to the presses yet, but its definitely blackmail material," L.J. added.

"Let me speak with the clone," I said to Deklar. I was feeling much stronger now. I had better start sorting through this mess.

"I should probably warn you," Deklar spoke up, "she's a programmed clone."

"What characteristics?" I asked heading down the stairs.

"Hatred, Anger, Intelligence, and Strategy."

"What type of personality package?"

"None." I turned to face Deklar, "None?"

"Yep, no fears, no favorites, she wasn't even afraid to die. She was programmed with a mission and the four characteristics. No fear of anything." I took a deep breath and reached the bottom of the stairs.

"We were on our way back," L.J. spoke, "and we noticed her ship. The DNA scanner picked up our DNA so we thought it was either you or V. We tried calling you. There was no answer but we were certain we detected our DNA on board. We called twice. When you didn't answer the second time, we attacked. Here she is."

"Pure luck we foiled Mavius twice today," Deklar said. I was thinking, "Or maybe it's a trap." No one else said anything, they were thinking the same thing.

We reached the bottom of the stairs. I looked at my clone. She just stared back at me with empty eyes. I could see hatred burning inside of her, but no soul. I wondered what it would feel like to have no fear whatsoever. It would not be life. There was no point to living if you can't be afraid to loose things you love. It wouldn't be human not to have any hope, nothing to live up to. I had long ago discovered that there was no meaning to life, you had to make one for yourself.

I just stared back at those seemingly lifeless eyes. I just stared and tried to imagine what it felt like to be her. I placed my hand on hers. She didn't move, but a disgusted look contorted her face. My face. I began to feel sorry for her. Just a little bit. Then it grew into compassion. I pitied her, she had life breathed into her, but she was not living.

I noticed a small change start to take form in her features. It was mild discomfort. She didn't move though. Then her features slowly started to contort into resentment.

"What the fuck!" She screamed and started to thrash. I pulled back and held up a hand to stop those who made a move to restrain her. She kicked and twisted until the chair fell over. She tried to kick free while profusely screaming all the curse words known in living tongues. It was no use. She could not free herself from what I had just given her. I was not sure how, but in that moment when my hand was on hers and I was looking into her eyes, I gave her love. That love would grow into a soul. It was something I could not explain, but somehow it had happened.

"She's crying," L.J. whispered with fascination, "she's not supposed to cry." It was pretty rude of us, staring at her as if she was a freak show. No one moved. I waited until my clone's sobbing had subsided. She turned her head towards me. Her eyes burned with a hatred that had the power to kill. She stared deep within my soul. I knew it was impossible though. She was not yet human. She could not feel my soul. Yet I was confident that one day she would be.

"Inject her with a sedative. Make sure she is tied down. L.J. and Deklar, you are to take her to the Service Unit on Neptune. She is to do community service. I'll send a message ahead of you."

"Permission to speak," Dragon requested. I nodded.

"Would it be wise to let Mavius know where we are and that we have his clone?" I answered confidently, "There will only be an uprising and system wide panic if we kill him. But I am sick of this run and hide bullshit, I say its time we gave him a piece of our minds."

"Should I call up the rest of the division with a formal consent to meet?" Dragon asked. I thought for a moment. Then I answered then through telepathy, something I had not used in a very long time, "First ask the counselor to grant a dismissal on the banishment granting us leave from our assigned planets. Then we will meet back at SHONDS on Mars." The three smiled. We have been scattered to the wind. Now it was time for us to reunite.

It was great to be back on Mars. The counselor was very hesitant, but things was getting out of control. It was safer for the rest of us to be reunited. Wayne and I waited in the meeting hall for the rest of the division. This is where I told him about Ken.

“I'm sorry I was really stupid and I don’t know how I didn’t see it,” I apologized. A part of me wondered if I did see it but just shut out the signs because I missed the attention. Or maybe I had been away too long, been away from a normal life and then tossed back into the mix. Then I was stuck there for a few years and my natural instincts started to get blocked. How else would Stregatori have found me?

“It isn’t fair,” I added, “Everyone else has to help clean up the mess that I made.”

“True,” Dragon agreed, “but something like this was going to happen sooner or later and all of us are still the target.” I smiled at him.

“So,” he said getting up, “I think you should stop kicking yourself,” he wrapped his arms around me and I laughed. He continued, “and let the inevitable happen.”

“So you’re not mad at me about the whole Ken thing?” I asked. Here, he paused thinking how to word himself.

“No, I’m not mad, but I am jealous. Phoenix I believe you that you really didn’t know what you were doing, I can tell by looking in your eyes. But they aren’t us and they did react to you and that I am upset about, but I’ll forgive. Just keep in mind that it is the same Earth where we grew up and out here we are freer in some aspects than back there.” I felt really stupid like a spoiled little brat out to destroy everything just so I could get what I wanted.

“You’re not a brat.”

“Was it that obvious what I was thinking?” I asked him. He held me tighter and I felt the world churn in happy colors and beautiful music.

There was a knock on the door that cut the sweet moment short.

"Come in," I called. Reluctantly, Dragon let go of me and eased himself into a chair next to mine. We had to remain professional. The door opened and Su-Lin came in, "Am I late?"

"No," I chuckled, "You're the first one here." She passed a small smile that faded quickly. I always wanted to ask her what was wrong, but I was confident that she would tell us whenever she was ready. Telling would be torture for her. It was her secret burden to bear.

"Ah yes," Su-Lin started sarcastically as she closed the door behind her, "back to being a slave of a life that is being forced to live."

"Amen sister," I agreed. She gave me a look and nodded. "Are we alone?" she asked both Dragon and myself. I nodded. She approached us quite close and quite informally. She pulled something out of her small uniform pouch strapped to her leg. She unwrapped the leather cloth that held it together and revealed two vials.

"I meant to give this to you three years ago, but you were exiled before I could." She handed the black vial to me, and the white one to Dragon.

"I am not exactly sure what is in them, but my guess is it is an alien essence that represents the phoenix and dragon spirits. I was told to tell you to mix them in water and to drink it, but I will leave that decision to you. Where I was, was a place I doubt our enemies have a connection with." In her mind, Su-Lin told us it was a place of profound serenity and peace. Another knock at the door prompted Dragon and I to hide the vials in our own pouches. More division members arrived. They all approached me and acknowledged me with a polite bow.

"Where are Will and Charles?" I asked no one in particular when the rest of them had arrived.

"Did you send a message to Charles?" Kirin asked with a slight mandatory bow of the head.

"Yes," Charles was declared an unofficial member. His behavior had improved but he was still more or less pessimistic about things. Before I could say anything more, Angela personally rushed in with a message. Something had to be wrong if it is her personally and not a messenger. She came straight up to me and lowered herself onto her right knee. With her head bowed low she handed me an envelope. I hated these formalities, they were such a waste of time, but I couldn't change anything. I skimmed over the report. At first I wasn't sure if I had read it correctly, so I double checked.

"Thank you Angela you can get back now," I spoke quickly. She left quietly.

"I have some bad news," I swallowed, "Charles and William are dead. The council was told that it was an accident. They were, can you believe this, being robbed supposedly. Great."

"How much do they know," Dragon asked. Being second in command, he did not have to bow or anything. Thank goodness.

"I don't know," I shrugged, "But we better get moving, they can come and arrest us with any silly excuse at anytime." I wasn't sure what we had to do, but I spoke my thoughts anyway, "We are held on contract not to leave the solar system. I have to return to Liva in less than two weeks. It is possible for me to arrange for all of us to leave. But here is the problem. Mavius is probably going to do something drastic to draw us out. With his authority he can easily frame us."

"Why is the council so stupid, they are practically handing him power," Dragon spoke up.

"I don't know," I answered, "I would like to issue specific orders for us as the governess, but if I do, it would seem too suspicious."

"Permission to speak," Zap requested.

"Speak."

"If you do, Mavius would leave us alone for good wouldn't he? I mean, he wouldn't be stupid enough to mess with the governess."

"I don't know," I replied, "I don't know if he has any higher friends who might make things more complicated than they already are." In my mind, I was already contemplating a coupe against Mavius as Phoenix. I know that as the Governess, my job was to keep the peace and change this galaxy into a better place. However, as Phoenix, I am responsible for the safety of Earth and the solar system. The council was becoming obsolete and Mavius was only getting stronger. He's up to no good. Problem was, I did not want to become another Cassius before Julius had become the evil dictator. Yet also, I cannot ignore the fact the Mavius wants me dead and my division gone. There was also the issue of the governess' volatility. The galaxy is still adjusting to her presence and too many people want her gone. Phoenix was going to have to be very careful and not let disturbances in Preyal reach Liva.

Closing the diary. Sometimes, scattered thoughts are best organized after being seen on paper. It can leave people with a fresh perspective after spitting out what was already done.

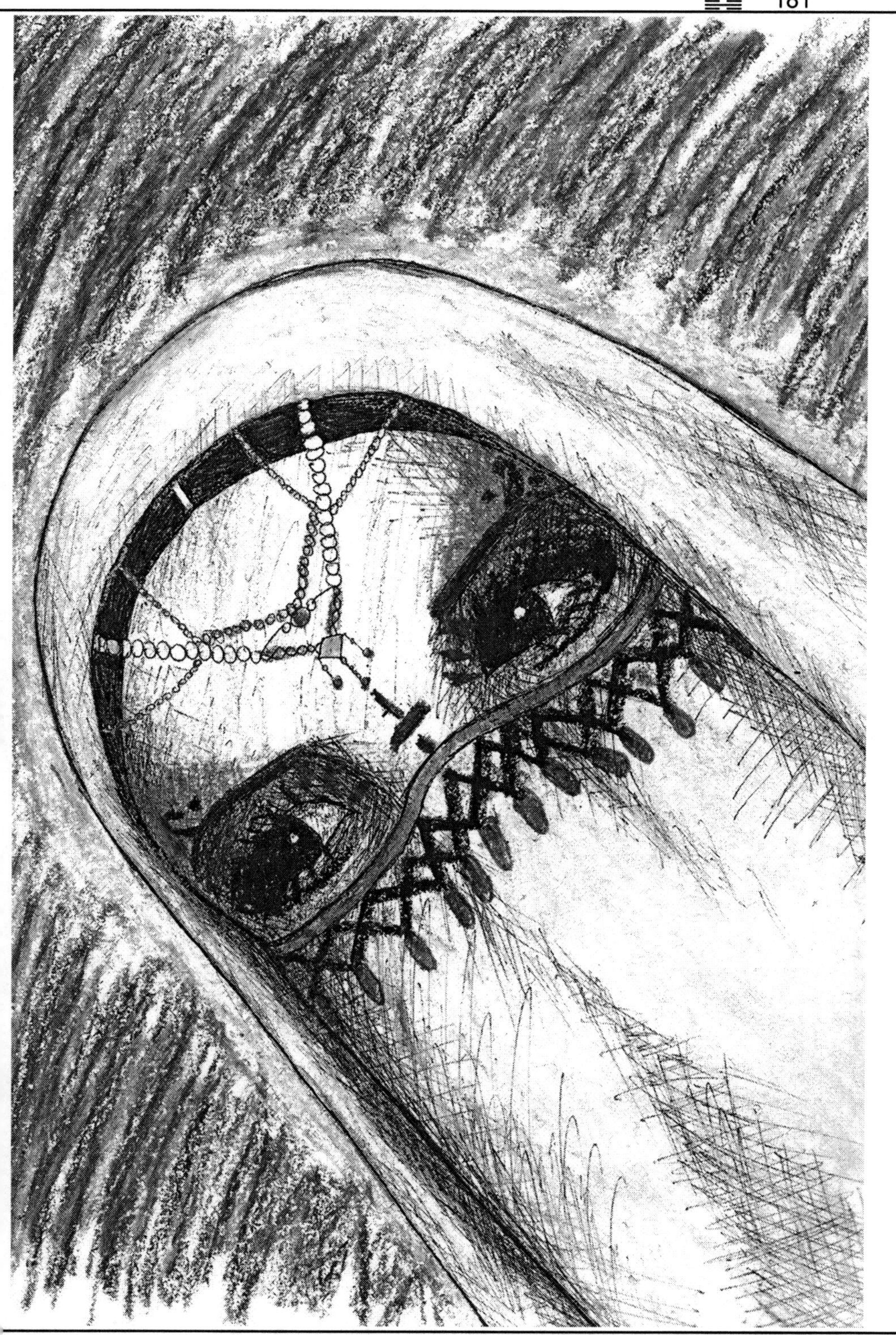

CHAPTER NINE

Ken was sitting at the SHONDS meeting hall with a smug grin on his face. His purpose there was there to aid division seventeen. He was amazed with all the capabilities he possessed after his Alteration. They explained to him that he would have an enhanced brain which meant that he would have a better chance at ESP. That in turn might lead them to his brother. Ken had accepted that his brother was against Hannah, or rather, Phoenix. Yet he was still not sure where his loyalties were to be. He knew that he should do what was right and help them bring him in, but it was his twin brother. For now, until he made up his mind, his goal was the same as division seventeen, and that was to locate his brother.

Hannah, he had given up on. She was still so beautiful. It was true she had very ordinary features and her figure was athletic but average, but there was a life in her eyes that screamed for his adoration. He had never felt this captivated before and was almost sure that she could be the one to spend the rest of his life with. Just as well, she was like all women. She was just teasing him and she was married. What a bitch.

Jessie had spoken alone to V and Angela on the topic of Ken. She had some unsettled feelings, “Do you really expect him to betray his brother?” she had asked.

“Well, it's complicated,” V answered, “he didn’t care for him when he crushed on, you know,” V said when she wasn’t sure what name to use, either Hannah, Rosi, or Phoenix, “but finding out that she’s hitched might have an adverse effect. Still, she claims she owes it to him to at least trust him.” Jessie rolled his eyes, “If she says so, but I am keeping my guard up.” Angela nodded in agreement. Sometimes, Phoenix let it get too personal and it became inconvenient for everyone.

The secretary of the province of Nurmana was at SHONDS again. After his carelessness with Old Matt’s soldiers, he had been to SHONDS less and less. This time, there were no commands, just a message for them. He spoke to the powerful Phoenix as if she were a useless peon. He was protected by the law and did not fear her.

“You are not to act against Mavius no matter what,” he commanded.

“But he wants us dead,” Phoenix replied flatly.

"Where is it written?" he demanded.

"I don't care what you have to say, everyone knows it, why isn't anyone doing anything about it?"

"There's no solid proof," he began.

"I will not be like the old Dragon and be forced to send my people into danger."

"You cannot disobey a decision made by the council," he scolded with disdain while pushing an ugly scowl across his face.

"The council is ruled by Mavius," anger was starting to interlace into her voice.

"Then you will have to be tried and pay the consequences of alternative action." His voice was final. Phoenix glared at him. Her anger was rising incredibly fast. She fought the urge to tear him to shreds. He must have sensed it because fear flashed across his face. It left when he realized that even though she was physically more powerful, she was still under his command. Sometimes things might not be fair, but they usually worked in his advantage.

"Leave, now." Phoenix demanded.

"You can't tell me," he began. Phoenix backhanded him, "I love my people so you take your fucking politics and get the hell out of SHONDS." Forgetting that he pretty much owned SHONDS he cowardly scurried back into his escort craft and drove away in a hurry. Phoenix stared after him. The redness was fading from her brain. She realized that once again her anger had won over her and she used it again like when she killed all those people who tried to burn her in her apartment. That was very bad. Old Matt never got angry and neither did Natasha. Maybe she just wasn't mature enough. Being 25 didn't mean that she had all the experiences needed to command her division. All she knew was that they were all she had

.

Ken squeezed his eyes shut and concentrated. He was on Jupiter. Phoenix and Angel, which was L.J.'s code name, had taken him to some sort of religious ceremony. These ceremonies were held because some people believed that they could communicate with the dead and others believed they could hear the thoughts of those who lived far away. Phoenix knew that it had to do with the poles and their alignments creating a magnetic pulse that aided in telepathy. She explained this to Ken as they lit their candles. A pale green flame danced upward to the beat of the music. He was very quiet. Ever since he had met Dragon and knew that Phoenix's love for him was unbreakable, he had chosen solitude. He was stubbornly abiding to the archaic concept of love and marriage as a contract of possession.

Dragon was very gracious to Ken. He just nodded and acted as if nothing was amiss. However, on the inside, he wanted to punch him. Just a hit. That should cure all his frustration, but he kept himself under control. If he was to blame anyone, it would be Rosi, but he didn't have the heart to. This whole thing was an accident and he should just let it go. Ken's attitude was the real agitator.

The three of them had held their candle and walked in a long curving line with hundreds of other spectators in robes. The robes were the colors of Jupiter's clouds. There was soft orange and brilliant reds mixed with a smooth yellow and a hint of mineral green.

Ken could feel something. It was Ben and he was angry. This was amazing, it felt as if they were in a common mind. After walking in the long lines, they were broken up into groups and they went under a huge canopy to contact whoever they wished.

"Ben!" he called out with him mind in amazement. He felt Ben twitch as if his attention was distracted, the anger faded a little bit.

"Who's that?" Ben had said.

"Holy shit bro! Its me! Ken!" Ken smiled when his brother heard him. Angel and Phoenix looked at each other. Phoenix nodded and they each took one of Ken's hands. He didn't notice at all, he was absorbed with his brother.

"Ken? Where are you what's going on?" Ben demanded.

"I got this alteration thing too and they needed me to find you, why what's wrong?" Ken asked. Neither of the Bevon twins realized that Angel and Phoenix were listening to their conversation.

"I'm so glad to hear you, listen up buddy, I've been trying to find you too, I've got this deal that you can't pass up. I just hope you still aren't stuck on that Hannah."

"Nah."

"Good, listen, where are you? In Texas still?"

"No, I'm on Jupiter, can you believe that?" Ken said.

"Jupiter? I'm here right now, I can come pick you up. Can you describe anything around you?"

"I'm at this religious thing where they're all holding candles and trying to talk to the dead."

"Oh that's easy. Can you get anywhere that I can easy see you,

I'll be flying there."

"Yeah there's a hill that don't have too many people on it, I'll go there," Ken said.

"Alright, I'm heading out right now, I'll need to concentrate so I can't talk to you anymore."

"Fine," Ken opened his eyes, "I heard him!" he cried aloud to Phoenix, "That was sweet!" Phoenix smiled at Angel, they remember when they first discovered their telepathy.

"He said that he's back on Earth looking for me," Ken lied. Phoenix glared at him, "Ken," she began.

"I think you guys should go, I want to learn more about Jupiter," he lied. Phoenix got angry, "Ken!" she shouted. Some people turned to stare but looked away when Angel glared at them. Phoenix continued in a quieter more restrained voice that was equally as strict, "We know he's here and he is looking for you on the hill, further more, you aren't allowed anywhere without being escorted by one of us.

"You were listening?" Ken challenged, "That's a violation of my privacy."

"Out here, you don't have the same rights," Angel said flatly.

"Yeah and that little lie of yours there could have cost you your life," Phoenix's tone was final. Angel cuffed him and the three marched up the hill.

So Ben did know they were listening. It was an ambush. More people died. Lives that went to communicate with the dead and the lost souls ended up losing their lives that very day. Phoenix and Angel lost track of Ken. Phoenix felt stupid and irresponsible. She was not yet back into the swing of things. The three years had made her mind mushy and instincts rusty. She was going to have hell to pay. This time, it was not explaining to an authority figure the details of what went wrong. This time, she put in danger the people who supported her. No matter how L.J. tried to comfort her, Phoenix could not forgive herself and her stupidity. She had underestimated the power that Mavius gave to Ben and now they lost the only way to track them.

I am Rosi's desk at her home on Mars. I have papers strewn about me. My lonesome owner is standing sadly by the window. If I were not made of wood, I would have flesh. In this flesh I would have found my eyes. They could be blue, or maybe even green. From these eyes I can see my Rosi. Her face is sallow and she is about to cry. She would never let herself cry. So I would take her tears and let them flow from my eyes instead. These would be the same eyes that can read the lonely little note that sits on top of me.

Phoenix,

I hate to be the bearer of bad news, but a friend of mine is investigating a death on Neptune. Your clone, the one that faked being the governess, is dead. A jet craft hit her. They say it was an accident but my friend doesn't think so. Were they after you? Or did Mavius find out she failed? I thought I should let you know.

All the Best,

Deklar

This evil little note is what caused her pain right now. If I were made of flesh and not wood, I would tear it up for her. If the note were flesh and not wood like me, I would strangle it. Thus, never ending this cycle of pain and suffering where vengeance is a deadly plague that slaughters life.

Shh. She speaks. My Rosi is speaking to herself.

"She was so good. She changed. She could have done so much more." I did not understand what she just said. She comes back from the window. Her eyes are still dark and lonely. She sits down and brushes the note aside. Placing a fresh piece of paper on my wooden, not flesh, surface. She begins to write. I can feel the pen on my surface, and now I understand her sadness.

Deklar,

Thank you for the information. I understand the dangerous situation. Even though she was not the most model citizen when we first met her, she had turned into a saint. I have been tracking her progress. She has a large number of faithful followers on Neptune. She has helped many broken people start new lives and is very self-sacrificing. I cannot help but shudder at the hopelessness of this world, this galaxy, at times. I sincerely apologize that we are all in contact with each other and all that this division has to offer is danger. I wish as our leader I can make things better so people like her will no longer have to die.

All the Best,

Phoenix

My Rosi places the pen down and folds her arms on top of me. She puts her head down and lets out a slow sigh that brushes across me. In the flesh that I do not have, there would be arms that would wrap themselves around her. I could caress her hair and out of the mouth that I do not have, I will tell her that everything will be alright.

Rosi was miserable. The clone did not have a name when she died. Rosi named her at the funeral. Her name was Hope Forre Peace. In the time of a little over a year, Hope had grown into an incredible person, blossoming into an angel. She had many followers but only one formal student. Her name was Leffi and she was a recovered abductee from Africa. Leffi was miserable when Hope died. She wandered around aimlessly, trying to discover the reason for misery in life. Not long after, she ended up training with Angela at SHONDS.

They whole event blew over without any officials knowing the governess was temporarily replaced. Almost immediately after the incident, the real governess implemented the first iron-fisted law since her ruling began. She placed limitations on cloning. Each cloning procedure had to be reviewed by six system medical boards and approved unanimously. This was a secret message out to Mavius as well. At these early stages in the game, the two were poking at each other from a distance, like splashing water, testing each other.

Existing clones were allowed to stay since they were ex post facto. The reality was that Phoenix could not part with her sisters. She often questioned if her decision was selfish, but she knew the answer would come later.

Obviously Mavius had obtained the DNA for the programmed clone from Wrie. It was all her idea to cause Phoenix anxiety thus adding to her confusion. Dikara the governess had no idea of Wrie's existence. She thought Mavius was the mastermind behind everything and was actively searching for a motive. Angela and the new technician, Simon, searched endlessly, but nothing in Mavius' records gave more than a two percent desire to contest with the governess. There was nothing to do, but wait until new events revealed themselves.

To her flattery, the people of Liva loved the Governess dearly. Dikara had spent a lot of time in her first few months conversing with the natives and learning their culture. They saw her to be a genuine being and supported her endlessly. It was only within a matter of a few years before they created a planet wide alliance to protect her.

Tanyui (Yeylacore)

Tanyui looked nonchalantly at the peculiar man. He introduced himself as Huinor Stregatori. He said he was from the Quandonta Galaxy and he worked for Governess Dikara. Tanyui kept thinking about her mother in that woman's hands. Stregatori would be lucky to escape with his life.

"Is there anything else her highness wants?" Tanyui referred to the Governess in a mocking tone. The timid young Tanyui had long since disappeared behind her visage of power and control.

"Nothing more, I am here to negotiate the return of your beloved mother," the man replied. Tanyui was barely able to maintain her cool disposition.

"Very well, go on." The man smiled. Little did Tanyui know, she was going to be replaced by two human rulers who were formerly known as the Bevon brothers. "In return, we ask that you leave the throne and appoint two new leaders we have already chosen." Tanyui hesitated. That was an enormous sacrifice. Who knows what type of people her empire would be left with? She opened her mouth to refuse, but what came out was, "Yes." After all, wasn't the domination and jurisdiction she acquired just for getting her mother back? That was her weakness and it led her to ruin. Tanyui and her mother were banished from Yeylacore and they sought refuge at another monarchial world called Cariosse. This was where Zurntain Maotvrie lived. When Zurntain's father passed away, the old king had left the planet to rule with Zmaena Maotvrie, his oldest child and Zurntain's elder sister.

There were three genders for the humanoids on Cariosse. There were the positively charged, the negatively charged, and the neutral genders. The positively charged gendered carried the sperm, the negatively charged carried the egg, the neutral was the womb that carried the child for fourth months and nursed it for seven months after birth. Zmaena was negatively charged and called "she." Zurntain was positively charged and called "he." The neutral gender was referred to as "it" and was the most highly respected of the three. Children were seen as valuable on Cariosse and conceiving was a long and formal process usually initiated by the negatively charged gender. They would first find a neutrally charged gender and offer them gifts so they would carry the child. Once they accepted, the negatively charged gender must provide for the neutral charge during the entire gestation and incubation period until the child can leave. If it is a positively charged child, it is raised by the negative charge. If it is a negatively charged child, it is raised by the positively charged. If it is a neutral gender, the incubating neutral gender keeps the child in it's care and trains it to be an incubator.

The incubators were highly respected as gifts from heaven, for, without them, there would be no life. The positively charged genders were the ones with the simplest role. They would give the seed to the negatively charged gender through intercourse. It stays inside of her until her egg is fertilized. Then, within four days, she must transfer it into the neutral being's body or else the zygote would abort since her body does not have the proper facilities to nourish it.

Zmaena was a totalitarianist. She worshiped the neutral beings as gods and spoiled them terribly. Even the ones who did not want the attention had it forced down their throats. Those of the positively charged gender were given very little attention. Zmaena's own gender was given the most power and authority when it came to decision making. Needless to say, her little brother Zurntain didn't like this very much. To make matters worse, Zmaena didn't care much for foreigners and treated them badly, trying to force them away from her planet.

One of these aliens was Tanyui. If not for Zurntain coming to her rescue, she and her mother would have perished immediately. Zurntain found them one day being harassed by locals. He brought them back to the palace. The palace was enormous and his sister had no idea they were there. He rebelled against her in any little way that he could, bringing Tanyui and her mother in was just a small thing.

Years later, Tanyui's mother died a natural death, and her heart left empty, she turned to Zurntain. Fascinated by her being a different species and able to conceive without a third gender, he gave her his seed and watched her belly grow. Everyday he would measure it and wait patiently for the fetus to kick. It was not long after that word traveled to his sister. She grew furious and when Zurntain was away, Zmaena had Tanyui killed.

When Zurntain returned, she placed the dead baby at his feet and asked him to explain himself. He looked at the dead thing that he had marveled as a miracle. To him, his sister had destroyed a symbol of their species' evolution. She thought she was protecting that which was sacred and ordained by the gods. She didn't see things the same way he did. To him, being able to conceive with only two genders was completely unheard of and Tanyui was a goddess from heaven. Tanyui was an anomaly and Zmaena had destroyed something sacred. He was so angry it felt like his head could pop off. Pushing guards out of the way, he went on a rampage destroyed what he could. Afraid to hurt royalty, the guards let him be. He found himself near the militia. He stole on of the two valued intergalactic spacecrafts and left his wretched planet and his sister's tyrannical rule.

Zyolious Sarces

After leaving Salineptra which became too still and sterile for her tastes, Sarces found herself on a prosperous trade planet, Turnika Jos. She was contracted for a job in security. This was the furthest from home than she had ever been.

Landing was breathtaking. Like the blimps on Earth, Turnika Jos landed their trading ships on poles. The ship would lock onto the pole then slide underground to disembark either passengers or cargo.

Sarces had never seen so many buildings and ships in her entire life. It was almost as if she have wandered into the future. The strangers were pleasant to her. They all held an air of sophisticated self assurance and confidence but were not self-indulgent. There seemed to be order free from chaos everywhere she turned. The whole planet seemed to run on courtesy and self-control. As far as she could tell, there were no brash last minute decisions.

Like all new troopers, Sarces was put on patrol to protect Turnika Jos from attacks. They were all explained the situation between Yeylacore and the Trials Galaxy. What they stressed the most was the visit they were expecting from the Governess next week. Everyone was supposed to be on their highest guard because the Governess was a highly controversial figurehead. Anything could happen and they had to be prepared.

The day before the visit, an awkwardly piloted spacecraft crashed into some landing poles. Even though they had the area fixed and operational within hours, the pilot was to be prosecuted after the visit.

The visit from the Governess went smoothly. Sarces caught a brief glimpse of her on the television screen in the prison. She was stationed to guard the reckless pilot. He was swearing in a foreign language.

"What?" Sarces asked passively. He then spoke in the tongue of Turnika Jos which was something they had to learn on his planet in order to deal with the traders.

"I said stupid female rulers, they should all die!" he called out hotly at the projection screen showing the Governess. He didn't know at the time this was the same Governess Tanyui hated. He was thinking of his sister, Zmaena. Sarces studied him neutrally. His eyes were wild like a cornered animal ready to fight to the death. His scraggly dry bluish white hair stuck straight out in all directions.

"Something happened to you, didn't it?" Sarces spoke softly in her usually gentle tone. His look did not change. He wasn't going to let her in on his secrets, his life. He hated all women. It was obvious to even him that Sarces was a negatively charged being. They were all the same. Even Tanyui had crazy mood swings and was evil at times. What set her apart was her physical capability to reproduce without the neutral gender.

"Where are you from?" Sarces asked again softly. He turned away. Sarces looked him over one more time, then turned back to the television to idly pass the hours.

"What is that?" Zurntain asked Sarces without realizing he had spoke out loud. He saw on the television viewing port a negatively charged being giving birth. There were more beings like Tanyui?

"That is a woman becoming a mother," Sarces replied with no emotion.

"What is a mother?" he asked. Sarces looked at him curiously, "don't you have a mother?" Zurntain looked confused. Sarces tried again, "it takes two sexes to make a baby."

"No, three," Zurntain spoke. Sarces looked at him deeper and studied his physical characteristics, "You are not from Cariosse by any chance are you? I have read about them."

"Cariosse is home, yes," Zurntain replied. He temporarily forgot his disgruntlement towards the negatively charged gender.

"Ah, that explains it, you are unique. All save five species in this Galaxy reproduce with only two genders. The male donates the seed to the female. I believe you would say, the positively charged gives to the negatively charged, then the negatively charged keeps the positive and becomes neutral to carry the child." Sarces studied his face, he was thinking deeply.

"You've never left Cariosse, have you?" she asked. He shook his head, "do you be neutral too?" he asked. Sarces nodded, "My species has only two genders too, our negatively charged gender is the one that carries the baby." Zurntain's eyes lit up, "I give you seed! Us make child!" he exclaimed. He was still fascinated by the process of dual conception versus tertiary conceptions.

Sarces let out a loud laugh, "I cannot conceive if I do not love you." Zurntain looked confused, "Love?"

"Yes, a ritual where two partners are bonded together and can only reproduce with each other," she replied. His innocence and ignorance intrigued her greatly. She felt badly for him, he had been kept ignorant.

Zurntain felt terrible for being crude to Sarces. She was another goddess, capable of acting as both a negative and neutral charge. He wanted to learn more about her and how her body systems functioned but his vocabulary in the Turnika Jos dialect was lacking.

After his trial, Zurntain was sentenced to public construction work and imprisonment for a year. He didn't mind, he had nowhere else to go. It just so happened that Sarces was his officer. She became his friend and taught him many things. She taught him all the languages she knew, the martial arts knew, and about the other species she had come in contact with and their lives. The traveling she had done taught her much and he listened eagerly like a child. Grateful to have met her, he continued to view her as a goddess in disguise. After his sentence was finished, he joined in to work with her on Turnika Jos, guarding the planet, learning about the galaxy around him.

Selena

Natasha stood barefoot in the cool blue dirt tinged with green sands. She watched Sally playing with her father. The eleven year old was tapping beetle bugs with the end of a stick and watching them jump away. Out of nowhere, Rosi wandered into her mind.

"Oh Rosi, I'm so sorry," Natasha said to herself. Into her mind, the scene played again. Her husband was at work and Sally was at school. Natasha was sitting at home meditating and reminiscing when a knock came at her door. To her surprise, it was an old friend. Marcuno sat her down and explained to her what he was asking of her. He told

her in a low voice his suspicions concerning the governess. He told her everything, confiding in her as an old soldier would. He told her about the army he was building, and of the people who he asked to join him. It was the same case Ara was following a few years ago concerning the missing people from Earth. It was Marcuno who was "kidnapping" them. Natasha listened calmly. When he was done speaking, she placed a hand on his knee. She locked eyes with him in her firm gentleness.

"Marcuno, our little Rosi is the Governess." At first, there was nothing. Then a spot of light touched his face. Natasha observed with curiosity as the light grew into confusion, and then finally, pain.

"Our little Rosi? Little Dove?" he asked like someone who just learned they killed their own child by accident. He swallowed hard, "Are you sure?"

"Yes, she told me herself." Suddenly, both Natasha and Marcuno sensed something. Within a split second they were at the window. Natasha threw it open and they began scaling down the side of the building as some darkly dressed figures wandered down her hallway. They had reached the ground by the time the figures broke down her door. They saw the open window and rushed to it. Looking down, they coul only see a sea of people, and knew that Natasha was lost in there.

Marcuno left immediately. Natasha took Sally out of school and begged Geoff to leave work. She left Jupiter without a trace and moved to Neptune. She was afraid to contact division seventeen in any way, shape or form. She feared for the young members. No doubt who ever the enemies were wanted to use Natasha to get to them. The best she could do for them, was to lay low.

Neptune had the same metallic islands and bridges as Jupiter with the same artificial atmosphere around each island. Sally and Geoff didn't take long to adjust. Natasha begged Geoff not to ask her to explain. She did what she had to. He was very upset with her for a long time and sought women outside of his home. In time, he finally understood that she was like all women he knew and she had her secrets too. He went back to her and begged for her forgiveness. Natasha smiled the smile of a person who had been jaded. After being ground down by division seventeen, what more could she expect? It was the same smile she had given when saying goodbye and when Old Matt turned the division over to Marcuno.

Natasha was not worried about Marcuno anymore. They were both protective over the younger members of the division. She hoped that Marcuno did not try to contact Rosi. It would be very dangerous. She did not know what he was planning, but she hoped that he had reconsidered his views on the Governess.

"Geoff, its getting late," she called out.

"Coming!" the two walked back towards her. She watched the beauty and purity and savored the moment. The blood on her hands and in her heart melted away for a moment and she was in perfect bliss. Together, the three of them walked towards their vehicle in the parking lot. There were a few other people walking around, enjoying the lovely evening as they were.

Then, out of nowhere, a ghost appeared. Natasha's heart secretly jolted in her chest. If she would have kept it still, she would have gone under the telepathic radar of L.J. but it was too late. L.J. turned and saw the familiar face. She pretended like it was nothing and just kept walking the opposite way.. Natasha let out a sigh of relief. L.J. sent her a telepathic message, "Don't worry, I won't tell Rosi where you are, she just wanted to know you were okay." L.J. had tracked Natasha out of her own free will. The old soldier's position was still safe.

Marcuno stood facing Jeremy. The two were locked in a deadly gaze. Jeremy was Mark's equal and they had been plotting for years against the governess. Mark had just told him he didn't want to anymore.

"What happened Mark?" Jeremy asked with great disappointment.

"I just can't, there are more strings and aspects than I had originally anticipated," he replied solidly.

"We can't let you leave, you can't get out, you know too much. We have to kill you," Jeremy said sternly even though he knew the threat was empty when it fell onto Mark.

"I understand," Mark replied compassionately, "but you are going to have to try. I know you can't just take my word that I won't leak you out, but I don't think you can kill me either." Jeremy looked at him. He was right. They bonded as blood brothers and swore an oath to each other before all else.

"Why did you have to do this, Mark? Weren't you also worried about the younger members of your old division serving the governess?" he asked.

"I can't tell you," Mark replied. He was done speaking, "I am going to go now." Mark turned and left the room. Jeremy stood silently.

Why did they want to overthrow the governess again? Was this personal war costing friends and allies?

Jeremy shook his head. He was making it too personal. They were doing it for the galaxy, not themselves. With centralized power, it usually ends in tyranny. The governess was going to have ultimate authority in a few years. If they don't remove her now, it could be too late. Better no ruler than an oppressive one.

Marcuno flew in his jet craft with no destination in mind. A strange array of melodic thoughts played themselves through his mind. What about the younger members of division seventeen? Little Phoenix was really the governess? How did this happen? Why and when did it happen? Wasn't the galaxy fine running on its own? Yes, there were high criminal and unnatural death rates, but you can't force power like that.

Suddenly, Marcuno knew what he had to do. Knowing Rosi was the governess was the last piece of the puzzle. With that in mind, he flew towards one of the rebelling planets and sought out a man known by the name Wirga. He introduced himself and shared his beliefs against the Governess with Wirga. Slowly, they became friends.

CHAPTER TEN

Division Seventeen took no action against Mavius. They merely reassembled and were attentive to his actions. Mavius ignored them and when the council asked him what to do about the division blatantly disobeying the order to remain off duty and inactive, he replied, "Nothing." The people in the system were starting to sense something was wrong with their new leader, but there was nothing for them to do because there was nothing they could pin on him.

Even the councilman who aided division seventeen was confused. Everyone was certain the Earth's guardian division was to be punished, but Mavius told everyone to leave them alone. The division knew better. Their actions were being scrutinized. Everyone was waiting for something to happen yet no one made the first move.

Rosi was 26, Wayne was 28 and for the sake of their families, they took their vows to each other on earth. A year later, a girl was born. They named her after Ara which flattered the aunt. Rosi remembered her vow and contacted Yolukia.

"I am sorry dearest, it is not I who does not value your child, but I must take into consideration how her gender is view by the other galaxies. Many of them are stubborn and are just not ready to accept a female leader as you are experiencing in your galaxy right now."

"I understand," Rosi replied in a relieved voice. She didn't really want to part with her daughter either. With Wayne, they shared a home in New York, but were seldom there. They mostly lived on Jupiter. That was where Ara attended daycare as well. The novice parents raised her in the best fashion they knew how. What Rosi hated the most, was how much both she and Wayne were away from their daughter. There was just simply no way around it.

Ara was a lot like her aunt. She was cheery and sugary all the way through. As a matter of fact, it was Ara who watched her most of the time since was there on Jupiter anyway. Darrel was asked to baby sit from time to time but he declined saying that he knew nothing of childcare and wouldn't know what to do when it came to diaper changing.

It was when Ara was two months old when her mother came home to find her missing. Ara, the aunt, was just a few moments away on her way to Rosi's place when Wrie called her impersonating Rosi. She told Ara that she was going to stay home after all. During this time, baby Ara awoke and was crying. The kind neighbor, whom Rosi had given a key to, went to go check up on her and brought her to his own home. Stregatori, who did not locate the baby, returned to Mavius without her. He got a thorough verbal lashing. Wrie took the action as a minor miscalculation. It wasn't a huge part of her plan and she can go on with the hitch.

When Rosi turned home, she was in a panic and had just picked up the phone to call someone when the neighbor brought Ara back. He scolded Rosi for leaving the young baby alone and told her she was a bad mother. Rosi didn't hear anything. She kissed her child over and over. To her neighbor's great confusion, Rosi kept thanking him. He went home and left the two alone.

"All humans are crazy," he made the excuse to himself.

It was very difficult for Rosi who lived in perpetual fear over her daughter. She had conversed with her sister Ara and knew that someone had called pretending to be Rosi. This meant someone knew about her daughter. This frightened Rosi and Wayne terribly. There was no place safe for them anymore. Ara would be old enough to stay at SHONDS when she turned six, but what about before now? Bearing tears and fear in their hearts, Rosi and Wayne eventually asked their parents to watch her. It was a silent planet and it was a strictly held law that no one was to interfere with life there. That was how Ara came to take turns living between the two sets of grandparents.

By this time, tension against the Governess had grown to a dangerous level. Something was going to happen, everyone could feel it. Rosi was terribly paranoid and frightened for her daughter and her families on Earth. Why did they even have a child anyway? She knew the answer. It was just the next step. People were supposed to get married and have kids. She didn't really think it through. It didn't matter, Ara was born and it was too late for either of them to have regrets.

After saying a heart wrenching goodbye, the mother and father left baby Ara to continue with their other life. Division seventeen was flying to Liva with Phoenix in the lead. This was just a disguise. They were called in as extra protection for the intergalactic meeting the governess was holding. This was also how the governess was secretly getting to the meeting. Everyone always expected someone else to know where the governess was and expected that they merely didn't have the clearance to that kind of information. It had never occurred to them that Phoenix could be Dikara.

"Calling Phoenix of division seventeen," a male voice came over the radio from Liva.

"Speaking," Phoenix replied.

"Orders from the Governess, head towards Turnika Jos and escort Yolukia to Liva."

"Roger that," Phoenix replied. She turned her formation away from the planet and her soldiers followed her. What was going on? Something was wrong! Yolukia was visiting? How come he never contacted her? She turned the radio to their private frequency, "Did all of you hear that?"

"Roger," everyone replied.

"What's going on?" Angel (L.J.) asked over the radio, "You didn't plan that did you? You would have told us right?"

"Of course I would have!" Phoenix called back, "I don't know, but we have to escort Yolukia. Just keep on your guard."

"Did they clone you again?" Sunshine (Erica) asked hesitantly.

"Maybe," Phoenix replied, "but it would have been very difficult." Thinking hard, Phoenix radioed back to SHONDS, "Angela, send Leffi to Turnika Jos, we will meet her there. Do a search on approved clones in the past five years, since before the governess began ruling."

"Any specific DNA scan?" Angela asked.

"Mine," Phoenix replied.

"Leffi is on her way, I will have results to you ASAP."

The group flew in silence, each thinking there own thoughts. Their ships were being tracked from Liva. Whoever was plotting this, knew their location at every given second, they had to obey. They all felt like a fish who took the bait and was struggling on the hook. Nerves were jangling and Phoenix started to feel a desperation take hold. She should have been more cautious. The lives of the division members were in her hands.

But wait! What if it was one of the division members who was betraying her? What if it was all of them? This thought had not occurred to her yet. It made her even more anxious. She took a deep breath and told herself to calm down. This is what the opponent wanted. She had to keep her mind still. It didn't matter though, the idea naturally spread throughout the rest of the division like a virus. Everyone suspected someone else of betraying the division. The bond of trust was breaking and they were vulnerable out of fear.

When they approached the planet, a young man's voice in a

smooth Turnika Jos dialect radioed Phoenix, "Please land in coordinates 87-91." The division complied. When they entered the complex, a young man with pale blue hair greeted them.

"Hello, my name is Zurntain I will be directing your stay until you leave along side the Ruler Yolukia." Phoenix nodded in agreement. Everyone was tense. A hot heat of resentment was building up amongst the division members. Zurntain took them to the armory room and let them be. He returned to the communications office where Sarces was in contact with the approaching ship carrying the ruler of the local galaxies. The other two individuals in the office were aiding her. Zurntain sat down at his own desk and picked up the reading he was doing on his pocket projector. It was a little flat screen that displayed digital books.

He had asked Sarces to find this book for him. It was a study on herbal remedies of the plants native to Cariosse. There was so much he did not know and that was what fascinated him the most. He was so completely engrossed in the book that he almost missed the call that was coming in.

"Gray Sector, Zurntain speaking, how may I help you," he answered on the videophone. The woman on the other side nodded gently, "I have a call from the Governess herself, are you ready to receive? A hot flash of resentment coursed through Zurntain. He hated the Governess, hated her. It didn't take long for him to learn that the Governess that had visited during his first day at Turnika Jos was the same one Tanyui had told him of. She told him about how the wicked woman kidnapped her mother and used it as leverage against her. Zurntain swallowed hard and looked around, everyone else was busy.

"Ready to receive," he said in a dry voice. The screen blipped and changed over to a darker setting. A woman with a veil on was looking straight through his soul with dark eyes filled with pure evil. She was just the way Tanyui had described her to be. Zurntain wanted to hit the screen and poke out the poisoned eyes, but he kept calm.

"I need to you tell Phoenix to return to Liva. She is to leave Dragon in charge of the operations on Turnika Jos. I am in need of her personal service here, and only hers alone. Understand?"

"Yes your honor." The screen blipped again and shut off. With steely control, Zurntain got up and walked towards the armory.

After the man with the pale blue hair left, everyone stood still. No one dared to move. Even though their telepathy was blocked off, everyone sensed that there was a suspicion of betrayal. Neroz (Dave) lifted a gun, and point it at Wolf (Travis). Wolf looked at him out of hurt anger. He knew what he was thinking. He was the newest member and he was dragged in without consent, therefore, he was the least likely to be trusted.

"Neroz, lower your weapon," Phoenix spoke softly. Neroz felt a pang of guilt. Phoenix was the most victimized here. Wait, was she? His father's words melted away and his initial dislike towards her set into his gut again. He lifted his other gun at her head. Immediately, Dragon stepped in front of Phoenix, "lower your weapon soldier."

"How do you know she isn't out to destroy us all?" Neroz demanded his second officer.

Dragon did not answer with words. He sent a telepathic sentiment to Neroz letting him know that Phoenix loved all of them. Neroz laughed wickedly, "That is just bullshit!" Everyone knew that as a first rule, soldiers were not supposed to feel, so why should Phoenix? While Neroz was distracted, Wolf pulled out his own weapon and pointed it back at him.

"Guns down." Phoenix raised her voice and stepped out from behind Dragon. She appreciated his concern, but she was still leading officer.

"Or maybe it's both of you!" Neroz was getting hysterical accusing his two leading officers. Dragon's brother, Deklar, his cousins, Kirin and Zap! walked to stand beside him. The five cloned sisters of Phoenix went to stand with her. Suddenly, Neroz realized his folly. They were all family. None of them would hurt each other. He realized how much he looked the suspect at that moment.

Suddenly the door opened. Neroz turned suddenly. Wolf kicked the gun that was pointed at him out of Neroz's hand. Kirin wrestled the other one away.

Zurntain was a little taken aback. His own disgruntlement towards the Governess faded for a moment. The division members had weapons drawn at each other and they disarmed one of them right in front of him. He paused, feeling awkward intruding on an obviously personal moment. It was like walking in on a friend's mom and dad fighting.

"I am told by the Governess that Dragon is to assume command here and Phoenix is to return to Liva," he dictated at last.

It was shortly after Phoenix had left that Leffi arrived. Zurntain asked for permission to escort Phoenix to Liva. Phoenix denied him, what a ridiculous question! She couldn't trust anyone. Still, Zurntain followed her at a distance. He thought Phoenix was unaware, but she kept her mind trailed on him the entire way. She learned that he was not out to get her. It was the Governess he did not like for some confused reason she could not decipher. She had a feeling that he was somehow drawn into this mess, but he was not her enemy.

Leffi could sense the tension in the room. Neroz and Wolf sat apart from the rest of the group. She looked around and took notice that Phoenix was missing, so she approached Dragon.

"Leffi reporting, sir," she saluted him. He saluted in return, "report of results."

"The only living clones of Phoenix completed within this galaxy through the last twenty seven years are the five present here," she reported swiftly. Everyone was astounded. What did this mean? Did this mean Phoenix was really plotting against them? Or was this something bigger than themselves? Something beyond this galaxy? If it were Phoenix, then they had just let her out of their sight.

"Any new orders, sir?" Leffi asked. Phoenix had requested her presence no doubt in case they needed some high skilled hacking done on the spot. Leffi was now a field tech but she had no idea what had just transpired.

"Not until we are called by Phoenix," was Dragon's response. Nothing could be read from his tone and an ill feeling tightened in Neroz's gut. They all knew the relationship between the two leaders and they hoped Dragon was making the best decision.

Wrie sat silently by herself in the royal chamber. The dark velvety walls absorbed any white noise there would have been and reminded her of a womb she was never in. She had arrived on Liva before Phoenix had intended to, and put the last of her plans into motion. She had invited the ruler of the local galaxy groups to visit. Her excuse was that she was going to relieve the council she was set up with and rule independently.

Her invitation to Yolukia was to come witness the celebration relieving the council members. She was also going to secretly send division seventeen to attack Yolukia's escorts. She knew Phoenix would never attack Yolukia, she would tell them there were traitors amongst the escorts. To the rest of the world, this would look like she were attacking Yolukia, and that is what Wrie as the governess was going to announce.

Then the rebels, who have had all this time to form an alliance would become agitated. The Milky Way loved Yolukia even though they did not agree with his action of implementing a governess. The protective nature would kick in and the rebels would move. Wrie would fake perishing as the governess. Without someone to overthrow and uproot, the rebels would turn their attention to hunting the division members who dared to attack Yolukia. On command, Mavius would tell his faithful dogs on Yeylacore to teleport the planet Yeyla to replace another planet in Quandonta. Then, they would initiate the explosion they had been planning. The mass confusion and explosion would be far from Liva and even then, there was a secret safe house built in the center of the planet. As the cosmic dust in the galaxy realigned, Wrie would go into hiding. When the ruler of the local galaxies was dead and no one to threaten Wrie's rule, she would emerge as the leader to pull Quandonta from chaos. This way, everyone would worship her.

She knew what the search results on the clones would show and she intentionally sent Phoenix with her division to Turnika Jos. This would give her time to build suspicion. She called her back so her division would plot against her in her absence. Dragon would support her, as would his sibling and cousins. They would remove Dragon and the others. Then they would be left to fight amongst themselves in a weakened state. It was beautiful. After Phoenix was removed and Yolukia was dead, all order would be gone, and she would be free to step in and create the perfect world. She would be free to sort things as she wished, to start anew.

Most people didn't think for themselves anyway. Everyday, people were always consumed with what they needed to do, what rules to follow so they could get ahead. No one ever stopped to think about what they could be if the rules didn't exist. She was born without rules, she was free to see and to do as she liked, because she believed that she was right.

"Phoenix of Preyal's division seventeen reporting for the governess," she called in as she approached Liva. There was a pause.

"We did not call you, the governess is resting in her chambers," came the response. A pang of hot fear shot through Phoenix. She kept calm.

"Requesting permission to land," she called back.

"Denied, we are to keep tight security for a top secret visitor, you understand."

"Yes I do, I was support to escort him until I got called back here."

"Not accepted, you were never called, please leave the vicinity or we would have to terminate you." Highly annoyed, Phoenix complied. Turnika Jos was too far to make the trip back, better wait nearby and carefully watch the progression of events. Phoenix aimed her craft a much smaller and younger planet that was primarily vegetation and first tier evolutionary animals. There were not supposed to be any humanoids on the planet. Every now and then Livan authorities would send a security teams to scan for anyone who might have crashed and were in need of aid. No doubt they would have just finished a scan of the planet to make sure there were no threatening squatters. But as Phoenix flew towards the planet, her onboard scanner picked up the signals from some Livan ships. It was for added security. Yolukia visiting was a very big deal. She decided to go to another planet and landed on it's moon. There she sat in her craft, waiting patiently. She sensed the young man by the name of Zurntain land a few hours later on the other side of that very moon.

The remaining members of division seventeen did not get a chance to speak to Yolukia. He was quickly and secretively transferred to another ship and the division were given orders to follow. They followed commands without question. Neroz was alienated by the group, as was Wolf. This upset both of them. They wanted to turn and leave, but there was no solid evidence that there was a plot inside the division. It was still engrained in them to follow orders like a robot. It was merely a temporary incident where they forgot they were not allowed to think and started to act upon personal suspicion.

The slow traveling ship was approaching Liva. Dragon and division seventeen were not the only ones to follow and protect Yolukia, there was the Turnika Jos security team as well plus a crew from Liva who were running the show. The leader of the Livan crew was named Fbel. They rode in a neat formation. Leffi traveled with Dragon in his craft.

"Division seventeen second officer, this is Fbel," he hailed to Dragon.

"Speaking, what are your orders."

"You are to rendezvous with your first officer on the moon Hicturzel."

"Roger." The division broke from the formation and headed towards Phoenix.

Yolukia looked out the window. His noted that his goddaughter's division was separating from the group. He did not find it strange. Perhaps she was going to get ready to receive him on Liva as Dikara. He counted the ships. One was missing. Now that was strange. Who could it be?

Dragon approached Hicturzel and spotted Phoenix's craft on his scanner.

"Following Fbel's orders, we are here to meet you," he hailed to her. Phoenix turned the radio to their private frequency, "There is someone on the other side of the moon, it is the young man who met us back on Turnika Jos. He followed me." The information received, they all landed by Phoenix on the sparsely vegetated moon. She exited the craft, and they all followed suit. They were parked in a circle, and the thirteen of them, Leffi included, stood amongst the ships and spoke softly.

"I am not going to dwell upon what happened on Turnika Jos," she spoke firmly in a low voice, "but I will give all of you my trust. Don't you see, whoever is plotting knows us better than we do and wanted us at each others' throats. I have grown with all of you and I am sorry to have made mistakes like losing track of Ben, but I promise you, I am doing my very best not to let you down. Dave," she looked deeply at him using his real name, "can you trust me? Can you trust all of us?" Neroz looked back at her. He suddenly felt guilty for letting the earlier thoughts get to his head. In his heart of hearts, he knew they were all in this together.

"Yes I can, I am so sorry for what I did." He was genuine, he opened his heart and let the others read it. They were satisfied. It triggered an effect that was contagious like yawning. They all opened their hearts and they realized they were all innocent in this mess. Whoever the culprit was, it was not one of them. Silent apologies were said and accepted, the wounds were patched up.

"Now about this fellow who followed me, we should go have a look," Phoenix said. She selected a few people to follow her. Phoenix, Kirin, Wolf, and Joy went to find Zurntain while the others stayed behind.

The four traveled on foot, but with their accelerated bodies, it didn't take long to reach young man who was sitting in his craft reading a book. Silently they snuck up on him. Smoothly, as if acting as one entity, Phoenix and Joy popped open his craft's door and Kirin and Wolf wrestled him to the ground. Kirin pushed her knee into his left armpit while Wolf pushed into his right. Su-Lin held his legs. Phoenix stood on his knees and balanced gracefully as he tried to struggle, but he was pinned.

"Who are you again?" she asked.

"Nobody," he replied nervously in a pinched voice. Phoenix scanned his mind, "You don't like the Governess, why is that?" Zurntain panicked, he felt himself staring death in the eyes as he looked into the woman's eyes. They were oddly familiar, like he had seem them before, but the fear was clouding his thoughts.

"I never said that!" he retorted. They were going to kill him. Oh God they were going to kill him! So this was how he was going to die? At the hands of the Governess' servants?

"Don't lie, we can read your mind," Phoenix said. Zurntain had long stopped squirming. Now he started again, "No!" he cried. All he wanted to do was avenge Tanyui for all the wrong she had suffered. In his mind, he saw her dogged face, her worn expression, the pity mixed with love he felt for her flowed back.

Joy caught the images in her head as well. He was picturing a girl that was strangely familiar. She brushed it aside, it must have been something in herself that shared a similar sentiment.

"Calm down," Phoenix spoke firmly, "just tell us your story, and we might not hurt you." Zurntain broke, he felt so helpless.

"Alright. There is this alien girl I met on my home planet, I was very close to her. I fell in love," he said using the word Sarces had described to him, "She told me about awful things on her home planet, Yeyla. She told me how awful the governess was, taking her mother. I wanted revenge, I didn't know how or what I was going to do, but I wanted to do something for her to avenge her suffering. Please don't kill me! I am a fool!" He had tears in his eyes. He was very scared of these four people. They were more powerful than anyone he had ever met before. The woman standing on her legs was quiet and thoughtful. She spoke after a few moments.

"What do you mean? The governess withdrew everyone from Yeyla after the civil unrest started, she wanted them to figure it out on their own," Phoenix said. Joy felt a pang of guilt. That was when she left to have Julian. She was glad Phoenix put it so delicately.

"Plus, the last ruler the governess was aware of in Yeylacore, was a man," Phoenix added. Zurntain nodded, "her father, she killed him because he would not negotiate with the governess to return her mother, a concubine. The governess kidnapped members of the royal family." Phoenix stepped off of his legs and the others following her lead released their restraint. Zurntain carefully sat up. He wasn't going to try to run, he was too afraid to. He didn't really think he was going to get anywhere.

"Tell me everything you know," Phoenix spoke gently. This eased Zurntain a bit.

"The girl's name was Tanyui. They were finally willing to give her back her mother, but only if she were to give up her seat as ruler. All she remembers were seeing two twin humans before she left. When she arrived on my home planet, she and her mother were in very poor condition. I took them in, I was not getting along with my sister. Tanyui's mother died peacefully and she and I conceived a child. I was fascinated that her species only had two genders. It wasn't until much later I learned my species was unique in having three genders. My sister was ruler and when I was gone, she discovered Tanyui had conceived with me. Tanyui and the child are dead and I left in anger. I ended up on Turnika Jos." After he was finished, the woman who was called Phoenix spoke again, "That is impossible, I know for a fact that the governess did not do such things. Who is they? Who are the new rulers?"

"I do not know, but Tanyui mentioned she rarely saw the governess, a man that was always with her acted for her most of the time, I do not know of the new rulers," Zurntain replied honestly.

"How do we know you are telling to truth," Phoenix challenged, though she knew full well he was being truthful. Perhaps the anxiety would prime further recall.

"He is telling the truth," Joy croaked, "I met Tanyui once at a bath house on Yeyla." Phoenix sighed, "Will you help us?" she asked Zurntain. He looked bewildered, he thought they still worked for the governess, "Of course not! I'd rather you kill me!" He was suddenly brave.

"You are not understanding me," Phoenix said, "the governess who committed all those actions, the one on the seat of the throne now, is a false one. We serve the true governess, and she is absent at the moment."

"What you are saying," Zurntain looked confused, "that the governess didn't do all that to Tanyui?"

"We don't know who did, but are closely associated with the true governess, and she was with us during the time you claim she sabotaged Yeylacore. She has no single man acting on her behalf. She has an entire council. She rarely shows her face."

"If you are going to bring the enemy of Tanyui to justice, I will serve you gratefully," he replied eagerly. He did not even question whether or not Phoenix was telling the truth.

"Not a bright one," Phoenix thought silently to herself. They hopped into Zurntain's jet craft and flew back to the others on the other side of the moon. They were all filled in with the story and questions flew back and forth.

"Was the man Mavius?"

"Could the identical humans be the Bevon brothers?"

"No, no, that would be too perfect wouldn't it be?" They went around in circles and were reaching no conclusive answers. Phoenix's radio buzzed, "Calling division seventeen leader, Phoenix, we have an urgent matter."

"Speaking."

"There are traitors amongst Fbel's soldiers, you are to take out crafts A-6, A-8, A-9, A-15, B-7, C-16, D-3, D-9, and D-12. We are hacking on further identities and may transmit further data to you at a later time."

"Roger." Something was not right. Phoenix relayed her incident approaching Liva to her soldiers. She looked at Zurntain, "you delivered the message to us that I was needed back at Liva, are you certain that was the message? Because when I arrived, they said no such command was given."

"Yes I am sure, a secretary told me it was a call from the governess and I saw a veiled woman." Phoenix chuckled, "No offense to you buddy, you are really not that bright. Someone the rank of the Governess would not show herself to you, especially in a video call." Zurntain turned red out of embarrassment and slight fury towards Phoenix' words. Nonetheless, he knew she was right. Why didn't he stop to think? He was too fired up over Tanyui.

"What if they're right?" Dragon questioned, "what if there really are traitors?"

"Whether or not there are, we can't let Mavius, or whoever is behind all this know we are onto them," Phoenix replied.

Zurntain and Leffi were asked to stay put. It was safest for them.

Phoenix and the rest of her soldiers piled into their jet crafts. The Livan system's sun was reaching it's first rays out to them and it looked like dawn would on Earth. Phoenix sighed, "It's going to be a long ass day." The others were silent, but they agreed. They could feel something heavy that was coming. Something they did not have any answers to, but were inevitably trapped in. At least now it was cleared up that no on in the division was a spy. They still had each other.

In a neat formation, they flew to meet Yolukia's ship. Phoenix flew in front. Behind her were Kirin and Dragon. Behind them, were two lines of jet crafts. Zap!, Deklar, Wolf, and Neroz flew in the top line. Sunshine, Moongirl, Tinkerbell, Joy and Angel flew in the lower line. As they approached the entourage, they received a warning. This did not surprise them anymore.

"Phoenix, you and your division are to stand down, do not approach any further," Fbel radioed.

"We were asked to escort the Ruler," Phoenix replied flatly.

"You have no clearance to be this near," Fbel retorted.

"What are you going to do, shoot me?" Phoenix asked. Fbel did not answer. Division seventeen broke formation and flew in front of Yolukia's ship.

"Phoenix, why are you not firing at the traitors?" the other voice radioed from a different frequency.

"We have our own tactics," she replied, and shut off that line.

"Permission to speak freely?" Zap! radioed Phoenix from their secure line.

"Granted."

"That was so fucking awesome!" he exclaimed. Phoenix smiled. Maybe being young and brash had it's perks.

"Leave now," Fbel radioed from his frequency. His voice was harsh, "You will be labeled as a threat if you do not retreat. We will open fire."

"You will do no such thing," an elder voice came online.

"Yes your honor," Fbel was quiet.

"We are no longer going to Liva," the older voice responded. Phoenix recognized it as Yolukia's faithful captain he always traveled with. She let out a sigh of relief. Yolukia was turning back. He must have sensed something was wrong.

"Division seventeen will escort us to where his Honor's personal army is coming to meet us. You are to return to Liva."

"Yes your honor," Fbel obeyed the captain and they disbanded. Phoenix and her division members moved out of the way to allow the Livan security crew to pass. The thirteen ships then surrounded Yolukia's and headed towards the edge of the Milky Way.

When they were safely out of Fbel's radio contact, Yolukia himself hailed Phoenix.

"Dearest little one, what is going on."

"Oh poppa!" she exclaimed out of frustration. She was bearing everything on her shoulders and it felt great to have an authority figure present, even if it were only online.

"It's alright, I just thought you wanted me to attend your ceremony."

"What ceremony! I don't know what is going on!"

"Weren't you relieving the council so you can rule alone?" he asked.

"No! I am not ready for that yet!" she cried, "I was on my way to a routine meeting with the council when I was radioed saying the governess needed me to go to Turnika Jos to escort you. I have no idea what is going on, we are all in danger." Yolukia was silent. When he spoke, his voice was tired and full of fear, "Listen dearest little one, there is something I have to tell you."

He never got a chance to. His ship was hit. There were unidentified stealth crafts firing from the front. The division members changed their scanners to detect movement. There were twenty or so crafts coming their way fast. The division members fired back and were doing well protecting Yolukia's ship when suddenly, their jet crafts died. Someone had installed a virus that killed their power. They spun out of control and flew in every which direction they were going.

"Poppa!" Phoenix cried out in fear, though no one could hear her. As her jet craft crashed into an asteroid and everything went black.

The person awoke in a dimly lit room. Where was she? Her mind drew a blank. She felt blank. Who was she? Sitting up, she realized she was alone. She looked at her hands, they were covered with black soot and dried blood. Suddenly, everything came back to her like a high voltage jolt.

"Poppa!" she screamed. She got up to run towards the nearest door but tripped and fell. Her legs were still broken. She cried out in pain as she crashed to the floor. There she clenched her teeth and tightened her fists, trying to breathe the pain away. The door opened and someone came in because of the commotion. They handcuffed her. There was nothing she could do. Her legs were not healed yet. They gently carried her back to the soft bed she was laying on. When the tears cleared away, she looked up into the face of Fbel. Behind him, stood a subordinate.

"Tell me he's alright!" she pleaded to him. He looked back at her sternly, no doubt he was judging her to be a poor soldier, but she didn't care. He remained icy even as he spoke.

"I thought something was odd. We did not return to Liva, we followed the ship at a distance. When you were under attack, we acted as well. The Ruler is safe amongst his own army and should return to the sanctuary of Juyvine shortly. He told me to give you a message, but I don't feel as if you should be trusted." He paused. Then added in the same tone Phoenix had used on Zurntain earlier, "tell me everything you know." Phoenix swallowed. How much did Yolukia tell him?

"My division and I were reporting to Liva after a summon. Before we reached our destination, we were radioed to escort the Ruler from Turnika Jos. We had arrived before he did and were waiting when we received a message. I was asked to return to Liva alone. I complied but when I arrived, I discovered that I had no such clearance and was not allowed to land. I found myself on Hicturzel where the rest of my division joined me later. We received an odd radio transmission telling us to eliminate parts of your crew. The voice claimed that there were traitors amongst you. We were not sure of anything so we merely flew along side your crafts. We had no intention of firing at your crew unless they took an offensive initiative. Even as we flew alongside you, a radio transmission demanded to know why we did not fire. I shut off both of your frequencies, and the rest you know." Fbel was quiet. He took out a key and removed Phoenix's handcuffs.

"If it were not the Ruler's personal captain who told us to stand down and respect you, you and your worthless division would be history by now," Fbel seethed. Phoenix swallowed. Where was the rest of her division?

"How could you be so careless?" Fbel continued to lecture. Phoenix did not say anything. This was just like old times whenever she would fail a mission and the generals would lash at her both verbally and physically. She failed an awful lot didn't she? She had let down a lot of people, didn't she? She became the perfect soldier again. She merely laid still as Fbel spat her mistakes back at her. She emptied herself of emotion. Even the pain of her legs automatically resetting did not cause her to flinch.

"Did you not do routine checkups on your jet crafts?" he commanded, "sabotage like that should not occur. You stinking humans really are idiots, aren't you?" he sniped. "I'll be damned if anyone every injects my vehicles with a virus like that! Your entire division lost power in the middle of a fight! And you were protecting the Ruler of the local galaxies nonetheless!" Fbel was furious. He let out a deep breath. He had not changed his posture the whole time. His arms were behind his back. His mood changed and his voice grew husky with concern, "There is something wrong with the governess." Phoenix's ears perked but she did not move. Not even to twitch her eye.

"The Ruler of the local galaxies wanted me to let you know that his council had made two clones of the Governess. They sent them to live in two separate dimensions. They were an insurance policy. He said you would know what to do with the information and told me not to question further." Fbel was quiet. Phoenix laid still. Her legs had stopped hurting. They were probably finished setting. A good ten minutes must have ticked by. Finally, she spoke, "where are the rest of my division members?"

"We are retrieving their remains now," he replied. A hot white fear started at the base of Phoenix's neck and spread upward. Deep in her heart of hearts where no thoughts could be heard, she said a silent prayer for them. On the surface, she kept her cool. She looked at Fbel, only, she did not use her own eyes. She looked at him the same way she would if she wearing the garbs of the governess. Did she dare tell him her secret? Would he laugh in her face and jettison her? Or would he take her seriously and become an ally? It was a huge risk. A terribly huge risk since the identity of Phoenix as the governess was never supposed to be revealed. But what about everything else that was involved? What if Fbel knew more about Yeylacore and just didn't know? Phoenix finally decided that whatever was happening around her, she couldn't figure it out by herself. Given the state of things, there was not much else left to lose.

"Fbel," she said sitting up. He looked insulted, she was addressing him informally. A common division leader like her should always address him as "Supreme General Fbel."

"Listen to me carefully," she said. He did, only because of

Yolukia and the trust he had placed in the human.

"At your knighting coronation on Liva, where the governess made you a Supreme General, division seventeen was not there correct? It was a top secret ceremony." He nodded once, sharply.

"The only people present were your wife and the other six generals, correct?" Again, a nod in response.

"And they understood the top secrecy of the event, right?" Phoenix kept asking.

"What are you getting at?" Fbel was growing impatient.

"Because I was the one who pinned the ruby medal to your chest and I know that your wife kissed you below your left earlobe and Struta was the first supreme general to shake your hand," Phoenix concluded. Fbel looked at her, was she trying to say that she was the Governess?

"I'm throwing you into the brig," he grasped her by the hair and dragged her towards the door, "you are insane and you are insulting her honor."

"Well then why the fuck does Yolukia trust me so much, as he trusts Dikara and placed her upon the throne?" she said firmly despite the discomfort in her neck and scalp. Fbel stopped. He jerked Phoenix's face around and held it beneath a sharp light. He looked into her defiant eyes. She was just a child. A human child. The governess was human too. He had never gazed deeply into the Governess' eyes for he was not allowed to. It would have been disrespectful. He looked into Phoenix's again. He let her go and she shook herself indignantly. He was not sure what to believe. What she was saying did ring true. Her account of the knighting coronation was accurate. Furthermore, there was indeed the trust Yolukia had placed in her.

"You better be telling the truth," he warned. Phoenix glared at him through her long black hair that was tangled before her face. Her piercing eyes glittered in the dim light like that of a feral animal, she had no fear of him.

"Find me my division members," was all she said. Fbel was not sure what to do. He had his hand upon his weapon. If she were really the Governess, he should comply immediately. But if she were an arrogant human child playing a wicked game, he should take her head without further hesitation. Then what about the message Yolukia had asked him to relay to Phoenix? What if the Governess on the throne now was really a fake? What if this was truly the real Governess? In the end, he turned and walked out the door. He would believe her for now, but he was going to watch her like a hawk.

All the division members were recovered and were in the process of healing. They were without transportation and stranded at the mercy of Fbel. He was cold towards them, but even he admitted that something about the current Governess on Liva did not smell right.

"You told him?" Kirin calmly asked Phoenix. She was a bit agitated. It was a huge secret.

"Kirin, we can't do this alone. I know Fbel is an excellent general and tactician. Just not having his trust one hundred percent is proof of that," she replied. The other division members were silent. They were all sore from their various crashes and it would be a good while before they were up to fighting again.

"What do they know of our situation?" Dragon asked.

"Fbel is communicating with Liva as of right now," Phoenix replied. The door opened and the supreme general himself walked in.

"I informed Liva that the Ruler of the local galaxies left safely and I gave them a brief account of the battle. They did not ask about you." Fbel left his tone open, waiting for Phoenix to question him.

"When was the last time you saw the Governess?" she asked.

"Before departing for Turnika Jos to escort the Ruler," he responded like a professional soldier.

"Do you know anything about Yeylacore?" she continued?

"The governess withdrew contact when the civil unrest began. There has been no communication since."

"Do you know a man by the name of Mavius?"

"No."

"What about Stregatori?" Phoenix pressed.

"He is a rebel leader but no real threat."

"Have you tracked his actions?"

"No."

Phoenix was silent. The imposter Governess was one of the clones Yolukia made, she was sure of it. She probably actively kept Mavius hidden and kept Stregatori from becoming a real concern. The door opened again.

"General Fbel, you should see this," a soldier said saluting his officer. He then walked to a television and turned on the news. The reporter spoke quickly in the lower left hand corner. Most of the screen was filled with photos of Phoenix and her soldiers.

"These *humans*," the reporter stressed the word "human" distastefully, "attacked the ship of the Ruler of the local galaxies. They failed in their attack but killed the Governess Dikara in the process." The photos changed.

"Supreme General Fbel and his crew are said to have aided in the demise of the Governess. The galaxy is put on alert to track them down and turn them in to the officials. It should be noted that these are professionally trained soldiers and one should exercise extreme caution when approaching them." Fbel and Phoenix turned simultaneously to look at each other.

"Now do you believe me?" Phoenix asked him telepathically.

Leffi found the division members hiding away on a backwater planet with the help of Angela. She brought them the obsolete older models of fighter crafts that were stored at SHONDS. Phoenix instructed Angela to go into hiding. She did not question Phoenix and obeyed.

"Phoenix, I would like to join the division," Leffi asked sincerely, "I can't help but feel as if I am fated for it." Phoenix had always been fond of Leffi and trust was not a question.

"I look to you as I had once looked to Hope," Leffi pleaded. Phoenix smiled, "I must ask the other division members." The other members were equally fond of her and acknowledged that they could use all the help they could get. Even though Leffi only had the basic field training, she was quick to catch on and learned as much as she could from the other division members.

Phoenix and Fbel wasted no time discussing what should be done. The first and foremost was to keep moving and to stay where the media was scarce. This put them at great risk since their own resources were dwindling. Fbel and his crew had not yet had a chance to reload back on Liva and division seventeen only had their obsolete jet crafts. Next, they had to figure out if indeed the imposter Governess was dead and locate Mavius along with all his henchmen. When Leffi did a hack a few weeks ago, she discovered that Mavius had twenty some men besides Stregatori working for him. Lastly, they had to figure out what was going on with Yeylacore.

The next step up. Be the best that you can be. Get all that you can get. Wasn't that the American dream? But what if you were not in America? Ken was solemn. Did they go too far? This was no longer about Hannah, or Phoenix, or whoever. This was about right and wrong.

He and his brother were asked to look after a system and safeguard it. They accepted it because it seemed like a noble offer. When they arrived, they were treated like royalty.

"Ben, I can't help feeling like there is a price to pay for all of this," Ken asked. Ben looked disturbed too, "Yeah I know what you mean." The man Mavius said he would contact them when the time was right.

"Oh shit bro, how did we get into all of this?" Ken asked with fear.

Dragon fingered the photo of his little girl. Her rosy red lips curled up in an exuberant laughing smile. She was beautiful. He hoped to God that she was alright. He hoped to God and said his most heartfelt prayer. He didn't know what he would do with his life without her.

The door opened and he sensed Phoenix entering. He sat still but reached out to her emotionally. She came up behind him and held him. She missed their daughter too. She wanted to nurse her and hold her and be a mother. She pulled her husband closer. Her breasts were heavy with milk and her frame was thick from having a child. Her body and heart ached to be close to her baby and to be in a tranquil situation where she was a nurturing mother and only a mother.

"At least we have each other," Dragon said in an attempt to comfort, but the words came out wrong. It only amplified the emptiness in both their hearts. They let out a deep sigh in unison as they sat together in their longing.

Phoenix commanded Kirin to lead the excursion to Yeyla. Joy volunteered to go, saying she had unfinished business. Phoenix was not sure if she liked the sound of that, but she granted the request. Leffi said she would go and Wolf agreed to it as well.

Fbel originally had 48 soldiers under his command and one assistant general. Once the news came on about their involvement in assassinating the governess, half of them went AWOL to plead their case on Liva. To their surprise, they were executed without trial. Now there were twenty soldiers with Fbel. Two of them volunteered to go with Kirin. Fbel and Phoenix decided it was too dangerous for both groups to stay together and that they should split up. They made plans to meet at an obscure location within a few weeks. Fbel and his soldiers were going to search for the imposter governess. Phoenix and her remaining division members were going to search for the other henchmen working for Mavius.

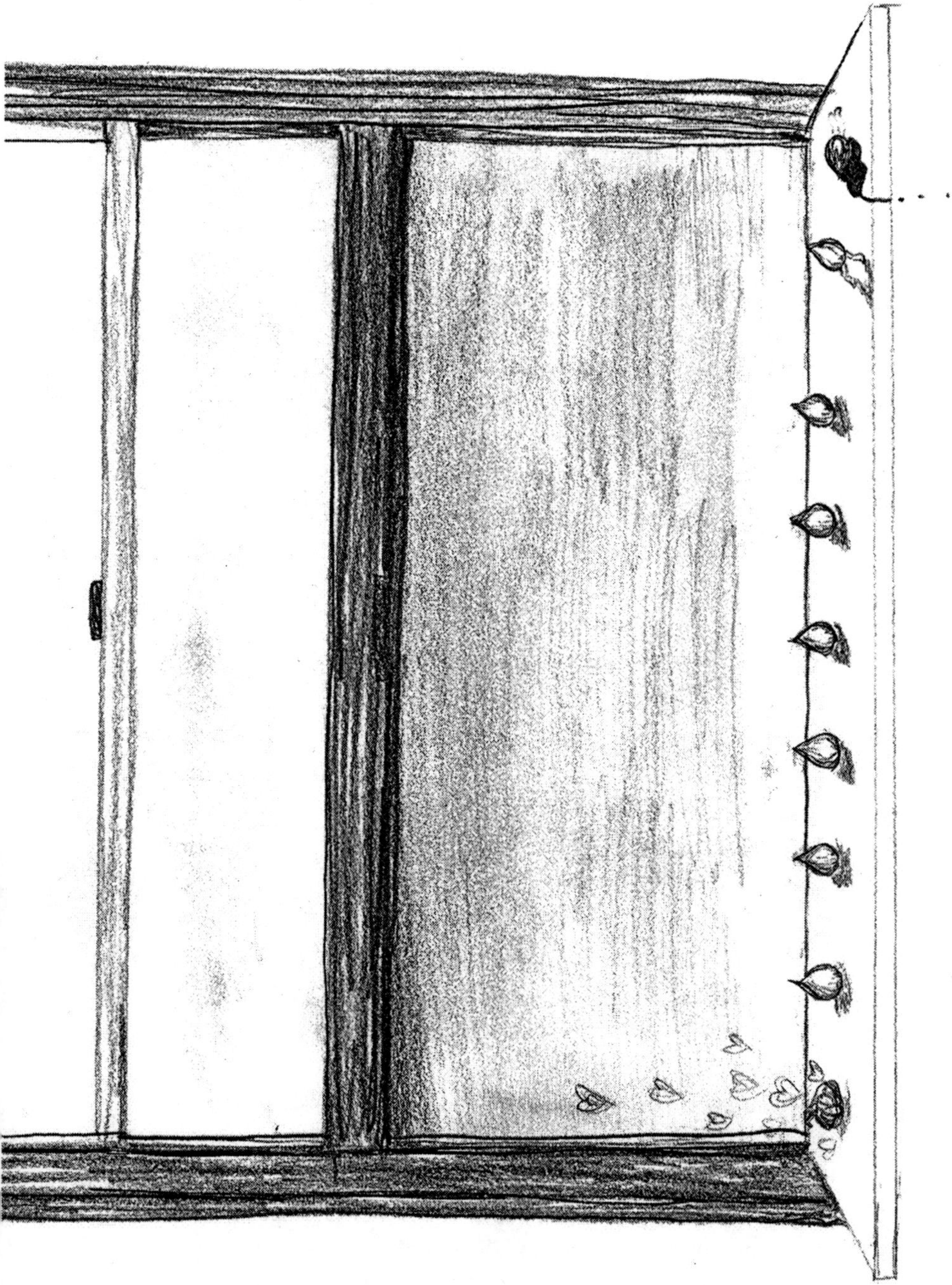

CHAPTER ELEVEN

Upon reflection, Rosi noted Marcuno did not stay long as Kirin. After Cora passed away and Old Matt made her Phoenix, she was laden with a disassociative emotion. It wasn't fear. She hadn't seen enough for fear, but something sat heavy on the little girl's shoulders. Maybe Marcuno knew he was going to retire soon, that was why he appointed Phoenix to accompany him on his trip to Turnika Jos. Rosi was nervous but very excited. They were going to be very far away. They were going to travel as civilians this time so Rosi had to get a visa. To her disappointment, it didn't arrive in time so she couldn't go. When Marcuno returned, he brought his little cousin, Palettia. Palettia and Rosi became friends right off the bat. Palettia's main purpose was to inform Rosi all about Turnika Jos. When Rosi's Visa finally arrived, she traveled with Palettia back to her home planet. She didn't fully appreciate Palettia's words until she saw the place with her own eyes. It was breathtaking. No wonder the planet was named "golden port." It was a complete smorgasbord of trade and commerce and held a little bit of every well known culture in the Milky Way Galaxy!

When Yolukia turned Phoenix into the Governess, she kept Palettia secretly close by. Palettia was her secret pair of eyes on Turnika Jos. Now, Phoenix sought her out for desperately needed information.

"I'm sorry dear friend," Palettia spoke, "I have no information. My heart goes out to you in your predicament and I will do my best to learn what I can." They shared a quick hug, then Phoenix quickly walked away and disappeared into the crowd. Palettia watched her go and a voice in her ear spoke like an evil conscience, "follow her." Palettia wanted to die. The wire hidden in her hair caught the entire conversation they had just exchanged. The three explosive devices sat beneath her cloths against her stomach as a reminder. Palettia hated herself.

"Rejianiticana!" Palettia suddenly called out Rosi's Jupiter identity in Martian, a language most people on Turnika Jos would not understand. "Run! They have a wire on me! They know everything about you, the woman who is impersonating you is from a different dimension and knows your future and how the course of your life spans out. The henchmen are Stregatori, Wirga, S-." Palettia's body exploded. Phoenix caught the corpse as it was falling to the ground. She tore through the screaming crowd and jumped into her jet craft to fly away.

Wrie paced back and forth. She was seething with anger. She had watched the course of the Governess' life from her own dimension before crossing over. She had calculated and simulated endlessly her intrusion into this dimension. Everything was perfect on paper! Everything had gone perfectly! It all started with that damn baby! The governess was not supposed to conceive for another two years. Stregatori was asked to kidnap the baby, but he had failed. Mavius was on his way to terminate him right now.

That was not all. The division did not continue to bicker among themselves on Turnika Jos, the reconciled! They were supposed to start fighting amongst themselves and half of them were to be imprisoned on Turnika Jos. Then the remaining were supposed to attack the Livan security crew with Phoenix. They did not. Why did they not? Were they not professional soldiers! That led to the Ruler of the local galaxies sending Fbel away. That wasn't supposed to happen either. Fbel followed them and allied with them. That meant more people for Write to worry about. The Governess had a tactician on her side, a Supreme General. This was not making Wrie very happy. And that girl! That girl with the kerchief on Turnika Jos, why did she run after the Governess like that, telling her the secrets? She was not supposed to. She was supposed to remain under Stregatori's control. Stregatori, it had to be him! He was the weakest link. No matter, Mavius was dealing with him now.

Wrie slumped onto the pile of furs in the cave. She took the herbal brew off of the fire and mixed it with a dash of liquor. Taking a sip, she was able to relax a little bit. Not much though. The real governess knew about her existence and Fbel was looking for her. There was no way they would find her where she was, but this did not ease her nerves. No matter, she would conquer all. She comforted herself with thoughts of the power she would acquire. It was so close, but why couldn't she taste it yet?

Palettia was dead. Phoenix had not gone back to Preyal since the chaos started. Now, she faced losing her friend who sacrificed her life to warn her. She told Dragon her decision to go to Neptune. He agreed that it was best she traveled alone. This would draw less attention. She held him close and said a tearful goodbye. With Palettia's body wrapped in old cloths beside her, Phoenix took off.

To her surprise, Preyal received her warmly. After Mavius moved on to being on the board of direction for the Governess (shortly before her faked death), true feelings towards him emerged without fear. There was an overall respectful sentiment towards division seventeen. They were sympathetic because Mavius had victimized them. The first time Phoenix met the man he had insulted her. Now he had killed her friend, Palettia. There was no way for her to feel sympathetic towards him.

She explained what had happened to Palettia to Dr. Spalling and Dr. Vector. To her relief, they said that Palettia's cells were still alive and there was a chance she could be brought back. Palettia would be operated on three times and would be in critical condition for months. There was no telling how much of her memory she would retain. Phoenix thanked them gratefully.

"As for you young lady, you had better get out of here, and don't tell us where you are going," Dr. Spalling smiled.

"Thank you, you are a good man!" Phoenix exclaimed. Before she left Preyal, she went to find Old Matthew.

"Oh goodness!" he exclaimed when he saw her, "what have you gotten yourself into? You are all over the news!" Phoenix smiled meekly. She told him everything, including her identity as the Governess. Old Matt let out a long sigh.

"Well young 'un, what're you going to do about it?" he asked.

"What do you mean?" she was confused.

"What do you mean 'what do you mean?' If this doesn't mean war, what does it mean?" he questioned her back. He sat back and let her digest her thoughts. She looked back up at him, "do you think I can find allies here?"

"It wouldn't hurt to ask," he replied, "but keep in mind, it helps to know your enemy before you act." Phoenix looked hurt, "Of course! You taught me that!" Old Matt just smiled. The two sat silently for a moment, letting the feeling of familiarity seep in. Phoenix felt at home, and she didn't want to leave. She knew she had to. Staying anywhere too long was dangerous. Old Matt would know how to take care of himself and Neptune was protected by the galaxy because of its highly treasured technology. She, however, was a danger to herself. No doubt there were people constantly tracking her, trying to find her trail.

"I had a dream once at SHONDS," Phoenix spoke in a hazy tone. "I was little at the time, perhaps just eight, I don't remember too well at this point. I was staring up at the night sky, at the Milky Way. It suddenly turned into a white beam of light shining directly through me.

There were voices and whispers around me. Sounds, but nothing that I could see. I was not scared but I didn't know what I was supposed to do. I woke up not long after."

"Those sounds and voices, were they not a warning of what was coming?" he asked. Phoenix looked at him quizzically, "What do you mean?"

"Were they not ethereal warnings?" asked Old Matt. Phoenix smiled broadly, "You don't seriously believe in spirits and ghosts do you?" she asked teasingly. Old Matt spoke quietly, "When you get older, you learn that what your five senses tell you, are not everything." A chill went down Rosi's spine. She brushed it off, "I told the dream to share a good ol' time feeling, now you are scaring me!" she chuckled loosely. Old Matt smiled in return, "I know, just be careful. Your life is laden with a lot more complications than mine ever was." Silently, Phoenix asked, "How do you know?" But Old Matthew did not master telepathy like the young soldiers. He did sense the question.

"Just remember what I told you about soldiers and warriors," he spoke softly.

Mavius was tired. He felt lost. He didn't know what to do, he merely did what Wrie told him to. He wanted this all to be over. Beyond that, he no longer knew what he wanted. What did he want? Right now, he had to, not want to, had to give Wirga his next mission.

"You are to hunt down Fbel. He is trying to destroy all the rebels with his private army. Without him, there would be no more opposition to our cause." Mavius reported the words. He had become a robot. The sounds escaped his lips, but he had no feeling. Wirga nodded, "Thank you, you have been a great help." They shook hands and Mavius left. Wirga thought Mavius was helping him do what he believed in. Mavius knew better, Wirga was as much a puppet to Wrie as anyone else doing her bidding. The only difference was what they thought in their heads.

"Marcuno, are you there?" Wirga called on his phone. The former leading officer of division seventeen entered along with a man Wirga had never laid eyes one before.

"This is my little brother," Marcuno explained. Wirga looked at the new man suspiciously. The young man had on a mean look and his blue glassy eyes stared sharply back at him. Wirga let out a laugh, "I like him!"

It was a close call. Marcuno was bringing Dragon to visit Wirga when they ran into Mavius leaving. The quickly ducked into a room and listened eagerly. The footsteps left steadily, growing softer. Wirga called Marcuno into the room and Dragon followed. He was introduced as Marcuno's little brother and Wirga let out a disgusting laugh. The man was so confident in his elusiveness that he never questioned Marcuno of trusting his little brother. He explained to them that even though the Governess was gone, their enemy wasn't.

"I was almost disappointed that we wouldn't have a chance to move, but an old friend of mind informed me about a general who used to serve the governess. Looks like he's trying to do her work. We are changing our target and going after him. Let everyone know."

"Will do," Marcuno gave a crooked smile. They turned to leave.

"Hey you!" Wirga called. Dragon's throat tightened. He turned around, "yeah?"

"What's your name?" Wirga asked. Dragon felt a rush of relief.

"Seth," He gave his father's middle name.

"Welcome aboard buddy." Marcuno and Dragon left quickly.

"That was a lot easier than I expected," Dragon spoke under his breath.

"I did the hard part and won his trust. This way I can always know what they are planning against you guys," Marcuno whispered back.

Dragon and Marcuno squatted next to a fire and held out their soup bowls. The old granny ladled some greyworm soup into them. The tip of her shawl fell forward and she quickly caught it. It singed a little, but she did not mind. Her hair was tied by in a scarf and her pale green skin tinged with white flecks had warts on it. She was small and rotund. When she smiled, she revealed a mouth of friendly crooked teeth.

Marcuno wore thick pants to protect his legs when walking through the underbrush. His light jacket had patches all over it from constantly being ripped. Dragon wore a thinner pair of dark blue pants. He had a small blanket draped around his shoulders to protect him from the cold. He fastened it with a button Rosi had given him. It reminded him of her whenever he missed her terribly.

The two of them were at a refugee camp. The rebels often stole money or robbed trade ships to bring them food. These were the people who naturally lost their homes due to industrialization every couple of decades. There was always a slack when old buildings were torn down and new ones were built. Those allied against the governess fed lies to the refugees telling them that it was the governess who made them lose their homes. The words would have a lot more effect if these happy humble people knew what a governess was. They were too busy making do and holding onto what they already had to care too much about politics. To them, the Governess was as far away as the next galaxy and did not touch their lives.

Dragon looked into his bowl and breathed in the aroma. He loved it here. A boy about seven years old kicked a can and the others went running after it. The boy had four eyes and handsomely bronzed skin. His eyes were vertical and full of light that danced whenever he laughed. He ran to the old woman serving soup when she called him. He referred to her as "Granny" and they both spoke the same dialect. Dragon did not find this odd. He found it astoundingly beautiful in his soul, how two completely different species were capable of behaving like family and both learning a language that was not native to their own. It made his heart warm. He sipped the soup. It was very strong and spicy but he liked it.

"Who is Fbel?" Marcuno asked in English, a language people didn't generally speak outside of Earth and Mars.

"He is the general that got dragged into all of this. When our ships lost power during a fight, he saved the Ruler. Somehow he got accused of killing the governess along with our division. He's stuck with us now," Dragon mumbled into his soup. Marcuno understood.

"So Wirga is not really working for Mavius, they just know each other?" Dragon asked.

"Right."

"How many people actually work for him?"

"Stregatori is the big one. He's the one manipulating and pulling strings on everyone else. Ucile is a coldhearted bitch, she tried to kill me once without even questioning me," Marcuno kept his voice low. "I think she does the assassinations for him, no one is really sure of her."

"Why did she attack you?"

"That is just how she is, she has five subordinates, most of them refer to her as 'Master Poison' and I don't blame them! Besides her, there is only Nek, but he is more Stregatori's helper that takes direct orders from Mavius from time to time."

"What would you do if you were us?" Dragon implored.

"I can only tell you all I know and what I think you guys should do," Marcuno began, "but in the end, it's all you guys now. You should not try to act like me, you have to find your own way." Dragon listened intently and learned about the plot against the governess that started when she was just a rumor, an idea of Yolukia's.

"So the rebels don't want to harm the Governess, they just don't want a tyrant?" Dragon asked. Marcuno nodded, "We were going to forcibly remove her from office and keep her imprisoned. We were then going to present Yolukia with our petition."

"But there are a lot of you allied together."

"We didn't really know what to expect of her forces. We thought that with Yolukia behind her back, it was going to be a bitter battle. Perhaps we have overly romanticized notions, but we just wanted to succeed the first time because chances are, we wouldn't get a second shot at it. This was before any of us stopped to really think about the situation. Most of us were just afraid of change."

"It was Natasha who told you about the Governess?" Dragon inquired further. Marcuno nodded, "I just couldn't go through with it. I felt stupid, here I was plotting against someone I might as well call my little sister. That's when I used my credibility, the name I had built up underground and wound up working for Wirga."

"What about your friend Jeremy?" Marcuno sighed, "Last I heard, he was drinking himself into a happy stupor at the news of the Governess' death. Now he is setting up a hunting party for division seventeen. He has it in his head that they went crazy and tried to kill Yolukia too but only got the Governess."

"That's not good," Dragon commented.

"No it's not," Marcuno agreed.

"Is that what all people think?" Dragon asked.

"No, some consider the division heroes for killing the Governess. Others think they are unrelated to her death but hate her for going after the Ruler. To those who don't know or care as much fantasized the division as angry gods and goddesses or demons. The story changes quite a bit. In the end, that is all they are, stories. Truth is never what the truth is," Marcuno blew into his soup.

"Are we ever going to clear up our name?" Dragon asked the question that had been nagging at his mind. Marcuno let a sigh that sounded like air leaking out of a flat tire.

"The name Phoenix is plastered everywhere now. Each place has its own version of the story. No, I don't think you will ever erase your existence in the minds of the people."

"It's only been a few weeks, won't this blow over?" Dragon voiced hopefully.

"That is hard to say, it depends on how you end it by finding the imposter and removing Mavius and all his ties." The two sat thoughtfully side by side like statues huddled over their bowls. The young boys kicked the can past them and paid them no attention. Dragon wished he could be carefree again.

Phoenix returned to the little backwater moon they were hiding on. She exhaled her frustrations as she pulled pins out of her hair. Looking for her brush, she ran into the corner of a small table. The pain added to her annoyance and she kicked it hard. It went flying against the far wall and smashed to pieces. Suddenly she felt guilty. She didn't have to destroy it. Old Matthew's words came into her mind and she shuddered at the thought of a higher power watching her, judging her actions.

"I'm sorry, table," she whispered under her breath. She gathered up the pieces and took it outside of the shack to use as firewood. Things were scarce, it was best not to waste. Her silky hair brushed against her face and she smiled lovingly thinking about her little daughter. It made her feel good to know that baby Ara was back in Preyal. Old Matt was close by and if anything needed to be done, he would do it. Upon returning inside, Phoenix noticed her brush was lying on the table by her pins all along. It were merely hiding behind a stack of charts. Bringing the brush with her, she walked back outside to search for Dragon.

The brush slipped over her scalp soothingly. It reminded her of Natasha brushing her hair. There was always something comforting almost as if she were brushing troubles out of her hair. Her hair was down to her waist now and it was completely blonde. It was a poor attempt at a disguise and sometimes she wondered why she had bothered at all, her face was shown on television almost all the time. The lame shows did simulations of her face with plastic surgery. They even did an image of what she would look like she would change her appearance to a different species. It was absolutely ridiculous.

"Hey Rejianiticana," Deklar greeted her. She smiled, "How are you?"

"I'm fine, I have to tell you something." Phoenix nodded and they walked towards the fire where Angel and Tinkerbell were helping Neroz make dinner.

"Marcuno paid us a visit and Dragon left with him," Deklar cut straight to the point, "Marcuno wanted to wait until you returned but my brother was afraid that if he saw you emotional, he would decline the mission." Phoenix was a little insulted, but then, he was right, she was pretty emotional at times.

"Where did they go?" she asked sadly.

"I don't know," he replied sympathetically, "and they didn't say when they would be back." He gave her a friendly shake on the elbow and went to go help his wife, Angel, make dinner. Worry crossed Phoenix's face. She walked past the fire into the grassy plain. She found a little patch of saplings and sat down in a clump to brush her hair madly in silent anguish. Humans feel, that was that, damn being a soldier.

When Angel went to find Phoenix, she found her staring soulfully at the ground. In her hand was a precariously clutched hairbrush full of loose blonde hair. Angel herself had dyed her hair red and waxed off all of her eyebrows. She sat down beside her sister and hugged her shoulders tightly. A little sob broke out. Angel kissed her temple. Exhaling a shaky breath, Phoenix let the first of her tears slide down her cheek. The pressure was getting to her. She felt as if she was trying to control the uncontrollable and nothing was working. She wouldn't mind so much if the consequences were not the lives of the people she loved. Now, she didn't even know where her husband had gone off too.

Angel stayed by her side all night and let her cry. The rest of the division finished their meals and went to bed. The dawn found Phoenix with swollen eyes and shaking shoulders, still huddled against Angel.

Su-Lin was Kinadr again. This time, her mentality was completely different from her last stay on Yeyla. As she stepped off of the ship, a wind came to greet her. It reminded her of Julian and a few tears stung her eyes. She swallowed them bitterly and pushed Groyu from her mind. She turned to Kirin, awaiting instructions.

They found a small boarding house that would take in all five of them. It was crowded, but the single mom desperately needed the money and she was willing to accommodate them. The two little boys were rascals and kept poking fun at their boarders. The mother was constantly scolding them. The soldiers merely ignored them and kept a close eye on the few instruments they had brought with them.

That night, Kirin went to spy in the palace. Kinadr wanted

to accompany her, but Kirin stated that if it were indeed the Bevon brothers, they would recognize her. So Kinadr stayed behind and Leffi went instead. It was too easy. Kirin and Leffi were hired as dancers to entertain the brothers. Not the most preferable job, especially for someone as stoic as Kirin, but it was the easiest and least suspicious way in.

Upon seeing them, Kirin and Leffi recognized the Bevon twins almost immediately. As it turned out, they didn't have to do much dancing. They sat and laughed and told jokes and fed wine to the boys. Kirin felt like a common whore and it disgusted her. Yet, she held back her emotions and tied down her thoughts and played along to being an empty shell.

"So tell me, how is it that we just get off the ship here and discover that this place is run by two humans?" Kirin teased giving Ben a provocative lick to her lips. Ben took a large sip of his wine and smacked his lips. He pulled Kirin close by the hips. It took all her might to keep herself from thinking anything negative and not strike him. She laughed hysterically like a moron and gently touched his chest. She smiled, but could not look into his eyes lest she tear him limb from limb.

"Well, we had some help, but natural charmers like ourselves were born to be rulers." Kirin laughed as loudly as she could hoping it covered up her thoughts towards them. Those fucking pig heads were nothing more than common losers.

"So what have you got planned in the next year? Any exciting projects?" Leffi spoke to save Kirin.

"You are a beautiful African princess," Ken said stroking her arm. Leffi looked at him coyly, "No, I'm from Baracece," she said truthfully. Indeed, her home was in Baracece, on Saturn.

"But you are human right?" Ken asked. Leffi nodded, "What about you? Do your future plans involve humans?" Ken ignored the question again, "Your ancestors were from Earth and they were from Africa," he told her as if the knowledge of her made him superior. Leffi wanted to slap him. Who cares?

"So how about it, does your future involve humans?" Kirin asked Ken. Ken stroked her cheek and Kirin gave him a playful twisted smile. It was all she could do to keep from killing him.

"We don't know, but we know it is something big," was his response.

"You don't know?" Kirin couldn't help but sneer.

"Do you want to be a part of it?" Ken asked leaning forward to kiss her. Kirin turned away pretending to be teasing. "Maybe," she said looking at him through the corner of her eye.

"Or maybe you can't handle the power?" Ken asked stretching back. Leffi almost choked on her wine while trying to stifle a laugh. Kirin had had enough of this. She slipped two pills into the glasses and both she and Leffi fed the wine to the boys. They were soon asleep and the two of them slipped away.

"Ew ew ew!" Leffi exclaimed when they were a safe distance away. Kirin nodded in agreement. She was comfortable back to being her stoic self again. She shrugged off the boys like an empty knapsack. As long as she wasn't there dealing with them, she didn't care. So the boys didn't know what they were there for. They had to just be puppets. There was nothing the rest of them could do except wait for them to act.

"Groyu," Kinadr demanded towards a man in a suit. He looked up to see another human. He was a little agitated. He remembered when he was the only human on Yeyla, now the rulers were human and Kinadr had to show up again.

"Where's my son?" he demanded. Su-Lin did not slow her steps and she did not respond. As soon as she was within swinging distance, she punched him in the face. He stumbled backwards and fell over with a surprised cry. Kinadr restrained herself and stood coolly as she watched him wipe the blood away in confusion.

"I hate you," was all she said. She turned and walked away. There was no longer a lump inside of her that burned with hatred towards Groyu. After all, he was just an idiot.

The gel-like gas substance that made up of Yeyla and the other minor planets in the system was a highly explosive material when exposed to enough heat. Their sun, the Core, was not very hot and the planets were far enough away that they were safe. There was a patch of planets in the Milky were that were the same gel-like volatile material. What Wrie intended to do was switch Yeylacore with an equally sized planet in the Milky was that was near the planets of the same dangerous substance. If she were to ignite the planets, she would cause a chain reaction. The shift in mass and the spreading of the heat was enough to annihilate structure on about a third of the galaxy. It wasn't enough to just want to rule the galaxy, she wanted to shape it as her own.

Mavius called upon the Bevon brothers a few days after their encounter with Kirin and Leffi. He took a sphere out of a box and handed it to them.

"Bury this at the softest part of the planet, as deep as you can," was all he said. The empty man left shortly afterwards. The brothers looked at each other. How were they supposed to do that? They hired some miners to do it for them. They responsibly supervised the entire procedure and were unaware of Kirin watching from a distance. Kirin called back to Phoenix and reported all she had witnessed. It wasn't long until they were all on Yeyla. All minus Dragon.

"Are you sure it was a heat generator?" Phoenix questioned Kirin. She nodded. "Then we are all in danger, start evacuating the planet," Phoenix said.

"How?" Kirin asked. Phoenix racked her brains. Nothing came up.

"Tell them the truth, start with the miners," Phoenix explained. Kirin nodded in consent.

"Lets settle this the old fashioned way," the gruff man breathed into Dragon's face. Wirga let out a laugh, "come on then boy, you aren't going to let him pick on you, are ya?" The man by the name of Stan was getting jealous of all the attention Dragon, or Seth was getting from Wirga. The man was too afraid of Marcuno to challenge him, but his little brother was a different story. Dragon did not want to fight him, but he knew he had to.

"Last one standing after five minutes," Stan spoke.

"One minute," Seth contested. The small group of people let out a cheer.

"Fine then," Stan agreed. Ten seconds later, he was on the floor and Dragon had his foot on his throat. No matter how he squirmed, Stan could not get loose. Time was called and Dragon released his hold. Stan glared at him through a dark face, "Again!" he screamed, "You got lucky!"

"Enough!" Wirga called. He walked up to Seth and patted his shoulder, "You're a strong boy! How would you like to stick my side?"

"I'd be happy to," he responded with a silly but empty smile and shook hands vigorously with Wirga. Sticking by Wirga meant he no longer spent time with the refugees. On rare occasions when he chanced to stop by, they still recognized him and greeted him warmly.

"Marcuno!" Seth finally found him. He had been wandering around the system for Wirga and it was hard to track him without radio contact.

"What is it?" he asked. Seth looked around. They were alone. Being extra cautious, he spoke in English, "I just got a secured message from Angela. She had tracked the division to see how they were doing and Kirin left her a message for me. The rest of them are at Yeylacore and there is some sort of trouble there. I have to stick by Wirga, is there anyway you or someone else you trust can go give them a hand?" Marcuno thought for a moment, "I'll see what I can do, keep hanging in there with Wirga, he is the most hidden of the rebel leaders and mixing in with him will no doubt benefit later. Maybe we can even make him an ally." Seth nodded in agreement and they separated.

It took Marcuno two days to track down Jeremy. The man was not happy to see him, "What are you doing here?"

"The Governess is dead, why are you still holding onto past grudges?" Marcuno asked. Jeremy let out a sigh, "you're right, what do you need?"

"I am about to ask you for a huge favor on something that could possible be as big as the governess," Marcuno began.

"I'm listening," Jeremy's interest was perked.

"Some of my old friends are in some sort of trouble in the Trials Galaxy," Marcuno paused. "How much do you trust me and my word?" Jeremy looked at him through hard eyes.

"I don't like that you left but you are a wise and honorable man and a great friend," was his response.

"Division seventeen did not really attack the Ruler of the local galaxies," Marcuno spoke slowly testing the waters. He watched Jeremy's features, they did not change as the words spread to his ears.

"Are you sure?" Jeremy asked.

"Yes, I know them personally."

"Then that is good enough for me. Plus, who can really trust the media these days? They put me on the list as working for that jackass, Mavius," said Jeremy. Marcuno smiled.

"Lemme guess, division seventeen is in the Trials Galaxy?" Jeremy concluded. Mavius nodded, "It's secret, do you know their faces?"

"I think so, I should be able to download their images," Jeremy added, "Where are they exactly?"

"Yeylacore, it is on the edge of the Trials Galaxy. They won't be easy to find."

"I bet they won't trust me at first, would they?" Marcuno shook his head, Jeremy was right.

"Tell Phoenix, 'sky rose' would you? And that Dragon is safe," Marcuno finally said.

"Will do."

"Is everything set?" Wrie asked. Mavius nodded. She went to the back of the cave and pulled out the tattered cloths she had stored. She put on the long dress, then the cape, then the hair scarf. Finally, she donned the veil. She pulled out a dagger and made long gashes in her flesh.

"Quickly," she commanded Mavius. Together, they pulled out the little chip that would teleport them back into the dimension where Wrie wanted to rule as Governess.

"Over here!" Mavius called out to a Livan security ship. Wrie sagged down to her knees and pretended to be wounded worse than she really was. The search party led by the rest of the Supreme Generals had been looking for the Governess' remains.

"She's alive! Down here!" Mavius hailed. Wrie was transported back to the 'castle' and was given the best of medical attention.

"When you feel well enough, would your honor mind giving us a recollection of events?" Struta spoke to her on his knee.

"Of course," she replied softly as Dikara would. "I don't remember much, but division seventeen was there. They were much stronger than any us had known they were. It was highly unnatural. I hate to do this, but label them as a dangerous enemy, and bring me their heads."

"Their heads?" General Struta was hesitant. That was a very strange request, "are you sure?"

"Yes."

"Could your honor write out an official decree?" he spoke trying to be cautious.

"It shall be done. I am tired now, please let me rest." Struta obeyed. He gave her a polite nod and retreated backwards with his head bowed. When the door shut behind him, Wrie threw off her covers and gracefully walked to the window. She looked out at the sky. Soon, it was all going to be hers.

Struta had no choice. He spoke to the other generals and told them what the Governess had said. They were all as equally shocked as Struta towards her request. Later that day, they all received the official written decree sealed by the Governess. Did Yolukia implement a monster? Maybe the rebels were right. Either way, orders were orders. They took turns guarding Liva and traveling the galaxy. Soon, word got out and rumors swirled about Phoenix and her division outside of the media. She became a ghost with unfathomable powers much like the pyre siren, Haiokasheeba that lived on the Solzan moon, Quar.

Phoenix awoke with a start. The heavy Yeyla air was clinging to the inside of her lungs and she felt like a wet towel from the inside out. It was not easy for her to adjust to this place and she felt sorry that she had ever sent Su-Lin here. The muggy light was spilling forth through the poorly curtained window of the seventh floor apartment. Around her was crammed half of the division. They were still asleep. They were either leaning against a wall with a weapon cradled in their arms or sprawled over each other. A country over, the rest of the division stayed with Kirin in command. They separated into two groups in case anything should happen to them.

The dream was fresh in her mind as Old Matthew's words poured back to her. Phoenix thought back to the way he had looked. She imagined it would have been what Moses looked like after he had seen God. Old Matt was serene, like he had all the answers he needed, but loved the mystery of not knowing best of all. It scared her a little bit, especially after the dream she just had.

In the dream, there were seven seeds sitting in a row on a window ledge. They were large, like a peach pit or an avocado seed. The one on the far left was wilting quickly and dying as it gave off an essence that looked like small pink and red hearts. From the right, two more seeds marched in on invisible legs. The one behind it suddenly tripped and fell forward onto what would have been it's face. Dark blood oozed out of the top, and it faded away as well. The other marching seed went up to the fourth one sitting from the right who was oblivious to anything around her. The marching pit kicked the fourth one a good hard blow, and the others that were sitting on the ledge shuddered along with it. Phoenix had felt like someone had kicked her heart and in the dream, she even gasped for breath. Then, things began to happen. The seeds danced around like they were crazy and the sunlight shining on them disappeared. They floated up into the air and began swirling around each other in disorganized orbits. The seed that kicked the fourth one turned black and emitted a red smoke. Phoenix could not help but feel as if she were somehow connected to all those seeds. She slowly became aware that as the first two seeds died, she felt a tearing inside of herself as well.

The black seed began pushing the red smoke at the other six seeds. This slowed them down and Phoenix imagined she could hear them gagging. Suddenly, the black seed began chasing one of the seeds in particular. It flew towards Phoenix, then turned and flew the other way. The others sat idly by, there was nothing they could do.

A black dog appeared. It gently swallowed the normal seed whole and Phoenix could almost feel it slide gently down the dog's throat. The dog then growled and attacked the black seed tearing it to shreds. As it was being torn apart, Phoenix could hear screams of agony and saw bloody limbs flying every which way. There was a tiny arm, then another. There was a pile of arms on one side of the dog, and a pile of legs on the other side. Right before Phoenix, was a pile of unrecognized heads. The torsos were raining down like shreds if paper. These were the bodies of all the people Phoenix had killed. The dog was fate.

Even though she was awake now, Phoenix felt the icy hand of dread hovering over her. She looked up expectantly but there was nothing there. Yet, she could not shake the feeling that something was going to swoop in on her. She walked outside in hope of finding fresher air.

"Phoenix," a voice spoke behind her. Bewildered, she turned to face a human she did not recognize. The dream lingered in her mind and her nerves were on edge.

"Who are you? Leave me alone," she accidentally gave herself away. She was loosing it.

"Are you Phoenix?" he asked daringly. He was really sticking his neck out. Phoenix wasn't thinking clearly enough to lie, "who wants to know?"

"If that is a yes, I will tell you," he contested. Phoenix was very tired of hiding and she felt something break inside of her, "yes I am." She then braced herself for an attack. None came. The man spoke again, "Marcuno sent me. He says to tell you Dragon is with him and fine. He also says you wouldn't believe a word I say unless I told you 'sky rose.'"

"What is it you have to tell me?" Phoenix questioned

suspiciously. The man took a deep breath, "you have my teams and myself on your side to aid you in whatever it is you need to do. The governess is dead, and we have no other purpose." The words warmed Phoenix. Good old Marcuno. Phoenix felt lightheaded. Perhaps it was the different atmosphere, or perhaps it was the dream, she felt very far from reality, as if a part of her was somewhere lost in another world. Her skin and all worldly possessions seemed not to matter anymore. This whole mix up seemed trivial, who cares if there was another governess. Shouldn't this mean she could go home and live a normal life? She suddenly felt that her responsibilities were no longer a part of her. It was as if she had fallen away from them and they were left wandering without a body.

Suddenly, an image flashed before her eyes. It was an image of her, sitting on the Governess' throne. Phoenix was not surprised. The girl had eyes as black as death and she was contesting Phoenix. Was this the girl that wanted her life? Was she sending her a message? Phoenix was very tired, but she knew she was not allowed to quit. She knew that her division members were just as tired as she was. Worst of all, she knew the imposter Governess was not really dead.

"The governess is not dead, I serve the true governess," was what Phoenix spoke.

"What do you mean?" Jeremy asked. He had long since started to feel there was something unusual going on with the whole situation of implementing a governess. The idea seemed dangerous and that was why he had wanted to remove her. He wasn't sure why he felt this way, but he knew something was wrong and it wasn't over yet.

"The Governess is being impersonated by another who is trying to kill her. We did not find out until it was too late and now the false Governess is sitting on the throne, waiting until it is time to set her plan into motion. She is planning on blowing up Yeyla, which is why we are here. We know her subordinates planted a heat generator in the center of the planet not too long ago." Jeremy jumped at those words, "well have you tried to remove it?" Phoenix shook her head, "It is too heavily guarded and we do not want to attract attention."

"What can we do now?" Jeremy asked urgently. Phoenix gazed back at him through the haze in her head, "nothing."

Phoenix scanned Jeremy's mind and knew he could be trusted. She did not admit to him that she was the true Governess, but she did tell him about the Governess when he asked.

"I am close to her," Phoenix began, "I know that she is trusted by Yolukia and even though she never wanted to be the Governess in the first place, she accepted. Her lack of desire for that kind of power was what made Yolukia trust her in the first place.

"What was?" Jeremy was a little confused.

"The fact that she didn't want to rule. Her council presents her with issues and she makes decisions."

"Doesn't she have supreme control?" Jeremy asked.

"Not yet. She isn't quite sure how to do the job. That is why she tours as many planets as she can to learn more about the Galaxy."

"What plans does she have for the galaxy?" Jeremy put in.

"None as of now, she needs to learn about it first. The council serves her every need until she is ready to assume control. She doesn't want that to happen though. She may always keep a council."

"How do you know this?"

"She told me herself."

"Where is she now?"

"Safe."

"I would like to meet her."

"Why?"

"Because I didn't trust her and wanted to remove her. What you say about her makes her sound grand, but I can't trust a person until I look them in the eyes." The two were quiet for a moment. Phoenix greatly respected Jeremy's sentiment. She eventually spoke, "do you trust my judgment of her?"

"I trust Marcuno's judgment of you." Phoenix understood. It was funny to her how her credibility relied on those around her who were more established. Fbel trusted Yolukia and aided her. With Jeremy, he trusted Marcuno. Either way, she was filled with gratitude.

Later that day, her head finally cleared. She called together Kirin and the rest of Jeremy's group.

"I am going to see the Bevon brothers," she announced. They all nodded.

"Start evacuating the planet," she instructed.

"Where should be send them to?" Kirin asked.

"We don't have clearance to place them on another planet yet, just keep them in the space ships at a safe distance if you have to. But at least try to contact the other planets and explain the situation."

"People are not going to want to leave their homes," said Jeremy.

"I know, but we have to try," Phoenix replied.

"When I spoke with the miners, they didn't believe me about the object being a heat generator. They are so far removed from everything that happens in the Milky Way," Kirin informed everyone. Phoenix nodded, "That is why I am going to see the twins."

Phoenix didn't care to keep herself secret anymore. Something inside of her changed after the dream. She went from passive and defensive into no longer fearing the consequences of her brash actions. She marched straight up to the palace. The first set of guards tried to restrain her, but she merely tossed them out of the way. Surprised by her incredible strength, they feared her and opened fire. The guns were normal lasers and caused her only minor lacerations on her skin. They healed within seconds thanks to her enhanced body. The guards became terrified of her and viewed her as a goddess. They quickly dropped their weapons and sprawled down on their faces begging for forgiveness. Phoenix ignored them and threw open the heavy palace gate.

She was tired of being a soldier. Following orders got you killed. It got the people following you killed as well. The people giving orders didn't even know what was going on half of the time. It was much better to be what Old Matthew had told her to be, a warrior. It was in that moment, her heart accepted that she would forever be a vigilante. She would no longer wait for orders, she would do what needs to be done.

"Benjamin! Kennedy!" she hollered through the large halls. A shot fired from the side hall caught her in the hip and sent her flying through a wall. Her hip shattered and her ribs were pushed against her organs. It hurt terribly, but it didn't matter, a few moments later, she was back on her feet as good as new.

"You rascal," she said when she found Ben holding a CP 4-9. He lifted the gun again but Phoenix's eyes stared through him, "put it down, Ben." He listened. He was suddenly very afraid of this strange woman.

"Who are you?" he asked in a quivering voice.

"It's Hannah," Ken said from behind him. Ben's eyes filled with surprise, "You dyed your hair!" he exclaimed.

"Hannah was never my real name, I am Phoenix of division seventeen. Anyway, no time for chit chat. You do realize you are aiding someone in the destruction of this planet, right?" The brothers looked at each other.

"We're innocent!" they pleaded.

"Look guys," she spoke solidly, "can we put everything behind us and focus on saving the people on this planet?"

"What do you mean?" Ken asked.

"I mean the sphere you had buried is an automated heat generator and this entire planet is made of highly explosive gel."

"So you mean we've been sitting on a pile of explosives?" Ben was exasperated, "holy shit! We have to get out of here!"

"Not yet!" Phoenix hollered. They were stilled by the power in her voice.

"You two are still the rulers, I need you to command everyone to leave the planet. My team and I will try to extract the sphere." The two nodded in agreement. Their life of luxury and fantasy just ended and turned into reality. They suddenly realized that if Phoenix did not show up, they would have paid with their lives.

"The civilians are safely on the other planets on the far side of the orbit," Kirin reported a few hours later.

"Good, we should try to extract the sphere now," Phoenix spoke, "Jeremy learned how to use the mining equipment this morning. It should be easy.

It actually was quite easy. Their nerves were on edge because no one knew when the sphere was supposed to activate. Everyone uttered a silent prayer and breathed in shallow gasps. When the sphere was dropped into the Core and consumed by flames, division seventeen and Jeremy's group let out an exhausted cheer.

Suddenly, everything changed mid-cheer. They all tumbled to the ground and the colors around them swirled together into an unrecognizable palette. It felt as if their skulls were being ripped apart and their appendages went numb.

When they awoke again, it was dark. Phoenix grit her teeth and painfully pushed herself to sit up. Looking around, she recognized the constellations.

"We're in the Archimedes system!" she exclaimed.

"I have a friend here," Jeremy chimed in excitedly.

Wrie sat waiting. Her patience was wearing thin. Someone from the Livan security crew was supposed to have delivered a message that a large explosion occurred at the other end of the galaxy by now. The automatic timer Mavius was supposed to have placed in Yeyla's main palace should have activated and teleported the entire planet into the

Archimedes system switching it with the planet Olive. The teleportation should have triggered the heat generator, which should have caused the planet to explode. The explosion was supposed to trigger the other smaller planets around it made of the same explosive gel. No one would suspect a thing since the Milky Way no longer had contact with Yeylacore. The teleportation and cross dimensional technology was accessible to Wrie alone in the Milky Way so she wielded it alone like a secret weapon.

Wrie tapped her foot. Why weren't plans going well? There was a knock on the door and Mavius entered.

"Tell me it's done," she demanded. He looked confused.

"Did Yeyla explode yet?" she asked agitatedly.

"Didn't it?" he was confused, "I thought you would have received confirmation by now.

"I did not." Another knock came at the door. Wrie calmed her nerves, this must be it.

"Come in," she called sweetly. The door opened and a soldier walked in. He kept his head bowed as he spoke, "Your honor, some of our contacts noticed a peculiarity in the Archimedes system."

"Oh," she replied curiously, "what is it?"

"The planet Olive disappeared and was replaced by a foreign one," he finished. Wrie was waiting for him to say more.

"We just thought you should know," he gave a little dip and turned to leave.

"What is the situation in Archimedes?" she implored forcibly. He turned back to her, "There is much confusion, we are trying to make sense of the situation. There are a few rebels on the planet, it seems to be under populated, the homes are abandoned."

"The planet is intact?" Wrie questioned further.

"Yes your honor," the soldier was confused by the question.

"You may go," Wrie dismissed him. He bow a thank you and left. As soon as the door was shut and Wrie had privacy, she turned on Mavius, "You back biting snake!" she threw him to the ground. He calmly covered his head to protect himself from her blows.

"I did everything you said," he managed to breathe out in between the beatings she was giving him.

"You can't do anything right!" she screamed.

「凤凰」
你杀掉了。
下雨了。
命
远的…
爱到死.
你一辈子

CHAPTER TWELVE

There was another dream. Phoenix was watching from a distance. There were some grew lumps. As the image grew clearer, she recognized them to be figures. Like a telescope, her vision zoomed in. Fbel, Old Matt, Marcuno, a few of Fbel's soldiers and division seventeen were circled around the woman holding her bleeding face. She looked up at her original the five other clones.

"Kill me now," she seethed miserably with hate touching every tip of her words. No one responded to her. They treated her words as empty. Everything went gray, and Phoenix awoke. A pang of longing shot through her as she sensed Dragon in her heart. Did he see the dream too?

They were on the planet Ceve and Joy was talking with a native as if they knew each other. Joy was smiling a genuine smile. It was something that had escaped her for a long time. Phoenix smiled too. A warm feeling spread throughout her limbs and Joy caught it. She turned to look at Phoenix. They smiled a painfully happy smile at each other as they connected in that moment. Joy had lost something precious to her and it was tied to this place. Phoenix could feel it. They gave each other their hearts and squeezed out the blood for each other to ease their sorrow.

"I love you," Joy sent telepathically to Phoenix. She smiled, "I love you too."

"Phoenix," Jeremy called approaching her. The connection was broken. Joy went back to talking to her friend and Phoenix turned to Jeremy. She got up and brushed the dust off of her dirty clothes.

"What is it?" she asked him.

"This is my friend Deritak and my brother Simon," he introduced the two young men. Phoenix smiled and shook hands warmly.

"They opposed the governess as well," Jeremy spoke. This offended Phoenix a little bit, but she bit her tongue.

"You mean the imposter Governess?" she asked. Simon and Deritak looked confused.

"I was getting to that, I was hoping you would tell them what you had told me," Jeremy chimed in. Phoenix did. She was feeling stronger as the number of her allies increased. When she was finished, she informed Jeremy of the plans her division had made the night before.

"We are going to remove the imposter Governess and reinstate the true one."

"It won't be easy," Simon warned.

"We know her defenses well, but we are going to need help with the Livan security crew. We have been trying to get in contact with former Supreme General Fbel but he was not at the last meeting point. We have no idea if he is even alive or not," Phoenix reported in a regretful voice.

"He is," Deritak spoke up. They three turned to look at him. What was he saying?

"Let me introduce myself," he continued, "I am King Deritak from a planet in the Helenic system. Fbel was seeking my help when a coup occurred on my home planet. He was imprisoned for helping me escape. As you know, I don't consider myself a rebel, but I do not support tyranny." He turned to Phoenix, "tell your Governess, yes, do rule with love, but she must remember to exercise control as well. I gave my people a lot of freedoms and stood apart from making firm decisions. Without strong leadership, my planet is falling victim to high crime and death. I am willing to help you because I feel as if the same thing that happened to me is happening to the true Governess." Phoenix nodded her thanks. Those were words she would never forget. Deritak stared at Phoenix for a while as Simon was tossing out a few ideas of what to do with the Livan security crew. Phoenix stared back at Deritak.

"Jeremy," Deritak spoke, "she is the true Governess isn't she?" Phoenix did not panic. She closed her eyes with a soft smile. Simon and Jeremy looked at Phoenix. They were exasperated.

"No," Jeremy responded hesitantly, "she couldn't be."

"Could she be?" Simon asked.

"Does it matter?" Phoenix questioned. It was then when Kirin approached, "We have to move," she announced, "Leffi picked up a signal, the impersonating Governess has left Liva and we suspect she is coming to this system."

At that moment, a strong wind blew across the plain. It was filled with blue music and it settled in Phoenix's soul. Time stood still and she breathed deeply. A tiny spark lit up inside of her in a deep hidden corner of her heart.

"I know what to do," she spoke quickly.

"Jeremy, Simon, Deritak, I need you to create diversions for the Livan security crew. My division and I are going after the Governess." The three men looked at Phoenix in a trance. When she spoke, there was an energy seething out of her, as if something in her already knew the outcome. Like she was reading the secrets of the universe. It made them shudder, but it comforted them as well that at least someone had faith in the situation.

Phoenix looked at the three men and saw right through them. They were all good people. They wanted to fight for something that was a noble cause. They wanted a reason for existence. They had no real grudge against the Governess, Mavius was the one who put it into their minds that she was going to be an iron fisted ruler selfishly consuming the goods of the Galaxy to benefit herself. Now that they knew who she was both physically and characteristically, they were gladly willing to fight their noble cause for her. She was real, she was material, not just rumors and empty threats.

The three men knelt down, "Governess Dikara," Jeremy spoke, "we will serve you until the end, no matter how bloody, or how peaceful." They rose and bowed deeply to Kirin before leaving.

"You told?" Kirin asked in surprise. Phoenix looked at her smoothly, "I didn't, they saw me and knew."

The twelve members of division seventeen quickly packed up their items. A small tube of lipstick fell out of Sunshine's bag and landed at Phoenix's feet. Inspired, she picked it up on a whim and drew a design on her left cheek. She tossed the lipstick back to Sunshine. She looked at Phoenix carefully. She too, drew a design beneath her left eye and tossed the lipstick to another sister. All six of them drew a different symbol on their cheek to identify themselves.

"It's our own war paint," Ara said solemnly. Without another word, the division members jumped into their jet crafts.

"Kirin," Phoenix radioed, "we are to try to bring down the false Governess in an isolated area. The less media coverage, the better."

"Roger that."

Struta's soldiers watched the Governess leave. They were to watch Liva while Mavius escorted the Governess away. She did not want any others to follow her and this made Struta nervous. Something just didn't feel right. Though the other Supreme Generals were hunting for division seventeen, Struta felt that it was the governess he should not be trusting. Quickly he scolded himself for such terrible thoughts. The ship was out of sight. Struta turned and went to the control center. There, a group of off duty soldiers were sitting around conversing.

"Where is division seventeen from?" a soldier asked another.

"I heard they were humans, that means they are from Preyal."

"Preyal? What are they doing here?" the first soldier asked again.

"I agree, it seems disgraceful," the second soldier replied.

"What does 'Phoenix' mean anyway?" another soldier chimed in.

"Not sure," the first soldier responded. An older soldier spoke up, "It means Pheinl, a bird that dies in fire." The soldiers let out a round of laughter.

"She probably will die in our crossfire!" a soldier called out in amusement.

"She is strong, don't underestimate her," Struta said before walking out. The soldiers were quiet. It wasn't long after that the Livan security crew created their own nicknames for division seventeen. The females were all called Queiltas, which meant "warrior." The males were Queidso Pheinls, which was merely the masculine form of the same word. When preceding the word Pheinl, it implied that they were the owned by the Pheinl. Thus the males were jokingly called the "warrior slaves of Phoenix." From that point on, Phoenix was known as Queilta Prima and her sisters the Queilta Ablotas, the warriors enslaved to sisterhood.

Smoke screens and illusions. That was what the truth was. It was a game of cat and mouse to see who could pull the most number of blind maneuvers. It was to see who had the best sand thrown into the others' eyes. The facts were just words, it was not reality but a delusion. Besides what was lost in translation, there was all that was lost in transmission. The communicators broadcasted words. The words were dictated by those who were trying to control the situation. The words usually landed on the heads of soldiers, loyal dogs who were punished if they were to stop and think for themselves and not their masters.

They were no longer going to be soldiers. The last command Phoenix gave them was to toss off the garb of blind obedience and follow their instincts. A burning fire boiled deeply in her gut and transmitted throughout her entire being through her blood. She felt cold all over. Her division and herself were raped of their respect. Their integrity and faith in following orders was brushed aside as if they were bones for the dogs. This would not do. This would not do at all. She was coming back full of a passionate emotion charged with vengeance. It coursed through all of them like a poison.

The world of the tangible was just that. It could easily be controlled and manipulated by those who were dictated and handed the most power. Whoever had clearance could not be questioned of their actions. This world, was disgusting. Trust and honesty became nothing more than words. There were no rules, only the fake lines drawn by fake people to keep the fearful in their place. Shedding their garb of fear, Phoenix questioned, "Why did they fear?" Being trained as soldiers, they were accustomed to think rationally, objectively. Being forced to swallow themselves and their emotional substance, was not rational, and did not dictate the best course of action. Hang it all, they were going as vigilantes and Phoenix was going to put the real Governess back in her place. She might not comprehend Yolukia's reasoning, but he wanted Dikara ruling for a reason. She had faith that the answers were a time primed release programmed inside of her somehow.

They cited the ship with the DNA signature of the Governess inside. They opened fire. Five ships flew out, but did not last long. Mavius tried calling for backup but Leffi jammed the signal. Deritak, Simon and Jeremy were attacking areas surrounding Liva and kept the Livan security crew too busy to actively keep track of the false Governess. It was all going to be over soon.

Phoenix and her five sisters boarded the ship. That was all they needed, there were not too many others on board. Kirin stayed behind with the rest of the division on guard. Stregatori was dead but his assistant Nek was still serving Mavius. He lead a small group of soldiers to attack the intruders. The Queilta Ablotas shot the guns from their hands.

"Look at me," Phoenix demanded in a black voice, "you can fight me or die, or serve me, and live." To her disappointment, all but two of the disillusioned soldiers took their own lives with their trex coated daggers. Nek stood before the great Phoenix. He had heard about her. In his mind, she was an indestructible spirit from the Netherworld. He thought he was being brave standing up to her. He thought he was dying for a righteous cause. He thought it was the real Governess he was protecting. He thought and he believed all the lies that were fed to him. Sometimes, even warriors lose their way when they chose to see what others' saw, and not what their own eyes and hearts tell them.

Phoenix took his life. He had wanted to die. He wanted to feel as if he were a martyr. She merely granted his wish. It didn't matter who he was serving or protecting. He felt like it was a virtuous cause, and that gave him peace.

The Queilta Ablotas stood clear as they blew off the door to the navigational room. As they expected, the people from within opened fire. Tinkerbell tossed in a bomb and the ship jolted. Control was lost and they crashed into an asteroid. Only the physically altered beings survived. Phoenix was the first one to gain consciousness. She pulled herself together and dragged her pain filled body around. Finally, she found herself standing above the creature dressed in the Governess' garbs.

When Wrie opened her eyes, her body was wrapped in heavy shrouds of pain. She could not see clearly. When her vision cleared and her body was almost healed, she looked up into a face that was her own. Phoenix stared down at her, unmoving. Her body was tense with anger. The anger near consumed her, but she managed somehow to keep her cool. This was the clone that tried to kill Yolukia, this was the clone that tried to kill her loved ones and herself. She was going to die today. The sudden thirst for blood was an unusual one for Phoenix. She had never wanted to kill before, it was merely what she had to do.

Wrie looked back up at the Phoenix. She thought amusingly to herself, “This is the one and only.” Unlike Phoenix, Wrie felt empty. There was a hollow inside of her and it was filled with cold. Everyone else had failed her. By herself, she was going to have to get her hands dirty and kill all of the others who shared her DNA.

Wrie stood up. Phoenix did not budge. Taking off her veil first, she revealed the same face as Phoenix. She removed the scarf over her head to reveal short chin-length hair. Looking into Phoenix's eyes with her own poisonous ones, she mocked her. The insult bounced off of Phoenix. She was there to fight and would not be distracted by words. Wrie removed the Governess' cape from her shoulders, then the long dress. Beneath it, she was in a jumper.

One filled with fire. One filled with ice. Behind them, the Queilta Ablotas were in combat with Mavius, Ucile, and the remaining soldiers. Ucile was a tough one. She took out three of the sisters at once. This left two of them to defend as the others forced themselves to heal quickly. It wasn't until everyone teamed together to fight Ucile did they triumph. As she died, her scream released the souls of all those she had killed. Mavius sat watching the entire scene. The five sisters approached him. He watched with empty eyes as they surrounded him.

He sad nothing. He was a shell. Unless Wrie commanded him, he had no more reasons to live.

Wrie struck out first. She kicked Phoenix in the face and before the Queilta recovered, a second kick landed in her throat. Phoenix fell a step back but kept calm. She was going to study Wrie's movements. Again and again, Wrie struck out. She was trying to instigate Phoenix to fight back because she wanted to study her movements as well. It frustrated her that her original merely stood there, taking her hits. Phoenix stared back at Wrie. The lipstick symbol on her cheek was mixed in with the blood that covered her face but her eyes still burned with a calm and steady hatred. Wrie lashed out with a deadly strike towards her solar plexus. Phoenix finally moved. She grasped the false Governess's wrist and with her free hand grasped her throat before the woman could react. She held her face close and breath a deadly curse into her empty soul, "I hate you."

Phoenix had never felt this way before. All the suppressed emotion from the time Sarah died came pouring out in a single blaze of hatred for this creature that shared her skin. It was, indeed, a sort of hatred towards herself. She hated herself for not waking up sooner and listening to Old Matthew. The challenge he issued them to know the difference between a soldier and a warrior was indeed a subliminal command to tell them to free themselves and to think for themselves. Phoenix hated herself for not knowing sooner. She hated herself for feeling so helpless at times and she hated herself for not being able to live up to others' expectations. She hated, and she hated, and she felt the fire growing stronger. She stared into the empty poisonous eyes so full of burning ice. She ignored the lashes that struck her until a small meteor collided nearby. To Wrie's luck, they were thrown sideways. Phoenix tumbled into a shallow crater and Wrie slammed into Mavius. The other sisters were scattered in all directions.

"Quickly, give me that gun," Wrie instructed her puppet as the Queilta Ablotas hurried onto their feet and were running towards them. Mavius looked up from his trance. Phoenix crawled out of the crater in time to see Mavius shove a dagger into the false Governess' throat.

"No more commands," he said with a peaceful smile. She gaped at him. She tried to mouth words, but they only came out as a windy howl.

Kirin and the rest of the division approached at this time and landed. They had a hard time getting to through the asteroids and meteors flying around. They exited their crafts and gathered around.

The trexia was working through Wrie's blood. She stared deeply into Mavius soul, "traitor!" she shrieked. It came out as a high-pitched whine. He smiled innocently towards her like a child who got the bike he wanted for Christmas.

"Goodbye, Wrie," he said soothingly. It wasn't long until her face turned purple and wilted into a dark blue. She was gone. The smile lingered on Mavius' face. Everyone was still. Was it over? Mavius moved slowly. He fell onto his knees, then collapsed to the ground. He stared at the blood on his hands. His mind suddenly felt free and he came to realize everything that had occurred over that last couple of years while under the control of Wrie. It was all his fault. If he had not accepted her ideas as his own, none of this would have happened. Slowly, he turned to look at Phoenix.

"I'm sorry," he said. He slowly picked up a gun and unloaded it. The spectators watched cautiously as he took one of the bullets. He dipped it into Wrie's trexia filled blood and then loaded the bullet into the gun. Mechanically, he lifted the gun and pointed it in his head. When he fired, the trex poison did its job and he passed away. Wrie's blood killed him, as much as her words had prevented him from living.

Phoenix exhaled. She was exhausted.

"What do we do with the bodies?" Kirin asked.

"Leave them," Phoenix replied with wrath. The division said nothing, they did not move since they were all engulfed by exhaustion. Phoenix retrieved the Governess garment Wrie was wearing. "I should be getting back to Liva," she said in a gentle tone. The warriors nodded. A sense of accomplishment and relief washed over all of them in that instant. Phoenix breathed deep and looked up into the darkness. Which way was Liva? What lie ahead? When was Dragon returning? There were so many questions and not enough answers. It didn't matter anymore. She was going to think for herself now.

It was peaceful for Phoenix on the return to Liva. Her rage had died down and she was breathing easier now. Kirin and Neroz piloted the larger ship while the others flew in protective formation. In her mind, she was going over all that would need to be done. The galaxy was a mess in more aspects than they knew about. There were communication problems and trust issues. She was going to have to work hard to clean up the Galaxy. Yolukia had appointed her too soon. Or, perhaps it was just the right time. The experience with the false governess taught her a lot.

"Unknown jet crafts approaching," Kirin called. Phoenix's ears perked. Kirin hailed to the ships, "Approaching jet crafts, please identify yourselves." They waited patiently, but there was no response.

"Please identify yourselves or we will label you as hostile." No sooner had Kirin spoken did their ship jolt tossing Phoenix to the floor. The others were wearing their seatbelts. The remaining division members flew towards the oncoming attackers.

"I'm going to fight," Phoenix said.

"That's a bad idea," Kirin offered, "You are the Governess again." She was right. Phoenix went up to the cockpit and strapped herself into a seat.

"Livan security, this is the Governess, requesting emergency back up," she called.

"This is General Struta, we are on our way, please give us your coordinates." Kirin gave the coordinates, but the attacking ships retreated.

"Enemy ship has retreated," Kirin reported to General Struta, "but still requesting escort."

"Roger." The division sat nervously. There was no telling who the other ships were. Where they attacking the Governess? Or did they think they were attacking division seventeen? They rode silently and steadily at their slow pace towards Liva. A few moments later, General Struta hailed on the radio.

"Your honor, requesting knowledge of your safety, we sense enemy division seventeen ships surrounding you but we will not be near enough to attack for another twenty minutes." Phoenix looked at Kirin.

"Division Seventeen is not the enemy, they are escorting me," Phoenix radioed back. There was a pause, then, "Then let me speak to Director Mavius." Phoenix felt a hot grip on the back of her neck.

"Director Mavius is deceased," she replied. Besides truth, what else was there to tell.

"I am requesting proof of your legitimacy as Governess," was what the radio said in return, "Offer proof before we arrive or we are annihilating all of you."

"You will do no such thing General Struta," another voice cut in. It was Fbel!

"Who is this?"

"This is General Fbel."

"General Fbel, you were labeled as a traitor and we were told not to trust you," came the response. Struta was hesitant in producing the last comment. He knew Fbel quite well, they trained together at the Academy on Liva. He trusted him more than the Governess herself.

"Listen Struta," Fbel switched to a private line and spoke directly to General Struta. "The Governess for the past few months was an imposter. Division Seventeen and myself have been safeguarding the true Governess and that is her on the ship returning to Liva."

"How do you know?" Struta questioned suspiciously. He was even beginning to suspect whether or not the voice really belonged to Fbel.

"I know it is her, she remembers pinning the ruby medal to my chest, she remembers Layka kissing me and she remembers you being the first to shake my hand. How could anyone else know something like that from a closed ceremony?" After hearing those words, General Struta smiled, "It's good to have you back old friend!"

Together, the two Supreme Livan Generals escorted the true Governess back to her ruling planet. Phoenix breathed a sigh of relief. When was this going to be over so she could hold her little daughter in her arms? That was all she longed for at the moment.

Liva was a small dot in their window. It was growing larger by the second and everyone was glad to be back. Suddenly, the Generals' soldiers broke formation.

"Hostile crafts approaching, be on your guard," came over the radio. Kirin managed to steer clear of the attackers in the clumsy ship until more defense flew from Liva. The Governess made it safely back to her "castle." She was locked behind sturdy walls surrounded by professional soldiers who were willing to give their lives to protect her. She was flattered, but as Phoenix, she secretly worried about the well being of her division. She was kept in the dark. Only after the battle was over would she receive any information.

Wrie was suspended in white light. She was waiting for something, that much she knew. She couldn't move, but she didn't want to either. There was an eerie peace that covered her entire being, which was no longer made of flesh. Her eyes were closed, but she had no eyelids and she could still see. She merely drifted.

Slowly, she was aware of presence. Was it her? Or were there little creatures running about? Was it a divine light? Was it God? She was not scared of anything anymore. It was all over, and she knew that she was dead.

"Where did I go wrong? How did I fail?" she asked herself. Then, an answer seeped through her mind like an icy breath and blew the words to answer her.

"When you traveled cross dimensionally, it changed the course of life on both sides. Both yours, and hers. You would have been better off staying in your dimension, and she would not have been marred by you. She is you. You were trying to kill yourself. If she dies, you die, as all of her clones. Twice, when she has been close to me, she went back to the world of living because of you and the others rooting her there. Her ties to you and them are so strong it brought her back to life."

"Does she know this?"

"No." The knowledge meant nothing to her. Wrie drifted painlessly inside a gigantic void of bright nothingness, in a trance. Her being was dissipating, being dissolved by the white light like an acid. Soon, she was no more, forever gone. She was in the vortex of wandering spirits and hers was not a genuine one. Thus, she had perished peacefully and left no residue.

The teleportation and cross dimensional traveling technology were handed over to the authorities in another galaxy, but not before Leffi saved the data for Angela. The Milky Way was only clarified to use artificial storage dimensions. Travel between existing dimensions was forbidden. Phoenix chuckled. Rules were so funny. It usually ended up cutting out the people with self control and handing power to those who didn't deserve it. Phoenix had no guarantee that her division members would not abuse the technology. It was true that it gave them a leg up in most predicaments, but it did not warrant the misuse of power. They all understood and knew they had to watch themselves.

Yeyla was returned to it's rightful place and peace was finally made official between the Trials galaxy and Milky Way galaxy. The Bevon twins were granted the right to stay on Yeyla and they were received as heroes for evacuating the planet before the teleportation took place. All of the unaltered beings on the planet would have passed away when the teleportation occurred. Most of the people on Olive did pass away and it was a sad time for the people in Archimedes. The twins offered their loyalty to Phoenix and promised to help where ever and whenever they were needed.

Jeremy, Simon, and Deritak were also allied with Phoenix. They had changed their views drastically since they had gotten to know their Governess. It took the fear out of them and was replaced with understanding. After fighting side by side with Phoenix, they were much more confident and comfortable with the Governess. Thus, she gained loyalty amongst the people along with her own security crew on Liva. Peace seemed to fall over them and things were slowly returning to normal.

Division seventeen had an extraordinary reputation. When Wrie was trying to hunt them down, she caused a number of different rumors to be spread. The only singular attitude shared towards the division, was one of awe betwixt with fear. No one knew exactly what the leader Phoenix was like. Some thought Phoenix was a man with three heads while others thought she really was a bird of living fire. There was nothing the Governess could do about these rumors except to let them die down whenever they would naturally burn out.

Wirga was furious. How did the Governess survive? This was not right! He would lose all his power to run underground activities with such an authority figure in place. He called his people and commanded them to attack the Governess' ship heading back to Liva. He gave Marcuno the lead and kept in contact through radio.

"Seth, I want you to fire at the main ship," Wirga commanded. Dragon was dumbstruck. Those were division seventeen ships surrounding the Governess' ships. No doubt that was his Phoenix onboard.

"Approaching jet crafts, please identify yourselves," his little cousin hailed over the radio.

"Fire now you dope!" Wirga screamed over the radio. Dragon carefully aimed at a small corner of the ship.

"Please identify yourselves or we will label you as hostile," Kirin called again. Dragon held his breath and fired. The division's old ships broke formation and flew at them.

"How could you have missed!" Wirga exploded on the radio. Dragon ignored him as the man yelled obscenities at him.

"Retreat!" Wirga finally called, "They are calling for security escort from Liva, return to regroup." As Dragon was retreating, he noticed Marcuno's body floating out in the vacuum. He opened the side port of his craft and pulled Marcuno in.

"You should have left me there as an assumed casualty," Marcuno spoke. He leaned back and studied the titanium rod running through his bleeding midsection. "Now I am going to have to fake dying in front of Wirga."

"I could toss you out right now if you'd like," Dragon replied with a wink. Marcuno chuckled, "Nah, that's okay. It gives me a headache being in a vacuum for too long." He pulled out a hidden flat communicator from the bottom of his boot.

"Hey Jeremy," he called, "long time no talk!"

Marcuno is an excellent actor, Dragon thought to himself. Especially since he grasped Wirga's sleeve pleadingly and said, "Please take care of my little brother for me." Dragon had tears in his eyes. They were not tears of sadness. He was biting his tongue to keep from laughing. The weird sounds coming from his mouth were mistaken for sobs.

"I'm sorry buddy," Wirga said slapping Seth on the back. Dragon coughed heavily and sucked in deep breaths. Thank goodness these people were such idiots. Marcuno was jettisoned and later secretly picked up by Jeremy. Not long after, Wirga sent them on a second attack on the Governess. He sent three times as many people. In the confusion, Dragon secretly shot at Wirga's own men and kept Phoenix safe. He could not help but notice some of his fellow division members went down and crashed into Liva. He prayed that they were alright. Wirga finally realized they were not going to get to the Governess and called another retreat. He was in a foul mood for the rest of the day.

"She has to go, we have to kill her, we can't just toss her out. Unless she is dead, these people will not cease."

"Don't you think that is just a little extreme and a little selfish?" Dragon asked.

"Nobody asked you Seth!" Wirga raged at him, "Even if I have to do it alone! She has to go! I don't care about the galaxy! I never did! Yes I said I did, but you wanna know the truth buddy? The truth is, everyone is selfish hidden beneath their noble causes. I want her gone so I can go on with my business as usual. With her around, it is only a matter of time before someone likes me gets the short end of the stick!"

"So you're going to kill her?" Dragon asked.

"Yes." The conversation ended. Wirga walked out.

Rosi awoke slowly. There was a soft dripping sound outside of the window by her bed. Looking out the window, she smiled at the lines left behind by the fresh morning dew. Only on Earth, nowhere else has she ever been made her so happy to be awake. On Earth, she can still live the delusion that she was a normal person, had a normal job, and led a normal life. Her skin tingled with excitement. The night before, she had taken a long hot shower when finally returned to SHONDS. She washed off all the soot that had built up during the last few months. She wiggled her toes and did not feel any slime. It was wonderful to be clean! They were in their quaint house in New York that was surrounded by brush and a few large trees. The sunlight danced passed the leaves and played through their windows offered a sense of magic as if they had a secret story to tell. Rosi wished desperately at times she could just stay home and listen to the stories. “No rest for the weary” she repeated Natasha’s words.

The two bedroom and one bath ranch home was old and rickety and she loved to hear the sounds of old wood clacking as the temperature increased then decreased. The peeling white paint on the outside had a beautiful patch of ivy that seemed to offer a fresh breath as it greeted the sun. The small kitchen had crooked mismatched cabinet drawers and the dishwasher scarcely harbored any wares. The refrigerator was filled with molding food and the small round kitchen table was littered with carry out boxes. The lone high chair that stood nearby was the only sterile inorganic piece of furniture in the otherwise homely environment.

The tub in the bathroom stood on four legs and had a cheap curtain thrown around it. The wall behind it was ceramic with a conservative stained glass window. On the window ledge was scattered a few small bottles and a large hunk of soap. The sink was small and stood before a medicine cabinet. The razor was left out and still had tufts of golden blonde mouth fuzz stuck in it. Across from the sink was a small toilet where Rosi’s underclothes decorated it like Christmas ornaments. Now she laid in bed with her little daughter and her husband.

Rosi reached over and brushed a lock of hair from the one year old’s face. She leaned down and kissed the little person that was wedged between her mother and father. The little girl yawned, exposing a tiny pink tongue surrounded by petal lips. She wiggled her little fingers and turned to snuggle against her father. Rosi looked up at Wayne. He smiled back at her through sky blue eyes. Carefully leaning over little Ara, she gave him a kiss.

"It's good to be back," she whispered against his lips.

"It is good indeed," he replied brushing her short hair back from her face. Rosi hacked off all of her long, dry, bleached blonde hair. The natural black was growing back in. It didn't matter. They were probably going to have to change their appearance again later.

"So what are we going to do?" Wayne asked her gently. Rosi leaned back on her pillow and gazed down at Ara.

"I don't know. I want her to stay with our family, but I know she would be safer on Mars or even Liva."

"What about Neptune?" Wayne asked insightfully. He was thinking about her schooling. Rosi bit her lip. She was overcome by a wave of sadness. She had wanted a baby so very much. When Ara was born, she was so in love she could feel her heart breaking. Now, the little girl was just too much for her and Dragon to handle. They had other obligations. She wished she could just quit, but quitting would be too dangerous, not to mention, not allowed. She could cease being a part of division seventeen, but not the Governess. She could stop acting on behalf of the galaxy, but the reputation that had built around the division was not going to fade any time soon. No, it was not safe to quit. They were in too deep. Too many people knew who they were and had a stake in their lives.

"I don't know," she whispered, "but we will figure it out." Looking at her watch, she turned to Dragon, "Oh my gosh! You've been on Earth too long! You had better get back to Wirga before he notices you're gone." Dragon gave his little girl a soft kiss in her downy hair and took a long lasting look at her. He imprinted her adorable face in his mind and sadly blinked away tears of emotion. He had a job to do, and he better not think of little Ara or he might give her away. He looked at Rosi. Her nightshirt hung astray and the muscular area below the clavicle showed the top edge of her pectoral muscles. He leaned forward and kissed the area deeply. He was going to miss them.

Carom and Sarilla

CHAPTER THIRTEEN

Sarilla of Liva

"Quandonta is a very large place," Sarilla said about the Milky Way Galaxy. Her voice held a kind of quiet awe that showed her respect. Her eyes trailed down to the shoes on her feet, "how do you know that they will ever find me?" Her brother lifted her face to his.

"Because you know Mother, what she wants, she will get." Those words were definite, short and truncated to iterate their definitude. The silence that followed was not an empty one. Through their gaze at each other, there was an understanding of the situation that only those who shared the same blood could comprehend. Sarilla looked away. Her eyes went over the expanse that lay before her. Stars twinkled gently at her like a lullaby. They were on a ship traveling from Liva to Turnika Jos. From Turnika Jos, Sarilla was debating whether or not to leave Quandonta. Her final decision was dependent on how much her parents wished to leave her alone. She glanced back out the window.

The five foot of Hydrexio glass was strong enough to keep cabin pressure stable at the speed they were traveling. She reached out her hand to feel the cold glass. It was a form of grounding for her, something tangible in her life. Her heart was a mess, she didn't know what she wanted, she didn't know her calling, at the same time, she was sure that she could not stay back and walk the path her mother had chose for her.

The Remotti race was one of many from Liva. They were different in that they placed females slightly above equal. This did not mean the females made the actual political interactions, the males still did. Yet, no one denied that it was the women who called the shots from behind the scenes. The hidden power of life was much more alive in women than it was in men. The men were very wise, but they did not know how to operate well behind the scenes, or beneath that which can be seen and heard. Her mother wanted her to take the position as dominant defender of the area they lived in. This meant that she would have to form a close bond, something like a human marriage, with a political figurehead. That was the tradition, one that would be heresy to disobey.

Sarilla was not yet ready for that kind of commitment. There was a calling out there for her in the universe. Her mother, a powerful healer in her area, was unable to understand. It annoyed Sarilla greatly that her mother, a powerful woman who can heal any physical malady, was unable to see what it was that plagued Sarilla the most. Of course, it was always her father that she shared the close bond with. He was a warrior. She was a warrior because of him.

She spawned from a large family. Two of her older brothers also went off to study to be warriors. Her second oldest brother was the only one who decided to be a healer like her mother. Her older sister was studying to be a philosophical politician. Her younger brother and sister were still too young to know what they wanted. Sarilla held the position as a Master of Defensive Arts. She wore her hair short like all the warriors, male and female, and had three rattails to signify that she was the third amongst her siblings to attain the position of a warrior. She knew that her path was with something by far greater than protecting a piece of land that harbored intellectuals that consorted with the Governess of the Galaxy. No, she should be out there protecting the entire Galaxy, not just the bigwigs who run it.

Her people were on Live long before the Governess was instated by Yolukia. Her race welcomed her into their country despite the rest of the galaxy. Soon afterwards, the planet was populated with politicians and members of her honorary council.

The Governess placed upon the throne was named Dikara. Bearing the traditional garb, she was covered from head to foot. Her eyes were the only parts of her body that you could see. Even those were heavily made up. There was no way for you to tell what species she was. That was the aim, for her to only be recognized by her power, not her roots.

Carom, her eldest brother, was the one traveling with her. Her second brother, Hsorht, was the one creating a distraction for her with their mother. He was asking her to train him in her healing arts so they were off in the mountains somewhere studying herbs. Sarilla's father had given her a small sum of money, and she was off to Turnika Jos.

There was a vast orgy of culture and tradition all over Turnika Jos. Species from all over the Galaxy and others beyond led busy lives there. From the small merchants selling their wares right in front of big corporation buildings to the intergalactic traders, the variety was astounding. The planet never slept. Landing poles for trade ships graced the sky and there was constant traffic. Large ships slowly eased onto the tips of the landing poles and used them as a guide to land somewhere nestled deep between the warehouses. From there, goods were divided and set upon smaller ships and transported throughout the rest of the Galaxy.

Sarilla's ship docked and slowly they trudged off of the ship. An announcement came on as they entered the cold and gray terminal. It warned them to be aware of possible attacks and told the new arrivals of the nearest bomb shelter. Turnika Jos as a valuable trading post often suffered futile attempts for destruction. The security was by far too great, Dikara the Governess made sure of that. The planet was imperative to the well being of the Galaxy.

There was graffiti on the walls and the stench of biological waste emanated from the four bathroom doors for the four primary genders. Though Sarilla and her family were noble class, she chose to travel in 3rd class because they did not have to give their names when purchasing tickets.

They spoke to no one. They didn't even looked at the hobos who came up to them with their hands cupped, begging for money. Her pack was slung precariously on her back, but the air she walked with demanded a certain degree of respect. Her brother held the same air, but he was more orderly. Carom's short hair was patted down neatly and his single rattail was in a tight long elegant braid down his back. This was a far contrast from Sarilla's unkempt weeds on her head and her dreadlocked pieces hanging down to her waist. No matter how they differed in their appearance, it was noticeable that they were both disciplined and well trained to contain themselves. Sarilla's appearance was merely a cover. She did not have the heart to part with her braids. It was a part of her family, her blood. Just because she was at a disagreement with her mother did not mean that she wished to sever everything she had with them.

They exited the terminal and Carom hailed a cab. They were off the meet with his friend Travis. Travis, that name sounded strange to Sarilla. Travis was to help her set up a new life. One that would be hard for her mother to track her down in.

Travis was sitting in his "hovel," his ground level cubbyhole of an apartment. This was merely one of his many residencies. Yet, he loved this one the most. It was so simple, a far cry from his life. He looked at his watch. Carom still had ten Earth minutes to get there. He was usually punctual. Travis was not worried. However, in two hours, he was due to rendezvous with his leader, Phoenix, for a mission.

For quite a while now, they acted out of what they thought was best. This occurred when a false Governess snuck into the Galaxy and was trying to take the throne from the real Dikara. Even though it was division seventeen that set everything right, it was not enough to clear the name of Phoenix. Her name was her burden. The division and all of their actions were blamed upon her. They were stilled marked as working for the enemy. The knowledge of their truth was one that was never able to impress upon the stubborn population. The propaganda had been embedded into the minds of civilians that they were stained. It was true, Phoenix and her division had killed thousands of people, but in the long run, they had saved the Galaxy from totalitarianism and massive ethnical cleansing on top of physical destruction.

Even though division seventeen has been called upon to assist the Governess directly on many occasions, they were still labeled as a threat. They were often cursed at and upon when seen in action. Travis often wondered what they would say if they knew that Phoenix was their beloved Governess. Masses of people were so idiotic.

He thought back to when he first saw Phoenix. He was dying from a terrible fall and she had looked so cold and unfeeling. He felt desperate and wanted to cry but the pain was choking him back. In the end, she saved his life and even though this new world he was thrown into was difficult, he was thankful towards from the bottom of his heart.

There were three sharp knocks at the door. Cautiously, Travis opened the door a crack. His body was tense as it always was when he was somewhere where he was not his true self. Carom was one of very few individuals who knew his true birth name.

"Who?" Travis spoke in English.

"T," Carom spoke Travis' single initial. He opened the door and quickly Carom and Sarilla slipped in. He shut the door quickly and quietly. The lights had been off and he left them that way. Through the thin curtains, a bluish light shined through. He embraced Carom with a forearm handshake of respect.

When Travis had shipwrecked on Liva while escorting the true Governess, Carom was the one who found him. He didn't care that Travis was a Queidso Pheinl, the name given to the male members of Phoenix's entourage. Carom helped him heal and kept him below the radar of authorities. They had discovered that they shared similar views and built a brethren relationship in the short time together. Travis was gladly repaying a favor.

In the weak light, Travis summed up Carom's sister. He understood the culture of the Remotti. The first determinant of authority was age, then gender. Sarilla was younger than Carom, but she was a female, therefore the two of them were equal. It was very apparent through their relationship in the way they stood and the way they spoke to each other. There was mutual respect and a bond that most families have lost.

Sarilla stood patiently. She knew that the man was judging her. She knew that she was in a place that was not her own and perhaps the society this man came from was patriarchal. She kept her face neutral and her mind open. When Travis was done looking her over, he offered her a small nod of acknowledged. She returned it.

"No time to waste," Travis said, "follow me," he already walked into a back room. After the two followed him in, he shut and locked the door and they were immersed in darkness. Travis snapped on the single bulb hanging on the sidewall. It was more of a closet than a room. There were no windows and no furniture. It was completely empty. Travis leaned over the floor. He took a deep breath and blew as hard as he could. Dust spread every which way and a thin rectangular groove showed itself. Travis took out swiss army knife from his pocket, a memorabilia from home. He popped open a blade and slipped it under the groove. He pushed all around the three foot by four foot rectangle and popped off the lid. Underneath, it looked like two filing cabinets had been built in on its back. There were two handles sticking up. Travis pulled up on one, and true enough, it slid open like a filing cabinet. He fingered through a few sheets and pulled out three forms. Setting them down, he recapped the cabinets and stomped all around the rectangle to push the lid back down. He then used his boot to sweep dust into the cracks.

Picking up the papers, he sat down cross-legged. The other two followed suit. Travis pulled a pen out of his pocket. After handing the top sheet to Sarilla, he started to write on another sheet.

Sarilla looked down, it was a birth certificate.

"You are now Eloria Ellen Dallis," Travis said without looking up. Carom had told Sarilla that Travis had often helped people switch identities. Sarilla's mind wandered. Who was Eloria? What did she look like? Was she dead and missing and only Travis knew where she was? Or did Eloria just wanted to escape her life like she did? Who was going to take Sarilla's identity? Travis scribbled on the second page and then turned both pages to face her.

"I need you to create a signature under that name," he said to her. Without thinking, Sarilla took the pen from Travis and wrote out "Eloria Dallis" in a flowery script.

"From now on, you will never be Sarilla Ce. You are Eloria Dallis from Wyoming. You were orphaned at age two and have no known relatives." Travis spoke to her without emotion and his eyes were sharp. She looked back at him unwavering. It was not a staring contest of any sort. They were both able to cap their emotions, that was all. There was no need for respect or dominance because there was a mutual understanding for the total lack of emotional expression.

Carom had to leave later that day. He was to get back before their mother returned. He hated having to deceive anybody, but he knew that Sarilla needed to be free and that his mother would never let her go. Their mother only saw potentials from one perspective: her own. Carom saw the need for Sarilla to escape, so did their father and Hsorht, Sarilla's second brother. No one else knew about her fleeing.

Eloria, that was her name now, was to live with seven other females in a housing facility and worked loading and unloading goods for a trading company. It was a temporary job Travis set her up with. She didn't plan on staying long so she kept to herself. There was no need to make friends and her roommates felt the same way. They all coexisted and got along fine because they were barely involved in each other's lives.

About two months later, Eloria had a solid job patrolling Turnika Jos and fending off attackers. This was by far more suitable for her calling and she felt at ease.

It was a typical day on patrol and Eloria sat in the theater room. It was merely a few scattered chairs and benches in front of a cheap projector screen to help pass the time. Right outside of the door was the launch area for the armed jet crafts. As soon as the alarm would go off, Eloria would jump into action in her assigned jet craft, her instructions would be given as she took off. So far, it was a quiet night. A dull movie droned on in the dark room. Spaz and Coloff were the only other two watching with her. They splayed their body parts out and tried to lounge the best they could on the old crooked chairs. Eloria was seated backwards in a chair with her arms folded under her chin. The others were playing cards at the far end of the room under a single lonely light. There were 10 people on duty at each base and about 20 bases in their district. They were well funded by the Galactic treasury. It would appear that they didn't do much to keep the buildings in shape, just the weapons and crafts.

Eloria pondered her life. She wasn't sure exactly what she was searching for. This was not meaningful to her at all, sitting here every night, fighting when she was told to. How bland could things be? Back home, she would be greatly respected and making political decisions for her life partner, or husband-like figure. Yet, that life would be one that locked her in. Here, she had the freedom of flexibility. She could change the course whenever she wished.

An alarm went off. Automatically, everyone ran to their assigned jet crafts. Eloria hopped into hers and was the first to the launch pad. Over the radio, her instructions were spat at her. They told her the coordinates of the attacker, how many of them, and what they were flying.

"Fighter crafts were hidden in trade ships, flying away from Hemirl Saitus, block four, hostage on board. Trade ships neutralized by ground troupes. Neutralize air situation, avoid destruction in metropolitan zones. 30 Dextros fighter ships from the Helenic System. Unknown arms and other weapons."

She was off in a flash. A few seconds later, the rest of her squad was beside her. They flew in standard two by two formation towards the mentioned area. In seconds they were there. Two other squads were already on the scene, and two more were fast approaching. The thirty ships in tight formation that looked all too familiar to Eloria. On Liva, she had seen them once. She was still a student studying at the Academy. In fact, it was shortly before Carom first met Travis. These ships were in the exact same formation as the ones attacking the Governess' ship. Eloria smelled trouble as excitement trickled in her blood.

There were now sixty Turnika Jos defense ships surrounding the thirty. They were trying to herd the ships away from the metropolitan zones. Strangely, the enemy ships did not fire back. There had been no more information on the hostage. Obediently, the thirty ships flew up, away from the planet. The radio spat out more orders, "When in clear distance, fire at will." Suddenly, before the last word was uttered by the radio, another voice cut through. It was odd since it was a private frequency. All security frequencies were private so as to not get confused with the trade ship frequencies. Not many people had access to the kind of hacking technology that could tap into a Turnika Jos signal.

It was a female voice and it was thick and rich. It was confident and cold holding a tone that demanded attention and respect, "Hold your fire, hostage must be retrieved, all troupes stand down and protect trade zones."

Eloria was confused. She had never heard this voice over the radio before. What should she do? It was the radio after all. She decided to stand down and saw that the other Turnika Jos ships did so as well. This eased her a little bit. They stayed within orbit of Turnika Jos obeying the radio, keeping their eyes on the departing ships. The thirty intruder ships kept a slow steady pace in leaving.

Without warning, their formation broke. They split in all directions. Eloria might have been the only one who saw a laser from nowhere hit one of the ships. It exploded. From the distance, a handful of velvety black ships flew towards them at top speed. Eloria recognized that formation right off the bat. One ship flew ahead followed by two that were equidistant. Behind them, were two horizontal lines of five fighter crafts each. This was the vigilante Phoenix division. Even though Eloria knew Travis was a part of the Division Seventeen, seeing them was still like seeing a ghost. The concept of the Phoenix division was more of an urban legend than reality. They were the unknown enemy that was only spoken of, but never seen. There are almost no photos of them. They were all erased from the databases and illegal to be shown. Even more so, the media was not allowed to broadcast them, they were under the protection of the Governess. Some say they are her secret execution squad. Most of what was known about them was merely passed down by words. So what were they doing here?

"Hey, Eloria," Coloff called her on his radio, "What the hell are we supposed to do?"

"I'm standing down until further instructions," Eloria replied thinking of Travis. He was her ally and within that division, she was not going to attack him. All the Turnika Jos ships sat and watched the battle. The rich confident voice that was on the radio earlier rang through Eloria's mind. Was that the legendary Phoenix? Until now, she had been as real to Eloria as the Boogie Man.

The thirty intruder ships were cut down quickly until about ten were left. The vigilante ships trapped the intruders between the Turnika Jos ships and themselves and were not letting them escape. Suddenly, Spaz's ship exploded. The intruders were attacking the Turnika Jos ships in a desperate attempt for diversion.

"All ships disperse, return to your base," the same rich voice came back calmly onto the radio. It was too late. About half the Turnika Jos ships were down and what was worse, they were spiraling to hit the planet. At a distance, there was a line of trade ships waiting to dock. The intruder ships did not attack the trade ships. Perhaps there was too much diplomacy involved. Eloria did not know, and it wasn't her business to know. This was the largest inconvenience she had ever encountered.

Eloria and the remaining Tunika Jos ships flew in evasive measures. Her training was by far more upscale than the other fighters. She shot at the large chunks of ship debris spiraling towards the planet. There was going to be a lot of damage. A lot of the buildings below had already put up their shrapnel shields, another item funded by the galactic treasury. The shields were made of titanium and were to protect from falling ship parts in case of an attack like this. Two docking poles were knocked over by falling shrapnel. That was not too bad. Those were easy to erect. Eloria looked back. Five intruder ships were left and they were engaging their top flight engines for fleeing. She could tell by the blue flare emanating from the engines. Without thinking, Eloria engaged hers as well and followed the chase amongst the vigilante ships. A huge rush flowed through Eloria as she shot at the intruder ships.

"Stand down," the rich voice over the radio spoke to her. She didn't listen.

"Cease fire or you will be cut down," it warned her again. She ceased fire, but not the chase. It looked odd, one Turnika Jos security ship amongst the velvety black vigilante ships chasing the intruders. Eloria did not let up.

The ships dispersed in an asteroid field. Eloria was well trained to handle any known ship. After all, she was the top student of her class at the Academy. She felt like a cowboy chasing these ships. She didn't fire, but she knew she was irritating them by keeping on their tail. These were skilled flyers, but she was better. This was the rush she had been searching for. If she would have taken the position her mother wanted her to, she would be spending most of her time plotting counterattacks and seeing very little action. This was the thrill, the chase, the very essence of her being. This was the adventure she wished to fill her life with. A recklessness that was somewhere deep inside of her broke free.

One last intruder ship remained but she noticed more ships like the intruder ships were coming at them from a distance. This might be a full fledged battle. A laser hit the tail of the last ship and it spiraled towards Eloria. She jerked her ship out of the way, but it caught her wing anyway. Together, the two ships spiraled towards a passing planet.

She was pissed that she got hit and that she couldn't join in the battle. She had no fear of dying, but was just plain upset that she couldn't kick some more ass.

Eloria smelled smoke. She could not open her eyes, but she could still smell. Something was burning and her ears were ringing. The incessant high pitched tone gave her a headache and she realized that she probably had a concussion. Her ears stopped ringing before she could open her eyes. She heard muffled words. They sounded urgent. With a soft groan, she dragged her eyes open. A peculiar looking girl with a kerchief on her head was speaking into her ship's radio. Eloria couldn't make out the words, but she heard the same rich voice flowing back from the radio. She shut her eyes again. The sound started to fade further away as she began to lose consciousness. Something was rattling. It took her a minute to realize that someone was shaking her. The smell of smoke became stronger and sounds became louder. When she tried to open her eyes again, a pang shot through her.

"Wake up," a soft voice flowed over her being. Eloria took a deep, smoke filled breath and braced herself. She opened her bloodshot eyes and looked up into the kerchief girl's face.

"We have to get out of here," the girl said urgently, "The beasts here in this jungle are dangerous. We have to find somewhere safe until Phoenix can find us and pick us up!"

Eloria tried to sit up. A jolt shot through her back and she let out a cry of pain.

"What Phoenix, she isn't really real, it's just an icon set up to instill fear in the population," Eloria mumbled without realizing what she was saying. The girl looked up startled. Eloria saw the fear in her eyes. There was something out there hunting them. Before they got to see the creature, a fighter craft set down and Travis jumped out. He and the kerchief girl loaded the wounded Eloria into the craft. It was a very tight fit in the cockpit, but the three of them managed. Within ten minutes, they were back on Turnika Jos and Eloria was under medical attention.

Eloria awoke only to stare at an IV in her arm. Her skin twitched the tiny hair follicles which was similar to human goose bumps. She hated needles. They always made her skin crawl like that. Quickly, she turned away and felt a pang in her neck. She ignored it. Physical pain was nothing to her as long as her mind was clear. The room was peculiar. She was on a small cot in the corner of a large room with many metal tables. The tables displayed a variety of weapons. Only about half of them did she recognize. Her curiosity was perked. She thought she had learned all the weapons of the Galaxy at the Academy. Seeing the foreign weapons led her to feel something just short of amazement. What did she get herself into?

Remaining calm and collective was not a problem for her. She tried to recall her last conscious event. It included a girl with a kerchief on. She was trying to remember if there was a threat of some sort. Before she could pinpoint anything, a girl walked in. She had large blue green eyes, by far too largely proportioned to be either Eloria's species or human. From those eyes, Eloria knew that she was the kerchief girl, a native of Turnika Jos.

"I see you are awake," she said in a silky delicate voice. She was very meek and mouse-like but she held an air of confidence and her eyes dictated her power. She seemed to be challenging Eloria silently. She no longer wore her kerchief and peasant skirt, rather a jogging suit. Her light brown golden hair was pulled back in a ponytail.

"Yes," Eloria replied hoarsely. The girl's hard eyes turned softer as she continued to speak, "I'm glad." She checked the IV that Eloria could not look at. A blonde woman walked into the room. She was shorter than Eloria but taller than the girl who had worn the kerchief. The blonde woman's frame was quite small, but she was well built and quite fit. There was a large contrast between her and the thin kerchief girl.

"Kirin," the kerchief girl addressed the blonde woman, "her back is definitely broken." It was then Eloria realized she was bound to the cot, which was more of a backboard. She remained calm. She did not feel a threat from these women, if they wanted to hurt her, they could have just left her to die in the jungle.

The blonde woman acknowledged the kerchief girls words. She knelt down beside Eloria. Something about her movements reminded her of Travis.

"You know our Wolf," the blonde woman was the owner of the rich voice over the radio. The word "Wolf" sounded like a drowning person's desperate gasp for air. Eloria did not know what language that was in, or what a "Wolf" was.

"You know him as Travis," the rich voice continued. Eloria was puzzled. She nodded, “what are you getting at?” she asked neutrally. Eloria noticed that the blonde woman had a visage of ice. Her eyes were dead, her face was dead. It was like speaking to marble.

“Phoenix noticed your abilities and would like you to join us. Travis vouches for you.” The blonde woman’s words were flat. There was no hostility, but nothing friendly either. The kerchief girl spoke again, “You have to understand this honor, no one gets invited in unless there is someone to vouch for them. Its hard enough just to get a vouch, but Phoenix is inviting you. Travis tells us that your brother is already one of their contacts on Liva.” This information was new to Eloria but somehow didn’t surprise her too much. Perhaps it was the friendship that Carom and Travis shared.

“This invitation lasts for the next twenty four hours. If you deny, you will merely be put to sleep, and you will wake up in a regular hospital with no proof of what you had just witnessed,” the blonde woman explained.

“We’ll let you think this over,” the kerchief girl spoke. They left together and Eloria fell back into her thoughts. Before she could contemplate, Travis showed up beside her.

“Hello, Eloria,” he said.

“Whats going on?” she asked getting straight to the point.

“You proved yourself to be most impressive, the way you kept up with those ships. Those were from the Helenic System.” The Helenic system was in the process of reform, they were also well known for their superior fighter jet crafts. It was also supposed to harbor the last threat towards the Governess. One of the leaders, Deritak, was constantly searching for the last rebel. Deritak himself was once a rebel, but like most people, he eventually changed his mind about the Governess.

“Where am I and who were those women?” Eloria asked.

“You are at a top secret base. We have alliances with most top secret governments who know that we are not the enemy and we never were. I can’t tell you more than that. The Turnika Jos woman is Palettia, she has been an insider for us for a long time and is like family. The blonde one is Kirin, she is the third officer in command and is usually the one in charge of base operations.”

“What about this offer? What does it entail?” Eloria asked.

“You will be one of us, and you will know our secrets. I trust Carom therefore I know you are not a spy. I checked your records.”

“How often do you invite people?”

"Almost never, I got dragged in to avoid death. Phoenix was trapped in a difficult situation so she gave me a chance to fight with her side by side. Most of the others have been with the division since the beginning. Palettia chose the life she leads. She can cease to stop helping us whenever she wishes, but she believes in us as we believe in her. Can you trust like that?"

"Why me?"

"Because your mind and fighting skills are superior in this Galaxy. We have our own ways of knowing. We have our sources. We know that you are one of the best. We also know that you have been tempted with other offers and the fact that you did not accept shows that you are in alliance with us." Travis must have been referring to the time when Eloria first graduated the Academy. She was offered a large sum of money to be a mercenary against the Governess.

There was silence for a moment as Eloria contemplated this offer. She had heard a lot about Phoenix and her dark angels. Her brothers spoke highly of them, and even her mother had a few positive words. They were shunned by society for leading the initial attack on Yolukia. However, she knew the truth that was never broadcasted because of all the chaos. She knew from underground sources on Liva, the truth that division seventeen was crucial in saving Yolukia. This still did not make it any more real to her.

"How can you trust me?" Eloria asked.

"Do you want to protect the Governess and what she is doing?" he asked. Eloria didn't have to say anything. She had the greatest respect for that woman and Travis knew it. When the real Governess was put back in power, all the confusion was gone. Life flowed back to the usual pace. The Governess Dikara was still continuing her chore and was cleaning up the Galaxy.

"I'm in," Eloria said.

"Good" Travis replied happily, "Now lets get your back fixed."

Eloria was suddenly thrown into a world of advanced technology. She experienced things that she didn't even know was possible. From birth, all noble citizens receive basic body enhancement alterations. This was because only the rich could afford them. The alteration upgrade she received from Phoenix's division was one that she didn't know existed. True enough, it was still in the prototype stage and they even flew her to Neptune in Preyal.

She obtained advanced healing powers and increased physical adaptability. She was told that even her aging process was to be slowed tremendously. Her telepathy was something she was going to have to build on with the other members. It was a form of advanced spirituality. Her mind was opened and she could channel a lot more of her focus into her thoughts.

She became acquainted with Kirin who was appointed as her primary trainer. Eloria was put through intense physical activity, by far more challenging than anything she had ever experienced at the Academy. Kirin referred to it as “Old School” a term Eloria was not familiar with. But answers were slowly dawning upon her and she did not need to rush them. There were plenty of other things to learn.

She also learned the history of division seventeen, the stories of the old members, where and how they got started. She learned of how they were soldiers once, blindly following orders. Eventually none of them felt right after a while and with the leadership of Phoenix, they broke away from the rules and extinguished those that were trying to overthrow Dikara. Phoenix still seemed to be a myth to her. It bothered Eloria a little bit that she hadn't met her leading officer yet. But she understood this was something completely different than anything else she had ever known. Kirin and Travis were real, and that was all she needed.

Kirin’s cousin, Dragon, was the second officer in command. Kirin told Eloria that Dragon and Phoenix were married. Eloria asked how that was possible because that was such an obvious vulnerability. Kirin exercised her power of authority for the first time, and did not reply.

Eloria was to be the fourteenth member. Her training lasted four Earth months. It was grueling and through it, she learned to respect the division beyond anything she could have originally fathomed. She was taught to use weapons from other galaxies. She was given top secret information. She trained in ancient martial arts and weaponry without firepower. She ran through top, state of the art training simulations and was shown the truth about how some systems were really run. Most civilians did not know, but Eloria now saw the truth. Phoenix’s division had their fingers in everything. They had thousands of contacts everywhere and in truth, they ran the Galaxy for the Governess.
They were her elite group of messengers who were privy to the real happenings behind the scenes. They were the real peace keepers. Palettia was their oldest contact. Palettia was the one who was secretly

in charge of keeping order on Turnika Jos. That was why she was kidnapped by the Helenic system fighter crafts. There were still a small handful of people out there trying to overthrow the Governess.

At the end of her training, Eloria had reached a sort of Zen. The problems she felt with her mother trapping her seemed far away. Her eyes were opened to truths and her soul was soothed. She felt like she was a solid part of Phoenix's division even though she had never met them. They were still operating away from her and only knew her by her code name, Gazelle, the English translation of Sarilla.

Kirin had another cousin in the division, Deklar, the Martian word for lightning. Her brother, Zap! was in too. This helped Eloria appreciate the amount of intimacy and trust the division had. Most of them were tied previously in bounds like the ones she shared with her siblings. Phoenix had five clones. These clones were one of the first successful clones in history. Their minds were not tampered with, they act and think like real human beings. Phoenix openly protects them and has beseeched the Governess to pardon them and prevent their destruction when cloning was outlawed. Eloria had heard from her father that the outlawing was because the Governess was cloned and a puppet had been put on the throne.

Those six, Phoenix and her clones, painted their faces whenever they went into action. They each had a system of patterns on their cheek that told them apart, otherwise, no one would be able to tell who was who. Leffi, the last member before Eloria, has her own back story. She was involved in a complex web with a clone of Phoenix's that was destroyed. Kirin did not share this story because she did not find it relevant. Those were the thirteen members that preceded Eloria.

"We need you now," Kirin said to Eloria while handing her a wristband. Eloria nodded and put it on her left forearm. When it sensed the computer chip installed in that arm, it activated. It ran on her body's natural energy.

"That is your remote for your personal voice activated ship, it also gives access to a personal storage dimension and all the other stuff we went over," Kirin explained. Eloria nodded and Kirin briefed her for the mission.

"You are going to be on my team for escorting the Governess. Dragon will be leading a team with his set of instructions and Phoenix will be leading hers. She assigned you with me in consideration that you will be most comfortable. Travis will be elsewhere, but you will be working with Tinkerbell, Joy and Moongirl. They are three of Phoenix's clones, who she prefers to call sisters." Kirin still retained the same marble face, not once had Eloria seen her smile. Kirin's old code name had been "Calm." Eloria noted how suitable it was.

"When do I actually get to meet these people I am supposed to trust to no end?" Eloria asked.

"When the moment is right, your trust is your real test. As of now, they are all needed elsewhere." Eloria forced herself to be satisfied. It made her uneasy how her leading officer was nothing more than an urban legend.

Eloria watched as Kirin helped the Governess into her special spacecraft. This was the first time Eloria had ever laid eyes on her in real life. She had always watched on television, but that was surreal. The television did not capture the exquisiteness of the shimmering dark blue cape with an elaborate Neptunian border. A fancy scarf was wrapped about her forehead and flowed down her back. A detailed decorative headpiece dangled from it between her eyes. Dikara always wore a different head piece everytimg Eloria saw her. At this close distance, she was able to appreciate the detail and complexity of the Governess clothes which was meant to reflect the woman's own detail and complexity. A solid veil was drawn over her nose with a matching border to her cape. Even her garb underneath, the sleeves were long and covered her hands to hide her identity. On her face, she wore heavy blue makeup with traditional Livan designs.

In a few moments, she had disappeared into her ship. Kirin was to fly that one. Eloria, or rather, her name was "Gazelle," now that she was on a mission, flew a fighter craft that was supposed to stay nearby. The other three fighter ships were also in the vicinity.

Gazelle had met the others that she was working with on this mission earlier. They were clones, or rather sisters of Phoenix. She secretly wondered if one of them was not Phoenix herself. They all had extremely different personas and were all very accepting of her. They trusted her, which made Eloria happy to no end and a lot more confident on the mission.

Things had not gone to plan. They had barely begun the escort when they were over taken. Now, the six of them sat as hostages in front of the Helenic system's underground leader. He ran all the crime, and was the last survivor of the coupe d'etat leaders against Dikara. Gazelle felt like a failure. This was her first mission and she failed already. The five of them stood protectively around the Governess who remained calm and did not say a word. She was well hidden beneath her garbs. Her eyes remained contemplative to the floor. She had a calm watery atmosphere about her, like nothing could surprise her. Gazelle felt nervousness in her gut when standing beside her. What if she wasn't ready to handle this mission? She had never been so close to her idol before. Oh goodness, what if she gets her killed?

Wirga entered the room. That was his name, the man who still won't give up on his old dreams of taking over the Galaxy. A man who had no control over himself, therefore he tries to exercise control over others.

"Your honor," he bows sourly to the Governess. To Gazelle's surprise, the Governess bowed back.

"And to what honor do we have of meeting again Mr. Wirga," she spoke in a soft and sandy voice seething with eloquence.

"You were careless today, Dikara," he was rude in addressing her without a title. Only those in ranks above the Governess may address her without a title.

"How so?"

"Traveling with so few escorts? You seemed to have gotten comfortable, you underestimate us. We are still here."

"I'm sorry." Her voice revealed nothing. It kept the same politeness and was tinged with warmth. She spoke with her head bowed. It was how she always spoke unless she was giving a decree. When she gave orders, her voice became powerful and booming. Whatever she said became law, but now, when addressing Wirga, it was feathery and fine.

Suddenly, at that moment, there was a scuffle.

"What is it?" Wirga demanded.

"Here!" a man shouted in the background, "a traitor I found trying to call someone concerning the Governess!" A man with scruffy dark blonde hair dragged Travis up to Wirga. Gazelle was confused. Something about the man dragging in Travis was familiar, but she didn't dare say anything. A voice spoke in her mind, "Relax." This was obviously telepathy. Something was going on and she didn't know what it was. Was this another simulation? She had no idea and for the first time since her youth, a tinge of fear crept at the back corner of her mind.

Were they setting a trap? Why wasn't she in on the whole plan? This had to be a test of some sort. She was not going to fail!

Wirga stared Kirin in the face. Kirin kept her eyes steady and stared straight forward.

"Do you know this man?" Wirga demanded her. She did not reply.

"Do you?" he shouted. She acted as if she didn't even hear him. He punched her in the stomach. She barely winced. That made him angry. With a slightly reddened face, he grabbed a metal stick of some sort, perhaps a crowbar. He swung heavily and hit her on the side of the head. Her torso twisted, and she moved her right leg out to steady her balance. A second later, she reverted back to her original position. Her face was still steely, only now with a red gash upon the side. None of the other division members moved. They were as still as marble statues. Giselle followed their example. Wirga walked up to Moongirl, "do you know him?"

"Yes sir I do you asshole, he is one of us," she sassed back. Wirga spat in her face. She merely wiped it off with her sleeve and laughed. Wirga came up to Gazelle, "You know him don't you?" Gazelle didn't know what to do. Moongirl had confessed, but her reply could be taken as sarcasm.

"It's okay, tell him," a voice in her head said. She was still unused to the telepathy, but she listened to the voice. She nodded tritely. Wirga grabbed her by her rattails, "You're serious." It was more of a demand than a question. Her neck was twisted awkwardly, but she nodded again, this time defiantly. Wirga pushed her head away.

"Off with his head, then theirs," Wirga said gesturing to both Travis and the Governess' entourage.

"Off with yours, bitch!" a voice came from the shadows of the dark high vaulted ceiling. A young man with neat hair dropped down and pulled out a large gun. At a glimpse, Gazelle guessed it to be a CP 4-9. Suddenly, there was chaos. Kirin shouted for her to stay with the governess. Gazelle obeyed, a gun was thrown at her, and she had defense again. Suddenly, there was a stand still. They were surrounded in the middle of the room but at least they had weapons. Gazelle recognized the young man with neat hair as Neroz. Sunshine and Angel, two of Phoenix's other sisters, were also there. Travis was beside them now too.

Wirga chuckled, "How do you expect to get out?" he tried to

sound confident, but Gazelle could read that his self assurance had been shaken. He didn't know how they had gotten through his defenses? The man with light blonde hair who exposed Travis walked calmly up to Wirga. No one suspected anything. Then the man put a gun to Wirga's head. A wave of shock washed over Wirga's face, "What is the meaning of this?" he demanded, "Seth, what is this?" The man with the gun rolled up his sleeve. He had a tattoo of a Dragon upon his right forearm.

"Genius," Gazelle thought to herself. She wondered how long it took Phoenix's second officer in command to work his way that close up to Wirga.

Wirga's face grew pale when he discovered his favorite right hand man was in alliance with his greatest enemy all along.

"You are coming with us, Wirga," Dragon said calmly and kept the gun to his head, "and we are going to do this without death." That would have worked if Wirga was not a stubborn man. He tried to knock the gun out of Dragon's hand but failed to even budge it. Dragon went to restrain him and the rest of Wirga's men moved into action. There were about twenty of them there in the room and more surrounding the fort.

There were some surprised shouts and when Gazelle looked around, she noticed that Leffi, Zap! and Deklar were also amongst Wirga's trusted associates. It was not a challenge at all to fight through the twenty people in the room. Gazelle kicked herself for not being aware of them. Her mind was not as sharp as she thought it was. She was told what signs to look for in recognizing fellow division members, but she didn't take notice. Now she saw through it all and understood that the Governess' capture was a part of their plan.

Wirga's men lay incapacitated on the floor. They were all paraplegics now with broken fingers. Phoenix's division doesn't kill if it can be avoided. The men were foolish to even try to resist.

They placed a few explosives on the walls and made a hole. With Wirga restrained and the Governess in custody, the division was making their way out as Wirga's henchmen were coming through the main entryway. Once outside, they had to make their way to the jet crafts. The most direct path was through an open field and that was as dangerous as fish being shot in a barrel.

They chose the sewer systems. Quickly without any confusion, they dropped below as Wirga's men came through the hole in the wall. Leffi and Deklar stayed behind and shot at those who were stupid enough to try to enter the sewer system. Gazelle wasn't sure how much of it was planned out and how much was played by ear, but she was holding her own end through all the confusion and she felt that was all she could do. Perhaps this mission was a test to see how well she can follow on a whim. Plans seemed to change a lot and she was at a disadvantage since her telepathy was not yet fully developed.

The walls were narrow and they could fit only one person at a time. Wirga was forced to go first followed by Dragon. The Governess was somewhere safe in the middle of the line. They made it to the jet crafts without much of a problem. Once the men saw that Wirga was in their custody, they kept their distance. The vigilantes quickly loaded up into two jet crafts keeping Wirga and the Governess separate and soon took off. They were aware that they were being followed at a distance by some of Wirga's men, but they did not get too close. Kirin told Gazelle not to worry, the whole lot of them would eventually disband without Wirga's influence. Gazelle was still tense. With them, there was no telling what was going to happen.

They made their way to Liva. Wirga's men stopped following a long ways back. Gazelle grew a little antsy. Theoretically she had nothing to fear because her mother no longer had a hold on her. But there was still some foreboding, some sort of entrapment in being back on Liva. What would her family say to know that she had teamed up with the division of Phoenix. More so, what would she say if she saw her mother?

Wirga's men had decided to attack out of nowhere. The division had to crash land on Liva. Gazelle thought humorously to herself that that was why Liva was so full of trees and rivers, it was for crash landings. They climbed out of the wreckage and and were preparing to hide in the trees.

It was not humorous anymore. Wirga held a gun to the Governess' head and was slowly dragging her towards his men and their ships. In the confusion of the mad run towards cover, Wirga had gotten too close to the Governess Dikara and took her hostage.

"You're on Liva, Wirga there's no where to go," the Governess said in her calm and loving voice. He was frantic and did not hear her. Gazelle's heart beat fast in her chest. No one in Phoenix's division moved, they all seemed calm. Then, a thought struck Gazelle, where in the world was Phoenix anyway?

No sooner had the thought struck her, Wirga tried to push

the Governess into one of his ships. Gazelle stared in disbelief. The Governess caught his arm and reversed the attack on him. He fell backward and grabbed at the Governess' hair scarf in the process. It came off tearing the veil with it, revealing her face. Gazelle recognized the painted marking on her right cheek. So it wasn't the Governess, it was Phoenix all along. Before Wirga's limited number of men could react, the rest of the division was upon them and soon, they were all dead. The woman, who was obviously Phoenix, picked up the hair scarf and readjusted it upon her head. She took the veil and reattached it to the scarf, once again concealing her face.

Gazelle felt a little bit awkward and lightheaded, but her focus was still there. This was her ghost, the myth she kept hearing about. This was "The Great Phoenix" in her actual form. This was her new leader that had devised this plan to pose as the Governess all along. Gazelle was so overcome, she was not sure what to feel. She watched as Phoenix picked up a gun and walked up to Wirga.

"You are childish aren't you, you will never change, will you?" her voice harbored a bitterness that seemed to come with age.

"No, you are not the Governess! No, it can't be!"

"You fear my one identity as Phoenix because you know I can destroy you, but yet you try to harm me as a passive woman, the Governess. You are truly despicable."

"You're a ghost! You're not real!" A part of Phoenix's power was her presence, her mere existence. There were legends of her immortality and a certain awe and fear that comes with the realization of her standing before you.

"I am more real than you ever were." With that, the Governess raised her arm and executed Wirga.

Gazelle watched in awe as Phoenix said a prayer and blessed Wirga's soul. This was obviously a complex woman. Gazelle was intensely curious as to what made her tick. Why did she kill Wirga after all this planning to try to take him alive? Why did she want to make him believe she was the Governess when she was going to kill him anyway?

By this time, Livan defenses showed up. To her slight despair, Gazelle saw Carom, her father, and Dabba, her other brother. They recognized her, but did not say a thing to her.

She caught their eyes. In that moment, tension released inside of Gazelle. They're eyes were accepting. She knew that they understood. She had found her path and she was going to follow it. They would support her to no end. It didn't matter what her mother had to say. This was her life now. It took her coming back to Liva and merely seeing her family's love again to understand that.

"Your honor," Carom spoke to the Governess, "is everything alright?"

"Yes, I am fine now. These people will escort me back to the 'castle' would you mind taking care of the bodies here?"

"Of course your honor, take one of our ships," Carom offered.

"Thank you, your services are greatly appreciated," Phoenix said. Gazelle felt a pang of resentment. Should Phoenix really be posing as the respected Governess? It is one thing for a plot to overthrow the enemy, but to lie to the Governess' army? Gazelle kept quite and they all headed to the ship Carom told them they could take. She looked back at her family one last time. Their eyes were full of love and understanding and she felt by far richer than she ever could and ever will.

Once on the ship, the entire division relaxed. Phoenix still wore the Governess' garb and sat quietly and nobly as if she were truly the Governess. She was quiet as the rest of the division formally introduced themselves to Gazelle. When everyone had exchanged a few words with the newest member, Phoenix approached her.

"So glad you could join us, you have amazing abilities," Phoenix said.

"Thank you, but, if I may, why do you still pretend to be the Governess when mission is complete? Isn't that disrespectful towards her?" Gazelle asked getting to the point of what was nagging her. Phoenix gave Kirin a look.

"I figure you would want to tell her since you like telling so much," Kirin said in a half teasing tone without looking up.

"My dear," Phoenix said taking off her veil to show her face, "You're name is Gazelle, that is the same creature as the Kirin, but you are differen't people. Sometimes, words, titles and names are just that. They cannot always reflect truth, but yet, they can make truth." Gazelle looked confused. Phoenix continued, "I met Yolukia as Phoenix when I was young. That was just a name I had first. Yolukia gave me another name and title making me the Governess Dikara. In the minds of the population, we are different people, but truthfully, if is just the same person occupying different roles. Just like you and Kirin, you have the same name, but different roles."

Eloria was silent in her thoughts. Phoenix sighed and spoke again, "I killed Wirga because he saw my two identities together. Otherwise I would have spared him. That was the reason for the whole guerilla plot, to bring him in peaceably. You understand that sometimes the truths is the biggest secret, the biggest lie." Gazelle could not hide the surprise on her face in discovering that her two most admired idols were one and the same.

It all suddenly became so clear. Yolukia loved and respected Phoenix, hence he chose her for the throne. The sacred knowledge behind the truth of knowing that Phoenix and the Governess was something that needed to be protected, even if it meant death. Plus, Wirga would have never ceased to be a thorn in their side and armed with such dangerous information, he could have created a lot of damage. He needed to be executed, because the Governess needed to be protected at all costs. Phoenix protected the Governess by severing truth and killing the knowledgeable enemy.

Gazelle looked deeply into Phoenix's eyes and truly saw her for the first time. This woman was not only her new commanding officer who gave her a purpose in life, but was also the ghost she had unknowingly been chasing her whole life. She embodied that higher purpose. Then to discover that she was equally the highly respected Governess was a little bit emotionally overwhelming for Gazelle at the moment. Still, she remained composed because she knew that this woman was already doing what Eloria had wanted to do all along. It was a great honor to be accepted.

With the veil back on, the Governess was handed over to the guards at the "castle." In silence, the rest of the division flew off to Mars. They had just executed a large mission. It was one that took meticulous planning to set up and was not quite perfect in the actual execution. That was alright, Kirin explained how most of their plans were never perfect. They always had multiple back ups. The entire division was so in sync with their habits they were able to change direction at any given moment. It would still take Eloria some time to catch on, but for now, she was a part of them and that was the first step.

The division was going to give themselves a little rest before they had to get back to keeping their ears to the ground. They were taking a break at their original training facility, SHONDS. Everyone loosened up and some Earth wine was opened. They exchanged tired anecdotes and were overall quiet. A peace fell over them that came with experience.

Eloria didn't say much either. She noticed that none of them talked of their families. No one of them spoke of their hidden lives. They only spoke of things in the past, projects that were completed and held little chance of haunting them. This just went to show that the future was never set in stone.

A few hours later, after she filed an attack report as the Governess, Phoenix joined them on Mars. She took a deep gaze into Dragon's eyes, holding his face in her hands. A moment passed by. Eloria had no way of knowing if they were conversing in telepathy or if it was a bond that required no words. She eventually turned her attention to her division, her new home. The ones who were equal to her in their destiny.

"Great job guys!" she toasted them. Then they all toasted the SHONDS institute. This was the first time Gazelle had ever been there, but it held sentimental value to all the others. This was where they grew up. This was where the original members trained from before Phoenix's time. This was a part of their history, and it meant a lot to Gazelle to be invited in. She was now a part of something with heart, something that was more than just a job. She was a part of a secret pact that watched silently over the Galaxy, protecting it as need be. These were people with immense power who chose to control it and not abuse it, putting it's use to good. They were the guardian angels of her home and now she was a part of that. Like them, she was to be hidden in the shadows. Her name would never be spoken. She would be known as a part of division seventeen and a dark entity. She was a part of a myth that had never been proven to society, but everyone could feel was out there looming behind each protective action. She was Gazelle, another dark angel of Phoenix.

Father, Carom, Hsorht,

I hope all is well at home. As you probably know by now, I have chosen a path. Don't worry, I know it is a good one. Please, don't write me, and I won't write anymore. This is because I love you and I wish to keep you safe. I have entered a world of immortality. Please don't cry for me, please don't miss me. I am always with you, but I must be dead to you.

Sarilla.

Carom put the letter down and looked at his father. His father's eyes were tired and Carom was sure his were too.

"Don't tell your mother," was all he said. Carom nodded. He folded the letter up and put it away.

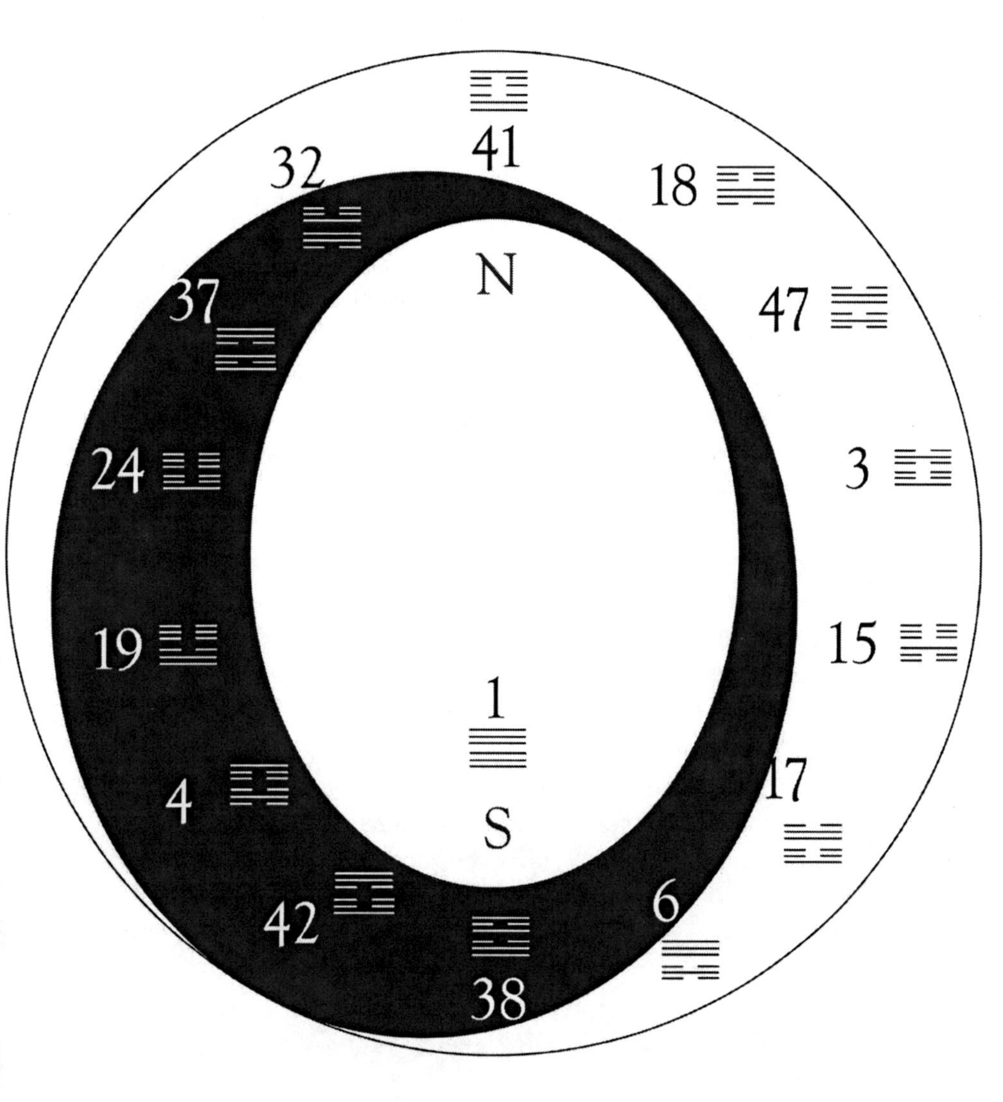

41
32
18
N
37
47
24
3
19
15
1
4
17
S
6
42
38

A sneak peak at <u>Book II: Celestial Warriors</u>.

After the peiod of extensive personal searching and growth in <u>Book I: Ontoo Neida Division Seventeen</u>, join the characters as they avidly begin to embark on their celestial journey.

(from Chapter One)

Leffi looked over to Travis. He scanned the ships' profiles eagerly. They were awaiting Simon's arrival with a shipment of weapons on Turnika Jos.

"Here yet?" she called over the noise. He shook his head. She went back to looking over the papers with Zurntain. He was the young fellow who had followed Phoenix to Hicturzel back when they had confusion with the Governess. He was gratefully helping them smuggle weapons. He felt he was doing it for a higher cause because D-17 served the real Governess and they were the ones that brought vengeance down on the woman who had harmed Tanyui. Leffi glanced up at the blue haired boy. She chuckled, "what are you eating?"

"Banana," he replied innocently.

"I know, but what are you dipping it in?" she asked. He helped up the jar. It was raspberry jelly.

"It's quite good!" he exclaimed, "want to try some?" Leffi laughed warmly, "no thanks, I prefer my bananas with peanut butter."

"You are both gross!" Travis chuckled, "I like my bananas with chocolate!" he added. Leffi laughed while Zurntain asked, "what is chocolate?" Travis searched his pockets and produced half a bar, "Here, you guys can have it."

"I love chocolate too!" Leffi cried accepting gratefully. She broke what was left in half and gave it to Zurntain. He held up the bar and looked with wide eyes looking at Leffi.

"What is it?" she asked.

"It is the same color as you, is it made out of your people?" he asked. Leffi gaped at him, she was offended. Then she gained her senses and realized that he had no idea what he was saying. He was as different as she was, if not more. She let out a chuckle, "No, don't worry, you can eat it, it is sweet." Zurntain wasn't sure, he knew that his taste buds were different from the humans. Still, he took a nibble. It was sweet! It was wonderful. Without thinking, he licked Leffi's cheek. There was no taste.

"Hey!" she flashed angrily, "damnit I told you its not made out of my flesh!" she yelled punching him on the shoulder. He was like a little kid! Travis was stifling a giggle.

"What?" she snapped at him.

"Nothing," Travis responded shaking his head. Zurntain sensed that he did something wrong.

"I'm sorry," he said meekly. He was still afraid of them. He remembered how strong they were. Leffi sighed, "I'll forgive you, don't do it again!" she warned. Just then, Simon hailed and Travis accepted the call. They were back to work.

(from Chapter Two)

They didn't even use the title of "division seventeen" anymore, unless they were in contact with SHONDS. The galactic media had spawned them a new name. They were the "dark angels" of the Governess Dikara and there was still a mixed sentiment towards them.

Erica was not sure if she liked so much media coverage. Some said that they killed at will, others say there were as gentle as angels truly were. Still others thought them to truly be supernatural beings and avoided them at all costs. Things were just happening too fast and she felt as if she had no time to catch her breath and adjust accordingly. She felt that there was a part of herself that she needed to ground and figure out first. Turning, she looked at her reflection in a glass window front of a store. She was on Earth, and it had just started to drizzle. The fuzzy rain was comforting and it gave her a nice warm feeling on that early autumn day.